A Matter of Fate

Ellie Heller

CRIMSON ROMANCE

F+W Media, Inc.

Published by
Crimson Romance
an imprint of F+W Media, Inc.
10151 Carver Road, Suite 200
Blue Ash, OH 45242. U.S.A.
www.crimsonromance.com

ISBN 10: 1-4405-6678-X
ISBN 13: 978-1-4405-6678-3
eISBN 10: 1-4405-6679-8
eISBN 13: 978-1-4405-6679-0

Cover art © istock.com/skyman8

Dedication

This book is dedicated to my husband Steve, who never got to see the finished project, and my sisters (in fact and by marriage) Julia, Nelly, and Beth.

A great deal of thanks goes to the critique groups I've been in over the years. From RWU to ERAuthors to Critters, Inc., you all have shown me the errors of my ways, helped me grow, and supported me on this crazy quest. In particular I'd like to thank Dr. Zee for metaphorically rapping me on the knuckles early on over my bad "that" and "it" habit, the Sunday Night Chat group—you know who you are—for bouncing ideas off of and being a source of inspiration, and the ladies of my current group for being upfront and honest, as well as wacky as all get out. I'd also like to acknowledge the wonderful editors at Crimson Romance who really helped me shape the final draft into the book you see today. As this is a work of fiction, some of the geographical locations around Lackawanna and Buffalo have been rearranged to suit the needs of the story. Any errors are entirely my own.

Chapter One

Her head bowed to the winter wind, Mona strode across the parking lot to the mall, her concern and curiosity about Raine now verging on dread. Since the frantic call from her normally unflappable friend, the scenarios flitting through her mind kept getting worse. Had she been mugged? Detained by mall security? Why? Raine had given no explanation, only saying she needed Mona's help *now*. Even if they didn't see each other much these days, their best friend bond was unshakeable.

The wind slid under her collar and raised goose bumps along her back. Fuck-a-duck, it was cold! As soon as she finished her training she planned to move someplace warm and get out of Buffalo. Not somewhere too far south though—her light skin sunburned far too easily to be out in the sun all the time.

Avoiding the revolving door out of habit—she felt trapped when she was neither in nor out—she yanked open the side door, thankful to be out of the frigid temperatures. All elves had their quirks, but she knew she had a few more than most. Growing up outside the Folk enclaves—where she might have learned about magic a lot earlier—hadn't helped.

Mona looked around, expecting to see the management office since she'd been directed to use this entrance. Instead she spotted Raine on a bench at the far end of the hall. Mona was relieved for a split second—until she took in her usually tidy friend's unkempt appearance. Poorly dressed for the winter, she had no coat and wore open-toed shoes and a loose, cap-sleeved sweater over a lightweight dress. Huddled over, legs and arms crossed, the thin sweater tented her body. If Mona hadn't known the woman, she would have avoided her, and not just because she could see the glow of evil intent surrounding her, but because Raine looked as if she'd been living in her clothes.

As she came closer, Mona's elf heritage allowed her to see the shape of the magic, although it was a bit difficult in the florescent lights. A spell had definitely been placed on Raine. And in her. Mona could clearly see both parts of the spell, the twisted, violent sigils, creating the intent of the spell caster, and the power runes holding and shaping the energy needed for the working. Mona would have cringed if she hadn't been stuck dumb with shock.

Oh no, oh no, this was all so wrong. Raine was mortal—aware that there were Folk, but mortal. And mortal or not, no one should have had a working like this on them, complicated with many intricate mini-spells encapsulated in the larger one. Mona was very, very thankful that Raine had called her. If anyone who created spells, and not just saw them, like she did, had touched the working it would have been a disaster. Even now she worried that Raine's actions may have triggered the warning beacon placed at critical junctures of the spell.

The magic in Raine would slowly kill her, Mona could see that much. Mona sucked in her breath at the shock. A world without Raine, no matter how infrequently they saw each other, was unthinkable. But what, if anything, Mona could do about it was unclear. She had to be able to do something. She was in training to be a Warder, to protect Folk and humans from misused magic. Even before her training a spell like the one Raine displayed would have drawn her to attempt to fix it; the need was part of why she'd been called to train. Mona took a deep breath; she needed to be calm. The working would shift—speed up—if Raine got overly upset.

"Raine?" she said once she was sure she could keep her anxiety out of her voice.

Raine jumped up. Standing, the heavily pregnant bulge of her belly became apparent. But last time Mona saw Raine—six months ago before her training had become so hectic—Raine was just starting to date someone and had reiterated that she was not doing the baby thing until she had a ring on her finger. What had happened? Now that Mona saw the growing baby, the spell was even more sinister, tied up in the tiny person inside her friend. Whoever set the spell either hadn't known about the pregnancy or worse yet, did.

"Mona!" Raine slapped her hand to her chest, hysteria lacing her voice. "You scared the crap out of me!"

"Raine, you okay?" Because, shit, this looked bad. Really bad. She couldn't believe it, but she actually wished her mentor, Smythe, was here to help her figure out how to deal with a spell of this complexity and magnitude. The old coot's pedantic lecturing when they were working was beyond annoying, but she'd put up with it in a heartbeat if he could help.

"Yeah," Raine said. She took several deep breaths. "I will be. Shit, no one's snuck up on me that bad in ages."

"Let's go in," Mona said. "Can I get you something to eat?"

Cracked acorns, that spell was convoluted! Nothing like the clear, linear ones with simple branches she'd seen before, this one looped and twisted like a tangle of yarn.

"I—" Raine jumped at the noise of the revolving door screeching.

They turned as a man in tan slacks and an unbuttoned blue blazer headed their way. In Mona's eyes he glowed with the same tainted residual as Raine. His spell was new and strong enough that she could almost make out the working despite the distance. Mona's read of his Folk abilities made clear he was a shifter, although he wasn't what the Weres called "strong," and didn't have the balance of elf and human blood needed to shift at any time. Which was good, because the last thing they needed was for him to transform in the middle of the mall. And he definitely had weak magical resistance, given the spell compelling him to act looked to be lightly set. Lightly set or not, the compulsion rune on the top layer honed in on them.

Raine gasped; the man seemed to have her worried, too. Without a word they both hurried to the more populated portion of the mall. If a mall on a late Sunday afternoon in January when the Bills were playing in their first championship game in decades could ever said to be populated. And, if the lumbering Raine was attempting could be called hurrying. Mona slowed down and placed herself between the man and Raine.

"Upstairs!" Raine yelled.

Raine swerved and headed up an escalator, tripping at the top. Mona caught hold of Raine's elbow to steady her, hissing as a painful tingle—a reaction to the spell—raced through her arm. A glance over her shoulder showed the man was gaining on them.

Their frantic pace attracted the attention of mall security; the guards closed in from the other direction, also dressed in tan slacks and blue blazers.

"Mona! In here!" Raine grabbed her hand and pulled through a door marked *Mall Personnel Only*.

The shock of touching the spell directly as she came into contact with Raine's skin threw Mona off for a moment. She forced herself not retch as she felt the perverted intent behind the sigils the spell caster had made to control the power runes. Raine tugged on her hand and Mona followed.

A security officer stood in the hallway. "Hey! You can't come in here!"

Mona let go of Raine's hand as they turned around. Another guard opened the entry they'd come through. Behind him stood the man who'd chased them, his blazer now buttoned and looking like he belonged. To anyone else's eyes, he would look mortal and safe; only Mona could see how different his being was compared to the security detail around him.

They weren't getting out without confronting either the security detail or their pursuer, who seemed to be biding time until the rest acted. The compulsion wasn't pushing him strongly enough to act rashly, which was good to know given the strength of the working surrounding him. Mona wasn't going to wait to find out exactly how long that would last.

Her best bet was to change the spell on him, consequences be damned. Unlike the complicated mess on Raine, this one didn't have as many components. She should be able to create a new spell by rearranging the order of the runes within the sigils. While she'd done it many times on inanimate objects, Smythe, her teacher, had yet to allow her to do this on someone while she was in training. Oh, Mona had tweaked a spell or two on people, changing the runes' orientation and tweaking precedence within a spell, much along the lines of what she hoped to do with Raine. So many things could go wrong on her first try, but the alternative was far worse in her opinion.

She was going to do it.

Decision made, Mona's hand twitched at her side as she suppressed the need to reach out and remove the threat the man represented. She'd only get one chance, so she'd better do it right the first time. In an effort to gain some time to study the settings, she started to talk. Babble, really—one of things she just did when she was uncertain and uncomfortable about her situation.

"Oh my god! I'm so glad you're here. My friend Jackie," she gestured at Raine, hoping her friend would pick up on the fake name, "she's being, like, *stalked* by the father of her child. She's told him she's keeping the baby and he isn't too pleased. Threw out all her winter clothes, ruined her car, and hid her purse. Like, as if being preggo by a numbskull wasn't enough, you know?"

Her babbling stopped as the man who'd pursued them tried to step around the guard in front of him. Mona sidled over too so he'd have to come through her to get to Raine.

Mona ignored the second spell under the first; she had to deal with the compulsion before anything else. She fought down bile as she deciphered the linkage between blood and food, then the one pairing giving pain with sexual pleasure. The last, hidden behind sigils so strong it was hard to see what lay beneath, looked like death and contact. She could only assume there was something in the sigils that would trigger the spell to kill him and anyone he touched.

Raine took over the chatter. Her hands now shaking, Mona kept them low and concentrated on what she needed to do. Luckily, with this strong a working, she didn't need contact to rearrange the spell. With so few options before her, she connected food to pleasure—the dude would probably get a hard on every time he saw a loaf of bread—and made them the ascendant pair. Seeing blood now caused pain; she hoped the guy had no plans of being a doctor.

The last set of runes were too volatile to move around, and very worrisome as the sigils were pulsing now that she'd changed the spell. She couldn't rearrange them but she might be able to pull them entirely out of the working. Smythe had taught her the theory of removal even if he'd never let her practice the maneuver.

Unfortunately, to do that, physical contact with the working would be necessary. A shudder of revulsion hit her at the thought of feeling the intent of the spell caster again, but she couldn't risk the guy running around like a time bomb.

I am immune to magic. This unique trait was the reason she'd been chosen to train as Warder, a needed immunity given she would be fixing spells gone awry as well as dealing with misdirected magic. The spell should not hurt her, not if it was directed at her. Directing a spell at other things that might kill her—like say, having boulders burst out of the ground and slam together like a ram's horns—could hurt her. Physical violence concerned her too, but the surrounding guards would hopefully intervene if he attacked. And, goddess willing, none of the magic she'd manipulate would show, keeping Folk secrets safe from these mortals.

Because protecting each from the other was also part of her calling as Warder.

Raine stopped talking and stood shaking, earning a lot of sympathy from the men near her. Time to get to work.

"Hey, did you get a chance to see the guy?" Mona asked as she stepped forward and grabbed the man's exposed wrist.

She pulled the rune set away, physically removing her hand to finish the separation.

The entire spell collapsed. A swirling whirlpool of new magic surrounded him, causing him to contort. The secondary spell! The working was a type of summoning spell, aimed at not just him, but some aspect of his magical ability. By all the thorns on the first rose, he was being forced to change into his den totem. Mona stepped back, appalled. This man was not strong, did not have the exact balance of elf and mortal blood to be able to change outside the full moon. He should not be doing this.

His face contorted in pain and the sharp smell of anxious sweat assailed her. This Were was going to die and there was nothing she could do about it.

In the blink of an eye his arms blurred and shifted to a puma's paws, but his shoulders remained human. By the goddess, this was obscene. The summoning spell was forcing him to take on his Were clan shape piecemeal, the strength of the spells causing a distortion in the air behind him as the energy they held was emitted.

But…this shouldn't be happening. Mona again read his magic ability; something in the spell was feeding magic into the change, like a power boost in an attempt to supplement an ability he did not have. Because of it he'd shifted far further to his puma than she'd ever thought he'd be able to, given his low level of elf blood.

His body stopped shifting and he was stuck with human bits mixed in with his feline body. His scream, a cross between a screech of sheer pain and a yowl, echoed down the hall. A vortex opened in the whirlpool of magic swirling behind him. Between one heartbeat and the next, his abomination of a body was sucked through.

Mona knew if she had still been in contact she would have gone with him, the final act of the spell.

She turned to check on Raine, finding her friend's latte-colored face several shades paler than normal, making her chocolate colored freckles stand out in relief. The smell of blood, sweat, and fecal matter hung heavy in the air, making even Mona feel queasy; she had to imagine Raine was hit harder. And magic—magic!—had just been done in front of all these mortals. Most would discount what they'd seen, but there was always one or two who picked up on what really happened.

Three men from security detail pushed forward. "What the fuck?"

Oh, hell.

"Imp! Please!" Even with the urgent, pleading tone of her voice, Mona wasn't sure the magical entities would answer her call. Still in training, she had no perceived social status. But if ever a situation called for the sparkling, pure magical energy creatures, this was it. Smythe had told her that in extreme circumstances, an imp might cast a spell for a Warder. Particularly should Folk be in danger of discovery.

"Please, I need memories altered to help Folk!"

Two small, bright, sparkly lights appeared, hovering high over the men's heads. Thank the goddess.

And their magic was already at work. The men stood frozen, with blank looks on their faces. Muttering a heartfelt "thank you," she took Raine's arm and dragged her out of the hallway.

Chapter Two

Raine wanted to run but Mona held her back—no need to draw more attention to themselves.

"Aren't you supposed to stop people from misusing magic? Isn't that your job?" Raine hissed as they passed another shop filled with valentines.

Mona was attempting to deal with her hair; the long, black curls had escaped her usual braid during their run and were getting in her face, driving her nuts. "No, I just clean up afterwards. I don't usually do anything to stop people from misusing magic. There are other people who do that."

"Well, it should be you. You might be new at this, but you have skills they don't have, right? And isn't it better to go after the source than clean up all the messes?"

Mona couldn't argue Raine's point. She'd tried to ask Smythe about it once and had simply been told that it wasn't her job.

As they walked, Mona sorted through the magic around Raine. She tried to study every single rune and marking. The working contained several nasty rune pairings, a few quite subtly hidden. There was deeper, angrier color at several of the junctures, making her think those parts would be difficult to move around. With this complicated a spell, Mona was hesitant to change any of the linkages, however she definitely could work around the sigils and make one or two pairs less prominent by manipulating the runes.

Decided, Mona took the opportunity to nudge, ever so slightly to the back, the set of runes creating Raine's compulsion to deny she needed help. The main rune had a lot of the angry red about it, and it took Mona more effort than she'd anticipated to change the position. After working so hard to reorder the precedence of just the one, she wasn't willing to move things around until she got a better handle on the setup. Particularly given what had happened to the Were.

"Raine, I can help you."

"Help me?" Raine asked, her tone clearly both worried and defensive.

Mona should have anticipated this. One of the sequences made Raine think no one could help, and conversely, another made her deny anything was wrong with her.

"Pick out clothes and stuff," Mona improvised. "There's supposed be a big storm headed this way, and you need to get ready."

"Okay." Raine was monotone.

"How about a cup of coff—? Tea! I mean tea, first." Mona didn't think Raine should have caffeine. And sitting at a table would give her a chance to really look over the spell and see if there was any safe way to tweak it.

The chain cafe had an entrance to the outside, which meant windows and an alternate exit should they need to leave quickly. Engulfed by the smell of coffee and yeast as they walked in, Mona realized how hungry she was. After convincing Raine she needed to go with peppermint tea, and getting them each a quick nosh, they settled into a table with views of both entrances.

"Raine," Mona said as she marshaled her thoughts, "I need to rearrange bits of your spell."

Raine slammed her cup down, a spattering hot liquid on the table.

"I have a spell on me? First that deranged shifter kidnaps me, then he rapes me leaving me knocked up. Now I find out he's put a spell on me, too? Why, that little piece of—"

Raine was an inventive and descriptive curser. She impressed Mona with her detailed description of how she'd remove, and then destroy, a certain part of his anatomy to make sure the "piece of refried crap with raw sewage for brains" couldn't knock up anyone else. Mona monitored the sigils to see if they triggered one of the mini set spells embedded in the working, but they remained the same, despite Raine's anger.

"Raine, deep breath," Mona interjected, as soon as Raine paused her diatribe. She held up her hand to stop her from continuing. "You need to be careful not to get too worked up. The spell has built in markers that react to your moods, particularly if they get extreme. Except for anger; for some reason that's ignored."

Raine seemed about to say something. Mona looked her in the eye and took a deep breath, continuing to do so until Raine caught up with her.

Moving things around was every bit as tricky as she'd expected, especially in areas where the orange-tinted red sigils directing how the runes energy would combine deepened to burgundy. In those places the runes were particularly recalcitrant. But Mona did her best. Careful not to brush against the sigils, she changed the orientation of some of the runes at the base of the spell. Raine ended up in less discomfort, although if she got fewer than six hours of sleep she'd be in pain. Mona made Raine's disinclination to speak, particularly of what had happened, into to an avoidance of quiet spaces. She also widened Raine's perception, so her fear of leaving the mall was now a phobia of rural spaces.

Done, she watched the working resettle itself around the new configuration. There were some bright sigils still glowing from earlier but nothing new seemed to have come active.

Raine finished the last bit of soup-soaked bread and sat back, looking content.

The bright sigils flared, then sparked before disappearing.

Not good, although nothing new took their place. Mona suspected it was a beacon of some sort, and if so, it was tied to the place, not Raine. This meant she needed to make sure Raine left the mall soon.

"I'm ready to go, how about you?" Mona asked, standing to see if Raine would protest or follow.

Raine followed, pensive as they left the coffee shop.

"Where do you want to go?" Mona asked.

"I'm not ready to face anyone, not yet. They're going to be full of questions that I'm not ready to answer."

"It's not your fault."

"Yeah, I know." Raine didn't sound entirely convinced.

Mona suspected nothing but time would heal that wound. "You're welcome to stay at my place."

"No, I need to be away from you all for a bit." Raine gestured vaguely, indicating some ill-set area of Folk. "I'll probably hole in up in a motel up by the falls tonight."

"I'm not sure you should be alone." Although if being around people she knew would make Raine more anxious, she might be better off alone for the next day while the new order of the spell took hold.

"I've been alone for the past several months. I'll be fine."

Guilt swamped Mona, if she'd stayed in touch, Raine might have gotten help sooner. Wallowing would not help. "Twenty-four hours, that's my limit. After that you're with me, or your aunt Betty. Got it?"

Raine smiled, they both knew her aunt Betty would smother her in kindness, no questions asked. "Between a rock and a hard place, huh? Okay, I can work with that." She stared at Mona before coming to a decision. "Please, can you hold off on saying anything to the pack just yet about that crazy shifter stuff? Surely one day won't make a difference."

Reluctantly Mona agreed, bartering her silence for Raine's agreement to let Mona buy her winter clothes.

Mona nattered on about inconsequentialities as she quickly assembled two outfits, along with boots—you couldn't go through a Buffalo winter without boots. She also added several credit company-based gift cards, as she was pretty sure Raine had no money and she'd need something once she left the mall. Admittedly it was worrying when the clerk threw a pair of matching Buffalo Bills stadium blankets and deluxe emergency car kits she had earned "free with purchase" to the pile. Her brother said twice was a coincidence and three times was a plot. Not that he was always right. But it sure looked like at least one of them would need the supplies.

Done, they headed out to the mall restrooms. Raine changed and came back out looking a whole lot more comfortable and ready to face the weather.

"You look fabulous!" Mona said.

"Thanks," Raine said, setting the bag with her old things by the trashcan. "I can't tell you how much better I feel wearing new, clean clothes."

"I know what you mean."

Mona watched the spell shift around again as Raine become more relaxed. Some of the sigils were brightening again. Shit, she needed to get them out of the mall. Leaving would help reinforce the new settings of the spell. When they reached the garage, Mona followed Raine to the lower level where Raine stopped by a tiny excuse for a car.

"Are you kidding? I don't think I've ever seen a car that small!" The exclamation was out before Mona could stop herself.

"Yeah, isn't it great? I never have any problems finding a spot. Even when those honking big SUVs bulge over the edge of a space, I can fit in." A frown crossed her face. "Guess I'll need to trade up for something larger soon enough."

They settled the bags in what passed for the trunk space before Raine slid the seat back and settled into the front seat, secured her belt, and checked the mirrors.

Mona stood in the open door and handed Raine the gift cards she'd picked up. She waved off Raine's thanks.

"Call me, all right? If I don't hear from you every couple of hours I'm going to come track you down. I don't care if I told you I'd give you twenty-four hours."

Raine shook her head. "Not every couple of hours. I'll check in with you when I get there, but I need a little time to figure things out. It's okay, isn't it? To be by myself?"

Mona didn't like leaving her alone, but doubted Raine would do anything drastic in the one-day window. Mona was more worried that whoever had set the spell might track her down. But…so long as Raine didn't set off the spell's beacons, she should be fine.

"Yes, if you stay calm, you should be fine. Just, call me when you get to the motel, okay? I'll feel a lot better knowing where you are." Mona leaned in and hugged Raine.

"Thanks, Mona. For—for everything," Raine whispered into her collar.

"You don't call me, and I will track you down. Like a dog after a bone." They both chuckled; Weres hated the saying.

Mona moved away and Raine shut the door. She started the engine, waved goodbye, then slowly backed out. Mona watched Raine until she turned and headed to the exit, fighting the urge to follow her. Raine was right; she needed the space to be by herself for a bit, even if Mona didn't like it. And now that she was out of the mall, she would be harder to find.

Outside the garage small, fine flakes skittered through the late afternoon sun. Mona looked at the steel-grey clouds edging their way across the sky toward the setting sun. Shit, what time was it? Mona quickly checked her phone. Damn. Too late for her to go home if she wanted to get to her shift at Fat Louie's on time. And crap, she had an assignment to read before she met absurdly early tomorrow with her teacher, Warder Smythe. After being bored for the first six months of her training, if the spells on Raine were any indication, life was about to explode.

•••

With the storm moving through, the bar had been quiet. For a long time the only customers had been her friend Francine and the date she brought to get Mona's feedback. The woman was as suave and sophisticated as Frankie, and Mona thought her friend may have finally met her match. Oh, and right before closing there'd been that elfing, about to emerge into power. That happened a lot now; elves whose talents were on the cusp of emerging would find her. She'd quietly grilled him on what he needed and agreed to meet with him during her next shift. Other than that it was the same old, same old, except her boss closing early because he was worried about his pregnant wife. When they'd left, Mona had hoped to be home by eleven. Between having to clear the snow off her car and then needing to dig a trench through the pile plowed next to it so she could pull away from the curb, it was almost midnight when Mona finally drove away. She headed home in the hope of getting a couple hours of sleep before she went to Smythe's.

The maintenance crew was out with the tractor plowing the lot of her townhouse complex when she turned into the back drive. Mona knew from experience that the rear access got cleared first because the shed that housed the tractor was there. Mentally making lists of things to do, she almost missed that there was something odd about her townhouse.

If she hadn't come in the back way, or if it had been snowing any harder, she might not have seen the two shapes in the snow by the patio exit. She thought she saw a glow of magic about them, but given the distance she couldn't be sure. Mona drove past her unit.

Damn. Okay, she wasn't sleeping here. And she wasn't confronting them, whoever they were; she was too tired and didn't have back up. Calling the local Were pack was out of the question. One, she wasn't sure how much help they'd be dealing with the goons, and two, well, they tended to be jerks and she avoided them as much as possible. Plus they'd want to know why the men were there and she'd promised Raine to hold off on telling the pack. If the shapes were still there when she came back tomorrow, she'd call and deal with their testosterone-laden leadership and comments on how helpless women were. But right now, no, thank you, she wasn't in the mood.

Mona checked the time. Twelve thirty-five. Far too early to head out to Smythe's and too late to call pretty much anyone who had little kids or babies, which meant most of her friends. Okay, then, it'd have to be her brother. She'd only be able to grab a couple of hours, given he was southwest of the city and Smythe was almost straight east, but something had to be better than nothing. Luckily she always kept a gym bag with a change of clothes in the car; part of her training with Smythe was showing up when spells went awry no matter what the time.

Nic answered on the third ring, annoyingly alert. "Mona?"

"There's a problem at my unit and I can't sleep there. Can I come crash back at the house tonight?"

"You need me to come over? What broke?"

Nic was an elf, like herself. After their mother left, he'd suppressed his abilities, which were quite strong from what Mona had read at one point, and ignored his heritage. Not fully ignore it as he worked for a secret division of the federal government monitoring Folk activity. He'd be less than thrilled to learn she'd come to embrace her Folk connections. Mona frantically thought of a safer reason she'd need to head over. "Nothing at my place; a plow hit the fire hydrant and the road's blocked."

"Even if you did get in, water's probably off. I'll go shovel the drive."

Tomorrow…no, today was already shaping up to be a hell of a day. She dreaded Smythe's reaction when he found out that she'd not done the assignment. Curmudgeon was the least of his bad traits. But given each region only had one Warder and he was it, she really didn't have a choice on teachers.

Nic had shoveled to the street by the time she arrived. She unclenched her hands from the steering wheel as soon as she turned onto the driveway, only then realizing how close they'd been to cramping. Her brother stood inside the garage, leaning on his shovel.

"Hey, sis," he said as he took her bag. "Were you able to find out when they expect the water to be back on?"

She blinked at his question and, knowing he caught her blink, covered for it.

"It's late and I'm short on sleep, so, no, I didn't think about calling. It's Sunday night, remember? Plus, they've likely got everyone available out plowing and shoveling."

Nic merely grunted and led her into the house.

Warmth enveloped her as soon as she entered. Mona had lived here from the time she was in fourth grade until she'd moved out a couple of years ago. Their mom had, with foresight, put the deed in Nic's name once he'd hit eighteen. When she'd moved on—almost a decade in one place had to be a record for their mother—Nic was out of college and Mona was almost in high school. Mom had made sure they had money to take care of things. Odd as it had been—and there were times when things got very odd, not the least of which were the hoops they'd had to jump through since their mother had given Mona her last name and Nic his father's—they'd managed. Mona had learned only recently that the elves traditionally gave their child the last name of the parent they felt would give their child better social standing. Apparently, that was one tradition her mother hadn't bucked.

Mona was glad Nic had redecorated since she left. The natural woods and blues and yellows in the kitchen were nothing like the brown and avocado she'd grown up with. Some memories she was happy to leave behind.

"You want something to eat?" he asked.

And some never left. What he was really asking was if she wanted him to stay up and keep her company. Particularly since she knew if they ate, she'd be cooking. Not because he couldn't, but because she loved to. She loved being in a kitchen, despite the fact that she'd dropped out of culinary school after a couple of semesters. Not that she had much time for it these days.

Imps were here, too? She blinked at the stove light. Yes, that was an imp. Were they always this prevalent and she'd just not noticed them, or was something going on? Had Nic somehow attracted them? Even though he ignored his magic, it was very strong; the imps might well have responded to it. Another thing to ask Abner Smythe about.

Nic was waiting for her answer.

"No, I'm bushed. Unless you want to stay up?"

"Nah, I should try to get back to sleep. I'm judging a regional Taekwondo bout tomorrow." He leaned over and kissed her cheek. "Night, sis. Let me know if you want me to come out and help with any clean up from the water being off."

Now there was an idea, she thought giddily as she trudged up the stairs behind him. She could have him come out and "fix it."

Mona hadn't read him recently, but the last time she did, he was still teetering on the precipice of coming into his powers. Knowing his rejection of his elf side, she didn't want any action on her part to be the catalyst to propel him into a life he clearly did not want to accept.

Exhaustion hit her in a wave as she flopped down on her mattress. She really sucked at this lack of sleep thing.

Her mind buzzed with all the worries she'd shoved back during the night: what was going on with Raine, how she'd now become a target, who could have set the spell. And, mostly, how much about the situation she was going to tell the Warder.

Sleep first, figure things out later. Mona rolled over, pulling the comforter on top of her, and decided that that was an excellent plan.

Chapter Three

Headlights flitting across wind-driven flurries, Mona turned the last corner of the tree-lined drive to find the entry of the Warder's complex in complete darkness. The dashboard read six fifteen. Hell, given the crappy roads this morning, she was lucky she'd arrived only a quarter of an hour after her scheduled lesson. She knew Smythe would be snitty about her late arrival, but turning off the lights seemed a bit extreme.

Yet another reason to wonder why she put up with his crankiness. If there was anyone besides the self-important old coot who wospell himself; warders uld teach her about wards and spells, she'd take them up on the offer in heartbeat.

But this, this was just wrong. Even the motion sensitive floods stayed dark when she pulled over to park next to a pile of plowed snow. One or two windows of the castle Smythe called home hung lit and disembodied in the ebony bulk of the buildings, so the power was on.

No, something was off here. As much as a pain in the ass Smythe could be, and some days she swore he made it into an art form, he wouldn't outright ignore her. He enjoyed busting her chops too much.

In the weak winter moonlight, the blue shadowed gate and the crenellated wall around the complex looked positively gothic.

Mona blamed the thought on too little sleep. Along with the sneaking worry that Warder Abner Smythe might be in trouble. She shook the worry aside; the complex was literally a fortress, built of stone and embedded with spells. Besides, clandestine images apart, the place didn't seem to show any evidence of an attack. Apart from the gated entry being dark, and the eerie picture the moonlight painted, everything seemed…normal.

But she definitely needed to check things out, just to be sure. She was too far away to see whether the guard spells on the walls and gate had been breached. First step would be to look at them and figure things out based on what she found.

Opening the glove compartment, she pulled out her flashlight, hearing Nic's smug "Aren't you glad I made you put one in there?" She'd never told his overprotective self how, after the first time she'd gotten stuck in the snow heading out of Buffalo to the Warder's to train, she'd made sure to keep one in the car. Particularly since she hadn't informed him about her training. So not going down that road with him. He chose to deny his folk blood; she didn't have a choice.

Mona bundled up and headed out into the lightly falling flakes. Her tire tracks were the only ones showing in the three-inch deep snow. Aiming the flashlight at the drive, she tried to find evidence of anyone coming by recently. Nothing obvious struck her, no lost hubcaps, no distinct furrows under the snow. Hell, she had no clue what she was expecting to find.

She cautiously moved toward the entry; the last thing she wanted was to turn her ankle. A strong breeze smacked her upside the head as if to ask what the hell she thought she was doing.

"Look, I'm just going to check the guard spells, then head back."

Crap, had she really said that out loud?

The wind slammed into her, so strong that another step forward became impossible. She stopped and the gale force gust stopped with her.

She was reasonably certain wind sprites were incorruptible by evil. And this wasn't a spell; no sigils or runes threaded the breezes.

Whoever or whatever had requested the sprites' help didn't want her to go any further.

Mona shone her flashlight over the frozen landscape. The gate stood perhaps fifteen feet away, the wall a touch more. Both were still too far for her to clearly read the myriad of spells scrolled upon them. She swept her beam across the ground, not sure exactly what she hoped to find.

A glint of pulsating red embedded in the dirt under the snow caught her eye. Mona cocked her head and leaned forward, angling the flashlight. Was that—yes, the glow came from magic.

Someone set a spell so it lay just under the gravel of the drive, hiding the telltale signs from her. Now that she knew where to look, she saw the working created a rectangle in front of the entry. If she'd driven up to the gate as usual she would have crossed into the field of the spell none the wiser.

The colors, including areas where it deepened, were exactly the same as the spell on Raine.

Mona shivered, and not from the cold. Given the little she'd seen, triggering the spell was a bad idea. How bad remained unclear. Several of the runes she did not recognize, her innate eye for reading them inexplicably blind. Warder Smythe had not yet covered these either. From what she could tell, the primary focus centered on stones and movement. An earth-based rune sat at the center. She reached out to trace the shape—sometimes doing so helped her learn the meaning, and if she knew the meaning she might be able to manipulate the spell to be less potent. The wind slammed into her side, upsetting her precarious stance. Arms cartwheeling as she tried to regain her balance, the flashlight arced out of her half-frozen hands and flew forward.

The earth rumbled and heaved. Mona shrieked in surprise as the ground buckled. *Move!* Shit, her flashlight must have crossed the plane and triggered the spell. She ran back to her car. Slipping on the wet snow she scraped her hands and knees raw trying to move quickly. Finally reaching it, she slammed her side into the rear bumper in her rush to get behind its bulk. Once safely behind the trunk she turned to watch. Pain burst from her bruised shoulder and her knees screamed protest at her crouched position, but she ignored the distraction.

Two giant slabs of rock surged up and out of the ground, slamming themselves at each other like whales at play before sinking back down. Except there was nothing playful about the shattered bits of plastic, glass, and batteries they left behind.

Mona fell, her ass hitting the frozen ground. That could have been her.

Her.

Smashed.

If the wind sprites hadn't stopped her from going forward… bile burned the back of her throat at the gruesome image. Oh! And had the lights had been on and she'd driven on like usual…

As if her thought triggered them, the floods above the entry flickered and the area was bathed in their warm glow.

Momentarily blinded Mona blinked away spots as she scrambled back to her crouch. No time to be sick, she breathed shallowly, trying to clam her frantic heart. Little puffs of breath hung in the cold air in front of her, giving her position away to anyone looking. Not like there was anyplace else close enough to hide.

The huge wooden door creaked open.

Smythe wobbled his way around the edge, the scant strands of his white hair bobbing as his head palsied. He took the few steps to the edge of the churned up area. She expected him to blame her for the mess because, goddess knew, anything that went awry when she was around was her fault.

He stood for a moment staring at the rubble, then motioned absentmindedly to where she hid behind the car. "Mona, you may come in now. You did adequately in your challenge."

What the…? That better not have been a test of her skills and reactions. Yes, she was tired of him pushing her to solve theoretical problems, when there was significantly more practical work they could be doing. Like restoring the wards around the Buffalo pack's neighborhood, which she'd been told not to touch, despite the fact that her fixing them in the first place was how Smythe had found her. Instead—except when a spell was threatening to expose Folk or harm someone—they'd spent the last four months with her memorizing rune families and his quizzing her on theoretical scenarios.

Although a spell to crush her was hardly theoretical. Mona shivered at the memory of the slabs crashing together.

His statement didn't make sense. One, he could not have se the spell himself; Warders were unable to bing magical energy and create the runes needed to make spells, they could only see and manipulate workings others had made. And two, the taint of the magic was evil. Forget about saying evil was a state and not a being; the magic had been drenched with pure malice of thought and action. Just like the spell on Raine.

And three, hello? What happened to it being her fault? He might be safe, nothing had breeched the walls, but something very screwy was going on here. Either she could go in and get dragged into whatever mess Smythe had brewing inside the walls or stay out here and avoid getting blamed for the problem. Right, stay it was.

"Mona?" His querulous voice rose at the end, sounding like the schoolmaster he was.

She didn't budge from her spot.

Smythe rocked, buffeted by the wind as he stood waiting. The sprites seemed displeased, which only firmed her resolve to stay where she was.

"You've been enough trouble already, running late and creating this mess."

Yep, there it was, the pile of blame being heaped on her doorstep.

Reaching out, Smythe manipulated the remaining rune and the pile collapsed back in on itself, leaving the ground more or less level. Like she needed further indication that Smythe, frail as he was, could take care of himself.

Smythe tugged his jacket straight, then dusted the hem. "Once you are over your tiff, you are to study chapter six, parts ten through twelve. Lessons, however, are suspended until such a time that I feel you have shown sufficient remorse for your actions. Contact me when you are ready to discuss improving your attitude."

He turned and shuffled back in, thudding the gate closed behind him. Thankfully he left the lights on.

Suspend lessons until she showed remorse? She wasn't a recalcitrant teenager and didn't appreciate being treated as one. Mona counted to twenty, just to be sure he wasn't going to pop out again, then scurried around and got into her car, shivering and thoroughly chilled.

What the hell had just happened? No matter how she twisted and replayed the situation in her head, she could make no sense of why the Warder would say the trap had been a challenge. Blame her, yes; downplay the danger, yes again; but to say he'd set the spell as a challenge?

Who the hell challenged a Warder? And why?

She had no clue.

One thing was clear—Warder Smythe was fine, no matter who or what had set that spell outside his gate. He'd shown no worry or concern. Things looked to be under control inside the complex, then. His adding the "contact me" also helped ease some of her worries, although she couldn't say why.

Knowing Smythe, there was the possibility that the sections he'd assigned held a clue or two. Of course, she'd need to shift through a lot of crap to find them. She wouldn't know until she got back to her copy of the encyclopedia at her house.

At the entrance ramp onto the highway, the battering her body had taken made itself known, her arm a constant siren of pain and her legs pulsating throbs. Her body started shaking. Exhaustion? Adrenaline drop? Didn't matter, best to head back home and get some sleep either way. No, wait, go to Nic's. At least he'd be out. She could grab an hour or two, then head up to meet with Raine.

• • •

Sitting on the couch, mug in hand, Mona eyed the phone on the opposite side of the coffee table. The device might as well been a mile away. Mona's right elbow thrummed with pain and both knees were stiff with a heavy cushion of swelling. Thank the goddess her elf blood meant she'd healed some already. She'd felt alarmingly like a human hockey puck when she'd gotten out of the car. Now she was just bruised, battered, and effing sore.

She didn't remember much after she left Smythe to sell his hot air of an excuse to the thin air. Driving back down to Buffalo. Stumbling in through Nic's front door. Landing on the couch, unable to sleep as shivers wracked her body. Calling Raine to check in, assuring each other they were fine and could wait to meet until the afternoon. As the panic receded, the hope that she'd have enough time to sleep and heal vanished faster than jerky at a shifter picnic.

Her cell phone rang, the loud blaring trumpets of a military march echoing in the living room. No excuses, she knew she needed to answer. It might be Raine, or even Smythe or the Pack with an emergency.

Ignoring the pain, she half stood to reach across the table.

The phone rang again in her hand. A shock buzzed through her fingers. Golems take it! Fumbling, she switched the phone to her other hand, shaking the tingling off. She glanced at the caller ID—no name and not a number she recognized.

She press talk and took a deep breath. "Hello?"

"Mona!"

A sour ball lodged in the pit of her stomach. Raine was frantic, and frantic wasn't good with the spells she had on her.

"Mona? Are you there? I need to see you!"

"Are you okay?" She pulled herself forward and sat on the edge of the couch.

"Yes, but something's come up. I'm not sure I can stay here." Raine sounded a tad calmer.

"Get out of there!"

"No, I have a little time, I'm sure. Please, just come and meet me here, okay? I'll feel safer leaving if I'm with you."

Mona didn't like Raine waiting, but getting Raine more frantic by arguing with her wasn't going help. "Where are you?"

"At the motel behind the Seneca Nation Casino." Raine audibly swallowed. "Mona, I remembered things about these guys. Things that'll help you stop the hurting and killing of Weres."

That explained why they were after both of them. "If you think you need to leave before I get there, don't wait."

There was a pause.

"I'm scared." Raine's voice was soft. "For me, for the baby. I—I'll try to calm down, but get your butt out here, okay?"

Mona had already picked up one of her brother's snowboarding jackets. She tucked the phone under her chin and slid one arm in, biting her lip to keep her moan of discomfort to herself.

"On my way. Just promise you'll leave if things get hairy."

"Yes. I—"

An automated voice came on asking for more money. Raine hung up.

Mona blinked at the phone in her hand. She pressed redial but was told the line did not accept incoming calls.

The urgent plea in Raine's voice pulled at her. A premonition, a worry, definitely something she'd seen in the spell on Raine told her this was not good, not good at all. Hurriedly, she opened the front door and headed out to her car.

The wind whipped past her and froze her nose solid within two steps. Shivering, she tossed her ruined clothes in the back and looked at the sky. Another storm was building up over the lake.

Mona couldn't wait to complete her training so she could finally do some traveling. On her brother's advice, she'd put off exploring the country until she had a steady income or a portable skill. Being a Warder was clearly a portable skill and there were Folk enclaves all over the United States. Of course, she'd have to avoid the southern plains—witches held sway there—but there were so many other places she could go. She'd start with the larger ones, typically located near Elfhaven portals, like here and the one near Reno. The idea of being somewhere warm was very appealing right now. She'd heard there was a small community outside San Antonio, too. Visions of dry scrub and Joshua trees along with the smell of sunscreen danced in her head as she rushed through the lowering gloom and across Grand Island.

Twenty-two minutes later, Mona showed her ID and picked up the spare keycard Raine had left at the front desk. She'd healed more on the drive over, rotating her shoulders and left leg as much as she could to help speed the process.

The maid's cart was in front of the door and the room was bare. Not good, not good. Looked like Raine had already left.

Mona flashed the card and went in. Raine's things were gone. More importantly, no imps were hanging around; they'd abandoned the place, too. After nodding thanks to the woman who'd ignored the whole thing, she noisily ran back down the stairs and out to the lot.

Shit, shit, shit!

She jogged around the building. Careful of her still sore knee, she slowed to cross the several frozen slick spots. No sign of Raine's small vehicle. Mona pulled out her phone and tried calling but got no answer.

Which meant she could be almost anywhere. Crap.

Okay, what to do. Mona went back to the warm lobby, trying to guess where Raine might have gone. There'd been no magical residual in any of the spaces she'd checked. Raine's room, the lot, the lobby—all were bare. So she had to assume Raine had left of her own accord. The clerk came out of the back room, frowning at her. He'd been a snit about giving her the keycard, despite her showing the proper ID and the clear note from Raine she'd seen on the desk.

Mona stood and crossed to the counter. She handed him a credit card. "I'd like to put my friend's room on my card please."

"Room number?" the clerk asked as he tiredly clicked on a keyboard set below the counter. As if he hadn't just given her the third degree when she'd asked for the keycard.

"Two-sixteen."

He glanced down at the screen and back at her. "Two nights already paid for. You want to do more?"

"Oh, no, thanks. Didn't realize she'd handled it. Can you tell me when she did? We seem to be crossing messages here."

"Sorry, can't."

Can't, won't. She didn't argue with him. A couple of minutes one way or the other weren't going to help her figure out where Raine had gone. And she had been here when she'd called, Mona was sure of it.

Not knowing what else to do, she headed to the lobby doors, with the vague idea of maybe going back to the mall to see if Raine had returned there.

Mona paused in the tiny vestibule, having heard the rear exit open. Maybe that was Raine. She turned to check. The bulk of two large Weres shadowed the hall, the essence of Folk and evil leeching out ahead of them.

She followed her instincts and ran, skidding across patches of ice on her way to her car. As she expected, they gave chase. Good, she needed to get them out of here and following her before they hurt mortals or exposed their magic. Mona wasn't sure which would be worse at this point.

She was backing up when they reached her. One tried to come around, hand aiming for her door handle. There was no doubt he was strong enough to rip the door open. Gunning the motor, she shot back, skidding across the icy lot.

The car spun three-sixty, clipping one of the goons hard enough that he thudded over the hood, his back slamming into the windshield before he tumbled off. The other backpedalled out of the way. She watched in her review mirror as he yanked his friend upright. The motel clerk stood by the door and was yelling at all of them, furiously scribbling down something—likely her plate. Mona eased up on the brake and tapped the gas. Her two assailants were already climbing into a Jeep double-parked in the fire lane.

As soon as she was in control of the steering, she hightailed it away from the lot. The Jeep wasn't far behind. Not good; she wanted them to follow her, but not this close. Her heart beat frantically and her hands shook. The trick was to not get caught, she had no illusion about the amount of harm the two would inflict if they got her in their grasp. The little bit of self-defense she knew wasn't going to help against a pair of hulking brutes. Try as she might, images of becoming battered and bloody played in her mind, sending panic coursing through her.

Mona hit yellow lights on every intersection, causing her pursuers to blow through the reds and finally attract the attention of a cop. Either her timing was excellent or the imps were helping.

They slowed down and she kept going, quickly losing sight of the cop's flashing blue lights in her rearview mirror. The distance meant they were less of a threat—now if she could just convince her panicked self of that.

South, over Grand Island toward the Folk enclaves near Lackawanna, seemed the best option. She'd agreed to Raine's request not to tell the Buffalo pack last night, but with unknown Weres chasing her and probably Raine, she'd be damned if she went anywhere else. There was no doubt in Mona's mind that these two were the same toughs she'd seen lurking at her place last night. Somehow they'd learned she'd helped Raine and were now coming after her.

The combination of the increasing rush hour traffic and sleet made driving more treacherous with each passing minute. She'd made it across the two bridges to the island without a sign of pursuit, but the Jeep showed up again as the Buffalo Skyway began, and the road started its rise over the surface streets. Dry-mouthed panic and a frantic heart were back full force. Dividing her attention between the incline ahead and her rearview mirror, she watched them swerve in and out of traffic, gaining on her.

Jerking her attention back, she found a solid wall of ice pellets heading her way and cars slowing down as it approached. She hit the brakes, the antilock mechanism kicked in, and the car stutteringly decelerated. Somehow the Jeep managed to pull alongside her on the left, tinted windows hiding the brutes' faces. A window lowered just enough for the tip of a gun to peek out. Any hope that she'd survive an encounter with them fled.

Mona jerked the wheel hard and bashed into the Jeep's side panel, sending it sliding across the skyway to the opposite side. Car horns blared and vehicles spun out as the wall of precipitation hit. Not waiting for them to sort themselves, Mona pulled over to the right shoulder and started backing up. Wheels humming on the safety treads, she only spared a few glances ahead to where the Jeep was still going forward on the far left, and the rest of the traffic was still snarled. Thankfully no one seemed to be injured, although at least one vehicle wasn't going to be moving anytime soon.

Going backwards down the incline was slow, the road behind, difficult to see due to the angle. The icy precipitation didn't help. But so long as she was heading away from the Jeep and that gun, she didn't care about her speed.

The itch of a large and forceful spell being worked made her stop. A huge ripple of magic, like a distortion of heat in the frigid air, arched out from the ground below the skyway to the wind turbines along the Lake Erie shore. The angry red tone color was all too familiar.

The immense metal and concrete structures shuddered on their bases.

Holy Goddess of the First Tree! Mona didn't know when a working of this size could have been set. She was fairly certain that she'd have seen that amount of magic on her way up and changed it, Warder restrictions be damned. Although, shit, if it'd been set down into the ground again, she may not have seen the markings from the elevated road.

The urge to help hummed in her veins. To shield Folk from mortals, or mortals from Folk, didn't matter at this point. Saving lives did.

Leaving the car running, she got out and ran around the front to the Jersey barrier at the side of the road, ignoring the honking. These people were in far more danger than just the traffic jam the Jeep had caused, and she needed to do something to protect them.

No time to read everything, Mona concentrated on the symbols that shone the brightest. She flipped the rune controlling movement to the side, slowing the working down. Then, before the spell fully took, she turned the size one upside down, halving the area it encompassed.

With a sense of dread and futility, she watched through the sleet as the spell took hold. With a loud bang and a flurry of sparks a blade from of one of the turbines sheared off. Glowing and unnaturally spinning like a drill bit, the huge metal spike arced slowly toward the skyway. There was no way to hide this, even to the mortals.

Car brakes screeched and metal crunched as the few cars that had managed to straighten out halted, trying to avoid the oncoming projectile.

People abandoned their cars and started to run back down the highway, screaming and carrying children, slipping and sliding on the slick roadway, desperate to get away.

Jostled and cursed at, Mona stayed where she was, watching, waiting. Finally a symbol rose to the top of the spell. Motion. She might be able to pull the rune out and lessen the amount of damage from impact. An impact that would happen soon—very soon.

Perhaps she could tweak the location of the target. She followed the trajectory, only to see the Jeep-boys were out of their car and running along the opposite edge toward her. Still off a way, they were already aiming their guns at her, ignoring or oblivious to the danger hurtling toward them.

Time was running out. Mona tapped the symbol, stopping the blade's spin and slowing momentum behind the blade to the weight of free fall. Something must have alerted the men, because they stopped and looked back over their shoulders, turning fully around in the next step, guns braced and aimed at the new threat.

With no way for her to get off the overpass in time, she needed the protection her car afforded. Counting seconds, as if she had a clue when the blade would hit, she hurried back to her car as fast as she dared on the slippery slope, worried she wouldn't make it in time. As she climbed in, the road shuddered, rocking the chassis. She turned off the engine.

The sound of nails scraping a blackboard magnified a hundredfold shrieked out as the tip of the blade ground against the concrete. Covering her ears, Mona leaned into the steering wheel.

The barren stretch of road where the skyway leveled out, imploded under the impact. The concrete tumbled, and the cars rose and fell as the skyway buckled.

The car ahead of Mona was hit by the car in front of it as the sedan slid back. Mona sat back up and crossed her arms in front of her face a moment before her airbag exploded.

Fuck, that hurt.

The car swayed along with the overpass, but her section remained aloft. As the jostling slowed, the airbag deflated and she could see again.

The blade stuck straight up in the dusk tinted sky, the road on either side gone.

If she hadn't sent the Jeep careening across the road, and there hadn't already been a snarl-up, more cars would have been on the collapsed section.

The Jeep.

As if her thoughts had conjured them, the goons climbed up from the askew section in front of her. Dust swirling around them, they pulled their guns out of their holsters. Whoever had sent them was determined to end Mona's interference.

Mona saw the second part of the spell too late to save them. The same summoning whirlpool of magic she'd seen at the mall formed, giving her an ill feeling about what was coming next. This time, though, she knew where to look and could see sequence of runes and sigils. The mage had set the spell to pull the Weres and their innate magic back, whether or not they survived the shift.

With all her heart she wished she could change the spell, erase it from being, but the linkage between the runes and sigils was too complex for her to manipulate without risking getting sucked in as well. This time she could see the coils of magic strengthening the spell and giving it the energy needed to change the men. She also saw some type of shield so mortals wouldn't see this aspect of the working. Why the mage who had set this wanted to hide from mortals was something to consider later.

A tentacle of magic wrapped itself around each man. Their bodies jerked at the contact. As soon as she realized what was going to happen, Mona closed her eyes and ducked under the dash.

She could imagine all too well the mutant change of their bodies, followed by the evisceration of their innate magical energy once they were stuck half-man, half-beast and defenseless against the creator of the spell. Someone was harvesting the power of the failed change. The idea was sick.

Nausea roiled and she lost the fight with her stomach. Fumbling to unbuckle her seatbelt, she shoved the car door open and lost what little contents her stomach had on the ice-laden blacktop as sleet pelted her head and back.

Who could force Weres to change like this?

Why was he then harvesting the failed attempts?

What the hell had the power to make such a working—or even knew it could be done? Suddenly being shot by the spell caster's henchmen seemed minor compared to the evisceration of the Weres.

Dammit, Raine was right. They needed to track this person down and stop him, not wait for him to continue creating spells that killed Weres. And she still needed to find her friend.

Of course, she had to get out of this alive first. But the pavement was still unstable and she was still in too much pain to move. All she could do was wait.

Finally summoning the courage to look out the front windshield, Mona discovered the chunk of concrete that the pair of spelled Weres had stood on was gone. She doubted anyone with Folk abilities had survived the second part of the spell. Her vision blurred when she realized how close she'd come to being in that group. Somehow her unique ability to have spells slide over her had kept her safe, even though she had Folk blood.

Shivers wracked her body.

Pulling out the emergency and stadium blankets from the fateful kit from the mall, she bundled under them.

•••

"Stay in your cars."

Someone was shouting instructions through a bullhorn. She rubbed her eyes. Darkness was rapidly falling across the steel-clouded sky. Red and orange lights strobed across the gutted landscape and flashed in her rear view mirror. Another blinked from the cubby in her dashboard.

How had she forgotten she had a phone? Picking up her mobile, she saw eight missed calls and no messages. Every one from her brother.

She tried to reach him, but her call went straight to voice mail. Her phone blinked a warning; the battery was getting low.

He must have been at work and close to the collapse; his office in the federally-owned building wasn't too far away. He'd been close enough to know she was in danger. Just like the time she'd been placed in the wrong group at a Taekwondo match and he'd shown up after racing across the college campus due to a feeling she was in peril.

The bullhorn, closer now, repeated the instructions from the safety of the ground below the skyway.

"Please remain in your cars. Help is on the way. We will come to you. If you can hear this message, turn your hazard lights on. Please remain in your cars."

Gradually Mona became aware that Folk were helping in the rescue effort. Not just any Folk, but a full elf if her reading of the magic was correct. Unlike the nastiness of the spell on the Weres, this was warm, sunny, and grieving with every life lost.

The only person she was aware of who might feel that way was the Maven, the ruler of Folk in the area, although Smythe had never introduced Mona to her.

The storm had passed and the wind finally died down when she felt the Maven's touch directly. It was an odd feeling. Somehow she felt both comforted, like someone had rubbed her shoulders, and uncomfortable, like the person's hand was too hot for her body to handle. Something about it reminded her vaguely of Nic, but she couldn't say why. Her brain was far too fuzzy to figure it out, despite the little bit of self-healing ability she had, and the sensation passed quickly enough that she began to wonder if she'd felt it at all.

Very soon a rescue worker made it to her car. After a quick check of her vitals, it was determined she could probably walk herself down, with aid of course.

At the bottom of the ramp she was checked over by a nurse and gave a heavily edited statement to the police. Released, she settled in a corner of the tent and tried Nic again.

"You get out okay?" was his greeting when he answered the phone.

"Yeah, thanks. How did you know I was in the collapse?"

"Just knew." He shrugged off the ability as if it was nothing. Something was going on; he'd never been this blasé about anything that might be tied to his Elf heritage. "You okay going back to your place tonight?"

And he definitely sounded like he didn't want her at the house. Unable to worry about it now, she added this bit of information to her long list of things to examine later. Along with the Maven being there and explaining the lack of remnants of her assailants.

"Yep." Well, no, but she wasn't going to tell him that.

"Okay, call me in the morning if there's anything you need," he said, adding softly, "Glad to hear you're okay."

"Thanks."

She heard the vague mumbling of a female voice in the background. Her curiosity would have been more sparked if she'd had any energy for it.

Mona tried Raine again. No answer. She called and left a message at the Buffalo pack leader's house, telling them to contact her immediately, but not giving details. Past time she let them know, in hindsight she'd been foolish to promise Raine not to say anything. The pack could be compromised given how many spelled Weres she'd run into. She left a less harshly-worded message on Raine's aunt Betty's voice mail as well. Despite the frantic worry over where Raine was and how she was doing, Mona didn't know who else to reach out to. Except the Warder. She should let Smythe know what she'd seen. But uneasiness settled in her stomach again, a sign she'd learned to pay attention to. There was definitely something off with Smythe, until she knew what it was she hesitated to contact him.

When had her life gotten so complicated? She rubbed the heels of her hands over her eyes, trying to focus, realizing her face had a bit of rug burn from the airbag deploying.

Opening her eyes again, she realized she didn't have anywhere to stay tonight. Or any way to get there.

There were a couple of last resort options, like Raine's Aunt Betty, but she didn't want to call in those favors. Crappy end to a crappy day, it looked like.

Mona wrapped her sore side securely in the blanket one of the workers had given her, knowing the warmth would help, and looked around the area near the triage tents, on the slight chance she knew someone. Worse came to worst, she'd take the first aid workers up on their offer of help.

No luck.

No, wait; a glimmer of a spell caught her eye. At one of the columns, at the very edge of the wreckage, stood a group of Folk, hidden behind a diversionary spell and examining bits of magic.

She could only hope they were the good guys; it certainly seemed that way from their actions. Either way she should head over. Her ribs and shoulder ached with each step she took. Damn, she'd been hit hard, possibly even fractured her shoulder if she still had this much pain hours later. Somehow she'd managed to hide it from her original rescuers and the nurse at the foot of the skyway, although she didn't remember intentionally doing so. Exiting the tent, she assured the women monitoring the victims she had a ride home. She only hoped it was true.

The Folk continued to work until she got quite close. Ah, the edge of a spell. Mona looked it over. Yes, it would let her through just fine. She stepped across and all activity stopped.

A row of unwelcoming, but not necessarily unfriendly faces turned toward her.

One man, the one she'd seen directing things, stepped forward. Were, she was pretty sure; she had no energy to spare to read him. He was quite tall. Mona, at five six, could fit under his chin with a bit of room. Even in the bulky clothes, he looked powerful and sleek, reminding her of a prowling cat. Mona wondered if he, unlike the three men she'd seen forced to change, was a strong-blooded Were, and could turn into his den's totem at any time. Somehow she thought he could, despite being unable to check.

She hoped she was never put in the situation where they would find that out.

"You are?" His strong Brooklyn accent threw Mona for second.

"You're from New York?"

He remained silent, but a small grin teased the corner of his mouth.

"Oh, right." She executed a short half bow, no saying how much protocol he expected. She bit back on the hiss of pain the movement caused her shoulder and ribs. Stupid, stupid of her. "I am Mona Lisa Kubreck, trainee to Warder Smythe."

The group behind him eased their stance, although he stayed still.

"I'm Were Protector and Trainer Josiah Carthage Dupree of the New York Were Training Center. Welcome."

"I think I'm supposed to welcome you, since you're in my territory." The thought slipped out before she could think it through.

The smile almost broke out then, but was suppressed. His brow arched, as if querying whether she was going to do so.

A wave of exhaustion hit her and she steeled herself from swaying on her feet. As much fun as all this was—not—she was too tired to be tactful anymore. "Right. Welcome. Thanks for coming, glad you're here. Look, do you have a way to get out of here? I'm stuck without a ride, since my car is up there." She gestured with her free arm at the wreckage of the ramp.

The playful light left his face, replaced by a "don't give anything away" mask she knew too well from her brother Nic. Well, at least they'd gotten past the careful banter.

"I'll take you. Tiffany, you're in charge until I get back. Hyram, I want you to continue to look for any signs of Folk."

"Try a little further up, by where that triangular piece of roadway is missing," she said, gesturing. "I know two Weres were blown away by the spell there."

Another inscrutable look from the Protector. Without taking his eyes off her, he waved at his group. "Take Menlo and go. Be careful. You'll be out of the spelled area."

He walked up to her, then past. "Let's go."

Mona didn't move. He realized it when he turned to ask her something and she wasn't there.

Scowling now, he came back. The man did have an expressive face; she briefly wondered how he'd look with a smile. With a sensual mouth, medium brown hair with blond streaks, and tawny eyes, probably too darn fine for his own good.

She really needed to get some sleep. Her exhaustion heightened her attraction to him. Tiredness made her defenses low, she needed distance before she did anything stupid. Like jump in his bed. Sleeping with a Were, this Were, would be a colossal mistake. They were far too dominant and controlling and she liked doing things her own way. He was already acting as if there were one set of rules for him and a different one for her. That was so not going to *happen[AA1]* .

"What?" he asked once he'd crossed the spell line again.

"Either you use that damn protocol you had me go through or you don't. You can't have it both ways, formal one minute and then so informal, you're rude the next."

A short silence, then, "Would you please come with me? I can take you out of here."

"Yes, thank you. I appreciate your offer."

Mona would have swept off, but she was too tired to do more than stagger. He grabbed her unencumbered elbow with a muttered, "Let me do the honors."

If she had thought about it, she would have realized there would be a long walk. The group was on the lake side of the skyway and any cars would have to be on the far side.

They'd made it past the collapsed inner lanes of the skyway when he spoke again. "You're wrong, you know."

"About?"

"About the protocol. It's a tool—one you need to learn how to use and manipulate. Most of the time, it's not an either/or situation, but a 'what will serve me best' one."

"I see, so using it to find out the full name of a person in a possibly hostile situation is okay, but not using it to aid that same person isn't? Which justifies being uncivil? Something's wrong there."

He muttered something about her not having seen uncivil yet. She pretended she couldn't hear him.

"I know you want to query me on how I came to be on the bridge, what I saw, and more. I hope, though, you can wait until I get some sleep."

"No, I can't, trainee. There's definitely something wrong going on with the Buffalo pack and I've been called in to find out what it is. I'll have an imp help you make a memory ball when we're in a secure place."

"I doubt it'll be complete, since I can barely remember my name."

"That's fine. I'd rather have it now, before you process what occurred too much, than after you've slept and your memory has already changed."

Man, she hated losing the argument, but knew he was right.

"Can we do it in the car then? Is your place far?"

He halted. "You're inviting yourself to my place?"

This time she was the one who kept on walking, forcing him to catch up, fighting the images of the two of them in bed. This was insane. She never reacted like this before.

"I'm not sure if the two guys I saw on the skyway were the same two who staked out my place last night. Plus there's something screwy going on at the Warder's complex, although Smythe tells me everything's okay. Not to mention every single Folk I've seen controlled by the magic has been Were, so heading over to the Pack House in Lackawanna is out. And that doesn't even cover what's going on with my friend Raine. Or my brother."

Mona wasn't sure why she threw in that last bit, except it seemed to fit.

"You do have somewhere you're all staying, don't you?" she asked. "The Maven—I'm guessing she's the one who set this up— surely arranged a place for you to stay. Or are you just crashing with the Buffalo Were pack? Although, since I'm pretty sure some of them are involved with this, you may not want to do that. And Maven's place is somewhere near Dunkirk, in the wine country—that's a good hour or more, too far to be useful, I'd think. No, there's got to be somewhere close you're staying."

Oh no, she was babbling and couldn't seem to stop. Something had made her nervous.

Right, the frisson of excitement that had raced through her when he'd asked if she was inviting herself to his place. Her mind had somehow imbued his simple question with sexual overtone.

Man, she really needed to sleep.

"I'll take that as a yes, you're inviting yourself to my place."

"Right." She clamped her lips shut.

Chapter Four

"Trainee."

Someone shook her shoulder. She batted at the hand.

"Trainee Mona Lisa," the female voice said.

She knew she grumbled something less than polite. She hated being called Mona Lisa. Mona was fine, thank you. The hand was back. She jerked her shoulder away and rolled into the back cushions of the couch.

A new voice, a male one, sexy yet irritating, said, "I got it, Tiff."

Silence and stillness at last. Mona snuggled back under the covers.

Which were immediately yanked off. "Mona, get up now."

She bolted upright and off the couch. She swayed, her not-quite-healed ribs protesting the sudden movement. Protector Dupree held her elbow while she regained her balance. She pulled her arm out of his grasp, irritated at the urge to lean on him. "What?"

"You've got an imp waiting," Protector Dupree said, gesturing to the hovering spark of pure magic. He was up and dressed and distracting.

"Oh?" She rubbed her eyes and blinked at the blue sparkler. This was the first time she'd ever had one appear with a message for her. It was one thing to find them hiding in lights or zipping by as they did magic, quite another to have the sparkling shimmer of one hovering in your face. A faint hope stirred that it might be from Raine, but it was quickly squashed. No way would her friend have access to one.

Coffee. She needed coffee. She'd ask for some but somehow she didn't think the man would humor her. Protector Dupree stood at her other side, nearly as close as the imp. Disconcertingly close given sleep had not accomplished what she hoped and diminished her attraction to him. A step to the side, and she felt better. The imp merely moved along with her.

"Um, how do open it?"

"Ask it politely to tell you its message."

The suggestion took a minute to sink in. Mona thought back to how Smythe received his. Right, okay. The blue imp bobbed up and down incessantly, agitated by the wait.

"I am Mona Lisa Kubreck. Please state your message." She left off her title, and, oh, lots of things—like her family affiliations—but it worked.

"Mona, this is Smythe. Meet me at the collapse site at nine this morning."

The imp, whose effervescent brightness she'd been trying not to look at with her bleary eyes, spun twice then blinked out. Good. At some point, she realized the bridge was as good a place as any to look for clues about Raine. She had a sinking feeling that if she found the person who set the spell, she'd find her friend.

Mona rubbed her eyes, hiding the tears that had risen, and stretched her back. She was almost healed. "What time is it?"

"Eight." Protector Dupree perched on the arm of the couch. Whoever had first tried to wake her up—for some reason the name Tiffany sprang to mind—had left. Mona looked around. This was clearly an office, tons of computers and flashing lights. But no desks or chairs, just two couches. Good enough for the night. Now she could go back to tracking down Raine.

"Do you have access to the people who were rescued last night? I'm trying to find if a friend was there." But, oh goddess, did she hope Raine hadn't been there.

"We're putting together a list, I can give you access once we have it."

"Okay, Protector—" His full name, Josiah Carthage Dupree, ran through her head but she wasn't going to use any of those.

She'd sound like his fricking mother scolding him. "Wait, we didn't do that memory thing, did we?"

"Call me Cart, and no, we didn't. We need to, but not now." He stood and walked over to the now closed set of French doors to the hall. "Take a left and there's a bathroom with a shower; take a right and you'll find a living space and kitchen. I'll meet up with you in fifteen minutes."

"In the kitchen or the shower?" Oops. She'd meant to say bathroom, not shower.

His gold-flecked eyes locked on her and a frisson of excitement raced down her spine. Mona hoped those would stop once she got enough sleep. She'd heard Weres often experienced intense instant attraction and lust; she just never thought she'd experience it too. He seemed affected too, if the slight growl he emitted was any indication.

"The kitchen." He opened his mouth as if he was going to add something, but then shook his head and walked out.

She took a quick shower, even though she was putting on old clothes. Okay, she skipped the thermal layer and just put on her long-sleeved t-shirt, figuring that was closer to clean. With no way to blow dry her hair, she gave it a rough rub, leaving the jet black, corkscrew curls tumbling over her shoulders and down her front. She would let it air dry while she had a cup of coffee then braid it back up. Feeling more alert, she gathered up her outer layers and purse, then made her way to the kitchen.

Cart stood leaning against a counter, looking out the window. Brown hair that was light enough to be called dark blond, shined in the overhead light. Definitely feline; she wondered what cat he'd become.

She followed his gaze. In a crack between buildings she could see the lake. The view looked familiar but off.

Looking away, she scanned the counter for a coffee pot, surprised when she didn't see one. Actually the "kitchen" wasn't more than a bunch of counters, a small fridge, and a large table.

"Do I have time to grab something to eat before we go over?" With excellent timing, her stomach rumbled as she finished her question.

He startled. Mona didn't really think he hadn't noticed her, just been deep in thought.

"Sure, we can get something downstairs." He turned and faced her, his eyes fixed on the wet ends of her hair for a moment before sliding to her eyes. "Bundle up. The stairs are inside but just barely. You got a way to dry your hair? And your shirt's wet; it's going to freeze once we get out."

"I'll run back and give it another toweling. Do you mind going ahead and getting me some coffee? Please? Light with two sugars, three if it's a large." Mona headed back down the hall not waiting for his answer.

She rubbed her hair again, knowing that it'd be frizzy now from the mishandling, but what was a girl to do. Mona braided it up so she could tuck the whole thing under her hat. Rats, she didn't have a hat. She hurried back to the kitchen holding the end of her hair, grabbing a twist tie off the counter to keep the braid in. Bundled up she headed on down the stairs. "Barely inside" was right—rickety plywood walls let in the cold and wind, but seemed to keep out most of the precipitation. She opened the repurposed screen door to find herself in an alley she was very familiar with.

D'Alessandro's. She'd no idea they had an apartment upstairs. She'd worked in the kitchen for a while before she'd started training with Smythe. The chef had tried to talk her out of it and stay with him. Oh good, she'd definitely find something edible here.

"Hey, Howard," she said as she walked in the kitchen door.

"Mona! So glad to see you! This guy, he came for coffee, but he didn't say it was for you!" She got a robust kiss on each cheek from the chef.

Howard set to work at the espresso machine making up a large, sweet, milky latte as he asked Cart if he'd tasted her cooking yet then expounded upon what he had to look forward to. Once done, the paper cup and a paper sack emitting a cinnamon laden scent were thrust in her hands.

"Hey, you know I'm still training with Smythe?" she asked.

"Waste of your talents, but if you're happy, I'm happy. Now out. I need to get to work."

"What should I do with this coffee?" Cart asked as they headed over to his car.

"Keep it. I'll drink it cold later. Okay if I eat in the car?"

"Only if you share." By now the odor of cinnamon had pervaded the cabin. And she hadn't even shut the door yet.

"Say please," she said teasingly as she closed her eyes and took a deep whiff of her coffee. Mona couldn't help the moan that slipped out—the fresh brew smelled so good.

Mona looked over at Cart as he whipped his head back. He unclenched one hand from the steering wheel and started the engine. Hoo-boy. Yep, he was attracted too.

"We should go." His voice sounded a bit hoarse. He cleared this throat. "So, what's it like living in Buffalo?"

"I've lived here pretty much my whole life so I don't have a lot to compare it to. The town's not as busy as, say, Toronto—I was in school there for a bit. Other than that, we've got decent restaurants, a downtown area going through a revival, clean energy sources. Not sure what else you want to know."

Mona reached in the sack and pulled out a pasty. Or tried to—a thick, gooey glob came out. "Monkey bread, yum!" Mona ate the bit then pulled out another. She started to hand it to Cart before she thought better of it.

"I don't think you can hold this and drive, you'll get too sticky. Here." She held the bit up to his mouth. "I can give you a taste now though."

"I'll wait."

He had looked at the piece with hunger in his eyes, she was sure. Odd man.

"Fine, suit yourself." The piece was starting to drip, so she tilted her head up and dropped the chunk in her mouth. Stray bits of sugar coated her lips so she licked those off. Her fingers were getting very sticky, but it just seemed a bit rude to lick them and then put her hand back in the bag. Like double dipping. Yuck.

She ate a couple more as she looked out the window; the southern start of the skyway was approaching. "We're almost there anyway, aren't we?"

He grunted his assent, then pulled over, showed some type of pass, and went the wrong way down the service road.

In the broad daylight the blade looked like a massive dagger embedded in the highway. Cracks and craters radiated out from the center, an almost delicate pattern belying the instability of the concrete.

He parked and pulled her attention away.

"I'll take some now."

She handed him the bag.

"No, the other." He nodded to the one in her very sticky, sugar-covered hand.

Their eyes locked as she held the morsel up to his mouth. This time his growl sent tingles down her spine, heightening her awareness of him. Oh, wow, the attraction went both ways it seemed.

He enveloped her fingertips with his mouth, his teeth gently grazing her skin as he removed the pastry. Sucking gently, he cleaned the tips of her fingers before he licked the sugary remnants off her upper knuckles. His hand came up and clasped her wrist, turning her hand so he could trace a path of kisses across the center of her palm.

Her insides clenched and her pulse raced.

Okay, like most other women, she'd read romances. But she'd never understood some of the "aroused just by a touch" stuff.

Oh, boy, did she get it now.

Cracked acorns, she did *not* need this. He could so easily make her loose her focus, something she could not afford, not if she was going to find Raine. Not if she was going to finish her training and become a Warder.

Mona looked away, refusing to acknowledge how he affected her.

"It's killing me too. Let's get this job done." He got out of the car.

"Wait, don't we need to do that memory thing?"

He turned and stood in the open door.

"Mona, if I worked that intimate a spell in this confined a space we'd combust, and I'm planning to spend a hell of a lot more time combusting with you than we have right now."

Okay then, good to know she was right that he was attracted as well. As for the "combust" thing? She didn't plan for them ever to have time, thank you very much. There was no way she wanted that complication right now. She'd finally found her place within the Folk enclave, a place she'd wanted to be, but her mother had refused to "let her conform" to. She wasn't about to let her lust for him distract her from achieving her goal. And, if he was anything like the men in the local pack, he'd start to demand all her attention and her training would go to heck in a hand basket. Not happening, no way. She'd worked too hard to reach this point to give up on it now.

"Let's walk, and you fill me in." Cart looked at his watch. "We've got about half an hour."

Mona grabbed her things and headed out. The wind off Lake Erie rushed against her face, cooling off her flushed skin.

"Here." Cart snatched his watch cap off and set it on her head. "Next time we need to make sure you have a hat."

"I do, in my car."

He merely grunted and started walking toward the lake. Mona fell in step besides him, gathering her thoughts and enjoying the sun, bitter as the temperatures were.

"Everything started the day before yesterday when my friend Raine called."

Mona told him about the mall, then briefly mentioned meeting an elfling at the bar.

"You work at a bar?" No censure, just curiosity.

"Yeah, I'm good at it, I like doing it, and it's not like I get paid or anything while training, so I need the money."

Cart merely nodded and waved at her to continue. She told him about finding people lurking at her townhouse, going to her brother's to crash for a couple of hours, then heading out early to get to Smythe's. They turned to parallel the shore and Mona took a sip of her coffee.

"When I got to the Warder's complex, the place was dark. Not sure what was up, I got out of my car and walked over to the gate. Or at least I tried to. The wind pushed me back and I stumbled away. Somehow, though, I triggered a set spell."

Mona swallowed, remembering her fear. "The ground split open and these two huge slabs of rocks rose up from the corners of the entry and smashed themselves together. If I had been on the area of the spell…"

She shuddered again, and Cart put his arm around her shoulders.

"The thing is—and you know this—spells don't affect Warders, but a spell like that, which wasn't directed at me, but on things that could harm me, would have worked." Mona shook her head. "The color was the same angry glow as the spell I found on Raine as well as the working that destroyed the skyway."

She paused and let him absorb the implications.

"Anyway, I ran back to my car, which was in a safe spot, thankfully. The lights for the gate went on. I waited a minute longer, and the Warder stuck his head out of the gate, told me I've 'passed the test' and to go home and study chapters blah, blah, blah. I was so tired and shaken I just left and didn't think anything of it until much later." She paused. "I think—"

Cart held up his hand to stop her. "I do want to know what you've surmised, but not now. First tell me what happened, then we'll start putting the pieces together."

Mona proceeded to tell him everything else, from Raine's frantic call to being on the skyway when the working struck the wind turbines, to her worry about where Raine might be now.

After she was done, he went over details, making her draw out far more than she realized she'd remembered. Including the fact that the Warder had told her to study a particular section of the *Tome of Folk Lore*, a huge book she'd been using as a her training text. This, Cart seemed to find very interesting.

They looped back and headed to his car.

"You need to do something for me—don't tell anyone else all of this," he said. "I'm worried you might be in danger if someone realized just how many aspects of all of this you're involved in."

"And compared to Raine, I've barely touched the surface."

He shook his head. "I hate to say this, but it doesn't look good for your friend." Cart opened the car door and she climbed in, only aware of how cold she'd gotten once she was out of the wind.

"You've got a couple of minutes," Cart said after holding up a finger to let his crew, who'd spotted him and called him over, know he'd be there in a minute. "Finish up the monkey bread—you're far too short on sleep and will need the energy. I need to find out if my crew learned anything new before our meeting. After that we'll track down Raine."

Cart leaned in and gave her an absentminded kiss on the cheek, already looking over at his group. "Don't leave here without me."

He shut the door and headed over to where his crew stood, examining the spot where the blade had entered the concrete.

Mona sat and gulped coffee, trying to get her equilibrium back, and finished off the monkey bread—not because he said she should. She dug out her phone, couldn't hurt to try Raine again. Damn, it was dead. Surely one of the Weres had a cell she could use. But there was no time to ask—the clock read 8:56. Time to go.

Workers still crawled over everything, and a pair of ambulances sat waiting. She doubted there had been a stop in activity since they'd left.

Warder Smythe arrived almost at the same time she did, crossing to walk alongside her. She caught his arm in his first stumbling step. She wasn't about to let him fall out of spite.

He looked awful, as if he'd aged ten years since she last saw him. Caught up in helping him, she didn't realize they'd gotten close to the group until the sensation of crossing their concealment spell caused her skin to goose bump.

"What happened the other day?" she asked, stopping them on the other side of the working, hoping here, away from the complex, he'd say something.

"If you'd been on time you wouldn't have been in the wrong place at the wrong time." He let go of her arm and walked toward the group. "Announce me," Smythe said, his voice more tremulous than before.

Cart's entire group turned at their arrival. Clearly a Were protocol she wasn't aware of, this waiting to face the person coming until they were close enough to speak.

"May I present Abner Smythe, Warder of the Niagara Region."

Cart stepped forward and bowed. "Warder Smythe, it is an honor to meet you, if unfortunate that there is a need to do so. I am Training Master and Were Protector Josiah Carthage Dupree "

Smythe jerked at the name, although Mona didn't think anyone else thought it was more than a worse than usual tremor.

"I am leader of the Upper West Side Pack," Cart continued. "Second in command of the New York Leadership Council and past president of the North American Pack Training Council. My investigative associates all answer to me."

Wow, she could learn something from him. Like the fact that he'd omitted a lot of information when he'd introduced himself to her.

"Good. Someone who knows something. What do you think of this here?" Smythe used his cane to point out a faded bit of magic.

They went off, leaving Mona to trail behind them. Sometimes Cart would look back at her, careful that the Warder didn't catch him. She'd nod yes, or no, or shrug her good shoulder depending on how her memory matched up with Smythe's analysis.

The rest of the group crowded around, staying close so they could hear the Warder's raspy voice. Cart picked up the habit of subtly repeating what Smythe had said.

They hadn't gotten very far when "Maven" was whispered down the line. Fighting the urge to turn around and watch the woman's approach since Weres clearly didn't do so, Mona followed their lead and did her best to neaten her appearance. About to turn around, Smythe pulled her aside, his grip on her forearm painful, even through her winter coat.

"You need to stay in the background."

He released her arm and they turned to rejoin the Weres.

The Maven was still several feet away, and she wasn't alone.

Nic?? What was he doing here?

It was Mona's turn to place her hand on the Warder's arm to detain him. "That's going to be difficult, as the gentleman with her is my brother."

"Then stay here and don't get introduced."

Not in your life, buster. "I think my staying back is more likely to draw attention. Plus, if I am with you, you can determine who I meet."

He gave a sharp nod. "Fine then, come along. You're still suspended. Don't say anything."

Maven Titania was every bit as imposing as Mona thought she would be. Not that she was large—she barely came up to Nic's shoulder—but her carriage and the amount of magical energy swirling around her, not to mention the absurd amount in her, created a palpably strong sense of being. Despite her hauteur, there was a kind look on her unlined face. Regal, yes, but she was more pretty than beautiful.

She drew to a halt in front of the group, Nic half a pace behind. Graciously she inclined her head as a majority of the group bowed low before her. Warder stiffly bowed just his head, as did, Mona noticed, Cart. Mona settled for something halfway between the two extremes.

"Warder Smythe, Were Protector Dupree, we thank you for your prompt response," Maven said, her voice surprisingly raspy and mellow.

Smythe shuffled up to the front of the group. "Indeed, Maven Titania, it is very clear why you called us. Such a working as this…" His face flushed and his thin jowls shook with anger as his arm swept out to encompass the destruction behind him. "We'll get to the bottom of it."

"We have every confidence in your ability to do so," said the Maven. She caught Cart's eye and her smile twitched.

Clearly they knew each other. Mona watched as the energy around the Maven became less frantic.

"Come, Abner," the Maven said, her tone much less stiff than before. "Show me what you observed."

Smythe hesitated, his palsied hands fluttering with words he wanted to say. Finally he turned and addressed Mona. "You will join us."

He clearly didn't want her to stay behind and talk to Nic. Interesting. Behind him she saw Cart signal to the Maven that he wanted Mona to stay.

"The young woman and Protector Nicolai Lombard will join us in a moment," the Maven said, blithely overruling him. "They share family."

Protector? Mona wondered when the Maven had given him the title—and if Nic knew it meant he was about to be immersed in the Folk heritage he'd long denied.

And, oh crap, was that his magic swirling around the Maven, protecting her? She needed to talk to him about his emerging powers and the link he was building with the Maven. Thankfully, Smythe didn't argue.

"Oh, yes, I have been told, good." He gave Nic a deep bow then shuffled off toward the wreckage, pointing. Cart looked back and forth from Mona to Nic before sending his group off to gather more information.

He said one word, "Careful," before joining the Maven and Smythe.

Chapter Five

The trio was barely out of earshot when Nic hissed, "Why didn't you tell me you were working with Folk?"

"Why didn't you tell me you knew the Maven?" she retorted.

"What other high ranking Folk in the area would I be monitoring?"

Right, she'd forgotten his real job, the one for the government agency that monitored Folk in the area. Of course he'd deny it to his last breath to anyone else, since his branch didn't officially exist, just like Folk didn't officially exist.

Crap, crap, crap. His latent magic pulsated, beating against the constraints he'd placed on it. She certainly hoped he, or at least the Maven, was aware of his pending immersion into Folk life.

"Wait." Nic's gaze, when not focused in anger on Mona, had been constantly sweeping the area. "Someone else is coming to join the merry band."

Indeed, a woman was picking her way across the strewn concrete toward them. Mona and Nic rejoined the rest of the group. He leaned over the Maven and whispered something to her.

Taking her cue from the rest, she turned when they did.

The woman was in her late twenties, perhaps a year or two older than Mona. She looked a bit careworn, but sharp intelligence showed as her gaze shifted back and forth between Mona and the Maven while they waited for her to introduce herself. Cart jerked his head at the Maven.

She swept a deep, proper bow, hand flourishes and all, then remained bent at the waist, waiting for the Maven to signal she could rise. Only after she straightened did she speak. "Maven, I come in response to your message to the Buffalo pack."

"And you are?" The Maven's voice was laced with annoyance. Mona didn't blame her; the pack was stuck in the past with women holding no place in the hierarchy. Sending a woman in response to the request was almost a slap in the face to the Maven.

"I'm Averill, of the Buffalo Pack." Her tone was even, as if she hadn't heard the anger. "Several of my family including two of my brothers and one cousin each served time as leader. When your message to the pack leader went unanswered the imp brought it to my house."

The pack leader couldn't be found and this woman was now the representative? Mona was dying of curiosity, but it wasn't her place to ask. The woman was certainly strong enough to be a pack leader, even though there was some blockage or something around her totem. Probably had repressed her shifting, something Mona had seen before with women of the Buffalo pack.

"Averill, if the imp delivered the message to you, you are clearly a leader," the Maven said, a smile on her face.

"No, Maven, I haven't been trained to do the job." Something about Averill's tone made Mona think she was gritting her teeth and holding in an old argument.

"Yet the imp, when unable to find the person you have designated as leader, went to you," the Maven said, pressing her point. "Despite any perceived lack of training, it recognized you as the current head. You do realize, very few would question an imp's call in this situation."

If the woman heard the chastising tone, she simply ignored it.

"I don't question the imps choosing to deliver the message to me. However, unlike the imp and those present, I'm aware of an…inability to reach pack elders as well as those who have held the leadership position."

"You can't reach the pack elders? When was this discovered?" The Warder didn't keep the worry from his voice.

"And you are?" Leader Averill's voice was polite but cold. Smythe had been unusually discourteous.

Mona fought between amusement that Smythe had committed a faux pas and worry over what was causing him, a stickler for protocol, to have discarded propriety several times now.

"Were Leader Averill," Maven said, gesturing to each person as she spoke. "If I may introduce Warder Smythe. Mona, who is with Smythe. Protector Nic Lombard, who is with me. Training Master and Were Protector Josiah Carthage Dupree and his crew."

Averill bowed to each as she had the Maven, bowing longest to Nic. He shot the Maven a dirty look but held his peace. Mona returned her bow.

Smythe waved off the protocol, again.

Mona exchanged a look with Cart, who also seemed to realize how off Smythe was acting.

"Fine, fine, now, when did you find this out?" Smythe barked at her.

"We only discovered the extent of the problem this morning, after I got the message and made calls to other dens in the pack. Based on what I learned today, everything started about three weeks ago."

"Tell us what you can." Cart's voice was calm, non-confrontational, unlike Smythe's.

"We don't know much." Averill's grimace made clear she was unhappy about that state of affairs. "From what I can gather everything started when our current pack leader didn't arrive for the elders' meeting three weeks ago. The next in line went out to look for him. Only he didn't return, so the elder in his den went to look. When the elder didn't return, a male from that den asked the elder of another den to look for him, not mentioning the previous missing leaders, only their missing member.

"In turn," she continued, "every elder went out, each one approached by the den of the previous elder to go. This continued until a few days ago when they couldn't figure out who could go so the idiots—sorry, but really—stopped sending men out."

"I see," the Maven said.

They pretty much all did. The Buffalo Pack didn't adhere to the newer practice of having protectors with access and knowledge of all dens. Small and densely intermarried, the leaders had successfully argued fifty years ago when the change was initiated on a national level, that there was no need for them in such a close community.

Averill also had made clear, subtly, that the males hadn't told the females until a few days ago. Her guess was the women had put their foot down at sending anyone else out.

"The Buffalo Pack—" the Maven started, irritation in her voice. She paused, and when she continued her voice was once again musical and light. "Well, we will not dwell on what they were, instead we will focus on what they will become. Here, this'll help you."

The Maven touched Averill's forehead, and Mona could see a spell set to mark her as pack leader. "You'll not miss any more messages."

"I. AM. NOT. PACK LEADER." Averill's face flushed and she swept Maven a hurried and flustered bow, not nearly as well executed as her first. "Your Majesty."

"Averill," the Maven said. "You aren't trained as a leader, no, but you have other qualities that made the imp recognize you as one, including a certain doggedness I can't help but admire. I promise that you, and any other Were who qualifies, will be taught; some to be leaders and some as protectors because I am not going to put up with this foolishness again. However, until someone else is ready to assume the job, you are pack leader. I, and everyone here, will back your leadership should anyone challenge the imp's judgment."

Mona was the first to thump her fist over her heart and execute the half bow due a pack leader. The others followed, except the Maven—and Nic, who seemed to be taking his cues from her.

Stunned, and mouth agape, Averill stared at the group. A long minute passed before she clamped her mouth shut and ducked her head in acknowledgement.

"Were Trainer Dupree will make arrangements for your training to start, Averill. He will also make sure a proper protector station is set up," Maven said, her voice less strident than a moment before. "I will set everything up with him, so there is no question it is my will and under my authority. In the meantime, Smythe, please show Leader Averill our initial findings. I think it may be pertinent to her problem."

Averill still looked uncertain and shell-shocked. The Maven leaned in and said something quietly to her that Mona didn't quite catch. Whatever was said, a smile lit Averill's face. Then she looked over the wreckage and sobered. She stepped up to the Warder and started asking him questions about the collapse. Mona again trailed behind and did not contribute.

Time and again Smythe pointed out that the type of magic used, the signatures left, all pointed to Weres rebelling and losing control of their magic. Which simply wasn't true; someone else was forcing them into it. Mona found herself glaring at Cart's back, hoping he'd correct Abner, but he didn't.

By the time Smythe called a halt it was clear Averill was shaking with suppressed rage. Then Smythe, not Cart, summed up what they'd found.

"There is clearly evidence that Weres were involved, however it doesn't seem to be a single Were who did the magic." Smythe wrapped up his analysis. "Of course, Weres can, if they act in concert, accomplish a feat on this scale."

He made a sweeping gesture to emphasize the scope. Realizing what was about to happen Mona put her body behind his so he wouldn't fall when he lost his balance. Mona caught Cart's eye finally, but he gave his head a slight shake.

"I agree. No matter how you look at it, something is very off. We need to gather more information, though, and see if the disappearances and the collapse are connected." Cart's statement earned him a sharp glance from all the leaders except Smythe, who was fussily straightening his coat.

Mona watched as, almost as one, they all looked over at the turbine blade. The image of the men who'd been after her on the bridge rose and she shut her eyes. Finally Averill stirred.

"Maven, Warders, protectors." Averill bowed her head to each of them. "It is clear Weres were involved in this catastrophe. However, I lack the skills to figure out who and how. Even if I could, with so many missing, there isn't enough manpower to track them down."

Reluctant as Averill was to take the job, she certainly seemed ready to shoulder the responsibilities.

"Protector Dupree and his crew will fill you in on what they find," the Maven said, waving her petite hand graciously at the group. Cart nodded his agreement. "You will need to talk to each den and piece together a timeline of what occurred."

"I think it's time to leave things in their capable hands," Nic said as he took the Maven's arm. "Let us know if something definitive comes up."

"Oh, I..." the Maven started before looking over at Nic. What ever she saw there made her give in graciously. "Yes, please do let us know. Averill, I've set up a meeting with the New York City group at D'Alessandro's on the Saturday after this. I'll send out imps, but please let people know. Everyone is to come, we'll have something set up for the children."

Done, the Maven turned her blue-grey eyes on the group.

"Warder Smythe." The Maven waved for him to come closer. Smythe's frown deepened with every step. "Earlier today we rescued a pregnant woman who was bearing a Folk child. The birth looked to be difficult and there is a chance she won't survive. You need to find out how she fared and arrange for care of the babe if that is the case."

"It is my duty and honor," Smythe intoned ritually, although he was shaking.

"Thank you," the Maven said before she turned back.

A baby? Difficult childbirth? Mona swayed where she stood. Raine. She knew it was Raine.

Raine had been here, trapped under the overpass.

If only…no, she couldn't think that way. She needed to find out where Raine was and get to her. Cart left off talking to Averill and was already heading her way—either something in her face gave away her thought or he'd jumped to the same conclusion.

Warder Smythe unwittingly stepped between them. "I'll leave the woman and her baby to you. I'm heading back to the complex."

Cart was staring at Smythe's back like he was a puzzle with far more intricate pieces than expected.

Mona felt the same way, but bit her tongue. "I will take care of the woman and her babe," she said.

"Good, good."

Once Smythe was in his car she approached the group.

"Look," Cart was saying, "there isn't much more we're going to find out here, no matter what the Maven says. We need to help Averill with her end too. Hyram, Monique, Kofi, and Jens, you go with Leader Averill, stay with her and help support her new role with the pack."

He looked at Averill, who opened her mouth, then closed it with a sharp nod.

"The rest of you are off until midnight, when you'll be on duty for the next shift with Averill. The fresh group from New York should be here early in the morning, you're on until they get here.

Oh, and someone—Menlo—get in touch with Loch Lomond, he needs to be filled in."

Mona couldn't help but notice the second group was larger. Perhaps he expected more trouble as the word got around.

"And you'll be?" This from tall, thin redhead with the pixie haircut she thought was Tiffany.

"I'm going to be tracking down the woman and the babe. She might be the lynch pin. Everyone should plan to meet back at base at ten tomorrow morning, or as soon as the new group gets here. Don't hesitate to call for backup if you need it."

Base, Mona assumed, was D'Alessandro's.

Everyone dispersed and Mona and Cart headed back to his car.

"You think it's your friend Raine?" he asked.

"Yes. Lynch pin?" she asked.

"Sometimes large acts like this are done to hide a small thing in the midst, leaving us to sort through everything to find the one 'pin' that caused it to happen."

"You think that's Raine?"

"Possibly."

"Hold up." They were crossing a stretch where a lone portion of the skyway still stood amidst rubble to either side. Residual magic, yellow and warm, lingered although there wasn't a spell. "There's a line of magic from the Maven here. Actually, two sets; some shorter connected lines that look like they are going in and a longer one headed back out."

Mona had never seen anything like it; there weren't any runes or symbols, but there'd clearly been magic used.

"You can see that?" Surprise laced Cart's voice.

"Well, yeah, Warders can see magic even after it's done."

"Not like that. At least, not the ones I know and yes, before you ask, I do know a few, six fairly well and another dozen on a first name basis. Can you point out to me where the magic hops to?"

"Over there, see that clear patch at the edge? That was definitely a stopping point."

"I'm going to regret this but if the woman they found is the lynch pin, I want to see." Cart wrapped an arm around her waist, pulling her close. "Let's go."

Her body contoured into his, setting her nerves jangling and a frisson of something she deliberately mislabeled as annoyance through her. Blackness surrounded them for a blink. Two. Just as her mind comprehended there were shadows of something else in the darkness, they were in the spot she'd pointed out.

"Can we do that again?" she asked, curious about what she had almost seen in the void.

Cart looked at her then doubled over in laughter. Mona smiled, wondering what was so funny.

"Oh, Mona, you are a ruby among diamonds," he finally bit out. "Yes, we'll do it again. Just show me where the next spot is."

"Oh, right." Mona looked around; she'd been distracted by his wide grin. Easy to do. "There, under the skyway, a clear spot at about eleven o'clock. You see it?"

He nodded and wrapped his arm again around her waist. "Got to say, nice to know you aren't going to faint or throw up on me."

This jump was shorter than the other, and she didn't get past the initial shock of darkness to see what else there was.

"Where's the next jump go to?" he asked before she could say anything. She noticed he didn't remove his arm.

Mona looked around. There were no short hops going in here, only one jump coming to this place. But…

"That's odd. The long one goes through that pillar and I don't see a short one. I wonder how—"

Cart put a finger over her mouth, which didn't help the skittering of her nerves, although it did stop the babbling.

He unwrapped his arm from her waist, and then took two steps away. "That help?"

"Yeah," she said, trying very hard not to show how his closeness affected her. "How do those jump things work?"

"Okay if I explain later? Right now it looks like we're going to have to walk around the pillar."

"Climb is more like it. Oh!" She'd taken a couple of cautious steps along the side and gotten a peek at what lay hidden. "That's Raine's car! Under the slab."

The tiny car was nose in against the pillar; only a bit of the side showed from under the slab of concrete angled over it. No wonder the Maven was worried about Raine's survival.

"You see any magic on the slab?"

She shot him a dirty look. If she'd seen any she'd have said something. "Not from this angle. I think we'll need to go all the way around."

He nodded his agreement. "So, how long has your brother known Tania?" he asked.

"Who?"

"Tania, the Maven. How long has he known her?"

So Cart knew the Maven on a first name basis. Interesting.

"Well, he's been on her detail since he started with the agency." If he was a protector he had to know about the agency. "And he's been head of the detail for the past ten years or so."

"He's that guy?" Cart laughed.

"What guy?" Mona was pressed against the pillar, trying to find a little bit of clear, or at least clearer, ground to walk on.

"To quote my cousin: 'Thorn-in-her-side-agent-Lombard.'"

She had to laugh. "Yep, he's that guy. You should hear about her from his end."

Her laughter ended abruptly as a bit of rubble slid out from under her feet and she slammed against the side of the car. Pain radiated along her arm down to her elbow from her already abused shoulder. A whimper and a couple of tears escaped before she could stop them.

Cart was immediately at her side, holding on to her good arm. "You okay?"

She looked over at him, arrested by what she saw his eyes. Concern morphed to passion that rapidly became heat.

As he said earlier, not the time nor place for them to be getting into this. She closed her eyes and turned her head away.

"Mona?"

"Yeah, I'm okay. I just slammed my already bruised shoulder." She stepped away, using the excuse of looking up at the top of the slab. "You were right, we needed to see this, there is some residual magic here. Three layers. The top is the spell that collapsed the whole thing. Under that—"

She looked harder at the now faint runes and sigils and her stomach churned. Thrusting the unease aside, she tried to be clinical about what she saw.

"Under that is a spell bound by death. Someone killed a small Folk creature, perhaps a Stellgut or Greypas, for their magic. The creature had been bound here, their residue hiding the other spells." Which meant the whole thing could have been set for some time; she'd overlook the bit of magic residual a Folk creature had left. "The spell under that…man, this guy likes complexity. This is worse than what he put on Raine. Let's see, at the very bottom…"

The runes and sigils where faint, but still connected to each other and still there, separate but intertwined with the other layers. Here, too, there were places where the spell binding was darker, like on Raine's spell.

"Under it all was another, much larger trigger spell, this one for the turbines' working. I think, maybe, when a certain thing happened, those runes are faded and their energy spent, but when whatever criteria was met, the smaller trigger spell would release the energy bound by the connected spell—"

"The one set by the small creature's death," Cart said.

"Yeah, the magic released from that spell would then trigger the larger one, the one that caused the blades to sheer off. But there's something else here. It looks like someone's come through and shifted some of these, putting a delay in, a slight one, so there'd be a moment of warning before it all came together."

"Not your work?"

"No," she said as she stared at the original spell. She gestured, trying to remember each movement she'd made the night before. "I moved things once the spell was in motion, to slow it down. Then I changed the quantity to half. I think originally two of the turbine tops, or maybe three, were in the spell. I tried to stop the momentum too, but only managed to stop the blade from spinning."

"No wonder you were exhausted last night."

They stood for a moment looking where the spell had been. Mona knew they were both thinking of who could have come along and changed it, and was glad Cart didn't say it out loud. She had no idea if or how she'd defend Smythe if he mentioned him.

"Let's get out of here and see if we can track down Raine," he said. "If she's able to talk, I want to hear what happened from her."

Chapter Six

Mona fell asleep again on the way back to base. This time, she half woke up when Cart carried her in.

"Sleep. I'll wake you up as soon as we track her down. What's her last name?"

"Sumners." Mona barely registered that she was in a bed before she rolled to her good side and buried her head in a pillow.

. . .

"What?" Mona said as she batted at the hand on her shoulder.

"Cart said to wake you," said a woman's voice, "and to give you this."

Mona rolled over and took her charged phone from Tiffany. Of course she was pretty much calling all the women in the group Tiffany since they'd not been introduced. She ought to correct that.

"He still hasn't traced your friend and needs suggestions."

Mona stumbled out into the hall, blinking in the light.

Cart was sitting on the couch she'd slept on last night, phone in one hand, the other resting on a laptop. Spread out in front him was an array of carryout containers along with a stack of paper plates. Seeing food made her realize she'd not had a solid meal in days.

"Have you tried St. Stevens in Lackawanna?" she asked as she sorted through what was left. "They have a neonatal unit."

"No. They were actually next on my list. There's a box in the kitchen, the chef sent it up for you."

"Ask for Fergie in records." She pushed open the swinging door. "She monitors all Folk who come through."

Mona slid the box open. Oh, yum! Stuffed mushrooms in masala sauce. She took a bunch, managing to get the sauce all over the thumb holding the plate. Cart came in, giving the tail end of a message to Fergie before he clicked off the phone. Mona shifted the plate to her other hand and licked the sauce off while she waited. No sense in taking a bite if he was just going to start quizzing her.

"Sharing?" Cart looked up as she popped her thumb out of her mouth.

"Say 'please.'"

"You're killing me, you know that?" His voice had deepened and that look was in his eyes again.

"Stop it," she said, pitching her voice low in case someone was close by. "I don't have time for you and…and…that right now."

She crossed to a chair as far away as she could get in the small room, taking a big bite of mushroom so she wouldn't babble.

"You think I do?" he hissed back. "It's my job to track this guy, not yours. I don't have time to be distracted by your fine ass. I'd say we should ignore it, but personally, I think that strategy is going to bite us in—"

Cart clenched his jaw on what he'd been about to say.

"Eat up and get ready to go, since I doubt I'll be able to dissuade you from tagging along. I can't stay around here and do nothing." He headed out the side door to the hall.

Mona put her food down and followed him. "I'm going because it's my area to protect."

"It's yours to ward. There's a difference. You aren't qualified to track down this guy and you're a danger to others."

"So teach me." Mona didn't back down an inch, invading his personal space to prove the point.

They stood at the far end of the hall, just past where it turned before the bathroom. Behind them they both heard low voices and chatter as people came into the apartment from the entry at the opposite end of the hall.

"I don't know if I can."

"What do you mean 'if you can?'" Mona's voice dropped to a harsh whisper. "Aren't you some big hot shot trainer?"

His eyes narrowed and became flecked with gold. "I am some big hot shot trainer. But given that I'm fighting the need to press you against that wall and fuck you until you scream, I'm going to have to pass for my sanity as well as yours."

"So maybe we should just fuck and get it out of our system." As soon as she said the words, Mona realized sex with this man would never be that simple. Some part of her wanted more, and the intimacy would only increase that ache.

Mona swore he growled, not just a rumbling, but a true growl. "When I have you, we're going to have hours and be alone because screaming isn't going to be all of it." He turned and stepped into the bathroom, slamming the door behind him.

Mona bit back her childish retort—no reason to antagonize him further.

Great. Just great. She had a huge, strong Were lusting after her, one to whom she was just as attracted. She so did not need this right now. Her training came first; she wasn't going to risk losing her position and the connection to Folk after finally finding a place where she fit in. And she wasn't going to turn into Averil, a leader who had not been given a chance, because she was in a Were pack. No, being a Warder was both a calling and a way for her to embrace her Folk heritage, and she wasn't going to put that aside for anyone. Oh, she'd use his help to find Raine, and track down the person doing this. She wasn't stupid. But anything more was out of the question.

• • •

"Hey, Cart," Menlo called out, the phone in his hand.

Cart emerged from the hall, much calmer now that he'd had a few minutes to settle down, and joined Mona and Menlo in the kitchen.

"Some woman named Fergie said to tell you 'she's here.'"

Raine! The idea of food flew out the window; Mona would finally be able to go check on her friend, far more important. "Okay, let me at least grab a coat before we head out this time."

"No," Cart said, "you're going to eat and then we're going to go."

"Excuse me? Are you ordering me around?" Just like a male Were, give him an inch, and he thought he ruled the roost. She was not going to put up with it.

"Yes." He crossed his arms over his chest and glared at her. "The Folk at the center know to keep an eye on her should something happen, which I don't think will. They'll let us know. And you need to eat. I need to eat. Right now, if we run into a problem, I don't think either of us have the energy to help."

Mona didn't immediately respond; one, because she was too mad at him and two, because she was trying to assess how drained they both were. He was a little low, nothing adding the last bit of residual magic wouldn't fix. Good thing they were above D'Allesandro's, with so many Folk stopping at the eatery gathering stray magic was easy.

She flicked her hand at him, putting the now clean magic into the stream that clung to him. There, now they were all set.

"We're fine." Mona grabbed her coat off the hooks lining the wall. "Let's go."

"I'm in charge of this unit and if I say you're not fit, then you're not going." He stood, arms still crossed, barring her path.

"YOU. ARE. NOT. IN. CHARGE. OF. ME." With each word she poked him in the chest, right below the sternum, causing him to step back until he hit the counter.

With a panicked look, Menlo slipped out of the room.

"Watch it, woman." Cart's eyes narrowed.

Not taking his flack, Mona closed the minimal space between them, ignoring the heat searing her from knee to shoulder.

"Do I deserve the same respect as the other members of your team?"

"Yes." He spit the word out as if it was an anathema.

"Have I informed you every time I was tired, cold, hungry, or otherwise unsure of my ability to handle a situation?"

"Yes." He somehow made the word shorter than it had been before.

"Have you or your team been in danger due to my actions or lack of action?"

"Yes."

Mona stepped back, appalled, when it hit her. He'd told her all he could think about was fucking her.

"No way, buster! Your inability to not be distracted by your libido is not my fault."

He grabbed her hand.

His calloused palm covering hers, and she realized how close he was to changing. The energy they created had no other outlet. He closed his glittering eyes and his body started to bulk up.

Hell.

She yanked her hand out of his and wrapped her hands on either side of his face.

"Not now, Josiah," she whispered, his first name coming unbidden to her lips. He shuddered and her grip tightened. "Stay here with me."

The tension in his face eased, so subtly that if she hadn't been focused on him, she wouldn't have noticed. His eyes opened, once again tawny and gold-flecked.

With a growl he slid his hand under the thick mantle of her hair and captured her mouth with his.

Fangs still slightly extended, they grazed her lips, sending a rush of desire through her, making her press her now aching chest against him.

He deepened the kiss and Mona realized she was unwittingly getting a full imprint of him, reading his energy and abilities on a far deeper level than she'd ever read anyone before. As they kissed, his sense of self, family, honor all became embedded in her memory, became part of her.

Along with his raging desire.

Energy burst out from them, rattling the cabinet doors and causing the kitchen chairs to skitter across the floor.

A loud crash of glass made them pull out of the kiss, Cart turning them so he shielded her from the danger. She looked over his shoulder to see the brand new coffee pot had shattered.

Mona rested her forehead against Cart's back, trying to get her breath to slow down. The kiss had made her tingle in places she didn't know a kiss could make tingle. It had been fantastic, literally electrifying, and a really bad idea. He'd only get worse from here on out.

Her suggestion that they just get it over with was clearly dumb, dumb, dumb. She opened her eyes to find him staring at her.

"Better?" she asked as she absentmindedly gathered the released energy.

"For now."

"Good, I—" She turned away only to find a row of faces in the doorway.

Cart and Mona bellowed "OUT!" in unison, sending the group scurrying back.

"Let's get out of here." He brushed past her, grabbing his jacket as he headed to the door.

"And where are we going?"

"We'll grab a slice or two and eat them in the car on our way to the hospital. That suit you?"

"A slice of what?" Mona pulled the door shut behind her and heard someone locking it up.

"A slice of pizza."

"No place close does pizza by the slice, only whole pies. Can't stop downstairs or Howard will want to know why I didn't eat the mushrooms he sent up. You okay with fast food?"

He'd gotten to the bottom of the stairs and turned to look at her. "You're kidding, right?"

"Nope. You're not in New York City anymore, Toto." Mona took the final couple of steps. The thin storm door rattled as a cold wind whipped down the alley.

"Don't I just know it," he muttered.

"We can pick up a beef on weck—it's a local version of a roast beef sandwich on the best roll you've ever had," she said at his confused look. "There's a place around the corner. They should be quick, if they're not crowded. That work for you?"

"Yes. And Mona?" He looked her in the eye and the wonderful but distracting tingling sensation flooded over her again. "Thanks. I…I need to be in control when my beast comes out or bad things happen. You stopped that, and I'm grateful."

"My pleasure," Mona said, and then realized just what she had said. "Wait, I didn't mean it that way. Not that it wasn't nice. It was actually really nice. Actually, I did mean it that way, but not, you know, the other way. The I-want-to-do-it-again-soon way. I do think I want to do it again, but not soon. I mean, I'm busy, you're busy, and I have things to do and if we made the cabinets rattle with a kiss—"

Cart's grin transformed his face, if possible making him more handsome than before. Damned man. He placed a finger over her lips. "Next time, just say 'you're welcome.'"

Chapter Seven

As he'd been directed, Cart parked in the emergency room lot.

"Can I help you?" The security officer behind the desk looked Mona then Cart up and down, radiating irritation.

"We've been called in by Nurse Ferguson." Cart raised the pitch of his voice, somehow making him seem less threatening.

"Go to registration, someone will help you there." The guard went back to monitoring the camera in the ambulance bay.

They mentioned Fergie's name at the desk and immediately someone came through the locked door to let them in. They were led off to a room so small, the swing of the door took up half the space. Mortal emotions strong enough they left a residue, lingered here. Pain, despair, and grief all swirled around Mona. She grabbed onto Cart's arm, swaying from the pressure.

"If you'll just wait here, I'll let her know you are here." Their guide stepped out.

"You need to sit?" Cart asked.

Mona looked over at the miniscule loveseat that took up the wall across from the door. The miasma permeated the dull, washed out material. She shook her head. "Don't you feel it?"

Cart shook his head.

"I need to get out of here." Between her worry for Raine and the miasma in the room she was seconds away from retching.

Thankfully, the door opened and a guy in a security uniform came through. Mona saw a bit of magic in him. Folk, possibly from a Were grandparent. He bowed in greeting, clearly recognizing them as Folk, and waved them out to the hall.

"Please, follow me."

They walked with purpose down, through, across, and up a dizzying array of halls, elevators, and doors. After a bit Mona realized they were following signs to the birthing center. Cart constantly scanned the halls, as if marking each intersection in his mind. Probably was.

They were left in another room, this time far more spacious with two couches, a television, and little pamphlets on the side cabinets explaining everything from proper lactation technique to immunization schedules to post partum menu choices.

Raine was here, and was unlikely to survive. Emotions already raw, Mona clasped her hands to still their trembling.

Cart looked around the room, and headed over to the windows. Apparently okay with what he saw, he turned back. His gaze lingered on the literature display.

"So, how much Elf blood do you have?"

"What?" Mona asked. His question was akin to asking someone their salary. She frowned at him. "Obviously a lot, or I wouldn't be a Warder."

"I'm exactly half, but you know that." Cart turned back to the windows. "My mom is a full elf, a Titania actually; Dad didn't have a drop, which confounded her to no end since she thought he'd had some and counted on her magic to…um…take care of the rest."

Ah yes, the magic only a Titania has to supplement a not-full elf's ability and make him more powerful. And, rumor had it, allow them to control their fertility. She bet it had been a large surprise for his mother.

"Not sure why this is relevant, but my dad is a full elf. From Elfhaven, actually. Decided to adventure earth-side for a bit and met my mom. She was…I don't know for sure, but I'd guess pretty close to full. Raised entirely outside the elf realms. She never went and apparently had no desire to go. In turn she raised us away from any of the Folk enclaves. I didn't have much contact with Folk until I got curious about my heritage when I was in college."

Cart nodded and waved his hands that he wanted her to continue.

"Mom was brought up in a commune and was very adamant about not becoming a number on a page, so we're not on the books, despite father's desire to add us," Mona said. Most elves chose to enter their descendants in Elfhaven's lineage books, so their descendants would be looked after should something happen to them. In order to get listed, a magical evaluation was necessary, something her mother would not tolerate for her or her children. "From what I've heard from my brother, their relationship was very much a case of 'opposites attract.' Dad was called back to Elfhaven when I was three; I've seen him a couple of times since then. Mom waited until Nic was eighteen, then left. Haven't seen her since. Something thing Nic said made me think he thinks she's dead, but I'm not sure."

"But your father's still alive? Do you know—"

A soft knock and a woman walked through the door, leaving it ajar behind her. Lots of Folk in her. She raised a finger to her lips, shushing the pair.

"Mr. and Mrs. Howard," she said. "I'm afraid your sister isn't doing well. Please have a seat and Dr. Pinchon will explain the matter to you."

"Thank you, Nurse Ferguson," the doctor said upon entering, immediately dismissing Fergie. He did not have a drop of Folk in him. "Please, have a seat."

They did as he suggested. Cart wrapped his arm around Mona's shoulders then took her opposite hand in his; Mona needed the comfort.

The news, delivered in a staccato, matter-of-fact tone by the specialist, wasn't good. Raine, or Rebecca as she was on the charts here, was on life support. She'd had some possible brain damage due to lack of oxygen, but they wouldn't be able to tell the extent until she regained consciousness. Which they hoped would happen in the next twenty-four to forty-eight hours.

If it happened at all.

The babe seemed fine, and they placed its age to be about twenty-five weeks. They did stress a longer gestation would make a drastically significant difference in the baby's chance of survival outside the womb.

Right now they were walking a fine line between what was best for the baby and what was best for "Rebecca." There were no easy choices.

"Can we see her?" Mona asked.

Behind the doctor's back Fergie nodded, like she had done the right thing.

"Only one of you can go in right now," the doctor told them. "I'll let you decide."

"I don't know that I could see her face to face right now," Cart said. He turned to Mona. "Will you be up to it?"

Despite the roles they were playing, Mona heard the concern in his voice.

"I'll be okay."

"There's a window you can look in on while your wife's there, Mr. Howard," Fergie said, earning a frown from the doctor. "It's by the nurses' station, but since the other two rooms on that side are empty right now I don't think it'll be a problem."

They went down the hall, the doctor leaving them as they prepped to go in the area. Taking a deep breath, Mona entered the room.

The bed was in the middle of the space. Monitors suspended from the ceiling created a bizarre sci-fi-esque headboard.

Raine was on the bed, unmoving and breathing shallowly.

And covered with more spells than before. In the past twenty-four to thirty-six hours, whoever set the spells had been in the area and Raine had seen him. They'd set a death rune, inextricably laced in, and over the other spells, the entire shape the deep crimson of the most intractable portion of the spells.

And there was nothing, *nothing,* she could to remove it and stop her friend from dying.

Tears streaming down her face, vowing to find the fiend, Mona stood by Raine's side for a long time, looking over the tangle. She didn't dare do much and risk putting things in imbalance. The best she hoped to do was delay things and save the baby.

Mona took Raine's hand in hers, and immediately one of the tracking spells kicked in, sending out a silent alarm. She knew Cart saw it somehow, because she heard him mutter through the glass.

The beacon had been put on top of everything else and, uncharacteristically, was not attached to the earlier ones. Without thinking, Mona pulled it off. She couldn't leave it here, that'd defeat the purpose of removing the working, so she collapsed the energy as much as she could, imagined it as a ball, and put the whole thing in her pocket, where it made an untidy lump.

Knowing she now had a limited time before whatever was sent interrupted her work, she looked over the spells to make sure nothing had changed. A slight turn of a rune and the inversion of the one next to it was all she risked. The spell instantly acted more slowly than before, hopefully creating enough time so the baby would have a better chance of survival.

Mona let go of Raine's hand, leaned over, and kissed her forehead. She didn't think she'd see her laughing, smiling friend again.

Once out of the room she was enveloped in Cart's arms. His warmth calmed and frightened her. It'd been less than twenty-four hours since they'd met and she already felt connected to him. She should step away; she had a job she loved and he was a complication she didn't need. But right now she needed the comfort far more than she'd realized.

"She's not going to survive," she finally murmured into his coat.

She hated that she couldn't do anything to save Raine. Anger and frustration left her shaking. They needed to find out who this mage was.

Nurse Ferguson patted her back. "You did a good job just easing things for her, I think. Her monitors show her blood pressure is already down a bit."

"I tried to buy enough time for the baby," Mona said.

"We're hopeful that you did," Fergie said as she escorted them back down the hall. "Now wait here, and I'll fetch someone to escort you out."

Mona pushed her grief aside and made herself calm down. After several deep, shuddering breaths, she stepped away from Cart.

"Thanks."

"You're welcome."

His deliberately pronounced reply brought a faint smile to her lips as she remembered their earlier exchange.

The same guard came to take them back, and this time Mona recognized his Folk side to be a mix of mortal and fairy, unusual but not unheard of.

They hadn't gone far when a speaker called for specific doctors needed in the ER. The escort stopped and listened to his shoulder walkie-talkie.

"There are armed men in the ER. One may have made it into the hospital proper. I'm thinking we need to get you out now."

"That was quick, you just worked on the spell." Cart's soft aside made Mona feel bad about not telling him she had a tracking spell on her. She didn't want to risk his telling her to leave it and jeopardize the lives of innocent people. Plus the further away from Raine she could get it, the better she'd feel.

They hurried down the hallway, Mona and Cart leaving their jackets behind so their arms would be free. The woman who manned the security door to the birthing center moved from behind an open desk to a Plexiglas-fronted vestibule. After looking around the corner to the area they were exiting into, she let them out.

The guard left Mona and Cart by a bank of elevators.

"Follow the signs to the radiology unit in the basement. Some of the doors may be blocked; when that happens try going up a floor to continue on. Once you get to radiology continue down the hall to the double doors. One is marked with radiation symbols and the other says employees only. Go through the employee side and there'll be a door on your left marked linens. The room has an exit to the loading dock.

"Here." He dug into his pocket and pulled out two IDs of people who looked similar but not quite like them. "These should get you through most doors, just don't go into any of the surgery areas or cancer wards if you can possibly avoid them."

Mona tweaked the spells on each and now the pictures were exact.

Then they strode, walking urgently but not running, up stairs, down stairs, along corridors. Unlike their first walk, they didn't run into many people, most were staying put and out of the halls.

They did, however, run into locked doors and closed corridors that the IDs did not open. The calls over the intercom became more frequent. Soon it became clear that the announcements were naming sections Mona and Cart had just gone through. The spell in Mona's pocket was still sending out signals.

"You took the tracking spell with you, didn't you?" Cart asked, only slightly out of breath from having just gone up two flights of stairs at a run.

Unlike Mona, who was valiantly ignoring the stitch in her side.

"Yes, and I can't leave it. Do you have a faster way to get us out?"

"Can't jump, if that's what you're asking. There's a warding around the building."

She'd seen the runes, but hadn't read them deeply enough to realize there was a containment element.

"We're not splitting up," he said before she could even think of it.

"Okay, let's booby trap the path," said Mona.

They moved a meal cart behind the door to a stairwell making it almost impossible to open without sending the whole thing crashing down the stairs. In another stairwell several wheelchairs someone had stashed on a landing became a pileup for someone to fight their way through. Even though the emergency paging for "doctors" stopped, Cart, showing strength Mona could not even begin to fathom, flipped a cot across one of stairwell doorways, managing to wedge it in the process.

After that, they made their way to the basement. As they came to the bottom of a stairwell they checked the signs; radiology was clearly marked.

"Paging Dr. Armstrong, code silver in radiology."

Slowing down, they peered around a corner to see several guards, including the one from earlier, using zip-ties to handcuff the Were. The cuffed man also had a low level binding spell, something the half-fairy could set with out the others noticing.

Mona watched as the magical working on the Were pushed and shoved at the simple spell, distorting the edges and weakening the sigils. She reached out and tweaked the runes, avoiding those that were darker colored. She shifted things around and pulled the binding tighter by strengthening the power behind them.

The energy coalesced. Oh shit, the secondary spell, the summoning that would force him into his Were, then strip the energy, was taking hold. But this Were looked to have the balance to shift, unlike the others. She hoped he would survive.

"Drop him!" she yelled as she pulled their guard's hand off the Were.

They watched as his features distorted, the smell of blood and fear overwhelming the hallway as he was forced to shift. A wolverine as large as mountain lion stood in his place. Mona watched the vortex behind him.

A distorted face appeared, a gleeful grin sending shivers down her spine. The magic lassoed out to pull the shifted Were across.

The wolverine turned and struck at the phantom face. The entire spell collapsed and the creature vanished.

"Shit! That's the working you've been seeing?" Cart swore and pulled Mona away from the residual magic. "We need to get out of here."

The mortal guards stared at the spot then swung around, scanning up and down the hall, guns drawn.

"Thanks," the Folk guard whispered. "Now get out of here before they decide you aided and abetted his getaway."

He jerked his head in the direction they needed to move. Later Mona would need to track this man down and thank him for his help.

"There!" Pointing in the opposite direction the guard took off as if he'd seen something. The two mortals followed him.

Cart led them around one more corner, and finally to the laundry room where large wheeled baskets piled with bags of dirty linens flanked the walls. The loading dock bays were closed, but there was a small side door. The only problem was the large alarm handle across it.

"Do you think he's disabled it?" she asked.

"He may have taken the connectors off the main system." Cart pointed to a small matchbox-sized box along the door's header with wires running out of it. "But this type also has its own internal alarm, which will sound once we open the door. I'll see what I can do."

He pulled out an army knife and twiddled with the faceplate. Two seconds later the alarm sounded.

"Hell!" He grabbed her wrist and bolted through the door.

Already there were cruisers, lights flashing, streaking around the far edge of the building toward them.

Mona looked for the line of the warding spell…there! The working glimmered at the top of the driveway. Reaching out, she tweaked the edge closer. Two steps and they were over it.

"Jump!" she yelled.

Cart slung his arm over her shoulder, pulling her to his chest as a shot rang out and they entered the blackness.

This time Mona was able to watch as the blackness streaked past them and the world faded away. She'd been right, there were faint streaks of color creating specters of dark on dark. Radiating magic, they didn't seem good nor bad, just elemental.

Before she could process any more, they tumbled onto the bed back at Cart's room in the Were protector's headquarters.

Mona was flat on her back and Cart was on top of her, causing all sorts of pleasant, if un-actionable tingling in private places.

"Okay," Cart said as he nuzzled his nose under her ear and kissed her neck, "while I could live without the sudden departures we've had to do, I do enjoy the arrivals."

She definitely was aware of his reaction; it warmed her inner thigh.

"We need to get out of here!" Her shoves at his shoulder ineffectual. "I still have that beacon on me!"

"Crap!"

They scrambled off the bed.

"Can't go to Tania's, can't go…hell, I don't know anyplace close enough that's not associated with Weres!" Cart said.

"I do."

"I can't jump someplace I've never seen, Mona."

"Maybe I can feed you the information? There's got to be some way!"

His look turned inscrutable.

"The airport?" she asked since her last suggestion didn't seem to be workable.

"No, I've never been." Most Folk avoided airplane travel due to the disruption of magic fields the planes caused as they tore through the air. "How far is it?"

"About fifty miles."

"I'll try. No matter what I do, keep the image of where we should go in your mind."

"Is it too far? I can—"

"Just do it!"

Mona set the image of the coal burning plant on its rocky promontory in her mind and the pier that paralleled it creating a small bay. She could toss the spell in there. Due to the pollution, there were no Folk in the waters who'd be affected by the beacon and the factory's discharge meant it wouldn't be iced over.

She closed her eyes to better concentrate.

"Keep concentrating." He grabbed her face and kissed her. Knock-your-socks-off kissed her.

His magic enveloped her in a hug as warm as the hands on her face. Despite the temptation to melt against him, she managed to keep the image in her mind.

Once she determinedly ignored how his magic seemed to be permeating her pores, the image became clearer, a memory of wind and the waves against the rocks and seagulls screeching in the air.

Two heartbeats later he broke off the kiss and they stumbled into the frigid air.

She opened her eyes to see his gold-flecked irises had turned brown again. His thumbs stroked her cheekbones and his fangs were poking out from his lips. She sensed his exhaustion. He must be pulling on his animal side to keep going.

If she thought his body had been warm against her on the bed, it was nothing compared to the heat he generated now.

"Spell," she blurted out. She didn't want to have them tracked here. Particularly if Cart followed through on the intent his body radiated.

He let go of her face and closed his eyes.

Mona stepped away and made her way to the end of the pier, where she attached the beacon to a large rock and sunk it into the icy waters. The cold temperature as well as the depth of the lake would make the energy more difficult to follow.

"Let's get out of here," she said, turning back to Cart.

"Can't. I don't have any energy," Cart said.

Mona looked at him. It was true. And there was no residual energy here she could feed him.

"Okay…"

The water behind them erupted, spraying them with pellets of freezing water and ice. Mona screamed and ducked away from the deluge, moving back along the pier to where they'd landed, Cart right behind her.

Or so she thought until she turned to find him still standing back at the pier, legs braced and fists cocked, watching the water, muscles rippling under his overstretched t-shirt.

Mona looked back to where the water burbled from the explosion. Nothing came up out of the water, although flotsam churned to the top then sank again. No telling if they were from the bottom of the cove or had been sent along with the spell.

"Cart!"

He turned and looked at her. His face looked different, jaw elongated and his nose smashed into his face. Shit, he was on his way to shifting again. One of these times he'd fully turn and then she'd be stuck with a tiger. A tiger? Why did she think that? She was certain she was correct, but had no idea how she knew.

Maybe the kiss? Oh yeah, his magic had imprinted itself on her memory. She resisted the urge to read what she'd found out—his secrets were his to tell, not hers to pry open without his consent.

One final look at the water and Cart wearily made his way over to her. Mona saw how much suppressing his need to shift was burning up what little energy he had.

The wind picked up and Mona started to shiver violently. Cart picked up his pace and hurried to her side.

Wrapping their arms around each other they headed off the dock. Once in the parking lot, they were faced with two choices: a hotel or a diner. Of unspoken accord they turned to the diner.

"Open until one a.m. That should give you enough time to recharge, huh?" Mona said as they entered the front door.

Warmth blasted from a heater in the entry, bringing with it the smell of burnt coffee and fried foods.

Their waitress clucked over their condition. They explained it by saying they'd just dashed over from the hotel to wait for their ride, and hadn't realized just how cold it was. The woman shook her head at them as she took their orders, only slightly startled when they each ordered three course meals with extra sides.

Alone with their waters, Cart sat tapping at the table and glaring at the front door.

"What?"

"I need to contact my group."

She dug through her purse and handed him her cell. "Averill has a landline, why don't you try that?"

He grunted in reply.

Hot cups of chocolate were set in front of them. Mona wrapped her hands around the thick ceramic and sighed as the warmth seeped through. Cart spooned a couple of ice cubes into his, drank it, and asked for a second one. When it arrived he picked it up and headed off to the hallway by the restrooms to make his call. She could see him, but couldn't hear him. Interesting. She wondered why he'd left.

Mona looked around at the clientele, something she should have done when they'd entered. Very few people were hanging around in the after-dinner lull. Not one had any Folk blood. Outside of the one time she visited an airport, Mona couldn't ever remember being in a place so barren of magical energy. She tucked the anomaly in her memory and examined who was there. A handful of middle aged men, a scattering of women, plus a couple of college kids who'd taken over a corner booth and had papers spread out in front of them.

Which reminded her, tomorrow night at work she was supposed to meet with an elfling to assess his powers. She glanced back at Cart, still on the phone, a frown marring his face. He'd know how to handle the kid and his just-coming-into-powers situation.

There was sudden stirring as most of the occupants finished their meals and lined up to pay.

The waitress stopped by with their soups.

"What's the rush to get out?" Mona asked.

"Shift's about to start over at the plant." The soups were slapped down and the woman headed over to bus the emptied tables.

Too hungry to be polite, Mona dug into the soup. Like all good diners she'd found, this one had its share of Greek specialties. The avgolemono was particularly tasty.

Cart slid back into his seat, tucking her phone into his pocket.

"Anything interesting up?" she asked.

"The incident at the hospital is all over the news, more snow is forecasted, and someone will be here in a while to give us a ride back."

"Hmm," she replied around a spoonful of soup.

"Oh, and your brother and Tania are definitely an item."

"I guessed that might happen when I saw them. And she did name him her protector."

"You sure you're a Warder? You know, you see things not all of them do."

Mona laughed. "Nothing more this time than knowing my bro. That combination of protectiveness and exasperation could only mean one thing."

"I can relate," he muttered into his soup.

Mona chose not to reply.

They ate slowly, talking about inconsequential things like which *Star Trek* movie was their favorite—they both chose Wrath of Kahn—and arguing over which would be second. Mona was for the newer prequel while Cart slammed it as being for "the ladies." Agreeing to disagree, they moved on to whether the "fog bowl" or the "ice bowl" football game had been harder to play in, which segued into the ugliest uniforms of all time. Each new plate of food added much-needed vitality to Cart's body.

As he grew stronger, Mona waited for him to ask about the spell.

Finally, when the booths around them cleared, he did.

"I—" Cart paused. "Describe to me what you saw with that spell."

"The summoning one?"

He grunted.

"The runes, the power symbols, are a fairly basic summoning combination. But there's something about the sigils and the energy attached to the spell that is clearly aimed at the balance, which would make the Were strong enough to shift. Somehow the working is rearranging things and pulling out of the Were the ability to assume their clan totem, whether or not they are actually able to do so. There's this…this shock of energy, which…"

Mona sat for a minute. How would she describe it? Cart signaled the waitress for more decaf. When she left Mona continued.

"The energy scrambles their inner magic, then rearranges it to a new pattern. I'm not sure how, but their elf blood is supplemented in such a way that they closer to the correct balance, the one strong Weres have that gives them the ability change any time. But the energy…it seems like it's only able to help out so much. Some of the shifts I saw…they got stuck partially changed. It was gruesome."

"But that's the part I don't understand," Cart said.

"I get the impression that whoever is doing this, when he calls the Weres back and they haven't successfully changed, their magic is reclaimed, killing them. It's probably just as gruesome, but then, letting them live, that would be worse."

"No, I get that part, as horrific as it is. It's the partial changing."

Maybe it was because she'd never seen a Were shift before, but she didn't understand his point. Cart was frowning and staring blankly out the window.

"I don't understand."

Cart turned and blinked at her, his mind clearly somewhere else. "What do you know about Elfhaven?"

"Besides that's where my father lives? Not much."

"Well, some of the tales are true—the difference in how time passes, the beauty of the place. And some aren't—eating the food won't enchant you to stay. One of the true ones is that there's a grove, a transitional zone between here and there, which you have to pass through to get to Elfhaven."

Cart looked around the restaurant, examining each person there before continuing.

"Except for first generation Weres, who carry their clan totem inside them, when a strong shifter assumes an animal shape, it's assuming the shape of an animal who lives in the grove.

"You mean they swap out their body for an animal from Elfhaven?" Mona asked. She'd had no idea.

"Yes, except our bodies don't go to the grove; instead there's a special place in Elfhaven they appear. This isn't commonly known—I doubt even the Maven knows. And very few elves from Elfhaven are aware of the vault and its use. The shift starts gradually, as I'm sure you've seen, then there's a burst of energy as the bodies are transposed."

Mona didn't correct him. She'd never been invited to monitor the pack's run, since the Buffalo pack banned females. Or had. That would be tough to do with a female pack leader.

She thought through what he'd said and had to agree. "The piecemeal shifting doesn't make any sense. Unless…by the goddess, are there mis-formed bodies strewn around the grove?"

"No, I'm very sure the magic in the grove would automatically kill any such chimera. The goddess's will wouldn't allow the abomination to live. No, there's something else going on here."

"Okay, but how does knowing what is going on help us get the person doing this? On the one hand, knowing what your enemy is capable of is good, but if this is the same person who has decimated the Buffalo pack, and they're killing off Weres, we need to track them down whether or not we know the how of what they are doing, right?"

"True. Can you trace the summoning spell back?"

"No, something done from a distance like that, that's not a skill I have. I'm not sure the magical traces are strong enough for me to follow. Could Tania?"

"Perhaps. We'd have to get her in the right place at the right time, and then she'd likely do something rash. Or your brother would. Better to see if we can track the user down."

"We could…I could…" Mona gulped at what she was about to suggest. "I could stay in contact with the person shifting and get pulled back to the creator of the spell with them."

From the growl coming across the table, Cart was not happy with that plan.

"You have my imprint. You could jump to me."

"Still don't like it."

"We have to do something, we have no idea how many Weres he's changed or killed."

Cart rubbed his face. "Any idea how Raine fits into this?"

"The baby—" Mona stopped herself, not wanting to share Raine's secret then realizing she had no choice. "Raine was raped."

For a split second, Cart sat slack-jawed. "Shit, he's trying to kill his own baby?"

"No, I didn't say that. I mean, I'm not sure if he's been trying to capture Raine or kill her. As for the baby being his, we'll have to wait to find out after the baby is born."

"We need to get this guy."

"I know. First we need to find where he is." Mona rubbed her finger around the rim of her hot chocolate mug, hoping something would come to mind.

"That's not going to be easy. Imps won't go near him."

"Wait, how do you know?"

"Tried."

They both slumped against the cushions of the booth. Cart's energy was better, but Mona could still see he needed rest.

"You need to take a break. You can't track this mage *and* set up the protector station for the Buffalo pack. Both of them are full time jobs," Mona said.

"I'll find him. It may take me longer than I'd like, but I will."

Mona didn't doubt it for a minute.

The waitress swung by. The food was long gone.

"Mind if we stay and just have some coffee? Our ride's not here yet," Cart said, dimpling a smile at the waitress.

"So long as you're not the last ones out, it's no skin off my teeth. I'm last on anyway."

When there were only two tables left, they settled the bill but stayed at the table. Cart had regained some energy, but Mona wasn't sure it was enough to get them where they needed to go if their ride didn't show up soon.

"I need to work tomorrow night," Mona said, remembering she wanted to ask him about the kid. "You mind coming in to see me? There's someone I want you to meet."

Even across the table, she could feel him tense. "Who do you want me to meet?"

"Some guy who looks like he's on the cusp of changing. What is up with you?"

"I thought it was your boyfriend," he mumbled.

She kicked his shin under the table. "If I had a boyfriend I wouldn't be kissing and…and snuggling, and thinking about doing wicked things with you!" Oh no! A thought struck her. "You don't have a girlfriend, do you? I mean, you don't, right? Because I would take it really, really badly if you did. I mean, I know all this was kind of sudden, but you don't go around kissing other people when you're already in a relationship. Or at least I don't, and I hope you don't either. Oh, that'd be really awful—"

He leaned over the table, a delighted smile on his face, and covered her mouth with his hand.

"No." He paused as she took a breath. "And I don't go around doing 'things' with other women when I do have one. But as you already pointed out, this isn't the time."

Cart removed his hand. Mona kept her jaw clenched lest she start babbling again.

He looked out the glass door.

"Here's our ride. And, yes, I'll come with you to work." His relief at seeing the ride turned into a frown. He slid out the booth and stood waiting for her, having placed a generous tip on the table. "Typically the Warder should make arrangements so you don't have to work while training. But then, from what I've seen, Smythe's methods seem to have been anything but typical."

Mona teeth started chattering two steps outside the restaurant.

Cart opened the rear door and looked in at the driver. "Hey, Tiff, thanks for the ride."

Tiff nodded her head in acknowledgement, the overhead light shining on her deep red hair. "No problem. How'd the two of you end up all the way out here, if you don't mind my asking?"

Mona climbed inside and was surprised when Cart climbed in the back seat after her.

"Jumped. Mind if you hold off the interrogation until later? I'm beat and cold and am going to try to sleep for at least part of the ride back."

There was a blanket in the back and he tossed it over both of them, pulling her to the middle seat while he fastened his seatbelt. Mona would have protested, except she was too practical to give up his warmth.

"Sure. But don't think I won't ask you about it later."

A grunt was the only reply. Cart leaned against the door and rested his head against the seatbelt webbing.

Mona leaned against him, far more comfortable than the door any day. A sure sign of his exhaustion, he fell asleep before she did.

"Any place you want me to drop you off or are you coming with us?" Tiffany looked at her in the rearview mirror, gray eyes glinting in curiosity.

"Oh, I'm coming with you. I may not be integral to the team, but I am part of it, and will be until we find this guy."

"Good."

Chapter Eight

Tiffany had pulled the car into in the driveway of a Victorian home in Lackawanna and left it running, both of them tacitly agreeing that Cart really needed the sleep. Mona snatched bits and pieces of sleep in the parked car, while Cart slept soundly for an hour or two. The sky was still dark, but lights were coming on in the second story of the house. The building sat back from the road and was surrounded with set spells. Old ones, which Mona noted desperately needed renewal.

This was Averill's house. Judging by the people Mona had seen come and go, and the well-trampled path in the new snow, the new Were leader had been dealing with visitors most of the night. The two protectors stationed by the door were not reassuring, although they didn't seem to bother the imps that hovered by the lights. A large contingent walked by, waving at Tiff before heading in; the replacement crew. Tiff slid out and went to talk to the guards at the door.

That wasn't what pulled her awake. An imp hovered in front of them. Looked like rest time was over. This time she was the one to shake Cart awake.

"Um, Cart?" He bolted upright and looked around. She pointed to the creature.

"Not for me." He ran his hand over his face, then leaned over the front seat and pulled the keys from the ignition.

"I know that. Think I can go in and get warm first?"

He turned and looked at the imp, who bobbed gently over her shoulder like a lopsided antennae.

"Looks like it'll wait. And leave the blanket in the car, we may need it another time." He climbed out into the cold night air and she followed.

His need to present a strong front to these Weres radiated off of him. He was back into efficient leader mode. Cart headed in and the guards by the door let them pass with brief salutes. Tiffany walked back to Mona, her thin, six foot frame barely moving in the sharp wind.

"Don't worry, that was a civil conversation for him when he's short on sleep. Come on, I'll get you something hot to drink and you'll feel better." She escorted Mona up the front walk.

The living room, made larger by some magic the imps had, held a good dozen people. Averill was not in sight. Mona hoped she was getting some rest somewhere. Cart was over in the corner already answering questions the crowd put to him.

"Hey Teflon, heard you picked up a trainee, she getting in the way as usual?" a man asked, his snort letting everyone know how helpful he thought the she would be. The way he said Teflon made Mona think he didn't mean it as a complimentary nickname for Cart.

"I like to think I'm helping," she said as she walked over to Cart's side. This was the attitude she was used to from Weres, but it didn't mean she had to put up with it. "But who knows, maybe I'm just a big old pain in the ass. Because you know, sometimes attitudes become self-fulfilling."

"Nice," he said, looking her up and down like she was a toy he was thinking about purchasing.

"She's already placed herself under my protection, Herrick" Cart put his hand on Mona's arm.

"Maybe she doesn't want your protection," Herrick said.

Mona heard Cart's growl. Again, he was close to shifting. And she knew, just knew, that if he hurt Herrick because of his inability to control his animal, he'd pull himself off the detail citing his attack as a sign of instability. They so did not need that right now; they needed him focused and doing his job.

She turned back to Herrick, placing herself between the two men. The rest of the group, she noticed, had given their trio a wide berth.

"Do you have a death wish?" Mona asked Herrick. "Because tweaking a tiger's tail has to be one the most incredibly dumbass things I've ever seen anyone do."

She looked him over again, deeply this time, sensing his magic and intent. Irritation at Cart simmered through all of his sense of self. Evil wasn't embedded in him, the way it sometimes became in Folk who were not pure elves. A little remnant of a spell of ill intent, likely from a recent encounter, but nothing festering. His attitude toward Cart was nothing more than any biased jealousy would create.

"Step away, now," she said, "unless you want to be pummeled and battered to a point where you will be no use to anyone. Not that I'm seeing you're much of one now."

She glanced over the crowd, her focus still on inner magic and abilities.

"You and you." She chose two strong but well-grounded Weres. "Take him out of here."

They glanced at Cart first, who must have given his approval as they moved over and grabbed Herrick's arms.

"You don't have any authority over me!" Herrick said.

"I do," Averill said.

Mona wasn't sure when she'd arrived, but was she was very glad to see her because Mona had no idea if she did have the authority.

"I have the right to accept or reject the protectors who are in the group. I choose for you to be placed on probation and banned from the house. In three months you may appeal the ban if you wish. Take him out of here."

The two Weres dragged the barely cooperating Herrick out of the room and house.

"Thank you, Leader Averill." Mona thumped her fist to her chest in salute and recognition of the woman's position as Pack leader. "Now, if you have everything under control, we're going to bed."

Again with the growling. Mona turned and smacked Cart's arm.

"Really, do you Weres ever think of anything else?" This earned her a couple of chuckles. "Since we both need to sleep, we'll be doing so alone."

Mona turned to head down the hall, guessing it was toward the kitchen. The imp, which had followed her, darted out of the way.

"Actually I should deal with this imp first," she told Tiffany, who'd accompanied them out of the room. "Any place private we can go?"

"Try the basement. There's a futon there so you take turns crashing while the other gets some work done," Tiffany supplied.

Mona had to think that last bit was for the benefit of those still listening in the room. They pushed through the swinging door to the kitchen and a wave of heat swept out. Sleepiness hit Mona like a wall. She stifled a yawn.

"Is there any update from the hospital?" Hopefully one of the calls Cart had made last night was to fill his crew in on the need to monitor Raine.

"Nurse Ferguson said she's holding steady." Tiff showed them where the basement stairs were.

Cart, who'd been shockingly quiet until this point, politely asked Tiffany to check on them at noon if they weren't already up. Mona headed down to an old fashion rec room, sofa on the left wall, TV on a crowded bookshelf across on the right. The building was on a hill and patio doors dominated the wall across from the stairs.

"I'd open that imp before you sit down or it'll have to wait even longer to deliver the message." Cart crossed to the futon and maneuvered the frame so it was flat.

"I am Mona Lisa Kubreck. Please state your message."

"Mona." Nic's voice was loud and clear. "The cat's out of the bag on what it is you're doing. I expect you to fill me in ASAP."

Nic had learned to use an imp. Wow. Part of her struggled to grasp how far he'd come so quickly, while dying to see his magic levels now, and part was simply too tired to worry about it.

Not bothering to stifle her yawn this time, Mona sat on the edge of the bed and kicked off her shoes. Turning to lie on her side, she found Cart had slipped in behind her and already taken the wall spot. He pulled her so she spooned in front of him then settled a light quilt over them.

She scooted back into his warmth and immediately dropped off to sleep.

• • •

• • •

The richly sweet smell of hot cocoa woke her. But, oh my, was it bright! She squinted her eyes against the glare of light. Beyond the patio doors, the snow had become neon with sunshine.

Cart handed her a mug. "It used to be hot."

The chocolate smelled heavenly. She looked at Cart. Not only had he slipped out from bed without her noticing, clearly he'd been awake long enough to shower and change.

"What time is it?"

"Almost two."

"I thought Tiff was going to wake us up at noon?"

"We tried; you muttered something about a damn alarm clock and slapped Tiff in the face. We decided to let you sleep."

"Oh, sorry." She took a sip of barely warm cocoa, hoping the mug hid her embarrassment.

"When do you need to be at Fat Louie's?" Cart asked, setting his mug down on the desk. Mona set hers besides it and stretched.

Right. She had to work tonight. "Four-thirty. I should scoot out of here and run home. I could use a shower and a change."

There was yelling and a loud thump from the top of the basement stairs and Mona found herself flung back on the trundle with Cart on top of her, his hand over her mouth and his gaze fixed on the stairs.

Mona tried to ignore the warmth deliciously spreading through her body and focus on what was happening outside.

There were some footsteps, then a muffled chortle. Mona relaxed, while Cart remained rigid. It wasn't until they heard Averill's voice telling people to clean up their mess that he calmed down and took his hand off her mouth.

"And what was that?" Mona asked, continuing without giving him a chance to respond. "You had no right to do that. I was perfectly safe. You don't have to protect me. I—"

Cart put his hand back, then removed it again.

"Aren't there guards upstairs? Why would you think there was any danger?" she asked, unable to stop. "I need to know because—"

His hand clamped back over her mouth. "You're babbling."

She nodded.

"You're uncomfortable."

She nodded.

"Do you want me to move?"

She hesitated, and then nodded again.

"Really?"

He kept his hand over her mouth and kissed along her jaw line and down her neck, nipping lightly along the way.

She moaned his name into his palm.

"Uh-uh-uh, I'm not removing my hand until I'm sure you're not going to babble again."

He draped his leg over hers, boxing her knees between his. Heat burned everywhere they touched, sending tendrils of desire racing to her core. Any traces of cold quickly vanished.

"Ready?"

She didn't move. He lifted his hand.

"I—"

He clamped his hand back. "Nope. No talking." He raised his palm up.

"But—" she got out before he pressed his fingers firmly over her lips again.

"Quiet," he whispered. He slid his hand off, tracing the outline of her lips with the pad of his finger. His feather light touch skated across the seam.

She opened her mouth and gently nipped the questing tip.

He growled and pulled it away, sitting up. "This isn't the time or place." He raked his hand through his hair. "What do you need to get ready?"

Trying to adjust to his mood change, Mona took stock of what she had on. She couldn't remember when she'd last put on clean clothes. "Black shirt, dark pants, the usual other stuff."

Cart nodded. "There's a full bath through the door next to the bookshelves. Get started and I'll find you something."

"Sounds good." Mona bit her lip to keep the words from tumbling out. She held them in for one breath, two… "Can Tiff or someone else bring them down, though? You know, since we don't have a lot of time and I'm pretty sure I'll get distracted if you come in while I shower. And I think you would too, I mean I hope you would. No, I don't hope, I'm pretty sure you just would. Plus, there's that extra energy we create, no way to hide that, and wouldn't that be embarrass—"

Cart laid his finger across her lips. "I'll send a female down. Tiff's out finding a new place for the protector group since D'Alessandro has asked us to move. It was only temporary anyway—too small and too far away from Averill and her Pack."

He removed his finger and tweaked her nose. "And yes, privacy would be a good thing. Not sure when we'll get that. Life can be perverse sometimes."

"I thought that was imps. Like the imp of the perverse?"

"You called?" a voice said from behind Cart.

Cart whipped around, this time remaining standing as he shoved her behind him.

The voice, though, was one she knew, one she'd come to expect pulling a prank like this.

"Hey, Puck, you should know better than to sneak up on Folk like that."

"Yeah, but it's so much fun!" His chortle rang through the room.

She stood and stepped out from behind Cart, who was gaping at the barely two and a half foot tall barrel-chested man.

The Puck had chosen to dress in his disco finery today, complete with bare-to-navel maroon satin shirt and a thick, gold chain necklace nestled in the hair he called his "manly rug." The guy had more clothes than a hotel heiress.

"Puck, this is—"

"I know who he is," the Puck said, looking at Cart and straightening his cuffs. "We've met before, but it's been a while, I don't hang out in New York City too much. Although they've done a better job keeping the parks clean recently. You going by Josiah or Cart or something else these days?"

The two obviously had a history. Mona kept quiet, not wanting to get in the middle of things.

"I go by Cart, oh Eternal Keeper of Folk memory," he replied.

Hmm, Mona had never heard that title before, but it did have the effect of stopping the Puck from pointing the TV controller at various objects around the room, pretending to use it to move them around.

"Right." He set the unit back and turned around. "You two better ignore the canoodling for now. There are big problems around here, and you can't be distracted."

"We—" Mona started before Cart cut her off.

"Tell me more."

"Can't," Puck said. He picked up Cart's mug, sniffed at the drink, and pulled out a flask from some unseen pocket. After adding a healthy splash, he drained the mug.

"Won't?" Cart asked. "And that was my drink."

Mona watched them both as they took up eerily similar stances and glared at each other.

"It's not just the humanoid Folk who are affected. I can't."

Mona knew Cart well enough now to know that this was news to him.

"Fine," Cart said. "I assume you'll show up again when you can use your appearance to the most dramatic effect?"

"Gotta make it memorable or people don't listen. See ya then."

The Puck popped out of the room, much more loudly than he had appeared.

"How do you know him?" Cart asked.

"Part of my training was spending a couple of weeks with him." A frown crossed his face.

"What? Let me guess—not standard training for a Warder, but not unique. Look, right now I'm going to take a shower and get the image of canoodling out of my head. I was doing fine until he said that, you know. Of course, he is the imp of the Perverse, so he probably did it to put the image there."

Mona made it the bathroom door before Cart caught up with her, grabbed her arm, and spun her around.

"You mean we're supposed to canoodle?" Disbelief, uncertainty, and eagerness all carried in his voice.

"I mean we should admit it's going to happen, set it aside until it can, and get to work. Like he said." She looked at Cart. He had his moments of typical pack leader.

"You're not babbling." His thumb stroked the inside of her elbow.

"I only babble when I'm uncertain and uncomfortable. Now that it's certain, I'll be better." Mona pulled her arm out of his grip. "I'm also certain we should wait, so knowing this isn't going to happen soon helps my comfort level. Please send down some clothes, okay?"

She went up on tiptoes, kissed his nose, then closed the door, immediately pulling off her shirt. She was shaking from her bravado. Hell, she wasn't certain, but she was even more determined than ever not to babble when Cart cornered her.

"It's not certain!" Cart yelled through the door.

She yanked open the door. Mona swore Cart's eyes popped out of his head at the sight of her in a white cotton bra.

"What, because someone states the obvious, you don't want to have sex with me anymore? That's stupid, and I'm pretty sure you're not stupid."

His eyes snapped to her face.

"There're levels of stupid, Mona," he said. "And yes, part of me thinks 'canoodling' with you would be stupid now that someone has put it on their agenda."

Mona opened her mouth to retort, but he held up a finger, forestalling her reply.

"However, given how much we both want this, and it's very clear the feeling is mutual, it'd be far more stupid to ignore our attraction. You agree?"

Mona could only nod, fighting the need to pull him into the bathroom and have him join her shower.

His nostrils flared and he growled.

Dammed Were.

"I'll go find you some clothes." He turned and stalked away.

Chapter Nine

Cart finally noticed her silence in the cab of the truck. Mona had showered, gotten dressed, thanked Averill for coming up with some clothes—including a very warm coat!—which fit relatively well, and managed to grab a quick bite to eat before they'd rushed out the door to get her to work.

They'd been driving for about twenty minutes before he spoke. "You said stupid first."

Yeah, like that was going to hold water. Besides, she'd said she didn't think he was stupid. She'd since revised her opinion.

"Look, it would be stupid to have sex," he said, "but it would be more stupid not to, you can't deny that."

"Why?" she asked, despite herself.

"Mona, I have a life in New York City: a job, friends, family. A whole network that I rely on there. My pack is small, but I am their leader. I can't, and never have, imagined living anywhere else."

She nodded. Okay, and the point was?

"You are a Warder," he continued. "While I could live anyplace, you have to live in a specific place. A large part of me doesn't want to give my old life up. 'Don't be stupid and throw out your life's work' I tell myself. But then a growing-by-the-minute part of me says 'don't be stupid, there's something special and unique here, you aren't going to find this again.' And trust me, I've seen enough not-quite-right partnerships to know that this one is so good, it's practically a matter of fate."

Mona refused to comment on that, despite the joy at hearing him say he thought there was something unique and special between them.

"Maybe not fated," he continued as he turned the wheel hand over hand to go around a sharp corner, "'cause I hate that word, but definitely well favored by whatever beings foresee such unions."

"Like the Puck."

"Exactly. Which explains the energy and the quickness of our attraction and the fact that we are constantly thrown together. For instance, I tried to assign Menlo, who actually specializes in dealing with the psychology of emerging Folk, to come with you tonight. He's now stuck on some rural highway with a flat tire."

Mona thought about what he hadn't said, but implied. They could be fated, be Seele, be elf soul mates.

But that didn't make sense, given she had no magic. From what she'd heard, elf soul mates were absolute compliments to their partner, an equal or very near equal in magical abilities and bloodlines.

She had no magic. And Cart definitely had a lot. So that ruled that out. Which was good because she wasn't sure she wanted her lifetime tied to someone else's, or theirs to hers, much less the emotional and physical connection that occurred. Feeling when Cart took a punch? No thank you.

Although they could still be mated on a Were level, less binding in some respects but just as strongly fated.

They drove a little further, each wrapped in their own thoughts.

"One thing that scares the crap out of me, though," Cart said quietly as he pulled into a spot around the corner from Fat Louie's, "whether you want to call it fated or predetermined or goddess blessed, each couple so named has a hard task ahead of them."

Mona looked at his face; worry etched his brow.

"Good thing you're good at what you do."

He sighed, moved away, and opened the car door. "That doesn't mean we both won't end up dead."

Oh no, he was not going to go there. She watched him come around the front of the SUV, opening her door to join him.

"Really?" She could help but laugh a bit at the macabre scene he painted. "You're going to lay that crap on me? Okay, I guess I'll just have to be the one to make sure we don't get caught in that trap. Because, you know, I have all the experience fighting and stuff."

He grabbed her hand and helped her over the wall of snow at the curb.

"If we're going to rely on you, I better start planning my tombstone now," he joked, his mood clearly lightened. "How about 'fought well, fucked better?'"

Mona laughed. "Sure, so long as you tell your family first. Or how about 'fought better well fucked?'"

"Or 'better fuck, well taught?'"

"Or 'butter tuck, sell naught?'" Mona said, doubling over in laughter.

"Woman, that doesn't make sense. I'm trying to be serious here." Cart hauled her up and hugged her.

Mona's laugh died, although a smile lingered. "Oh and 'fought well, fucked better' is serious, Cart."

"It is in my family." He waggled his eyebrows and his grin promised her many things.

Mona wasn't quite sure she was ready for any of them. Or at least not mentally ready; her body had far different ideas.

He kissed her nose then let her go. They'd arrived almost forty-five minutes early, making excellent time across town. Mona wasn't ready to go in yet.

"Mind if we walk around the block?" she asked. "I feel like I've been running or sleeping for days now. I wouldn't mind the break."

"Sure." He tucked her hand in the crook of his arm and stared off in the direction opposite of where she needed to go. "Tell me about bartending."

So she did, sharing insights on the regulars and telling him about the elfings finding her there, one of whom she'd brought him to meet tonight. They'd made it all the way around by that point.

"No relation?" he asked as they walked by the plate glass windows.

"Not that I know of." Elf families were far flung entities, particularly since most elves, except those rare ones who did have a Seele, did not stay in long-term relationships and often had children with several different partners. Families were very extended by mortal standards since all the children of any person with whom one of your parents had a child with was considered a sibling. Distinctions of half, full, and step simply did not exist in an elf family. Good thing when elves were in a relationship, they tended to be monogamous, or it'd be even more confusing for everyone.

Adding in cousins made the family that much larger.

So Leonardo could be family. Mona should ask him.

He was already sitting at the bar, waiting.

Which would have been fine, except for the person who'd chosen to sit next to him. Something was off.

Cart bumped into her back.

"Anyone you know?" she asked Cart, pointing to the pair. "He looks like he could be in your family." His build and coloring were eerily familiar.

"Which one, the geeky kid or the older one?"

"The older one. The geeky kid is Leonardo."

"Not that I know of."

"He's trouble." To Mona his magic exuded a level of uncleanliness she didn't trust. Not enough for her to filter out, but enough that she was very uncomfortable.

Cart stilled. "Should we leave? I don't want to get mortals hurt if he's here for you."

"He hasn't spotted me yet. I don't think he was expecting me to come in accompanied or this early."

"Okay, wait here. I'll head in and see what I can find out. Do me a favor though, stand over by the edge of the building—you'll be out of sight, and if the window shatters I don't want you right in front of it."

Cart approached Leonardo. He offered his hand to shake, saying something in the process.

Before Leonardo could take Cart's hand, the other guy jumped up and pulled out a knife, placing it next to Leonardo's throat.

Mona took a step and in that blink Leonardo was gone. Shit, he'd probably jumped; she was also sure it was the first time he'd used magic that way.

Cart knocked the knife out of the guy's hand; his opponent didn't care, he was lunging for Leonardo's satchel. He grabbed it then jumped himself out, leaving Cart standing there and the few customers looking at him agape.

Mona ran to the door. By the time she'd yanked it open imps were flitting across the room, indubitably altering memories.

Cart crossed over and pushed her back out.

"Truck. We need to track the kid down."

They climbed over the snow bank and back in the cab of the pickup.

"I need an imp please," Mona said.

A slowly rotating spark came to light in her lap.

"I need your help please. A young elf named Leonardo just did his first jump from the bar down the street, Fat Louie's. He was the first person to go of the two who jumped out of there in the past couple of minutes. Can you please find him then report to Protector Dupree where he is? Please verify it is Leonardo since we do not want to follow the other jumper. Here—"

Mona held up her finger and concentrated on what she knew of Leonardo from the one time she'd met him. The imp came and brushed her fingertip, causing a not insubstantial shock to race up her arm. Mona hissed at the pain as it spread through her body. Her heart started to beat frantically and muscles ticked.

"Thank you," she managed to get out.

The imp stopped its slow revolution and faded out.

"I didn't know you could do that," Cart said.

She gasped and shook her hand, she hadn't known either, just acted on instinct. Now that she did know, she wasn't sure she'd be able to do it again.

"Mona. Mona! Are you okay?" He held her hand and examined the tip of digit.

"Just a bit of shock," she said around her chattering teeth.

"A bit, hell, you're reacting like you touched a live *wire[AA2]* . No wonder that ability's not widely known—it's dangerous." He slid his seat back and hauled her across the console.

He held her and rocked her until her heartbeat slowed to something close to normal.

The imp reappeared. "Creekside Village, unit one fourteen."

"That's one of the University at Buffalo graduate residence complexes," Mona said. She uncurled herself from where she'd been snuggled on his chest and sat up straight. "I need to work. Bills to pay, you know the drill. Go, and once you've tracked him down, come back. I'm off at midnight."

It was a typical weeknight, slow with mostly regulars. No one seemed to have any ill effects from the imps earlier, although Mona could see trace residue from their work. Vince's wife had gone into labor, so Mickey, the daytime manager was on duty. Just as the last customers left for the night, Cart walked in the door.

"Good timing, almost done with closing. Did everything go okay?"

"Yep, let me help and I'll fill you in." Cart took off his coat and hung it by the door. Mona would have to get more information later.

"Except for sweeping the floor, everything else is behind the counter and Mickey and I will handle that."

"Okay, where's the broom?"

Mona set chairs on tables while Cart came behind her and swept.

"We found him," Cart said. "Turns out it hadn't been the first time he'd jumped, he'd done it once or twice with relatives. First time he'd done it on his own, though. So he was surprised but not shocked when he ended up back at on campus. Roommate was a bit flipped."

"Where is he now?"

"On his way to New York."

Done stacking chairs Mona wiped the already clean bar, dreading the question she was about to ask.

Cart put his hand over hers. "No change on Raine. I checked before we came back in."

Relief washed through her. "Thanks."

Mickey came out of the back room and told them it was time to leave. Zipping back up against the bitter cold they headed out and waited for Mickey as he locked up.

"Where are Menlo and Tiffany?" Mona asked as they walked to Cart's. "Did Tiffany find a new place?"

"Yeah, the old Y. We've set up cots in the offices and there are two locker rooms so we have a place to wash up. Plus we can use the gym for a big open office, which we like. A bit rough now, but long-term looks good."

"That's a great space to set up as a headquarters for the Buffalo Pack protectors. I didn't realize it was still livable inside, it's sat so long. There's that wing which used to be rooms for rent, although that's been boarded up for a while."

"Yeah, we can definitely work with it. Not sure what we'll do with the pool though."

"Ask Randall for help, he'll see to it."

They'd made it over the curbside pile and were at the truck. "Randall?" Cart asked.

"The Puck, his name is Randall," Mona said as she climbed in.

Cart slid behind the wheel, quickly starting the engine. "I'd forgotten you'd know the Puck's name. He doesn't like people using it, which is why it surprised me."

Mona rubbed her palms together as they waited for the engine to heat up a bit. "Yeah, well, I'm pretty sure that has more to do with the fact that he likes the power calling him the Puck gives him, than his dislike of the name. Although, yeah, he's not too fond of the name, is he?"

Cart laughed. "You're going to be calling him Randall now, aren't you?"

"Every flippin' chance I get. You try living with the control freak for a while. He was worse than my brother, and that's saying a lot."

Still chuckling, Cart pulled the car out of the spot.

"Hey," Mona said, "I'd like to try to swing by my place to pick up a few things. You up to it?"

"Hmm, you think it's safe?" Cart asked they stopped for a red light.

"I think the goons who were waiting the other night were the pair I saw on the skyway, and they weren't strong enough to set a spell. And since the target was more Raine than me, I guessing my place is off the radar."

"Okay. But if it does look like something is set or someone is waiting, we're leaving and coming back with some of my group."

It wasn't a question, so she didn't answer.

"How long have you been working at the bar?" Cart asked.

"Started as a waitress the summer after my first year in college, then I moved to bartending and I've been working at least two nights a week ever since. That's…what? Almost ten years."

"Same owner?"

"Yeah, Carmen. He has a touch of Folk in him and grew up in a Folk neighborhood. He was happy and worried for me when I told him I was training as a Warder." And because he cooked the books, but Mona didn't mention that. She was reasonably certain it was for relatively benign reasons. "Take a left here and go to the second entrance, the one marked clubhouse. That way we can drive past the rear of my place before we head in."

No goons were hanging out in the back or the front, and no magic or spells that she saw. One thing about her house, it was solidly in a mortal community; very few Folk were around. Good in that it made it easy to spot the goons, bad in that if she ever needed help there were not Folk close by.

"Looks good to me," she confirmed.

Cart parked on the short ramp to the garage door. Mona got out and keyed in her code, Cart standing beside her and scoping out the area. Her smashed car was sitting in her garage. Someone must have moved it, she suspected the Puck. With the entire front end crumpled, it wasn't usable, something she'd have to deal with later. She closed the garage door behind them, she pulled out her spare key from under the jug of windshield wiper fluid near the front of the space.

Cart took the key.

"Hey!"

"So the guys couldn't set spells, that doesn't mean they couldn't do other things."

He cautiously opened the door and peered around before flicking on a light.

Mona looked over his shoulder.

"I didn't pick you for such a neat nick…that could be a problem."

Mona grabbed his shoulder and held him back. "I'm not a slob, but this isn't how I left the house."

They tiptoed around the corner to her now pristine kitchen. A vase of flowers and a note were propped up on the counter. She looked at Cart. He shrugged, so she crossed over and picked up the paper, holding it so he could read it over her shoulder.

I cleaned it up for you. Stay safe.—Nic

Her shoulders slumped in relief.

"Nice to have a brother who'll handle things for you. Can't have been in power long, or I would have heard something." Cart's stomach rumbled. He unzipped his jacket and slung it on the back of a chair before he headed over to the fridge.

"He hasn't. I mean, he's just now coming into power," Mona said as she piled her jacket on top of his.

Cart's sudden stillness made her look over. He stood, hand on the handle, arrested by her statement. He stared at her for a minute.

Worried? Angry? Mona couldn't figure what he was feeling; perhaps he wasn't sure himself.

"You mean Tania's pulling his power out and pushing him into acknowledging it? He okay with that? You okay with that?"

Mona fiddled with the flowers, refilling the vase in the sink as she thought through her answer. The bright red tulips were some of her favorites.

"I think he'll be okay with it eventually. Despite the fact he's ignored his own heritage, he's used his knowledge to get a job monitoring Folk, so it's not like he's forsaken it entirely. Plus, he's been unhappy and edgy about work for a while. I truly expect, once he recognizes what's happening, he'll see working with Tania as a protector is a much better fit. Although…he can be oblivious about some things, it may take him a bit to figure out what's going on."

"How strong is he?"

Mona realized his question was more how she thought Titania's augmenting of Nic's power might affect him after it was withdrawn.

"Well, he's a full blooded elf and he has a ton of magical ability, so I'd guess plenty strong even before whatever mojo Tania works." She set the flowers back on the counter and didn't look at Cart, suspicions on just how much power her brother might one day have too close to the surface for her to face him right now. "With Nic, I've always figured it was more of 'when' he'd start to fully embrace his heritage, not 'if' despite his refusal to take part in Folk society." Mona thought about Nic and his life. "Besides, he and Tania have been doing a bizarre arm's length dance for a bit. Not sure either of them was aware of it. But I'm guessing they're both going to be super aware very soon."

Cart's response was a loud grumbling of his stomach.

"Let me grab a couple of things and we can head back."

"No reason to, we can crash here tonight," Cart said from inside the fridge. "I'll take the couch. You cook or something? There's a lot of odd ingredients and sauces in here."

"Spent two years at a culinary institute after college," she said as she sorted through the stack of mail on the counter, bill, bill, solicitation, bill. "Enjoyed it but decided long-term the life of a chef wasn't for me. I wasn't that dedicated."

They were alone, in her condo. No Folk about to disturb with the energy they were likely to create.

Mona blindly stacked the envelopes into two piles. Should she say something? Hell yeah, the Puck wasn't going to control her sex life.

"You don't have to crash on the couch."

The bottles in the fridge rattled as Cart slammed the door shut. Before she could turn around he scooped her up in his arms, causing her to shriek, and the envelopes she still had in her hands to scatter across the floor.

Oh my, his eyes were turning again and he'd become so hot his body practically scorched her where she touched him. Mona flushed. Desire for him sent tingles from the inside out and flushed her with heat.

"Good, because I really, really didn't want to." He strode out of the kitchen and to the stairs.

"Wait, you have some kind of protection, right?"

"I am a protector," he replied, his grin wide at his humor.

Mona slapped her hand on his chest then left it there, enjoying the feeling of his warm skin though his shirt.

"My crew has been sticking condoms in every pocket of every jacket I own since the very first night."

Mona laughed, embarrassment tingling her cheeks. "Smart of them."

"I only pick the best."

They reached the landing and Mona pointed to her door. Cart set her down and reached for the handle.

Mona placed her hand over his. "You okay with this?"

She took his nonverbal reply as a yes.

Chapter Ten

A combination of the warm sun on her face and a hand caressing her hip woke Mona. She turned away from the sun and snuggled toward the hand only to find Cart was on top of the covers and dressed. And wide awake, the bastard. Exhaustion had claimed them far earlier than either had hoped. But before then…Mona smiled and stretched at the memory. Wowza.

"Have you heard anything from the Warder since our meeting?" he asked. "I'm getting worried."

And there went that mood. But she understood Cart's reaction, once she thought about it. Not having heard from Smythe was worrisome, particularly given everything that had happened since they'd last seen him.

"No, I haven't, and you're right, it's very odd," she replied. Looked like she'd be getting out of bed sooner than she thought. She stretched and rolled over, the smell of coffee hitting her mid yawn.

"You bring a cup for me?" She sat up and wrapped the sheet around her bare torso.

"Sorry, here." He handed her a mug of already light coffee absentmindedly.

Mona took a sip. He'd even added a bit of sugar. Oh, and he'd used the Kona blend. Excellent.

She inhaled the smell and took another sip. What had they been talking about? Oh, right the Warder. Shoot, she still needed to read that assignment.

"Yes, it's worrisome, but look on the bright side, this gives me more time to catch up on my reading homework. Although, we haven't scheduled my next lesson."

"We got some time, you want to do it now?"

"Let me finish waking up. Not the most captivating of reading material as it is."

Cart slid off the bed and started pacing. The room was generously sized but he made the space seem small as he passed from dresser to window and back again.

Who knew having sex would make the man a focused, analytical machine? Mona gave up on thoughts of morning-after nookie.

"I've been thinking through what I know," he said. "And what I want to know. And I'm realizing there's a gaping hole in my knowledge."

"What is it you want to know?"

"Stuff before our time."

"You could ask the Puck. Hey! It was just a thought." Mona had to laugh at his rude gesture.

"I could also ask my mother, but that's not happening."

Mona turned to set the mug down on the bedside table and slid her feet on the floor. "How about an aunt or someone else of her generation?"

"I—" Cart's response was bit off.

Mona looked over her shoulder to find him staring at her bare back, nostrils flaring. Maybe not so focused on work after all.

He closed his eyes and turned his head away. "I'll wait for you in the living room. Take your time."

"You don't have to go."

His eyes remained scrunched shut. "If I want to get any work done, I do. Trust me, though," his lids popped open and his grin became feral, "if I didn't know we'd have plenty of time together to make up for missing this morning, or I didn't have this worry hanging over my head, I'd be on you in a heartbeat."

Mona shook her head at him. Men. Well, okay, not just him; if he stayed in the room she probably wouldn't be getting any work done any time soon. "You better go then, since once I get out of the covers I'm going to be as naked as a dryad."

"But a heck of a lot prettier."

The compliment warmed her down to her toes.

"I'm going to take a quick shower, be down in twenty."

He grunted and closed the door behind him.

She didn't make it downstairs for over an hour. Cart joined her five minutes into her shower, cursing his imagination the whole while.

"I think," he said as they walked hand in hand down the stairs, "I'd better head back to my group soon, or I'm not going to get anything done."

"You hear anything about Raine?"

"No calls this morning. Have to think no news is good news."

"Before we head back, I want to go over my lessons to see if there's something there that'll help before we go. And grab a bite to eat, since we keep skipping meals."

"Why don't you tell me the pages and I'll look it up."

In the kitchen, Mona wrote down her assignment: chapter six, parts ten through twelve and chapter seven, section eight. Was there more? She stared blankly at the wall, trying to remember.

Oh, by the goddess, there were a lot of imps hanging about.

A lot. She'd never seen this many except when she'd been with the Puck. They flocked to the man.

Something about the large gathering of randomly moving lights reminded her of the shifting colors she'd seen when she'd jumped with Cart. Was that where imps stayed when they weren't flitting about? She held out her hand and an orange one, floating like a piece of thistledown, hovered over her palm.

Cart came in and set the large book down with a slight grunt. He headed over to the coffee pot. "Hey—"

Mona held up her hand and cut him off. She pointed to the imps.

He jerked back in surprise, darting a glance at her then back to the dozen or so hovering imps in each corner.

"Hmph." He walked back to the table and sat by the book.

"Wait, that," Mona waived her hand at the sparkling entities, "is more than a 'hmph.' Particularly as they caused you to forget to get coffee."

Cart looked at her notes and started to rifle through pages. "You know about that fated and meant to be stuff the Puck was implying?"

"Yeah."

"Well, that," he jerked his head at the corner above the cabinets, "is probably why he wanted us to wait."

Mona looked at the mass of shimmering lights again. "We did that?"

"A sign of the goddess's approval." He flipped one page back and forth, double checking the information on her list.

"Cool." Mona couldn't help but smile. They'd created enough energy for imps to come to being. Puck had never been clear on the process, all she knew was a lot of magic energy was needed.

"If you say so."

Mona didn't know what was bugging him, but she'd have to assume he'd tell her when he was ready.

"You are not going to rain on my parade, Cart. We helped imps come to being. In my book, that's cool. So, unless there's more?"

He stopped flipping the page. "They shouldn't be here, not yet," he grudgingly muttered.

Mona went and joined him at the table. Cart frowned down at the page and didn't look at her.

"Why?"

He scowled at her, his brow furrowed. "We didn't mate."

"No, but every time you kiss me, really kiss me, none of this peck on the cheek stuff, we send off enough energy to rattle cabinet doors. Figures we'd make enough energy, whether or not we did whatever stuff it is we need to do to mate, to create imps. Although, until this stops, we should be careful where we have sex." Mona stood. "Good thing you're not above D'Alessandro's—you'd never get any if you were still there. Eggs okay?"

"I don't think—"

"Look, is this energy imp thing going to happen no matter what we do?" Mona asked as she pulled items out of the fridge.

"Yes."

"Do we have any control over it? Aside from not having sex—and between you and me that's not going to stop. You couldn't even keep yourself from joining me in the shower after you said you were going to stay away." Good, the unopened salmon hadn't expired. Mona set that on the counter next to the eggs. "I say don't sweat what you can't control. Figure out why it's happening, okay, but don't freak out that it is happening. Because, you know, freaking out doesn't solve anything, you only—"

Cart's hand clamped over her mouth and his warmth pressed against her back.

"You're babbling," he whispered in her ear. "I wonder what made you uncertain and uncomfortable. Not sex, we're past that. Is it mating?"

Mona nodded.

"The mating ritual?"

Mona shivered in anticipation. From what she'd heard, each one was unique but all the women she'd heard talk about it agreed. Best. Sex. Ever.

"I'll make sure I plan something special then." He kissed her neck. Then he stepped away, swatting her rear with the hand he'd removed from her face. "Until then, I'm hungry, woman. Feed me."

She slapped his wrist as he walked away. Understandable why he'd distracted her, and himself from sex, but damn! Now she was going to be thinking about mating with him far too much. Picking up a potato she went to the sink. "After that, you expect edible food?"

"I'll have to hope your sense of skill outweighs your sense of indignity." He stood at the table, running his finger down the page the book was open to.

"Let's see," he said, picking up the list. "Chapter six: Those positions usual and customary in Folk culture filled by such persons born with special gifts or those who have such gifts bestowed upon them." His voice took on slight northeast accent, making the title sound humorous.

"Uh-huh, read through that earlier." Mona washed then peeled the potato.

"Part ten is Warder, customary qualifications; eleven, typical duties and jobs; and twelve, specific information regarding the ward."

"Wait, what ward?" she said as she slid a now clean spud over the mandolin, making nice, thin slices for her galette.

"You know, the bad elf you are most likely going to have to spend your life keeping captive and out of the area of any Folk."

"Contain the big bad elf; not funny, Cart." Although it was a funny idea. Shifters could turn evil, but full elves didn't. So why not have a big bad elf to make up for it? "Really, what ward are they talking about? The neighborhood one? I know there is a very faded one around the area most Folk live in, it's getting to the point that there's not much left for me to repair. I keep meaning to ask Smythe about having the Maven reset it. And I definitely need to do the one around the Lackawanna pack house."

Mona set the shallot down on the cutting board and quickly skinned it.

"Mona, put down the knife."

Cart had again moved silently to her side. She put it down before she thought to ask why.

He turned her and held her hands. Eyes flecked with gold stared at her. "I wasn't joking about the elf."

"Of course you're joking. No one can be expected to dedicate their entire life to keeping someone in captivity."

He remained silent.

Oh shit.

"Wait, a 'bad' elf? Elves are never are born with innate evil in them," she said. Never. The goddess kept them pure.

"That's true for most elves, yes—but only because once a generation or so the goddess allows one to be born with all the evil they would have. And a Warder is born to keep that elf from everyone else. Although there are more Warders than wards, if Smythe wanted you to read that section, I assume he thinks you'll have one."

Mona slumped against the counter. She couldn't fathom it. Spending her whole life keeping someone captive.

Although…that did explain why the complex was way out in the middle of nowhere. So much for moving close enough for pizza delivery.

"I—" She couldn't string a thought or sentence together.

Cart sat her down and got her a glass of water.

"Look, I'll tell you what I know, then we'll try to make sense of what Smythe has down here."

Mona nodded.

"First thing, it isn't like you keep the ward down in some dank dungeon. It's not the fault of the ward they have been born with this way, so the Warder tries, as best they can, to give them freedom within the restrictions of the complex. I've seen everything from suites whose gadgetry would make a teen green with jealousy to sumptuous villas reminiscent of a sultan from a tale."

He went on to say how she still would do her other jobs, she wasn't restricted to the complex at all hours. Other Folk and even some mortals could be trusted around the ward, once it was clear how the evil would manifest itself.

"That's why you said I had to live in a specific place," she interrupted. "I thought it was because, like a Maven, I have an area I am responsible for, not a person."

"Think of it this way, if you had a child with a severe handicap, you'd make sure that child was cared for well into their adulthood, right? It is somewhat similar. Folk produce a child with special needs and it is your unique job to take care of it."

"Because I am the only one who can. Magic doesn't affect me."

"That's a large part of it. However, and this is always the case, the Warder has a special skill set with which counter to the skills of the ward."

Mona mulled that over.

"But—how old is this ward? Do I get them as an infant? Full elves have long lives, won't it out live me?"

"Part of the special binding typically extends your life to match your ward's." He chaffed her cold hands. "Look why don't you read through the chapter and I'll finish cooking."

Too numb to do anything else, she pulled the book over.

The first paragraph jumped out at her.

When I first started writing this book, I had recently begun my Wardership. The subsequent dearth of material upon which to draw information from led me to collect such and put it together for others to use. What I have collected is by no means a complete manual, merely it is as complete as I could make it in the ten years I have labored.

Mona flipped to the title page of the book.

There, at the bottom: *Boston: Ticknor and Fields, 1886.*

Her brain unable to calculate how old Smythe was, well beyond one hundred years, she turned back.

This was wrong. Something Cart said didn't jive with that date.

"Wait, you said about once a generation an elf is born that must be warded, right? But then, shouldn't there have been another one between Smythe and me? It's longer than a generation, even for elves."

He was standing at the counter whisking eggs. "Sometimes it skips a generation. Perhaps the previous ward is still alive. Sometimes the person is unwardable and is killed, but that's rare. From what I understand, once a generation is a general guideline. Sometimes a ward is born a little sooner, sometimes longer. There'll probably be more about the frequency in the chapter. I think, too, it has to do with the birthrate. The fewer babies, the less likely you'll have a ward born. Makes sense, and with all the intermingling with mortals, less elves have been born."

Right, only someone whose bloodline was at least fifty percent elfin was an elf and able to manipulate the energy Folk called magic. Of those only elves that were almost pure blooded—Smythe had put it at eighty percent elf lineage—could never be turned to evil. It was the group between the fifty and eighty that caused the most problems. And witches, but Mona wasn't concerned about them right now.

Cart poured the eggs with a flourish into a hot pan and then turned his attention to the second skillet he had on the stove. Mona turned her attention back to the book.

Ten minutes later, when Cart slid a plate on the table next to her, she still didn't have any answers on when or who or how, just a headache induced by the archaic language Smythe used.

And Mona had a plate of unappealing looking pink streaked, green-flecked eggs in front of her.

"It tastes a lot better than it looks," Cart said as he helped himself to a forkful.

Looking more closely she saw he'd scrambled the salmon, shallots, and dill into the eggs and served them over hash browns.

"What, no cream cheese?" she quipped as she filled her fork.

He smacked his head. "I knew I forgot something."

He grinned, clearly thinking she was kidding. She was, about the cream cheese, but it needed something, so she got out the crème-fraiche and drizzled it over the stack, then topped the whole thing with a light coating of cracked pepper.

Cart followed her lead.

It was pretty darn good. A couple of slices of fresh, cold firm tomatoes and it would have been superb.

"Thanks for making something. I was getting tired of food on the fly," Mona said as she stacked the dishes in the dishwasher. They'd avoided talking about wards and Warders through the meal.

"You did half the work." Cart added his plate to hers. "We do need to head out. I need to get the reports from my group and knock a few heads and it's already almost noon."

Mona agreed. Ignoring the problem that she couldn't wrap her head around seemed to be working for now. Or at least it was until Cart draped an arm around her and asked if she was okay.

"I think so. It's a lot to process. Let me go throw some things in a bag and I'll be ready. Hope you don't mind if I assign hauling the tome to you."

"No prob."

"Knew I'd find some use for having a manly man around."

He waggled his eyebrows and she ducked out of his embrace.

"Stay downstairs," she ordered as she headed up.

He gave an overly exasperated sigh then turned to wash the pans.

Mona changed, again, belatedly remembering it was Thursday and she was supposed to meet Nic for their weekly dinner. She packed a bag with several outfits, no telling when she'd be back, adding in extra socks and the boots she had taken off last night. Or had it been Cart? She smiled at the memory. It had been Cart.

When she made it back downstairs Cart was already in his coat and using her cell phone, he'd never given it back. Funny, despite his keeping it, he hadn't seen him on it much, come to think of it.

"No, no imps around these guys. I know you don't like phones, Menlo, but that's what we're going to have to use. Uh-huh. Uh-huh. I'm on my way in see if you can stall them. I'll be—"

He looked at Mona.

"Ten minutes," she supplied.

"Ten minutes. Yes. Yes. Yes, she'll be there too. No, not the Maven. We'll wait to bring her in until later. She's dealing with something else now. Yeah, well, trust me, it's related, and I'm not just saying that."

Mona zipped up her coat then held her hand out for the keys. He dug them out and handed them to her. Apparently he'd already carried the heavy book out to the car.

He stayed on the phone, one call after another, until they pulled into the lot of the old YMCA. He snapped the unit closed. "The imps took it upon themselves to delay my calls until noon," he said.

As if they needed further proof someone was meddling to get them together. She'd tell the Puck her opinion of his antics next time she saw him.

"You know," she told him, "you can ask an imp to take a message directly to Randall saying what is okay with you and what's not. I'd suggest not letting him have his way too easily or he'll walk all over you."

She heard most of Cart's message to the Puck as she pulled her bag out of the back. It'd be effective, if it didn't tick Randall off.

Cart caught up to her on the steps, phone put away and the large tome cradled in his arms. The place was pretty busy, given it had been up for less than a day. Hyram stood just inside the door beside a manned desk that was clearly a check in point.

The lobby was circular, pleasing to Folk if unintentionally built that way. The three-story area was capped with a dome, which Mona could see needed cleaning as well as a renewal of spells. Interesting, though, that there were even spells there.

"They've set up a room for you on the third floor, and an office on the second, Cart. The Warder and his trainee have a couple of rooms set aside down here, past the gym. Herrick's set up workstations down the hall to the left. He's expecting you there."

"Thanks, Hyram. Here, take these." Cart handed the heavy book and Mona's bag to him. "And put them in the Warder's rooms, out of sight preferably, then come join the meeting. You have someone to cover the desk?"

"Wait, can you take my coat too?" Mona shrugged out of it, hesitating a minute since she did seem to be taking off suddenly, without a coat, a lot recently. But what could happen to her in a protector station? She handed it over.

Hyram gathered everything together. Mona hadn't realized he was so much larger than Cart, but he carried everything with ease.

"Take the hall to the right, first door on your left. It's behind those windows." The wall of glass Hyram gestured to took up one side of the entry rotunda. "We haven't cleaned them off yet."

Not that they could—they were spelled opaque. They headed down the hall.

"You want me to clear the windows?" Mona asked.

"When I open the door." He reached for the knob. "Now."

Mona rotated the clarity rune clockwise.

People stilled around the workstations and tables that filled the room as activity ceased. Half were looking at the now clear windows and half had their attention on the door.

"Geez, Leader Josiah, you sure like to make an entrance," said Herrick from his position along the wall. "And about time. What's this about not using imps for messaging?"

Somehow Mona didn't think it accidental that all the desks faced his. The guy had control freak written all over him.

"Pretty simple, no imps," Cart said. He looked around the room, he had everyone's attention now, his presence controlling the pack in a way Herrick's never would. "The person who did this is manipulating them. Stopped all my messages for a while, which, I can tell you, turned out to be a pain in the ass."

Mona filed the information away, wondering when he'd learned that, as she watched Herrick. His magic had the slightest taint of evil to it, the stain noticeably larger than before. Cleaning the cancer out now would be better than waiting.

"And Herrick," Cart added, "despite the fact they've named you head of the policing side, call me Cart, everyone else does. Now, I want to see the chart my investigative team has on attack locations as well as families attacked and I'll add to it. Do we have a conference room?"

"Hold on a minute," Mona interrupted. "Cart, Herrick, when was the last time either of your crews was cleansed?"

Not that she'd ever done the check on protectors, given Buffalo didn't have any, but Smythe had her read the procedure and explained it. Protectors routinely went through a cleaning of their essence so foul residual that might cling to them from their work was removed. Usually the procedure was done after, and sometimes before, they went out to handle someone whose magical essence was severely tainted.

Although Herrick was a small step beyond what she'd been told to expect, the procedure would clean him too.

"We don't need cleansing," said a voice from the back of the room.

"Glad you volunteered to be first," Mona said as she walked through the crowd and grabbed the arm of the tall, African American woman who'd spoken. "This is not negotiable, and you all know it. If I see the need, you have to submit. Or you can be placed in solitary until your appeal is heard."

The woman tried to slip out of Mona's grasp. Mona reacted, stilling the magic in her, which had the effect of slowing her movements. The woman was, for all intents, frozen in place as her body moved at a fraction of what it usually did. But, oh, how interesting this was! For she wasn't a Were or even an elf. She was a witch.

Mona had been told about witches, early in her training. Here in the states they'd claimed a large chunk of the southern plains, from Utah to the Mississippi, and mostly they stayed there except for small covens in New York, Chicago, and San Francisco. But once in while one got a wandering foot, and showed up in unexpected places. The woman's magic felt different. Definitely part of her, but not so much in her body, like elves and Weres, more mental. Interesting. Worrisome, since even holding her for a short amount of time might cause some damage Mona couldn't anticipate.

"The longer you hold out the worse it is going to be for you," Mona told her.

"Kofi, submit or I'll be sending you home on administrative leave. Again," Cart said from behind Mona.

"Funny thing is I don't see any residual on you, just a crappy attitude." Mona hadn't realized she'd spoken the thought out loud until someone snorted at her words.

Kofi nodded her head imperceptibly, and Mona unfroze her.

"Good, I'll do you, then the bosses," Mona said, pulling up a chair for her to sit on. No way she'd be able to reach Kofi's head standing, much less half the crew. "After that, whoever is in line first will get to the meeting room earlier and be in on the strategy session."

"Line up behind Herrick," Cart said as he stood in front of the man. A general scrambling ensued.

In the cover of shuffling around, Kofi whispered to Mona. "You won't change my personality, right?"

No, but this would be different given how tied to mental processes Kofi's magic was. Mona would need to do more of a surface check, but then any external evil taint would be on the exterior, she thought, so that'd be okay.

"That'll only happen if what is causing your attitude is tied into the residual. Don't worry," Mona smiled at her, "I think every group needs a nay-sayer, keeps people on their toes."

Mona placed her hands on either side of Kofi's head, fingers slotting into place between the tight braids. Unsurprisingly, several imps, including an orange one that looked remarkably like the one from her kitchen, had come to hover near her. Something, she didn't know what, made her think these were some of the new ones she and Cart had created. Mona could only guess she was now in a cone of silence, but she didn't want to pull her attention away to check, so she kept her voice low.

Kofi's magic felt fine—restlessness, worry, and resentment laced the energy, but nothing evil. "Kofi, if there is something you can do to get more training, look into it. Your magic is underused."

A startled look crossed the tall woman's face. "I keep saying I need to do more and they say I haven't shown potential yet."

"If 'they,' whoever 'they' are, wait for a sign of your potential, it'll be too late, because at that point it'll explode out of you. Clearly they're not taking into account that you'll evince your magic differently because you're a witch. I'll mention it to Cart." Mona lowered her hands. "You're done. Go give them hell."

Cart stepped up next.

"You have a nice talk with Kofi?" he said, confirming there was a cone of silence. Rejecting the chair, he sat on the edge of a table so she could reach his temples. It also forced her to step between his knees to reach him. As if the crew needed any more of a hint they were together.

"She needs more training. Pull strings and get her some or her magic will get out of control."

He, too, looked startled. "But—"

"Not everyone shows potential the same way. I'm guessing Kofi served for several years, doing well, before she started asking for, then demanding, training and getting cranky when she didn't get it. Her potential should have been picked up then. Besides, she's a witch, she's going to do things differently."

"Right, we'll have to contact the New York coven to see how they can help. Thanks, I'm so used to her fitting in, I'd forgotten she wasn't fae."

"Not safe to do with a witch, even if they are on your side."

Cart only nodded and looked thoughtful.

Mona placed her hands on his head. "I'm only doing this for show. I would have noticed if any evil was clinging to you already."

"Ah, and I thought it was the sex that had given me the extra energy."

"Both." She couldn't help but grin back. She lowered her hands. "Now go kick butt."

He jumped down and, mimicking her, placed his hands on either side of her head and kissed her, pulling away before things got too intense. The man was clearly marking her as his in front of his people. She'd complain about Weres and their desire to publically claim their property, but she understood the need riding him. Plus it felt damned good.

He let her go.

"You do realize you didn't need to do that, they all know," Mona said as she willed her heart back to its normal beat.

"Yeah, but I wanted to." Grinning cheekily, he stepped away and toward the door.

Herrick turned to leave with him.

"Herrick, everyone's got to do it, that includes you," Mona said loudly, knowing the imps would have removed the cone of silence with no one in her space.

He came reluctantly into her space, Cart patting him on the shoulder as he passed.

"What's up?" Mona asked. "I can't imagine you don't know how important this is."

"I get extremely nauseous from the feeling. The crew knows I'll be puking my guts out afterwards."

Mona looked him over. He was a man's man. She expected he had a pack of cigars stashed next to the recliner he watched football and hockey from.

"Is the Warder who does this in New York male?"

"Yep."

And that explained a whole lot. The process could feel like a very intimate touch and, while she didn't think he was homophobic, he would be intensely uncomfortable with a man's caress.

"Well I'm not, so this should go better for you." She put her hands on his temples.

One of the logistics she hadn't thought through was where to put the bits of foul energy she pulled out. Someone had, though, since the orange imp lowered itself to her hand once she pulled the taint away.

"Thanks," she muttered. The imp felt like a small spark of static electricity as it took the magic. Not much, a minute or two and she was done. She removed her hands and stepped back.

Herrick grinned at her.

"Wow, I feel better. Guess I did have some stuff." He stood and stretched, cracking his back. "Maybe I ought to get transferred so you can do that all the time."

"Sorry, I am a one man gal, and I've found my man."

Only two more had any substantial residue. Even those she pulled nothing from said they felt better after having her look at their magic. She guessed it was like going to the dentist—having clean, smooth teeth felt nice even when no other work was done.

She was starving when she finished up with Hyram, whom she was told was the last until the night shift, a skeleton crew for now, came on. Checking the time she saw she had a good four hours until her dinner, so she'd need to eat something or risk passing out.

"Any food around, Hyram?" she asked when she was done.

"Yeah, there's a full kitchen, and they laid in supplies, but not a lot of ready made stuff."

No problem, she'd make something up. She'd had enough of pack politics and personalities for the day. Better to let Cart find out what he could, and ask him later.

Chapter Eleven

The kitchen might be stocked, but the place hadn't been properly cleaned in years. Again, though, Mona found imps waiting to help. Good thing since the site was too new to have a family of brownies in residence like Smythe had. While they worked she went to look at what was in the fridges. No walk-ins, just a wall of industrial sized units. After opening every top and bottom door and moving on to the freezers, she started pulling things out. The counter was sparkling.

"Thank you again, imps," she said to the two remaining ones who seemed to be working in the bottom of an oven. They shimmered green then disappeared.

As she cooked, she gathered her thoughts. Cart was, in essence, right. Having a ward would not be that different than, say, if she had found out she had a child with a severe disability. Plus, she knew she'd have the added advantage of the support of the entire Folk community to help care for him, or, more correctly, help her as she cared for him. Or her.

Mona sighed as she scraped the minced chanterelles into the bowl. She needed to go re-read the parts on a ward, but she still wasn't ready to deal with the reality.

Mona had the mushroom barley soup on the stove in two big pots, one batch with cubed roast, beef stock, and tomatoes—the tomatoes were, in part, to make it easier to see which had meat—and one without, as well as several loaves of a fast-rising bread proofing on the counter when Cart found her.

"You doing okay?"

"Yeah, I think so. Still taking me a bit to process it."

Mona filled a sink half full of soapy water and set the Hobart mixer bowl in it to soak.

"Leave it, someone else can clean up."

Not about to argue with that, she removed the apron she didn't remember putting on.

She joined the group in the dining area and had her own soup served to her.

The crew bounced ideas off each other to figure out if there was a pattern to who had disappeared from the pack. Clans, trades and age all were put out and discarded before they decided to put the idea aside. Mona enjoyed the chaos of the group but was more than ready to leave when she was done eating.

"Thanks for making food for the crew," Cart said again when they were in the hall.

"No problem. I tend to cook when I am anxious."

"I thought you babbled," he said as he took her elbow and led her around a corner and down a long corridor.

"No, that's when I'm uncertain and uncomfortable, remember? Anxious, worried, that I cook for."

"Good to know," he said.

"So, anything you want to share now that you know two of my worst quirks?"

"Me, I don't have any quirks," he said, his too cheeky smile belying the point.

"Yeah, right." She followed him, quickly getting lost in all the turns and half staircases.

"The group hasn't made much headway tracking where the leaders headed off to," Cart shared. "The information from the pack is different for each person who went to meet him, giving us too many leads for our manpower to follow up on. Most, though, were north, toward Canada so we're concentrating in that direction."

"Near the falls?" Raine hadn't gone somewhere safe when she'd headed up there, she'd walked into the lion's den.

"Seems reasonable he'd be near a major source of natural energy."

Mona had no response to that. He was right, she should have thought of it.

"Any word on Raine?" she asked.

"I called Nurse Ferguson before lunch, she had nothing new to report except to thank you for buying the baby more time."

Mona abruptly stopped in the middle of a hall they'd gone down at least once before. There was a door hidden in the wall here. From the guarding and secrecy spells, it looked like a Maven might have used this as an office at some point. With all the spells around, it was clear the building, before it'd been a YMCA, had been used by Folk. Mona reached up and fiddled with the working, renewing the guarding part and deemphasizing the secrecy. Some secrecy was good, but this would make it difficult for some people to remember the room's existence once the door was closed. Actually, she could see the spell being very useful. She memorized the sequence of runes.

The door, which had been blurry to her eyes before, shimmered and solidified.

"I thought you'd be able to do it," Cart said his eyes on the newly appearing door.

"Changing spells is what I do, Cart."

"Yeah, but no one's been able to find the room since Hyram shut the door after he put your stuff in."

Mona looked over the workings again. "Who chose this room? They had to have seen it."

"Kofi went through and did the initial assignments. Yes, before you say anything else, I realize now it isn't just skill anymore that guides her and I have arranged, or am arranging for, training for her, once this gets done."

"Glad to hear it."

He opened the door and took a quick look around before holding it wide for her. "Shall we?"

The outer room looked like a waiting room, just large enough for a couch, table, and magazine rack. What made the room special was the waterfall feature in the corner, complete with a small tree and plants. Imp magic glistened all over it.

"I don't remember her saying anything about the fountain," Cart said as he walked over to take a look.

"I'd guess it wasn't here before. I think, eventually, the imps plan for this to be the Maven's room again, so they wanted to set up something so all Folk could access her. For now, while things get settled, I'm sure it's okay for us to use the room."

Mona walked through to the next room. Surprisingly contemporary furnishings sat in the sun lit room. Looking up she saw there was a large, clear dome letting in as much light as possible. As if she needed further proof this would be the Maven's room; as a full-blooded elf who'd come into their powers, the main way the Maven renewed her energy was with sunlight. She wondered how Nic would deal with that.

Her book was on a desk facing the door and her bag on a chaise set under the window. Mona kicked off her low boots and sank her feet in the rich rug.

"No curtains, the windows are spelled, right?"

Mona looked at them. "Old spells that aren't quite working. The Maven will want to set her own, so I'm inclined to just leave them."

"But you could fix them."

"But I'm not going to." She crossed over to the only other door and found a bathroom with a shower and lots of white marble.

"I need to freshen up." She opened up her bag and pulled a couple of things out.

"Wait, what?"

"I have dinner with my brother every week. And no, you can't go. I'm not up to dealing with two men thinking they need to protect the women in the room from each other. I'll never get anything accomplished."

Cart grunted and looked at his watch.

"Oh, no." She strode to the bathroom door. Stopping, she turned to find Cart immediately behind her. "I am not canoodling with you here. I'd be embarrassed to leave a residual of magic energy in a place the Maven was going to use."

"But—"

"Excuse me, are you working on a case or not?" She crossed her arms and canted her hip. "I've got to say, I can't decide whether or not I'm flattered by the fact that you are distracted by sex every time we are alone."

"Me either, but part of me is convinced I need to make memories now, since every time we separate I'm worried I'll never see you again. Doesn't help that with the full moon tonight, my beast is close to the surface and he doesn't want to let you go."

"We haven't separated in days! Until last night, I've been in the same building as you since we met."

"Doesn't matter."

Mona took his hands in hers. "You're wrong, it does." Mona held tight when he tried to pull away. Realizing part of his anxiety was due to his being low on energy she fed him some of the magic she'd unconsciously been cleaning since she'd entered the room. "Worrying that a thing might happen, when you have as much magic as you do, can cause it to happen. So you need to stop."

Mona sighed, released him, and grabbed her coat. Staying here with Cart was too much of a temptation for both of them. "I need to get going. Is there a car I can borrow?"

Mona saw him mentally bracing himself to let her go. It was both sweet and annoying. She could only hope he'd get over his need to monitor everything she did before it drove her nuts.

He dug some keys out of his pocket. "There's a tan all-wheel drive car in spot fifteen, use that."

He held them up and out of her way. "I'll be out running with the pack. You have to promise to leave a message when you get back so I know you're safe."

Mona kissed his cheek and agreed, plucking the keys out when he lowered his arm to hug her. He flipped her into his lap and convinced her he was not settling for anything close to a peck.

"I do have to go. If you want, I'll call you when I get there and when I leave."

"No, that's okay. I'm pretty sure you're right. In the grand scheme of things, our being together is useful, but not monumental." He did sound as if he was still trying to convince himself, but she let it slide.

And she knew she was going to try to call him anyway.

"Okay, I'll be back around eleven. Have fun on your run."

"Let's go, before I haul you back and pin you down."

Mona headed down the hall, Cart right behind her.

"Just as well you're here, or I'd get lost," she said as he took her elbow and steered her in the correct direction.

"Yo, Cart, some dude here to see you." The voice echoed down the hall.

"Who is it?" he called abruptly.

"Some dude from the Buffalo Pack."

Something wasn't right. "Didn't Averill say all the able-bodied men were missing?"

She had never seen someone move so fast. Cart took off down the hall before she'd processed that he'd moved at all. She raced after him knowing it was likely this Were had a spell on him too.

Cart and two other protectors wrestled with the man in the main rotunda. They moved around so much it was hard for her to get a read on him. No time for finesse, she just had to hope her changing things didn't trigger the same summoning the Weres she'd encountered had.

Her stomach roiled at the thought.

There, the rune for endurance was riding on the top of the spell and thankfully it didn't have the darker residue that made it difficult to move. She flipped it and he went down under Cart's next chop. Now speed rose to the top. She flipped that too as she yelled, "Stop!"

Amazingly, they all stepped back. The Were was pitifully flopping on the floor but she was not about to change back the runes.

"I've reversed the strength and speed aspects of the spells," she told Cart.

He walked over and hunkered down by the man.

"Wait, don't ask him anything—he's got some nasty things tied to speech. Let's see…" She looked over the spell. She'd been incredibly lucky with the two she'd chosen to turn as they were linked to so much else.

Having learned her lesson she looked deeper.

"Get him out of here! He's got some kind of beacon on him!"

Cart picked the man up and slung him over his shoulder. The two other protectors who'd been fighting stepped further back.

"I don't think so!" Mona was not going to let Cart face whatever was being called.

Acting on instinct alone, she gathered the residual magic from the fight and spell. Somehow she fed that magic into Cart. He ran down a corridor, and out to the back lot of the building. As soon as he passed the old barrier, Mona grabbed the back of his t-shirt. Blackness swirled around them.

"What the hell are you doing?" Cart yanked his shirt out of her grip.

"Helping you!"

They were in the living room of an empty house, the stunned Were Cart had carried now slumped unconscious at his feet.

"It's not helping when I have to take care of you too."

"You don't have to take care of me, I'll take care of myself."

Still snarling, he grabbed her hand. This home had a ton of residual magic, an elf adept at spells had lived here and left. Not that she was able to do more than recognize the potential before they were jumping again.

Mona found herself dumped like a hot potato when they arrived. Her bottom smarted.

"What the hell is your problem? I'm trying to help here!"

"You're distracting me!" he whispered back. "Now shut up before you get us both killed."

Mona stalked to the opposite corner of the small, decrepit shed he'd brought them to. To the far left, through the door-less entry she could see a house under the full moon. Further than across the street, for sure, but close enough that they'd be able to see movement. Cart must have known whoever lived in the house and thought it was a safe place to leave the spelled man.

She studied the building closely as she rubbed her arms in an attempt to get warm, unsure what Cart was waiting for. "This isn't the Were's fault, they don't have control. We need to track down the shithead who is creating these spells. We, as in I need to be there too."

Cart didn't look convinced. He turned back to watch the house, not responding to her statement.

"What are we watching for?" she asked, barely able to keep her teeth from chattering. She began bouncing in place to try to warm up.

"Well, we've got a bit of a predicament. I can't do what I was going to since, as you pointed out, they're not entirely responsible for their actions. On the other hand I can't leave them here to wreck havoc on any Folk that may be around."

"No mortals?"

"Not for some distance. Tania liked her privacy."

"Oh, if it's just the non-human Folk, I can take care of that."

"How?"

"I am a Warder, or at least one in training," she said between bounces. "I do know how to send alarms to the Folk, particularly creatures who we can't warn with words."

Mona stopped bouncing, closed her eyes, and remembered the tone, then did a flick that sent it out to reverberate along any magic lines in the area.

"Crap. I felt that." Cart shook his head and rubbed at his left ear.

"You shouldn't have, that tone is for creatures!"

"It's a full moon tonight, Mona, and I am not just strong and able to change, I'm a first generation Were. Right now I'm probably closer to creature than person."

"Shit, let's hope other shifters didn't," Mona said. "I don't think there are many strong Weres in the pack."

"I don't know if I have enough energy," he grumbled. "If I hadn't pulled you along with me, I might have enough for just me."

"Even with the extra I sent into you?"

"The...what?" He stopped talking for a minute. "How did you do that?"

"Later, just get us out of here. I'm getting a really bad feeling."

Too late—a mix of wolves, big cats, and other predators headed to the house. Right as they got there, the spell they had unwittingly carried caused the building to shake, then burst into a huge ball of fire.

Mona saw the spell, saw the simple runes, and reached out to turn them, thankful this spell, for once, didn't have any of the sticky residue.

Only to have her hand batted down. The bastard!

"Don't ever do that! If I have a rune in my hand you could wreck the entire spell and cause chaos." She turned her back on Cart. "I'm going closer. I want to try to send the whole thing, including the fireball, back to the maker."

"Don't go closer!"

She shot a 'fine! But don't interrupt me' over her shoulder and raised her hand again.

The large swirling she'd come to expect with the magic wielder formed in the sky above the house. Weres were dying in that fire, she was sure of it. She needed to move the fire away from the shifters if she was going to save any.

If she turned the homing rune that way and flipped the igniter rune that way…the ball of fire shot right at the swirl.

And so did all of the remaining Weres.

Mona stood numb, not wanting the bespelled shifters to get caught in the flames, not seeing what was pulling them along with the spell.

"No!" she screamed as the first of the shifters passed through the fireball on its way back to the face. The decimated remains hit the face and there was a huge flash of light. Everything—the swirl, the shifters, the face—everything disappeared.

She blinked in the pitch black, spots dancing before her eyes. Cart had jumped her out before she saw any more.

She tumbled face first onto the bed. He'd jumped them to the rooms above D'Alessandro's again. Shivers wracked her body, despite the solid warmth at her back. The frantic beat of her heart matched paced with the pounding in the chest pressed behind her.

She'd killed Weres she'd been trying to save.

"If you had gone in closer—" Cart started.

"But I didn't," Mona interrupted. And then, because she simply could not help herself, she started to babble. "We got out of there, didn't we? But those poor Weres! What if I—"

"Stop!" Cart's angry yell made her blink. He scrambled off the bed and stood, arms akimbo, tension in every line of his body. His face looking down at her was furious.

She sat up and stared at him.

"Excuse me?" she finally said. "You did not just tell me to stop talking."

"I did because you were going to babble incessantly about what happened to those Weres, which wasn't your fault. Oh, you may have killed one or two who might have been spared from the fireball, but only by random bad luck. The bad guy here is whoever sent them and the fireball in the first place."

Mona blinked at him. Killed one or two? As if that wasn't a big deal.

Perhaps to him it wasn't.

But she couldn't ever see looking at lives that way. Her job was to stop magic from hurting others. Instead, she'd killed two the people she'd been trying to protect.

She stood up and absentmindedly brushed her pants off. "I need to go."

"I think you'd better."

Mona looked at Cart. Anger still poured off him.

"I know why I think I have to go. Why do you think I need to go?"

His chest rose and fell as he took several deep breaths before answering.

"I've seen what happens when someone thinks their job is to protect everyone else but themselves and their family. They end up dying. I don't care if I'll be in physical agony because I've withdrawn from the person who I'm pretty sure is my mate, but I can't watch as you destroy yourself helping other people. Nothing is worth that."

Mona nodded, unable to form an argument with her grief over killing the Weres wrapping itself around her heart.

He took a step toward her and before his foot hit the ground he disappeared.

Unsure what to do, Mona wandered out into the hall and to the kitchen. Dinner was gearing up downstairs, the smells from the restaurant were almost overwhelming.

Dinner. She was supposed to join Cart and Tania.

One of the lights shifted and moved toward her.

An imp.

"I'm Mona Lisa Kubrek, state your message."

"Mona," Nic's voice carried in the empty room. "I need to cancel dinner. Something's come up with Tania—Titania, the Maven. I'll explain later. You should get in touch with Smythe, some odd things are going on."

Past time to track him down. The imp blinked out and another took its place. She directed the imp to state its message.

A quivery, out-of-breath voice said "Mona, four hundred eleven sixty, make note."

There was a heartbeat of silence after the imp sparked out. Smythe! He'd sounded odd, out of breath and almost incoherent. Where was he? Did he need help? Mona paused in the act of calling an imp to check. Cart was right, damn him, someone was messing with imps and she couldn't rely on them. Mona grasped on the one clue Smythe had given her. 'Make note.' He had to be referring to his extensive journals and records. Mona needed to tell Cart so they could track down the clue and try to find him.

She headed to the door then stopped. Cart had left.

Surely the protectors would help. Unless Cart had told them to keep her safe, in which case she'd be stuck at the station instead of doing something. Better, then not to say anything, yet, about the message and track down the clue.

Mona headed out, grabbing an oversized sweatshirt off the coat rack by the backdoor. It was going to be a cold five block walk to the new headquarters, but even with Cart walking out, she wasn't foolish enough to head over to the complex without some backup. Despite his assumptions, she didn't jump into situations without a thought to her safety. She just didn't plan to tell them the reason she wanted to go.

Chapter Twelve

During the walk over she'd gotten more and more antsy about Smythe's message. What did the numbers mean? There were too many possibilities, none of which seemed to fit.

The desk was manned with two Weres when she entered this time, neither of whom she knew. She wondered if any of this crew had had a chance to go on a moon run, if any of them needed to. Surely Cart would have taken care of it.

Indeed, as she waited, a half a dozen Weres headed out, chattering and excited and talking about the tricks they'd learned to hide their tracks in the snow and how hard it was to not mark the territory with everything so unclaimed. Tifft Nature Preserve was mentioned too, a good place for a group their size, provided they had control, which it sounded like they did.

"Hello," she said to one of the attendants. "I need to find someone from Protector Dupree's unit. Can you help me?"

The man gave her a look and dismissed her. "We're closed, except for emergencies. Is it an emergency?"

"Well, no…"

"Very well then, it can wait until the morning. The protectors are here to help, but it's unreasonable for you to expect them to jump just because you can't wait until the morning. Really, the Buffalo Pack has got to learn some priorities." This last was spoken more to himself than to Mona.

He glared at her. She smiled sweetly back.

"Protector…" She glanced at his badge, pinned to the hem of his t-shirt. "Matheus. I am glad that Cart, Tiff, Menlo, Hyram, and the rest of the crew have such an avid defender. However, perhaps first you should find out from whom you are defending them from."

Mona didn't realize how anxious she was to get going now until she made the pithy speech. Turning to the desk, she saw that Herrick was there, an annoyed look on his face.

"Matheus was doing his job, Trainee," he said before she could say anything.

What? She didn't see any foul magic about him so she was very taken aback at the attitude. No, without Cart there, he was acting like a typical Were and dismissing her 'hysterics'.

"Protector Leader Herrick, I cannot but think that if he'd asked who I was and found out that I am the *Warder's* trainee, he might have handled the situation differently." She emphasized "Warder" since his calling her "Trainee" had been more than a slight. "While I understand the need to vet requests to see the investigative crew, since I am working with them, my request for help to locate them is reasonable."

"Not at this time of night it isn't."

He just lost any chance of her being civil.

"I must insist that it is." Somehow she knew bringing Cart's name into the mix would only make his attitude more recalcitrant. Besides, she didn't want him involved in this.

"With Leader Dupree gone, I am the senior Were here and I say it isn't." He crossed his arms over his chest and stared smugly at her.

"Oh?" She did her best to hide the fact she was plucking at every recently laid magic thread she could find by using her hands to emphasize her points. Disrupting the energy was a silent call to those Protectors sensitive to magic. "You think that gives you the right to rule the place? To make decisions that will affect Dupree's unit? Last I heard, the investigative team and the policing team were separate entities. Have you, in your megalomania, decided they need to be joined?"

As she spoke, Weres started coming into the room, some hurrying, others in caution, from both units.

"You may perceive yourself to be the senior Were here, but you are not the highest ranking." Mona silently gave thanks to Smythe for making her memorize the endless lists of hierarchy. "I outrank you, as do, I am sure, several members of Cart's crew. However, even they do not have the authority you have sought to assume by putting the entire group under one umbrella. Right now, until the Buffalo pack has trained its own protectors and named a chief, you all are under the direction of the Warder and the Pack Leader."

Anger simmered out of him, then a sly look came over his face. "Yes, and she—"

Mona could not let him complete the sentence and possibly perjure himself. "She what? Be careful what you say. Remember I was there when she banned you from the pack house. Shall I call an imp to refresh your memory?"

He paled; everyone knew that what one imp knew, they all knew. Plus, Cart had said he didn't want any of the protector group using them.

"Fine, then." Mona turned to scan the crowd. "Menlo, Tiffany, if I could meet with you and the rest of the investigators, please?"

"Bitch." Herrick muttered. The acoustics of the room carried his pronouncement to everyone.

As Mona turned back there was a loud pop and lights began to blaze from every wall. But they weren't lights—more imps than she'd ever seen lined the rotunda.

Randall stood on the desk in a furious rage. The thirties gangster outfit completed the impression of lethalness. Mona heard several gasps.

"You are so far out of line, Herrick, you've just earned yourself a one way ticket to visit me. And if you think I'm mad, just wait until you meet the goddess. You don't mess with her designees."

He turned to the imps, who had coalesced behind him like a large sparkling cloak. "Take him."

They swirled around Herrick, completely blocking him from sight. Then they were gone, Herrick along with them.

Randall turned and looked over the crowd, his body relaxing and face easing into a smile when he saw Mona. "Hi, Warder."

"Hello, Puck." It was times like this, when he went from an overwhelming rage to charmingly calm that she remembered he was even less human than she was.

He flashed a large grin before somberly addressing the crowd. "Protectors, investigators." He stabbed his finger at the groups within the crowd. "Do your job. Now. The goddess is watching."

He flipped off the desk, causing people to scramble out of the way. In the middle of his back flip he disappeared.

On the one hand, Mona was a little annoyed at his jumping in and not letting her handle things. On the other, she wondered just what all was going on to make him interfere. Most Weres were lucky if they saw him once in a lifetime.

The problems in Buffalo clearly had wider consequences than they'd realized.

A few people stood still, looking shocked. Most, however, were already merging into groups and discussing things. Mona found Cart's crew heading toward her.

As a group, they bowed to her.

Crap, that designee of the goddess line was going to be tough to live down.

"Warder," Menlo said, confirming that he was in charge. Or maybe Tiff was and she'd asked him to speak. Mona cut a glance over to her. She nodded, her smile faint on her face.

Wait.

"I'm not a Warder yet."

"Pretty sure you are if Randall just named you one," he said, a grin on his face. The rest of the group grinned too. "Handy, that. I wonder if I could get his help."

Right, Menlo specialized in dealing with elves who were coming into power.

"Let's head to the conference room," Hyram said, looking around. "We can go over what we know there and add to the schematic Cart made up. Good job with the fireball. The little bit of intelligence we have says you put him out of commission. At least for now."

They started to turn.

"No." Despite all that had gone on, Mona still clung to her objective. The group turned around. "I need to get to the complex. That's why I was looking for you all. I need a buddy."

Tiff and another woman stepped forward.

"I thought you were in charge," she said to Tiff, who'd just directed the other woman to get their coats.

"Yes and no. Menlo and I share the job. Besides, Cart said guarding you was top priority, since things seem to happen when you're around."

Mona would deal with this guarding thing later since he was right about things happening. She hadn't fully articulated the coincidence in her head yet, but she did now. Crap.

Mona rubbed her face. No wonder Cart thought she was an accident waiting to happen. If he couldn't get over his worry… she wasn't going to think about that now. Restless energy and a sense of urgency had Mona pacing. "I need to get out to Smythe's complex."

"Anyone out there to keep an eye on the ward?"

"Not that I know of. But then, we hadn't started that part of my training yet."

The woman was already coming back with their winter gear.

"Let's go," Tiff said.

"Wait, all of us? We don't need three people."

"All of us. Emetaly," she waved a hand at her companion, whose long, black hair and hooked nose were reminiscent of a

Mexican native tribe, "is a first generation Were and can jump us out if need be. And I'm not not going."

"You can't jump in or out of Smythe's complex!" Mona said, exasperated that she needed to explain.

"Right, but if we need to jump at some point outside of it, she can do it. I can't."

"Fine." Okay, Mona saw the logic, given how often Cart had jumped her out of tight places the last couple of days.

Until recently, Mona had never understood why the complex was so far away from the Were enclave. Now she knew the forty-minute drive was to keep the ward removed from Folk and still keep the Warder close enough he could do the rest of his job.

And the skyway was still closed, so they had to go a circuitous route.

Then things kept delaying them.

Broken lights.

Long freight trains.

Disabled cars.

A massive pothole.

No one said anything—it was clear someone or thing was determined they'd not get there.

This, of course, made them all the more determined to do so.

The worst delay was when they got stuck on a road behind an accident where they had to airlift someone out. Two hours. Mona actually took a nap, once it was clear they weren't going to be moving any time soon.

Dawn was streaking the sky by the time they got to the turnoff for the Warder's driveway.

Mona pulled over at the second to last turn in the drive.

"We should leave the car here and walk the rest of the way," she said, fighting to keep her worry from her voice. They'd all taken turns driving and cat napping when they could, but none of them were anything near rested and up to speed. And the way things were going, they'd need to be.

"We got any rations, Emetaly?" Tiffany asked, tucking her short, wine colored hair under a knit cap.

"Yeah," Emetaly reached into a satchel that was on the back seat. Mona had used it as a pillow one of the times she'd tried to rest. "Let's see what tasty treats we have in store today. Eggs Benedict? Hash browns? Belgian waffles? Ah, yes, I see they've opted for the almond butter and coffee bean option, my favorite."

They ate their protein bars and washed down the thick taste with sips from the one bottle of water that'd been packed. Mona almost missed the rations from the emergency kit.

"Okay," Mona said once everyone was done. "Let's check this place out."

Mona's tire tracks from earlier in the week were still discernable and they followed the path as the drive made its way through the stand of trees shielding the complex from the road.

Tiffany stopped where the path ended in a large area of trampled snow. "Which way?"

"To the right, but let me lead. There was a trap here earlier in the week, and I need to make sure it's gone."

They halted at the edge of the clearing around the walls, the full set of buildings in view. The high, crenellated stone wall and the turrets on the corner of the inner buildings looked medieval in the frosty morning air.

Of course, they looked medieval in any air, but something about the crisp blue sky made the slate spires atop the building look far more sharply out of time than they had before. Tiffany and Emetaly stopped and stared.

"That is awesome. A castle in the middle of a forest in upstate New York. Definitely the most…um…warrior-like Warder compound I've seen," Tiffany said. She scanned the area in the front of the gate. "That's where the working earlier in the week was, right? I can see the residual from the disturbance in the ground. Not seeing anything now, though, are you?"

Emetaly and Mona shook their heads.

"Any way in besides the gate?" Tiffany asked, gesturing to the large wooden doors mounted deep in the keep's outer wall.

"No." There had to be a back way, but Mona didn't know where it was.

Tiffany shrugged. "Then let's go."

This time Tiff led and the other two followed.

She skirted well wide of the churned earth left from the spell Smythe had said was a test. Once at the gates Mona noticed the runes on the warding spell were rearranged.

"He's changed the spell. You won't be able to come in with me."

"What? You're kidding right?" Tiffany reached to run her hand over the door, as if that would give her information.

Mona's yell of "Stop!" coincided with the arc of energy coming off the planks of the door.

Tiffany flew back a couple of feet and crumpled to the ground. Her breathing was shallow and her pulse, when Mona thought to feel for it in her neck, rapid.

Emetaly lifted Tiff's hand and carefully pulled the remnants of her glove off. An angry red welt ran across Tiff's palm, but the glove had protected her skin from the worst of the heat, if not the energy of the power.

"Go, jump her back," Mona said. "I need to stay here and see if the Warder's left me a message."

Emetaly bit her lip, clearly torn on what to do.

"Look, it's pretty clear no one besides me is going to get in. If I think anyone is trying, I'll call, imp restriction be damned."

"Okay."

Truth was, Mona wasn't sure she would be able to get in, but she was going to try.

Mona watched the spell as she approached and reached out for the handle. There, to the right, was the part she needed to change. She tweaked the rune, opened the door, and tweaked it back. "I'm in," she called out. "Go! Get her some help."

Mona felt the surge and knew they were gone.

Chapter Thirteen

The circular drive was barren. No snow on any surface. Mona had forgotten how odd the effect of the three large castle-like buildings with the pristine cobblestone drive looked after walking through the snowy forest.

She crossed the wintry lit courtyard to the Warder's house. Mona realized very quickly gaining entry was a lost cause. The spell had been twisted and turned in a very convoluted string—it'd take her all day to loosen it enough just so she could figure out what she could change to get in. The good news was she was pretty sure nothing was going to get out.

Okay, off to the middle building then, which housed a large library and warehouse. Saying the classrooms on the third floor were too old and dusty to use, the vast book-filled second floor was where most of her training had taken place. Aside from his journal, Smythe kept logs of most events in the Folk community, from births to marriages to the date and location he'd fixed a set spell. They were more like lists than narratives and very, very dry reading. Mona hoped to find something in the library to explain Smythe's cryptic numbers as well as "make note" of them in the current diary.

She headed up the side staircase to the vast and chilly room. The stone walls and high arched windows reminded her of an ivy-clad prep school she had attended for a year. That was before her mother left and Nic switched her to public school.

Fortunately there was a much smaller reading room off to the side, in an alcove made by the exterior tower. The circular space held the desk Smythe used and the table Mona studied at as well as comfy seating. And a potbelly stove, old but still working.

Mona closed the door. After making sure the flue was open—she wasn't going to make that mistake again—she started a fire from the wood already laid in. A set spell made the cast iron fixture more efficient.

As the room started to warm and the scent of wood smoke filled the air, Mona took off her coat and sat at the desk. She'd check the Warder's journal and add a note on what he'd said in his message.

But the top left drawer, where Smythe always placed his book, was empty. So was the one below it. And the three on the right hand side.

Nor was the small leather clad volume on the shelves to the right of the desk where the pervious journals were kept.

Or the floor, or under any of the cushions of the couch or on any of the side tables in the room. Not there.

Would it make more sense to look through the older journals or to look in the larger room for the current one?

Library.

Mona shrugged back into her jacket, did what she could to bank the fire, and headed back into the vast book-filled space. Smythe had a journal for every month he'd been Warder. Add to that the fact that he'd been doing it for over a hundred years…that was a lot of journals she was going to have to do through.

She pulled out the oldest, brittle with age and flaking.

She read the first journal entry date.

March 21, 1812.

Abner was even older than they realized if his first journal was two hundred years old.

Nothing seemed relevant on the pages she checked. Births, deaths, trades with the natives. Mona carefully slid the journal back and pulled out the next.

Nothing, nothing, nothing.

Three hours later, she was starving and still hadn't found the book or stumbled onto anything that might help decipher the numbers.

Giving into her hunger pangs, she headed down to the kitchen hoping to scrounge something to eat. There was a large bag of string cheese sticks in the fridge sitting all by its lonesome on a lower shelf. The freezer had been cleared out as well, although three pints of frost covered soup remained stacked in a corner. In the cabinets, a case of fusilli sat next to an institutional-sized box of toaster pastries. Smythe always had them around, although, come to think of it, she'd never seen him eat one.

Standing in the empty kitchen, Mona was struck by how off things really were. Usually brownies kept the house stocked with at least enough for Abner to eat, plus food for anyone who worked here.

But there was nothing. Even most of the serving ware was gone—a handful of mugs, a saucepan, and a bowl were all that remained. She had no sense that the brownies were about at all.

Mona felt like she was trespassing in an abandoned home. But the answer to the clue Smythe had sent was in all likelihood here, she was sure of it. Knowing she was on the right track didn't assuage her guilt she hadn't told anyone of his message. Only one way to deal with that.

"I'd like an imp please."

Nothing happened. She counted to twenty and tried again. Nothing.

Mona pulled out her phone. No reception. How was she supposed to check on Raine? Find out if more spelled Weres showed up? She was torn, sure she needed to be here, and unwilling to be disconnected from everything that was happening. Focusing on the big picture helped, along with the worry that if she left, she might not make it back. If the goal was to get the person spelling the shifters, her best option was to stay and use the journals to attempt to figure out what the numbers from Smythe meant. The protectors knew where she was. If they needed her, they would figure out a way to come get her. Determined to find something, she grabbed several cheese sticks and a toaster pastry, and headed back upstairs to the bookshelves.

Mona passed several days in a stupor of reading, eating when hunger hit and sleeping only when she couldn't keep her eyes open any longer. Worry over Smythe and Raine, as well as the shifters the madman seemed to control, became a constant companion, one that urged her to keep looking, keep going. Her tiredness served as an excellent buffer for thoughts on Cart and his declaration that he couldn't be with her. Not to mention the sadness that he hadn't even shown up to check on her. She simply tried not to think and worked her way through over two thousand books.

The sun was streaming through the windows when she woke up from a cat nap nearly a week after she got there. Mona sat up and rubbed her face. She slid her phone out from under yet another journal to check the time.

She'd not found anything, despite stacks of notes on the pages she'd checked and today was the day the Maven had set for the Lackawanna pack meeting. Mona didn't understand how her feeling that she'd find something here could be so wrong. She'd wasted days when she could have been with the protectors, helping them. With nothing to show for her work she started bundling herself back up and grabbed her keys.

Which were next to a journal.

A journal that had not been there when she went to sleep.

Looking around, she saw the faint trace of imp magic—which was unnerving, given none had been around the entire time she'd been there.

Gingerly, she picked the book up, holding it by the binding. There was a spell running along the side of the cover; the markings looked like Randall's work. Understandable, then, why the magic hadn't awakened her—she trusted the Puck implicitly, pain in the ass that he could be.

Although, maybe she shouldn't. Not that he'd mean her harm, but protecting all the non-human Folk would always come before any friendship they had.

Only one way to find out.

Bracing herself, she opened the book.

Images, words, feelings all bombarded her. Information, scenes of Smythe's life, came at her at the speed of sound, and she felt like she was standing in the middle of the largest, busiest place she could ever imagine, where people and beings rushed up to her, acknowledged her, then rushed back away.

The assault of sights and sounds and scents overwhelmed Mona to the point where they were her whole existence, and her body a memory.

Then the sensations stopped.

She breathed deeply.

Her heart stuttered.

Blinking, she focused on the room around her, she'd seen this room built, furnished, lived in.

With an almost audible snap, everything found a place to settle in her memory. All the learning that Abner had not yet been able to give her was with her.

A knowledge bequeathing spell. Apparently it was the one spell that could be directed at a Warder and actually work.

Which meant Smythe was dead.

Mona didn't remember grabbing her things and running down the stairs or out of the library, nor the start of the tremors that shook the ground and buildings. Her newly acquired memory told her, however, that she needed to get the hell out of there before the place fell like a house of cards.

As she had when they were by the Maven's old home, she sent out a note of warning to the non-human Folk in the area of the danger. She'd not seen any but that didn't mean they weren't there.

The gate was already askew when she went to shoulder it open. As she squeezed through the foot wide gap between the huge wooden slabs, she heard her coat rip.

Then she flat out ran, stumbling as the earth shuddered from the impact of the massive slabs falling. Collapsing against the car, she took several deep breaths, the cold air searing her lungs.

That had been far too close a call.

She checked her phone, noting she had a bar or two of reception along with the time. While she'd been absorbing Smythe's knowledge, an hour had passed. Strange. It felt like all the memories should have taken longer and, at the same time, that only a minute had passed.

Should she contact someone? No. She wasn't going to tell anyone Smythe was dead over the phone. She was about to put the phone back in her pocket when a text came through from Nic. *Meeting at D'Alesandro's six p.m. Need you there.* Tucking her cell away, she got in the truck.

Thankfully the engine started and she was able to turn around and get out.

Then, at the end of the drive, like a curtain waiting for her to pass through, there was a sheet of falling snow.

If the drive up had been frustrating, this was far worse. Visibility was poor, traction non-existent. The snowfall only let up as she neared some of the busier intersections of the rural highway, where gas stations and fast food outlets seemed to crop up suddenly in the lessening snow. The snow stopped all together when she hit the outskirts of town.

Some part of her recognized the pattern meant the system had somehow been tied to non-urban areas, likely to do with hindering non-human Folk. She'd never have known that without the information Smythe imparted. Having this unexpected knowledge was going to take some getting used to.

Despite the let up of precipitation, she drove carefully the rest of the way, wary of another ambush to delay her arrival.

Three blocks away from D'Alessandro's she found the delay she was expecting.

Simple, yet diabolical.

The fire hydrants had burst, sending huge plumes arcing across street, and coating everything in a fifty-foot radius in water. In the below freezing temperatures, the water quickly turned to ice. Controlling the car as best as she could on the incredibly slick road, she slid over to the edge, got out, and determinedly, she set out on foot. She needed to get to the meeting before they were done. By the time she made it to D'Alessandro's, her half frozen hands could barely grab the knob on the door.

"Mona!" Gabby, the night hostess started toward her.

Mona waved her aside and moved into the warmth of the building.

"I've got to get to the meeting." Shivering and dazed, she knew she had to take that last step.

Suddenly drained, and realizing just how much she'd been running on adrenaline in her trek from the car, she teetered and stumbled down the back hall to the meeting room, each step painfully difficult. Gabby fluttered behind her, offering *help[AA3]*; Mona had no energy to accept or reject. One last burst of energy and she shoved her way through the door.

As if in slow motion she saw Nic and Cart both vault a table, although Cart magically hopped the last few feet to get to her side first. Nic and Tania appeared a hairsbreadth behind him.

Sagging into Cart's arms she felt some of her energy restore— she must've been pulling it out or he was unconsciously sending magic into her.

Message. She had a message she needed to deliver to the group.

"The Warder, he's dead!" She hadn't meant to shout, but the urgency to tell everyone created volume.

Her voice echoed through the stunned room.

"HOLD!" Randall's voice rang through the room. "Maven, there is an imp here for you."

In the silence a faint and feeble light glimmered to being in front of Tania.

"I'm Maven Titania, please start your message when ready."

A couple of raspy breaths, then, "Four hundred eleven sixty."

The Maven gasped. Nic put his arm around her, "We still don't know what those numbers mean."

Mona was so thankful to realize Smythe had sent them the same message.

The Puck gently scooped the fading light out of the air. He cupped the imp in his hand, an expression of deep sorrow on his face.

"Little Spark, you have served well and are an honor to the well spring of knowledge from which you sprung. Go in peace."

The imp flickered then shone brightly through the spectrum of colors before fading out. A low keening filled the room, the note tinged with infinite sadness.

Mona sat in the chair someone had kindly put behind her. An imp had died. More than anything else, and there had been a lot of other things, the death highlighted just how severely something wrong was occurring. Imps didn't die. Everything she'd learned from Smythe was telling her this was impossible. Yet it had happened.

Randall looked up at the group, his expression fierce. Crap, she knew he was going to do a binding and she was in no shape to argue him out of it.

"Maven, you'll find who is doing this and bring them the swift justice of the Folk." His stentorian tones echoed through the hall and no doubt beyond.

Tania did something, a tweak of magic that morphed into a full spell. There was a slight flare and the magic settled. Mona gasped at the suddenness and the beauty of it. She felt like she'd been reading runes and symbols in block letters and now was looking at them in what her Dad called copperplate, elegantly curved writing that celebrated the beauty and symmetry of the work.

Between one blink of the eye and the next Tania was in an outfit fit for a Queen at the Elfhaven court. Mona, along with most of the room, stared in awe at the jewel encrusted tiara and crimson sash heavily decorated with medals. She actually heard Nic gulp at the sight of the gossamer dress. Not much was left to the imagination.

The scepter in Tania's hand only added to her regal appearance. All around, Weres knelt or bowed or curtsied. Mona started to follow suit, only to find Cart clamping his hand on her shoulder and keeping her in the chair.

Tania regally nodded at everyone, gesturing immediately that they rise, a small smile playing on her lips as she waved and bowed her head to the children in the back.

"With the Buffalo Were Pack and my protector as witnesses," Tania said, turning to face Randall, who Mona could tell was trying to hide how impressed he was by the Maven's actions. "I agree to search for the one who has harmed the imps, and has imprisoned and coerced the Buffalo Pack Weres."

The Maven had been told, or perhaps already had known, about the spelled Weres. Mona was glad Randall had pushed Tania into taking action on what clearly was no longer just a pack problem.

Tania's voice rang through the room and, like Randall's had earlier, beyond; such a pact would be heard by all Folk within several miles. Which made Mona wonder if any of those they sought would hear the binding.

"Seek those who'll help you," Randall said.

Tania's eyes narrowed with annoyance. Mona could tell she didn't like Randall's request but wasn't going to turn him down. She ran her fingers down her sash, stopping at a small pouch that had been pinned on. Oh my. Mona could read the contents through the bespelled fabric. Fairy dust.

The pinch she took was infinitesimal and she kept her finger in her palm to keep it from floating away. A few particles sifted out and hung iridescent in the air. Mona watched as Tania's magic reached out and swirled with the floating bits.

"May all who shall go forth with me to confront this being be marked and made known," Tania ritually invoked.

Somewhere a memory from Smythe rose up of a similar action in a long ago time, but the image faded before Mona had done more than recognize the similarities of posture and word.

Tania lifted her hand, palm up, and blew gently on the dust as she turned in a circle. Prismatic sparkles lingered in her wake. Once her revolution was complete, they flashed brightly and surrounded Mona.

"Hi, Warder." The Puck grinned, momentarily dropping his fierce persona. His mood swings were starting to worry her, because as soon as his gaze left her, he became solemn again, his bushy eyebrows drawn in a straight line. "Mona Lisa Kubrek, you have been chosen."

As soon as Randall finished, the particles left and immediately reappeared as glittering particles surrounding Cart, who stood by Mona's seat.

"Training Leader and Protector Josiah Carthage Dupree, you are chosen," Randall said.

Then the dust did an odd thing—it went to Nic, flying around his head and then spiraling down his body, but left to circle back to the Maven before the Puck intoned his name.

A slight hesitation, then Randall said: "Niccoli Machiavelli Lombard, you too join in the pursuit of justice."

Mona sensed confusion from the Weres on Nic's participation. But unlike them, she was informed, in Smythe's dry voice, of two factors at play. First, with Tania committed, Nic, as her protector, was also committed, so his being named was not needed.

And two, he was still coming into his powers. There was a very good chance, once they settled, and likely by the end of their search, Nic would have a different title than Protector. The Puck would not bind him by title until his powers fully manifested.

Mona shook her head, not liking Smythe's didactic recitation of the Puck's reasoning. She noticed Tania looked taken aback that the dust was done but still stood straight as she said her part of the binding.

"With those called forth, I'll mete the retribution of the Folk on behalf of the imps and the Buffalo Pack Weres."

"So mote it be," Randall and Averill said in unison, each within their rights as leaders to bind her. In Mona's head a thready, reed-like version of Smythe's voice urged her to join in the binding, but she ignored it.

Silence spread out as the binding took. Mona saw the spell settle on Tania and more lightly on Cart. Nic was not tagged by it at all. Interesting. Of course, she wasn't either, but then that wasn't unexpected.

The crowd stayed motionless, stunned to have witnessed the stuff of legends; at least, she knew *she* was.

"Okay, let's get started," Cart said, his voice clear and loud. From where he'd moved behind her, with his hand on her shoulders, he started barking directions and people shook themselves out of their mesmerized state. His stance radiated irritation. At her? At the Puck? Hard to tell.

Nic came and eased her out of Cart's grasp; for a moment she thought Cart wasn't going to let her go.

"Let me get her out of the middle of everything," Nic said.

Cart removed his arm, but not before whispering into her ear. "You will never put yourself in danger like that again."

Cart moved away, not allowing her the chance to speak. Idiot man! While she had no desire to put herself in harm's way, she wasn't going to avoid her job because he thought she needed to be safe.

Fuming, she and Nic shuffled around the edge of the room, her muscles protesting with every step. Once she was seated at a table along the far side of the room, Nic got her a water bottle and told her to take several sips. The water helped, although she was still a bit shaky and furious. Mona asked for some food but he suggested she wait to make sure the water stayed down first.

Tania, she noted, had changed out of most of her regalia and was approaching them with a large mug of coffee in her hands.

"You okay, Mona?" Tania asked as she set the cup on the table next to her.

The reply wasn't automatic. She took stock of herself. She felt faint, definitely bruised, her palm bled from a scrape she didn't remember getting, her ears were ringing. And she wanted to give Tania's cousin a piece of her mind.

Things could have been worse. "Yeah, I think so. I—"

"Wait, don't say anything yet, Mona." Cart came up behind Tania, Emetaly by his side. She saw his barely contained rage even if no one else did. Although the shifters did seem to be giving him a wide berth.

"I want Emetaly to make a formal recording."

Mona ignored Cart and looked at Nic, who nodded at her encouragingly.

"First I need to know how Raine is doing."

"We checked and she's still in a holding pattern," said Cart. "The only good news is the babe is still healthy."

Mona nodded. "Any more attacks?"

"No. Current thought is that the fireball you sent back did some damage." Cart held his hand out to stop any further questions. "Let's make this record first, I'll answer your questions later."

"Okay." Mona took a deep breath. Cart had heard much of this already, but not Nic or the Maven. She had no idea how much he'd shared with his crew. "I need to start the day before the collapse of the skyway. I got a phone call from my friend Raine…"

Her tale came out between sips of the sweet milky coffee. She did skip some bits, like, oh say, having sex with Cart. Several of the Weres, including Hyram and Tiff walked by to check on her, but didn't interrupt.

Finally she got to the collapse of the compound, and then her walk this evening through the icy streets.

"Once I hit the broken fire hydrants it was tough, like someone poured buckets of ice over all the cars. The lot here looks particularly frozen."

Cart caught Menlo's eye. He'd been hovering at the periphery for the last twenty minutes or so. Menlo nodded and headed out.

Tania leaned in and said something to Nic when she was done. Cart stood on the other side of the table, arms crossed, his glare hard to avoid, so she didn't.

"How's Tiffany?" she asked.

"She's fine, got a bit of a burn but it's already healing."

"Good."

Tania headed to the other side of the room. Nic stayed with Mona but his attention was clearly with the Maven.

"Any chance I can have some food?"

Nic didn't look as if he'd even heard the question.

"Let me see what I can do," Cart said.

"Mushrooms, if they have them. Whatever is fine, though, I'd rather have something sooner than wait."

As soon as he left. Nic turned his attention to Mona. Not as oblivious as he seemed.

"Do you know what you're getting yourself into?" Mona asked before he could grill her.

"No. But I don't think I could stop it now even if I wanted to." He glanced over at Tania, who'd settled in by the kids' corner. "Everything okay between you and Dupree?"

Mona shrugged. She wasn't sure. "Just growing pains, I think we'll be okay."

"You need me to read him the riot act?"

"Nah, we'll figure it out." Some of what Smythe imparted helped her understand a bit of Cart's reaction to the death of the shifters in the fireball. She still hated that they'd died, but she understood a bit better why Cart had reacted the way he did.

Cart entered the room, hands full of food, only to be waylaid by Tania. Whatever she said helped ease some of the tension from his shoulders. He looked across the room at her. Mona held his eyes, unwilling, unable to look away. He could not dictate her actions, could not rule over her, and he needed to realize that. A smile formed and he crossed. Mona would have to find out what Tania had said. In the meantime, the smell of mushrooms masala wafted across the room.

"Any other news to pass along?" she asked Cart. Oh, she was still mad at him, but this wasn't the place to talk about it.

"You were right about Kofi. She blasted a hole in the wall. I took her back to New York and met with the local coven about her training. Just got back yesterday."

"Wait, I thought witches and Folk avoided each other." Nic moved out of Cart's way.

"Typically, not always," she said around the tail end of a mouthful of food.

"Get Tania to fill you in, this is stuff you need to know," Cart said. He snatched a string bean.

"Getting her to talk about Folk is almost impossible but I'll try." Nic swiped a bean as well.

Mona pretended to go after both of their hands with her fork. "Mine. You got to eat earlier."

"Yeah, but yours tastes better," Cart said unrepentantly as he filched another.

"That'll cost you. Go get me some more water," she said, covering her plate with her arm.

"My turn. So, what have you and Tania found out?" she asked Nic as soon as Cart headed to the waiter's station. There was a slight twitch in his shoulders that made Mona realize he had heard her, although he kept going.

He stilled. "About what?"

Now that was an interesting reaction. Before she could formulate a reply he started across the room. "Tania's done with the kids, I need to go." He looked like a warrior or something off to defend his property.

"I guess you didn't have any more luck than I did when I tried to find out what all they know?" Cart said when he returned.

"Nope." Mona pushed her empty plate away, feeling a lot better. Too many days had passed since she'd had a decent meal. She stood and stretched. Her legs were still sore, would be for a while she guessed, but she could walk.

"Let's see if tag teaming them works." Cart took her elbow and helped her across the room.

Tania and Nic were already heading out. Cart and Mona intercepted them at the door.

"I've got some not good news," Tania said, after stopping to wait in the hall, just past the door to the meeting room. "Apparently salamanders have been moving into the Were tribes."

"Salamanders?" Mona said trying to remember what she knew. Her new font of information didn't supply anything. "Aren't they harbingers of death and destruction?"

"That is how they used to be viewed," Tania said. "They actually are natural healers, with an uncanny sense of where they'll be needed next."

"So yeah," Cart said, "they do foretell bad things, but they don't bring it with them."

"They've been known to be wrong," Tania pointed out.

"No, not true, cuz. We've been able to avert disaster so they weren't needed, but the potential is always there."

She graciously bowed her head.

"They can be useful as an intelligence point, but they didn't tell us anything we didn't already know," Nic said, shrugging off their importance. Good thing he didn't see Tania's expression, because she was clearly floored by his remark. "Why were you two wanting us?"

"We're heading back to the complex tomorrow," Cart said. Not that he'd asked her. "We'll be looking to see if the collapse is linked to everything else. Will you join us?"

"I'll be there. Not sure about how useful Nic will be, it is magic," Tania pointed out.

"I'll be there," Nic said, eyes narrowed and jaw ticking.

"But it's a magic place, there's not much you can do," Tania said, a bit of worry and annoyance in her voice.

Oh! Tania was trying to keep Nic out of a dangerous area. Like that was going to work.

"I'm going. Randall said to stick with you, I'm sticking with you."

"Good," Cart said. "We'll meet you outside the complex at noon."

"See you there," Nic said. He turned and headed out.

A split second later Tania followed, body rigid and posture straight, clearly very mad at him.

"Glad I'm not in his shoes," Cart said. He popped open the door to the meeting room, glanced around, then pulled her further down the hall. "What the hell were you doing? Do you realize you were unreachable for a whole week? Anything could have happened."

Mona yanked her arm out of his grasp. "I was doing my job. Besides which, your crew knew where I was."

"Knowing didn't help. We need you to stick around. You're important."

Mona wanted to believe it was her, not the job, that was important. A thought struck her.

"How did you know I was unreachable?"

"I broke my own rule and had an imp go look for you." He grimaced and ruffled his hand through his hair. "Are you really okay? Tiff and Emetaly told me some of the incidents you ran into on the way up. And I have no doubt that you glossed over how bad the drive back here was."

Mona relaxed against the wall for a brief moment then gently pushed herself straight, needing to be strong for this. "Did they tell you Randall named me Warder before…before…"

Her last words came out as a sob. Dammit, she didn't want to cry!

Cart tucked her into his shoulder and rubbed his chin on her head while she bawled.

"And here I am, being an asshole. Sorry, I just—" He took a deep breath. "I just wouldn't handle it well if something happened to you while I wasn't around. Yes, I know I said I couldn't handle being together, but some things aren't going to change, and the need to protect you seems to be one of them."

He rubbed her back and held her close. "I think Smythe knew it was his time," Cart said after her initial burst had quieted. "He made the transfer spell, right? He lived an extraordinarily long time, Mona. He surely knew the risks of what he was doing."

Mona sniffed and nodded.

"I think Tania thinks his Ward died," she said.

"I think she's right. Although…" Cart hesitated before continuing on. "That may have happened a while ago."

"Why do you say that?" She stepped back and looked into his eyes, puzzled at the idea.

"My first thought when I saw him was he looked like a man living on borrowed time. The idea stuck with me." He shrugged. "I've learned to pay attention when that happens."

He looked down at Mona and stepped back, as awkward as she'd ever seen him.

"I, uh, need to get back and make sure they're staying on track. And I need talk to you about what happened with Herrick, but that'll wait until later. We need to talk, too, but first we're going to have to deal with whatever geas the Puck put on us."

He took another quick breath, likely to add to the list of things he'd been saving up to tell her. Mona flapped her hands at him, shooing him away.

"Go. I'll join you in a minute."

He nodded then ducked away.

Exhaustion clawing at her like a hungry pup, she sat down in the first chair she found in the room. Eventually most of the group stopped by a second time, checking she was okay and catching her up with happenings.

She was going to miss them when they were gone.

After the third time she jerked awake because her chin bumped into her chest, she made herself get up.

"Cart, I need to go," she announced to the suddenly spinning room.

In short order she found herself bundled up and put in a car.

"Backlash—"

"Over-exerted—"

Words swirled around her as she snuggled into the seat belt webbing and drifted off to sleep.

Chapter Fourteen

Mona tucked the duvet under her chin, comfy, cozy, and warm. A part of her didn't want to have to get out of the warm cocoon she was in. Another, more insistent part, told her she needed to get up now.

She was in the protector's station, her bag on the rocking chair in the corner. Cart was nowhere in sight. Rubbing her sleepy eyes, she got out of bed just as Cart entered the room.

"Shower, I need a shower," she said.

"Damn, and I wanted to wake you up."

He shut the door behind him and reached out for her shoulders. Mona stepped back. They weren't going back to status quo without a discussion.

"Too late now, I have things to do, places to be." She ignored his crestfallen look. "What time is it, and how long before we need to leave?"

He stepped back and put his hands in his pockets. "It's seven-thirty, I'd suggest leaving at nine-thirty, no later than ten."

"Good time for a shower. Then we'll talk. Is there an update on Raine?"

"Nurse Ferguson already called to let us know there's been no change."

Nodding, Mona grabbed her bag. It'd be important to find the right person to raise the orphaned child. Wait, was the baby her charge? No, that didn't make sense. Raine had no folk blood, so her child couldn't be the ward. She headed to the door then stopped. She didn't know where to go. Turning around, she saw Cart leaning against the wall, arms now crossed over his large chest, smile on his face.

"Okay, fine, where are the showers?"

He crossed over to her, wrapped his hands on either side of her face, tucked his fingers into her hair, and pulled her flush to his taut body.

There was a reason, something she'd learned yesterday, why she shouldn't let him do this, but she couldn't think of anything but the warmth in his eyes and the smile quirking one side of his mouth.

And the heat of his body searing her from shoulder to toe.

"Good morning, Mona," he said, between the kisses he scattered across her face. He pulled back, his eyes churning amber. "Are you feeling better this morning?"

Unable to stop herself, she slid her free hand up his chest and twined her fingers around the curls at the nape of his neck.

"Much better, but I really, really want a shower, Cart. More than anything."

"Anything?" He pressed her against the door.

"Anything," she managed to get out without sounding too breathy.

"Can I have a rain check then?"

"You think if we don't have sex now, you can get a voucher to have sex later?" Mona asked. "I don't think so. You need to earn it."

Especially after he said he couldn't handle how she did her job. He must have seen something in her face because he stepped back.

"I'll remember that."

"Shower? Now, please?"

With a very audible and visible sigh he let go of her. "One day, we'll have all the time in the world, and rain check or not, I'm keeping you in bed."

Mona didn't have much to say to that. She'd suddenly remembered why being with Cart was a bad idea. A really, really bad idea, no matter what the Puck thought. Images and memories from Smythe about the relationship between Warders and their wards crowded her thoughts. The transfer from him was still there, but at a remove, and not as intrusive as it had been yesterday.

Cart took her hand and led her through the labyrinth of corridors. He didn't seem to notice her silence or distraction.

"I'll come back in, what? Thirty minutes?"

Mona thought over everything she'd need to do.

"Thirty-five." She needed a little time alone, time to figure out how the hell to undo what she'd already done.

"Gotcha."

She ducked in the locker room. The room smelled of disinfectant and chlorine, and very faintly of wet dog. Mona found a bench and set her things down on it.

Cart.

Shit.

Mona closed her eyes and replayed what she'd learned from Abner.

An ethereal woman, one with the small bone structure of a European elf, a lot like the Maven, stood before her. Smythe labeled the woman "mate."

He also labeled her "ward."

And Mona could see why, the taint of evil magic was so deeply embedded in the woman she could almost see the imprint on her bones.

There were other memories of Warders, each mated to their ward. Each caring and loving them in private, keeping the world safe from them, and them safe from the world.

That was the bond others missed. Yes, a Warder guarded the Folk from their ward, but they guarded their ward from being used or killed by Folk seeing only their evil just as much.

Which meant either Cart was going to turn evil, which didn't match up with what she'd been told and now knew about Wards being born with evil, or he wasn't her mate. Nor, as she'd hoped, her Seele, the deeply bonded soul mate only those with enough elf blood experienced.

Okay, okay, why then did Randall seem to think they needed to be together?

"Puck!" She practically growled. Damn, but she'd been hanging around Weres too much.

Randall appeared, sitting on the bench next to her. Except when she'd stayed with him, she'd never seen him so casually dressed. Trousers, shirt, knit vest, he looked like he was slumming with Gene Kelly. With his shoulders hunching over and one leg bouncing so hard the bench threatened to vibrate, Mona knew he was ill at ease.

"Hi, Warder," he said. "I can't tell you much."

"Can't? Or won't?" she asked, making the same point Cart had days ago.

"Too fine a line," he waved off her question. He stood and paced the short length of the bench and back again. Lecture mode. She'd seen him do this many times before. "It's not like I haven't been dropping hints all over the place. There are big events going on here. If I say any more than that, my ass is going to be in a sling and I won't be able to help you at all."

"You've been helping? Really? 'Cause those cryptic messages and the dire vagueness? Not helpful."

He stopped and stared at her, arms akimbo. "I could just leave, I don't need this crap."

"Sorry, I just…" Mona scrubbed her face with her hands.

"Look, I'll let you ask me one direct question. If I can answer it I will. But you only get one."

Just one? But she had so many. She needed to find out about wards and Warders and the faces she saw when she jumped and Cart and imps and that evil, evil taint she'd seen on the spells.

Randall had crossed his arms over his barrel chest. The tapping of his toe echoed in the metal filled room.

She needed another resource that wasn't Smythe's tome.

"Is there a resource or book that isn't Smythe's where I can find out more information on Folk magic, particularly Warders and their wards?"

"Sorry, there's not a book."

"So there is some other resource?" At his sly grin she asked, "Someone I know?"

"Do you mean know or *know*?" He waggled bushy eyebrows. "Because there's knowing and there's *know*ing. On second thought, that's a second question, I'm out of here."

With an audible pop he disappeared.

Showoff.

The person had to be Cart. Of course. The one person she didn't want to be asking.

She chose a locker near the showers and was dried, dressed, and waiting by the time he showed up.

"Food's next on the agenda," he told her. "I've got the crew waiting in the kitchen."

The mention of food made her stomach feel like a hollow pit. The kitchen and being around other Weres sounded good to her. Once in the kitchen, her anxiety about Cart hit her full force. Mona slipped on an apron and started on breakfast. She cracked up eggs for French toast as the group talked about the meeting from the previous night. Apparently she'd missed Nic's recruitment speech, urging youngsters to grow up and be protectors. They crew was impressed.

As she started cooking everything up the discussion turned to leads and trying to figure out what the numbers meant.

"Do we have contacts up in Canada? The stronger the magic user," Mona said, "the greater the distance he can cover. And this guy seems like he'd be able to cover a great distance."

Mona had to turn her back to monitor the large griddle, so she only heard the chatter of excitement her comment caused and didn't see their faces.

Finished, she picked up her plate of hot toast and warm syrup, piled some fruit on top, and went to join them at the folding tables they'd dragged in from somewhere. The rest of the crew hastily stood and lined up to serve themselves from the platter on the stove.

"Once you're done we'll head out," Cart said as she sat. "We've got all the equipment ready."

In less than twenty minutes the half a dozen protectors going with them piled into an oversized SUV leaving Mona and Cart with the jeep they'd used the first day.

"So, how was New York?" she asked once they were settled in.

"Good. Nice to see the gang. There's only a handful of family. Less than a dozen of us go out on a run. And it is a run. Half of us stay human and 'run' through the park with the 'dogs' for an hour or so, then we switch."

"Oh, I keep meaning to ask you what happened with the guy who jumped from the bar." The bar! "Shit! I missed my shifts this week."

"Don't worry, Menlo covered for you."

"What?" Menlo? Although, now that she thought about it she could see him handling the bartending with his usual self effacing efficiency.

"That's how he put himself through grad school before he joined the force."

"Grad school?" Was it typical for people to go to college or more before becoming a protector? She had no idea.

"He has a PhD in psychology. In regards to your other question, Leonardo is doing fine. He's in New York now. We gave him a couple of options, and he seemed most interested in working in the archives, but it'll be a bit before we find the right fit."

"And Averill's doing okay?"

"I've sent Hyram over to train her. We've been butting heads, he wants more responsibility so I thought I'd see how he does. Now you tell me—what happened to Herrick?"

Mona did. Knowing Cart wanted to know what happened as well as the reactions of those around, she went into detail, including the fact that he'd called her a bitch.

Judging from Cart's flushed face and white knuckles on the steering wheel, it was probably a good thing Herrick was gone.

"You need to calm down, Cart," she said, a little uncomfortable with his rage.

"Can't help it, everyone in the family is overprotective." He groaned. "Which reminds me. My mother's likely to show up soon, since I happened to mention you when I was back home. I can tell you right now, she won't like you."

"Mention me?"

"Yes, she jokingly asked if a woman had put me in my foul mood and I said yes. In her opinion, you have a huge strike against you already. She not going to be happy that you're gorgeous."

Mona felt the heat of her blush sear her cheeks.

"And smart," Cart continued. "Not to mention you don't live in New York City, which is worse than everything else combined. I didn't even mention you're a Warder."

He'd given her an entre to ask about Warders and where they'd live and if he might change, but Mona couldn't bring herself to ask.

His grin was positively gleeful. "Actually, didn't tell her because your position means she can't use hers to intimidate you."

"Her position?"

"She's a Titania too, like Tania."

"But not a Maven."

"Hell no, too much responsibility and work." Only a slight touch of irritation tinged his voice.

"So she's a tad overprotective of her already grown son?"

"She's not the worst of my family you'll meet, but if you can handle her, you can handle the rest."

"Thanks for the heads-up, they say forewarned is forearmed."

"I only hope you feel that way after you meet her."

If she couldn't ask Cart about Warders and their wards, and if he might shift to evil maybe she could ask his mother. Right, she could see that conversation with a woman already predisposed to not liking her. *Do you think your son could turn into evil incarnate?* She was better off asking Cart.

Surprisingly few impediments sprang up, and they made excellent time, arriving well before Nic and Tania. As soon as they turned into the drive, Cart pulled over to the berm.

"We've got a ways to go yet. A good a quarter mile," Mona said.

"I figured as much. I want my team to carefully examine the ground, given what you ran into, and that's easier to do on foot."

A very good point.

They bundled up and got out of the car. The day looked to be warming up nicely. Still cold, but sunny enough that the ice clinging to the trees would occasionally snap and fall.

The group spread out making notes and comments to each other over what they saw and found. Mona tagged along, walking behind them. The tracks and shapes were getting distorted as the sharp edges blurred and softened as the top layer of snow melted into the one below.

Before long, Nic pulled up behind the two cars. Cart and Mona headed back while the rest of the crew kept their slow pace forward. Nic didn't wait for Tania to get out of the car. He strode over to where the group was examining something. Dressed like a commando with a tech fetish, he had gadgets, rope, and gee-gaws hanging from a utility belt around his waist and banding his chest. Mona hoped they if they needed them they would work around magic. Electronics could be finicky.

Tania came up to Mona and Cart, and deliberately turned her back to the group. As if they needed another hint that she and Nic had argued.

"So, what's the plan?" Tania asked Cart.

"Don't know. Yo, Lombard, you got a plan?" he called out.

Funny how Cart's accent got stronger when he was around his cousin. Tania's finger tapped out a rapid staccato on her crossed arms, as she was forced to look over at Nic too.

"Figured we'd get closer and see how bad the damage is before we make one," Nic called over from the group. "That enough to start?"

"Sounds good. Everyone's here, let's go."

On the walk up the drive Cart started asking more detailed questions on the complex and its buildings. He seemed a bit tiffed that Mona didn't know much about the construction and composition. Oddly, the information had not been included in the bits Smythe passed along.

"Cart?" Tania asked.

"What's up?"

"Is there anything in your training that might help Mona learn her job? Usually a Warder directly trains his or her successor, but since Abner isn't around…"

"Got it covered."

That was the first Mona had heard of it. Mona looked at Cart and started to ask him about it, but was forestalled by an infinitesimal shake of his head.

"My mother, Titania Margaret, that is, Aunt Meg," he turned back to Tania, "is due to arrive later. She'll probably have something of use."

"Oh?" Tania sounded disbelieving of her aunt's helpfulness.

Cart actually laughed. "Hard to believe, huh? But I bet she'll know something about who Abner was guarding and why. If only the gossip. And Mona can see Mom's magic, so we can start to narrow down who in the family might have helped build the compound."

"Hopefully if it was mother or grandmother, Aunt Meg will know," Tania said.

"It couldn't have been your father?" Nic asked. Mona wasn't sure when he'd sidled up, but there he was, pacing along side Tania.

"It might have been," Tania said, frowning. "I guess it would depend on when it was built. He died shortly after my mother and, as far as I know, rare as it is, I'm his only offspring. We should probably ask Aunt Meg that too."

Reaching the curve in the drive that lead to the entry gates, they stopped, along with the crew.

The gray stones looked like knocked over dominoes, all leaning askew and slanting, mostly, in the same direction.

Everyone stared at the huge pile of rubble beyond. The castle-like home was in shambles as was the converted stables. The only building left looking mostly intact, was the library. One of the team made to go forward.

"Wait." Nic's command had them all looking at him. "The only thing left standing, more or less, is this front gate. Given what I have heard of the destruction of this place, there's a chance it's still booby trapped—remember, Tiff? Mona, can you check to see what spells are still there? I can check for non-Folk methods if needed."

Mona turned and examined the gates, stepping close to see clearly. Odd, very odd; the spell was set more on the inside of the gate.

"I'm not sure, there is still trace magic there, and I can see a bit of the spell but it's unclear if the spell is to keep us out or something in."

"Is there another way in?" Nic asked. "A side entrance or emergency gate?"

"He did mention one, but I don't know where it is."

"I do." Tania supplied. "He showed it to me when I first became Maven. It was a while ago, though, so I'm not exactly certain."

She cocked her head and looked at the gate. The she turned her back and moved her hands in front of her, like she was placing imaginary objects. Shaking her head, she turned back.

"I'll have to pull up the memory I made," she said as she sent out a tendril of magic.

"Wait! You're not doing a spell, are you?" Nic's tone was laced with annoyance.

"Yes, you do want to know where the other entrance is don't you?" Tania replied, having halted her actions when he shouted.

"I do, but I don't think doing a spell is the way to do it," Nic said rather tersely.

"Do you have a better idea?" Despite her calm voice it was clear she was annoyed. She didn't realize, Mona suspected, that his worry wasn't over the magic, but over what might happen to her if there was an offensive spell.

"Nic, the spell's a passive one," Cart said. "The magic never builds enough, or goes far enough, to be detected."

"And I don't see any traces of magic this far out from the gates, bro," Mona said, trying to calm him down. "Seems like a safe risk."

Nic looked at them for a long minute. "Fine, do it."

Immediately Tania sent the faintest thread of magic out again and said the words to start the spell.

"My memory of my first meeting with Warder Abner Smythe begins thus: We exited the library out onto the front circle. Let's see, to our right sat the residence for him and his ward."

As she spoke she gestured, and faint images of each building sprung up. The library, the tallest building in the complex, reached up to Tania's shoulders.

"To my immediate left was a large stone archway leading back to a small garden, and, then, along the left wall, what'd been stables and a carriage house but was now a garage and workshop. The middle of the circular drive was grass with a shade tree and a fountain."

Tania looked everything over, then waved her hand again. The scene all morphed into more substantial images, still not solid, but much more clearly defined, except the wall, which they could still see through.

Mona was amazed—she had never seen anything like this before. Given the gasps around her, she wasn't the only one.

Tania walked through the images and stood, relative to the miniature complex she made, in the same spot they now were.

"My recorded memory of my first meeting with Warder Abner Smythe, starting after we exited the library, went thusly…"

The buildings became a scale set, and miniature versions of Tania and Abner appeared in front of the library. Tania's voice spoke in the still air around them. Tania was in a long, semiformal day gown, stiff with embroidery. Their walk had a slow measured beat likely due to the formalness of the occasion: Smythe showing the new Maven his stronghold. It wasn't until Mona looked over to see how Nic was dealing with this that she realized Tania wasn't talking, the spell had recorded her voice.

Nic, like the rest of the protectors, watched with an air of awe and concentration.

"Have you had any call to train another Warder, Warder Abner?" the memory Tania was saying, her voice full sized despite the diminutive appearance. "I'm sure a new Warder would have much to learn from you."

They all saw Abner preen from the compliment, standing taller and squaring his shoulders.

"Maven, I haven't yet. Which, in all, is a good thing. Warders only arise when there is need."

"Oh?"

"Yes, indeed, Maven. That a Warder hasn't come forth to be trained is beneficial, since having one would mean there is a Folk out there who needs containment."

"And is that what Warders do? Come forth? You don't go seek them?"

"Traditionally, those who will become Warders come to the attention of the current Warder through their own actions. My fellow Warders say this is still the case, so I see no reason to go seeking anyone."

Mona knew Abner well enough to realize he was being blustery, as if he knew she had a good suggestion, but clung to reasons not to.

"I apologize, Abner, it is simply my curiosity that makes me ask, having known from a young age I would be Maven. Where are we going?"

The two were on the walk heading around the side of the library. There, hidden by the angles of the buildings, plantings, and two feet of false façade, was a small path between the residence and the library. The entry was entirely blocked from view unless you were on top of it.

"As part of the tour I wanted to show you the traitor's gate. Rather, that is what they used to call it. I think the current term is emergency exit. If something should happen and you need to get in without me, you should come this way. The entrance is under the crenellation with three missing bricks. Once keyed, if you put your hand on the wall where it is, the entry will appear. I'll need a token so an imp can set it up for you."

"Thank you for your foresight," Tania said as she undid the ribbon holding her hair. "Let us hope we never need it."

She handed him the strip and he bowed over her extended hand, before taking it and tucking it into his vest pocket.

"End the memory here," Tania intoned.

Her and Smythe's miniatures disappeared and the buildings began to fade away.

A slow beat of silence held everyone.

Mona knew she looked in awe as Tania waved her hand through the wisps of the reenactment still hanging in the air. With each pass of her hand the strands of the energy sank into the Maven. She then stood, straight and stiff, clearly uncomfortable and unwilling to say anything first.

Nic stared at her for a moment before nodding. "Right, then, the traitor's gate. Everyone ready?"

Cart gestured grandly to Nic. "Protector, I assume you have a plan."

Mona didn't doubt that Cart had one too, but for some reason he wanted Nic to lead this part.

"We'll split up, and check each side for evidence on who did this. Tania and I'll go counter=clockwise with you two." He picked a pair out of the group. "Two more of you go with Cart and Mona clockwise. Stay in the trees as much as possible. The other two stay here and guard our backs. If we need your help we'll find a way to contact you."

He held up his hands to forestall questions. "I suspect there are traps specifically set for large groups that we want to avoid. Plus, smaller groups can move faster. But no one should continue on by themselves. If the choice is go on alone or turn back, turn back."

Cart nodded his agreement as Nic spoke. Tania glared at his back.

"To make sure we all head for the same spot, see where there are two tall white pines, right next each other?" Nic continued, pointing at the tops that rose above the devastation. Everyone gave an affirmative sound. "We'll meet up there before heading in."

"Sounds good, but don't wait too long for the next group, as they may have all turned back," Cart said. "I'd suggest calling an imp to tell the other you've made it, but that strikes me as a bad idea."

Everyone nodded in agreement. Cart looked at the jumble of rocks and forest that we'd need to get through, then at Mona. "You up to this?"

"I'm as ready as I'll ever be," she replied.

"How about you, cuz?" Cart's concerned gaze captured Tania's. He was giving her an out if she didn't want to go with Nic, Mona realized.

Tania's response was to shoot him an annoyed look and walk away, leaving Nic and the others to catch up.

Chapter Fifteen

Walking proved difficult on their side. Beneath the melting snow was a layer of leaves, not to mention fallen branches, making the ground very slippery. Then there were occasional low, rocky outcroppings. They detoured were they could, but sometimes it was just faster to climb over.

At the third such climb, they lost one of their team members to a severely twisted ankle. Cart sent her and their fourth back, telling them not to send anyone else along after them.

"I'd rather have the gate guarded."

Once they were safely on their way Cart turned to Mona. "You see any magic?"

"Nope," she replied. "I can't help if there are any other types of traps, but magic I'll spot."

"We can't risk another injury. Let's stick to just inside the edge of the forest. It'll be faster and less likely that either of us will get hurt." Cart took her hand and started forward. "Even with all the parks in the city, I miss forests."

"When were you in a forest?" she asked, deciding not to pull her hand away.

"Scouts. Went to camp every summer from the time I was seven until I graduated from college. By then I was an assistant division director. Lots of the Were packs in the city had their own Scout dens." They both smiled at the play on words.

He held up his hand and she stopped.

"There's something." He slowly spun around. "Black bear I think. You talk and keep going, I want to make sure it's not a shifter."

Moving silently toward the trees he beckoned her to keep walking forward.

"You talk," he said, moving silently toward the trees and beckoning her to keep walking forward.

"What? I can't just come up with a monologue on demand."

"Here's a topic to set you babbling: I sent in my notice to the force."

His pronouncement had the desired affect. Shit, this was bad.

"You what? I can't believe you did that. Why? I mean, no, well, why is what I mean, but I am not going to go there now. What are you going to do? Not that I don't think you'd find something to do. If nothing else, Nic can put in a word for you at the agency. That is, um, assuming you are staying in Buffalo. You are staying in Buffalo, right? I don't want to assume you are, but then you were the one talking about fates and destinies. Which, you know, might be an issue."

No, no, not going there, not going to say she was worried about what her relationship with her ward might be. "What if I end up someplace else? There's no reason to assume Buffalo is where I'm going to end up. Particularly with your cousin here, she can do the warding stuff as well, actually, probably better than I can—"

He came running back and grabbed her arm, forcing her to keep up.

"Not a shifter but a sow, let's get out of her path."

Without waiting for her reply he let go her arm and Mona followed him on a crisscrossing path through the woods.

Finally, at a slow jog now, Cart lead them back toward the complex, angling far away from where they'd come in. Once they got to the edge, the White Pines Nic had designated were in sight. Cart slowed his pace, aiming them for the other side of the trees, away from the complex. They caromed around the corner, to find Nic in a defensive pose and Tania seated and serenely watching the direction they came from. Their companions were nowhere in sight.

Mona sank down to sit on a log near where Tania sat, in a beam of sunshine. The split trunk of the pine stood between them and the complex, hiding it from view. Later, she'd talk to Cart about his decision.

"You loose your escort too?" Tania asked.

"Larissa twisted an ankle not that far in and we sent her back with Tyrene," Cart replied. "As Nic said, having a smaller group made it easier to avoid any traps. Where are Frank and Lytel?"

"They found something they wanted to check out. I'm sure you'll get the details when we get back," Nic said pacing in front of them. "I want to go take a look at the wall. We've found the spot with the missing bricks."

Mona and Cart waved him along; he was clearly antsy and ready to do something. Tania joined him as he rounded the tree and disappeared out of sight.

"Did you really send in your notice?" Mona had to ask.

"Not yet, although I do have it written up." He stood and peeked around the tree. "And it's not really a notice, it's asking for a sabbatical while we figure out where it is you are going to end up. Then we'll figure out if I want to transfer to a local place or arrange for something else."

"Were you going to discuss this with me?" she said.

He stuck his head back behind the tree. "We are discussing it."

"No, we're not. You're listing your plan of action and telling me about it." Mona held up his hand to forestall his sputtering. "Although I agree that is better than your having sent the notice off before telling me."

Cart leaned against the tree, all six foot plus of him. A study in nonchalance, so he must be worried. "Do you object?"

That wasn't the point.

"No," she said. "I don't. But, there are complications—"

Tania's and Nic's voices raised in disagreement rang through the air. Cart stuck his head back around the tree.

"What's he doing? Is that—" He bounded off before she could tell him her concerns.

Mona rose from the stump, her legs protesting the movement. She'd ignored the discomfort while running, determined to get away from the bear. Cart stood next to Nic, looking at a contraption resembling a radar gun. Tania had her back to them, her hands sweeping the air in front of the wall. Likely checking for the feel of spells.

"I can't believe you have that," Cart said as Mona caught up to him. "We've tried to get some, but they're too new and aren't on the black market yet."

"They're also highly restricted—at least, this type is. Of course, officially, I don't have this one." Nic flashed a grin at them before going back to touch the screen. "Okay, let's look."

Nic walked to the left and squared himself to the still intact section of the wall. He braced the unit with both hands and pointed at the stonework. All of them, even Tania, crowded around him and stared at the blank screen.

Nic did something and green lines raced down the screen from top to bottom, crisscrossing and multiplying to create the illusion of depth and dimension. The room was pretty much square except for a series of lumps at the bottom.

"That's the first room, the one on the left?" Tania asked.

"Yeah, wait just a sec, it should fill in, yeah there it goes."

The green grid had been overlaid with tones of gray, adding a layer of detail missing from lines. They all stared at the images, particularly the human like shapes at the bottom.

"The lumps on the bottom, those look like two mummies," Tania said.

"There could be bodies there, I don't know," Nic said.

"Not alive?" Cart asked.

"Unlikely. They'd have to be holding pretty darned still for their breathing movement to not register."

They all looked at each other.

"Smythe and his ward." Mona was the first to say it. Had to be—who else would be in the complex?

"Are you going to be okay?" Cart asked Mona.

"You don't have to go in, you can stay out," Nic said.

"Nonsense," Tania decisive slash of her hand let everyone know what she thought of Nic's offer. "She knows they are just empty husks, their souls with the goddess. She'll be fine. Right?"

Mona looked at Cart. This wasn't the first time she'd seen deceased elves, but for it to be Smythe. The Maven was right, though, she new they were empty husks, Abner's soul had left its shell behind when he'd sent the spell to transfer knowledge to her. She could do it.

"I'll be fine." She shrugged. "And if I'm not I'll let you know."

Nic clapped her on the shoulder. "Don't be a martyr. If you need to step back, step back." He raised the scanner and the room came back into view. His finger traced a slightly darker area. "This looks like a room, not the hall, although there is a door there. It could be the way in. Let's see the next space."

He took several steps to his right and repeated the procedure. This time the image was of a hall. Although a couple of the vertical lines seemed to be wavering.

"Ah, that's movement, isn't it?" Cart said. "Those lines that keep changing."

"Yep." The image again turned gray and a hall with no apparent end appeared. "Look here." Nic pointed to a spot to the side. "There seems to be niches built into the walls."

Cart and Mona uh-huh'ed in agreement; Tania remained silent.

"The first set appears to be empty, but there could be something there that the radar isn't picking up. The second set definitely has movement," Nic said as his finger traced the places on the screen.

"Likely something that doesn't need daylight and can do without food for a while," Mona said, trying to figure what might be able to do that.

Tania and Cart looked at each other.

"Or something that uses the stones for food," Cart added. "How regular do the niches seem, are they the same height? No," he answered his own question, "the one in the front on the right seems to be a bit lower."

"It could be a stone golem, although it'd be larger than any one I've ever heard of," Tania said.

"Maybe a small mountain ogre?" Cart said.

"Or a quarry Wyrm," Tania said, "although I haven't heard of one this far from an actual quarry before. It could be any number of things. The only way to find out is to go in. Shall we?"

She stepped up, and started to place her hand on wall.

"No, wait! Go through the other side first," Mona said.

"A much better plan," said Nic.

"Why?" Tania asked.

"It's easier to open it now, before we see who is in the hall, than to have to come back later if there's problems," Nic explained.

"Okay, then, I'll do this one." She stepped to her left.

"Wait until Cart and Mona get back behind the tree, could you?" Nic said.

Cart stayed where he was, clearly more reluctant than Mona was to move away from the action. Mona grabbed his hand and dragged him back to the trees. Once there they both immediately peeked around the trunk.

"You really okay?"

"Yeah."

Nic nodded at Tania. She placed her hand on the wall; spiral tentacles of distortion spread out, pushing aside the stone until a jagged star opening was left.

"Cool," Mona said.

"Yeah, but not so safe to go through with those edges," Cart said. He stood on tiptoe trying to see around the two at the wall. "Where are the bodies?"

"What?"

"I can't see any bodies, wait—"

They watched as Nic reached out and tore down a piece of fabric scrim, which had been painted to look like the inside.

"Now that was cool." Cart was nodding to himself. "A bit scary that someone went to all that trouble, but cool."

"And there are the bodies." Mona could see the residual of magic around them.

Tania leaned over the edge and then stepped in.

"NIC!" Tania's scream echoed across the clearing as her head slid from view.

He lunged, landing flat on his stomach on the sharp stones.

Mona and Cart scrambled over each other to get around the tree. She felt magic build up in Cart.

"No! Don't jump!" she hissed at him as she grabbed his arm.

They watched as Nic slid a little further, then his body jerked. Tania gave a short shrill scream. They arrived in time to hear the soft thud of her landing.

"Tania!" Nic leaned over the edge and yelled.

Cart very carefully leaned over the edge of the wall and looked too. He pulled a small flashlight out and shined the beam down.

"It's muddy, I think she's okay, although she probably got the wind knocked out of her," Cart said. He shone the beam quickly around the room before turning it back to the pit.

For it was a pit. Mona peered over the edge of the wall and could see the ragged edge of the hole. Two elves in death shrouds were on either side of the hole. Which made her think the shaft was probably thirty feet or so down, as that would be the correct depth for burial.

She didn't think she'd mention that to Nic, he might flip.

Nic, in the meantime, was counting to ten under his breath.

"Tania!"

Another count.

Another yell.

"I'm going down no matter what. Even if she's fine, I'll need to do it so we can get her back up. It's still not safe to do magic here."

Mona didn't ask how he knew, but he was quite right, there was something off. She looked at the walls, trying to figure out what it was. The thick, planked door to the hall was closed. Whatever was on the other side, they still needed to deal with it.

"Here." Nic unclipped something from his belt, then unwound the rope he had coiled on his hip. "Make a winch so I can repel down."

"Right." Cart stepped back and looked at the crenellated edge of the wall.

"Tania!" Nic called again.

Nothing. Cart set the unit up and helped Nic rig some type of harness.

"Here." The soft call echoed up the hole.

Nic scrambled back to the edge and looked down.

"You okay?"

"I'm okay. Got my breath knocked out. Give me a minute."

Nic stood and finished tying up the knots. "I'm going down before she can say I shouldn't," he said in a low voice.

"Easier to just not ask sometimes," Cart agreed.

Nic climbed over the edge and nodded at Cart. He began to slowly go down while Cart fed him rope at a steady rate.

Mona kept an eye on the door and examined the room again. There was something to the side of one of the bodies, a book and some runes in the corner. Part of a containment spell, but not the main portion. That was through the door and on the other side.

And there was a scraping against they heavy wood of the door from the beings in the hall. She looked over at Cart. He shook his head at her.

The rope had stopped moving.

"Wait," Cart said in a low voice. "It'll take them a little while to get through. And Nic and Tania are more likely to get hurt if we make them rush."

Slowly, although it probably wasn't as long as the anticipation made it seem, more scraping sounds came from the door.

"Yo," Cart called down after a particularly violent push made the door shudder. Mona could tell he was worried—his New York accent was strong again. "You okay down there?"

"Almost ready to come up," Nic replied.

"Good," came Cart's voice again, "'cause we're starting to have a situation here."

Fairly quickly, Nic called up that they were ready.

The voices seemed to spur the beings into action because the beating at the door became furious. With a tremendous screech the wood splintered and a small gap appeared between the boards.

Briefly a blue-gray, scale covered hand along with a short, reptilian snout appeared before slipping back out of sight.

"Damn," Cart muttered. "I haven't seen that type of Wyrm before. Nic, I need you to hurry up!" Cart's voice was calm, but the urgency was clear. His head swiveled back and forth between the rope he was bracing and the door. With the next pass, the splintering hole got larger. He jerked his head at Mona, indicating he wanted her to leave. "Go back to the trees. If I need to I can jump to you."

She ignored him and stayed. He called "Hold on!" down to Nic, whose head was barely visible from where they stood outside the room. Stepping back, he secured the rope around the outcropping. He started to scale the wall, heading up to where the rope was over a crenellation.

"Go!" he yelled at her.

Mona ran to the trees, fairly certain that Nic and Tania were close enough to the top that they'd be okay. Nic was beyond resourceful.

She had to think that, or she'd be turning back.

Steps from the tree, a wave of magic washed over her, making her skin itch. Instinctively she threw herself flat on the ground and covered her head. Small projectiles staccatoed against the bark of the trees. When she looked up, thin quills were embedded deep in the wood.

Another surge, different this time. She started to scamper to the relative safety of the pines, backwards so she could see what it was and defend herself.

Mona's ears popped and Nic and Tania appeared, then collapsed onto the ground where she had just been. Nic immediately rolled off Tania and pulled out a knife.

"You could have warned me," Mona hissed. Okay, she knew it was an asinine thing to say, but if she hadn't moved, she'd have been under the pair as they landed. Like that was the biggest of their problems. Mona looked back at the complex. The faint outlines of a beacon spell hung by the opening, like a faded pennant. Except in this case Mona knew each act of magic would strengthen the spell until the beacon would go off and the mage's creatures would come.

"Nic, get down!" Tania yelled as she crawled to join Mona behind the tree.

He complied, managing to keep the knife out as he elbowed his way over.

"Did Cart say what they were?" Tania asked.

"'Damn, I haven't seen that type of Wyrm before' were his words." Mona shrugged.

"What's a Wyrm?" Nic asked.

"In this case," Tania said as she worked to free herself of the harness Nic had rigged up, "a reptile-like creature that can eat through rock. I want to get closer. Nic, I'll put a shield up but you'd have to stay behind me or you won't be covered."

"Let's go," Nic said.

Tania stepped out from behind the tree, and Mona saw her build a shield of magic in front of her. It was a beautiful spell, a single rune, wall, modified by a sigil controlling the size.

A surge of magic pressed against her again.

"Watch out!" Mona said as she ducked.

She heard the projectiles hit the shield with an angry ping of energy.

"Damn, those things came fast," Nic muttered.

Nic and Tania began to walk forward. Mona peered at them from between the two trunks, only able to see a small patch of the ground between her and the Wyrms. After seeing the deep holes left by the second set of quills she was happy to live with the limited view.

Nic and Tania stopped about ten feet out and scanned the wall. Cart had a large pile of slush set between two crenellations, the edge of which dripped onto the ground in front of the opening. How he'd managed to pile it up she didn't know and her hindered view didn't help.

Another brush of magic against her skin pulled her attention away from Cart. Tania knelt. In her hand was a knife and Mona saw the runes that would merge stone with the metal form. The flare of magic as the working took hold was strong enough that Mona shut her eyes. When she opened them again Nick sat crouched next to Tania, sucking and spitting from her finger, as if she had venom in it.

Tania jerked her hand away and he took a swig from his water bottle, which he spit out as well.

Mona looked back at the wall, wondering why the creatures were doing nothing during this time.

Tania looked over too, said something to Nic and they started forward, hunched over. The closer they got, the smaller they made themselves.

"Hey, there, rock munchers, come and pick on someone who can fight you, why don't ya?" Cart yelled suddenly, startling them all.

A slight shifting sound from inside the cave, but neither came out.

Tania and Nic were having a whispered conference slightly to the side of the hole.

Suddenly Nic stood and shouted. "Hurry up! We've got to get the goods out of here by dark. We'll get a great price for them only if we don't miss the deadline."

Tania scrambled to get the shield up and in front of Mona's foolish brother. Cart was braced to send the slush down.

Nothing happened.

"Wait!" Tania yelled at them both.

There was a tense silence before she spoke again.

"Wyrms, I am Maven Titania Greymantle, ruler of the Folk in this area. I promise to help you get back to where you belong, if you promise to help us discover who ruined this complex."

No answer.

"Tap twice if you both are willing to work with us," she said.

The dripping of the melting snow sounded like a gong in the silence that followed.

Two taps.

"Okay…um…thank you for your cooperation," Tania said. "For the safety of both sides I need to put a cooperative binding on you and on us. If you disagree at any point with what I say, tap three times and I'll stop. Again, tap twice if this is suitable for you."

Two taps came rapidly. Mona wondered at the intelligence of the creatures.

"If you'll allow me, I'd like to come close enough to see if I can heal you. Would that be acceptable?"

The creatures were hurt? She wasn't sure how Tania had come to that conclusion, but then, Tania was a lot closer.

No taps this time. They waited and finally a claw feebly reached up, grasped the rocks on the bottom edge. The elbow kept dipping up and down in a futile effort to raise the Wyrm's body.

"Oh, for Pete's sake…" Tania dropped the shield and strode up to the wall. Nic followed her more closely than a shadow.

She leaned in and started talking to the Wyrms; Mona could almost see the calm she was projecting at them. Cart swung down and leaned in to have a whispered conversation with Nic. He looked back at Mona at one point, then continued on.

Mona didn't mind being out of it. It was one thing to be immune to a spell directed at her, missiles, rocks, and bullets were another matter and, despite Cart's assertion that she put herself in danger without thought, she liked her skin too much to risk it.

Tania asked for the rope, breaking up the guys' conversation. She wrapped an end around her waist and climbed back into the room. Good precaution in case she fell again.

Once Tania was in, Mona crept forward. The now familiar feeling of a warm breeze brushing against her body as Tania worked magic strengthened the closer she got to the working. She was not close enough yet to tell exactly what Tania did.

Cart met her not too far from the doorway. "Glad to see you can listen well."

"Only when I agree it's the best choice. What's Tania doing?"

"Apparently they have some kind slow acting poison in them. Obsidian? And she's getting it out before they die from it."

Mona edged closer in time to hear the one talk.

"Do it," a voice croaked, high and raspy, like a lounge singer whose voice had stayed soprano. "I'll make sure he is taken care of."

Tania created a wire thin lasso of magic and removed the foul piece from the scaly skin of the male one the floor. Or at least Mona thought it was male, given what the other had said.

With beautiful economy, Tania used the line to slide healing magic in the puncture wound. Nic's hand was on her shoulder, and a strong line of energy passed from him to her. Mona wondered if Tania realized he was augmenting her. The thread was so faint, she might not have picked it up, had she not been so close.

A loud flatulation rent the air and Nic was sprayed with a thick, stinking mess. Oh dear, the Wyrm had lost control of its bowels. Tania's lap somehow only got a trickle, which she ignored.

Nic stood, dripped, and tried to shake off the mess. Ineffectually, trying to not spatter everyone, he shook one arm then the other. Globs fell with splats on the stone floor. Most of the excrement seemed to be on his parka, although there was a definite thick splash across both sets of knuckles. Plus some on his face, a wide arc on the right side from temple to chin.

Tania looked over at Nic and suggested he go scrub it off with snow. Not speaking, and holding his hands up and away from most of the ick, he turned to go.

"Yo! Cart! Nic needs a hand here!" Tania called out.

Tania explained to the Wyrms someone else would be in to help. Making room for Cart, Mona backed out of the entryway, keeping close to the edges and moving away from the gaping hole in the floor.

Cart scooped up a big handful of slushy snow then climbed through.

"Hey Rock Lady," he said and bowed to the Wyrm. He lifted his handful of slush toward Nic. "I can't tell you how much fun this is going to be!"

Nic did not move.

Shit! Something had happened and he was frozen in position. Mona moved closer—magic? She didn't see a spell.

"Nic?" she said. "Nic!"

Cart started to reach out to Nic.

"Stop!" Tania yelled as she scrambled to stand. "Don't touch him!"

Tania sent a tendril of magic into Nic, and relaxed only a fraction once it connected. "Imps! I need three imps! *Now!*" she demanded.

Three bobbed into existence at Nic's shoulders. And, oh dear, Mona could almost see the tracing magic following them. They needed to act quickly and get out of here before something was sent through the connection. Something she wasn't sure they were ready to face.

"Clean this mess off his face and hands, anywhere it touches his skin," Tania directed. Tania used her line like a beacon and directed the imps to the worst spots, starting with the crescent on the right side of his face. "Start here."

Each place she pointed, the imps came over to quickly touch it then went back to hovering by his shoulder. Nic's face and hands were blurred by rapidly moving lights.

While they did that, Tania was doing something to his body to heal it. Mona watched as a laser point of magic burned up bits inside him, in his veins, she thought. Mona had no idea how Tania knew where and what to do until she remembered the Maven had done a full imprint of him at some point.

His jaw worked first and he spit out any residual from his lips. Then his eyes blinked. He shifted his shoulders and began to lower his arms, causing the residue to start to slide down.

"Don't!" everyone cried, including the female Wyrm.

Nic put his hands back up.

"Go!" the female Wyrm said. "Take care of your protector. This one and his companion will stay and help me."

The Wyrm pointed to Cart and Mona. Cart bowed in response.

Tania didn't hesitate. She slid on a glove and grabbed the one wrist that had been cleaned. With a pop and a gust of magic, she jumped them both out.

Chapter Sixteen

The tracer spell was now starting to glow with a distinctly evil cast Mona knew too well. The runes were simple enough, but with the sigils convoluted by dark maroon markings, she couldn't change it around.

Mona looked at it again. Smythe's memories told her that the darker color she'd been seeing meant someone was reworking the spells. Whoever was creating them had someone helping him make them stronger. This was a kink she'd need to share with the group later.

She nudged the rune that monitored the build up of magic. Not even a quarter of a turn, but it would buy them a little more time.

"You, get someone to help us now," the Wyrm demanded of Cart.

"About that—"

Mona didn't know what Cart had been planning to say, but she needed to get them out of there so she interrupted. "Ma'am, I am the Warder for this area. I will help you. However, with our Maven being busy it may take us a little longer than 'right now.' We'd be better off moving you out of here and then seeking someone to help."

The Wyrm lying on the ground twitched, his leg jerking with spasms beneath him.

"You neglect to understand, I need to get us back so I can use our medicines to heal him." Even through the unusual accent her demand was clear.

Cart looked at Mona, consternation on his face. "Okay, I can get someone now," he said, "but it ain't gonna be pretty. Yo, imp, please tell Titania Margaret thus: Were Trainer Dupree needs

Titania Margaret's help immediately. Dress for outdoor, arctic, work conditions. I'll owe you one. Thank you."

The imps, who'd stayed after Tania had called them, spun around like tops and then disappeared. The tracing spell became clearer, but fortunately didn't activate yet. Each act of magic seemed to strengthen it. Better make sure they were ready to go when help got there, since that might be the final trigger to set it off.

"Here," Mona said as she climbed into the space, determinedly not looking at the shrouds, "let me see what I can do so we can be ready when help arrives."

Tania had removed the splinter but Mona could see there was still residue in him. And around both of them. Something was keeping them in this place.

Mona walked closer to the door. There, embedded in the lintel, were the remains of the spell, bathed in the same color as the rapidly growing tracer spell. Setting aside that observation to share with Cart later, she looked the lintel markings over.

Simple, neat, and hard to change; however the working was at its most, a basic containment spell and those she did know how to manipulate. Mona could move two of the points and set a new perimeter. So long as she didn't make the new places too close or even together, this should work.

"Ma'am—" Mona turned to ask the Wyrm a question and was cut off.

"You may call me Rushka, Warder."

Mona didn't know if that was a name or a title so she opted to bow her shoulders in acknowledgement.

"Rushka, a spell has been set around this space to contain you in this area. While I cannot disable this spell without injuring you, I can change the spell so that you and your companion would be considered part of the walls of the room."

"Which would make them free to leave this place, since the spell would adjust to the new room size. Nice trick," Cart said.

Mona wondered, again, just how much magic Cart could see. Far more than she expected.

"If I may have your permission?" she asked.

"No harm would come to us?"

Mona had to think this over. "I don't believe so, not from transferring the spell. However, I can't say long-term what the consequences of being thought of as a wall might be."

She waved a claw at this. "I can have the spell changed once home. You may do it."

Mona looked over the placement of the five points one more time, given she would need to touch the runes to manipulate them. The easiest perimeter rune was the one by the lintel, but that was also an anchor for the spell—indeed, their passing through the door had triggered the spell. How Mona hadn't seen it earlier, she had no idea.

Then there were the ones side by side over the wall they'd come in, and thus the gaping hole. Those would be almost impossible to get to.

She'd have to go with the two high in the corners over the shrouds. Lucky her.

Trying to figure out how to get to the corners without disturbing Smythe and his ward, she checked the tracking spell. No changes from the last time. Looked as if so long as they didn't do any magic, the spell would remain static.

"Cart, I need to climb up into that corner to get part of the spell I need to move. Any suggestions?"

"Well, first, I can't move the bodies, don't ask me to."

Even she knew the ceremonies and rituals enough to know he couldn't touch them—no one with elf blood could. Even the faintest touch might leave some residual magic that would cause soul to linger, instead of going back to the heart of the goddess as it was supposed to. The ritual was very clear. A plot had to be dug—by hand, no magic could be used—to the correct depth. Once dug, only then could an imp be asked to move the bodies. Even though Mona was pretty sure both spirits were gone, she wasn't about to ask him to do something she wouldn't do herself.

Although…she stepped close to the edge of the shaft and peered down. If it wasn't thirty-six feet, it was close. There looked to be a bit of magic at the bottom, but it was hard to tell from this distance. Besides, Tania would have said something, right?

She turned to find Cart standing besides her with a speculative look in his eye. He'd come over to peer down too.

"It couldn't hurt to ask, could it? I can phrase it so if it's not correct they won't move them."

Cart shrugged.

Shit, though, there was that tracking spell. She looked at the semi-opaque working hanging like a drift of fog by the entrance. Would calling an imp provide enough energy to trigger it? Probably not, given how much had already been done. With no other way to get the Wyrms out, calling an imp was a risk they'd have to take.

Mona looked at the Wyrm to see if she had any advice, but Rushka was bent over her companion, stroking his shoulder and whispering something to him.

"I'd like an imp please, for possible burial of these unnamed Folk."

Three imps appeared, startling her. Mona looked over at the working. No change. She looked back at the imps. No additional tracking runes seemed to be on these imps. No time to speculate why.

"Thank you. Can one of you please verify if the depth of this plot is correct, while another please see if you can verify that it was, indeed dug by hand?"

They didn't move but immediately both blurted out, "Yes."

Cart narrowed his eyes at the imps and shot her a wary glance. Mona agreed—something seemed off.

"Will the rites be observed if we were to ask you to place the bodies down there?" he asked.

All three chimed "yes" but threw off yellow sparks of agitation.

"Does a reason exist why it would not be in our interests or the interests of the families of the deceased to put them down there?" he asked.

They started bobbing frantically up and down, as if they were nodding but unable to bring themselves to say yes.

"Maybe we should ask if a reason exists why it would not be in the imps' interest to put the deceased down there?" Mona said.

"YES! YES!" The answer echoed through the space loudly, and they all, even the Wyrm, leaned back in shock.

"I will not ask you to perform a duty that is hazardous to you. Is there a way to perform the duty without hazard to you?" she asked, with little hope.

They spun blue, thinking on it.

"Wyrm help," one said.

They both turned to the Wyrm.

"Do you know how they might want you to help?" Mona asked, knowing the imps were unlikely to give them more information.

Rushka slowly rose, then shuffled over and peered down the hole. Showing no fear of falling in, she leaned far over, her tail twitching. She tapped the sides of the pit as far down as she could reach. Pebbles skittered and a chunk of earth fell. Sitting back on her legs and tail, she tapped the ground on either side of the pit.

"The area is unstable. Possibility exists that once the bodies are down, a spell has been sent to make implosion."

Mona noticed the imps were bobbing eagerly at this information.

"The sparklyflies, they know this. I can make stable so long as I am near, but once I leave it will fall."

"Does it take a lot of energy?" Cart said, clearly plotting something out. "If we needed you to hold it for, say, an hour, would you be able to do that?"

How long did he expect his mother to take?

"A little energy to set the spell and nothing to maintain," Rushka clarified.

"What are you planning?" Mona asked.

"Once the remains are moved you still need to scale the rubble, and I don't know of a way to stabilize it. Unless you could do that too?" he asked Rushka.

"The shaft and room will be stable until changed. I can maintain this stability. The pile is inherently unstable, I cannot maintain something that is not."

"Thank you for letting us know," Mona said. She turned to Cart. "If there's a chance everything will come down, or that we'd disturb the shrouds, I won't climb it. It isn't safe for everyone down here."

"Right. And we can't move anyone until you climb it. However," and he looked uncomfortable, in an I'm-not-sure-how-you'll-take-this kind of way, "I could shift, if you're okay with that. Once changed, I'd probably be able to keep my bottom feet on the floor, work my way cautiously up the pile with my front paws, then brace them on the walls. You could then clamber over and up me. Wouldn't be very comfortable for me, but it might work."

Mona looked at the corner—the ceiling was a good ten feet up and the pile of dirt and rocks went up almost to the top, not to mention the spread at the bottom.

"What do you turn into? A saber-tooth?"

"Nah, Weres can't be extinct animals, don't know why that is. Although I do have an uncle who turns into a Persian tiger, but then they weren't extinct when he was born. Me, I turn into a Siberian Tiger."

Cart would become an animal. A tiger. Something about it was just a tad creepy. She knew he was a Were, a first generation one, which were always strong enough to shift. Why she hadn't thought it through that she might actually see him change from human to beast, she didn't know.

"Will he fit in here?" This from the Wyrm.

"I think I will, ma'am. If it bothers you, though, I won't change. I'm sure we could come up with something."

"Your help will be here soon, yes? Maybe we should wait for her?" the Wyrm suggested.

"Well, there is a chance she might be here soon. But she's her own boss, so I wouldn't count on it. I think it'd be best to have you ready to go, so when my mother gets here she doesn't have to do more than get you back."

"I have no problem then. Does your mate?" She looked at Mona.

Mona decided not to correct the assumption. "I'm fine. Ready to have you do your part."

"Right," Cart said. "I think, Rushka, it might be safer to stabilize things before the imps pick up the bodies."

"I have already done so."

Mona blinked and realized a fine net of power in a color similar to the stone emanated from Rushka.

"Mona, could you direct the imps?" Cart asked.

She had called them so it was up to her to do the next part.

"Imps, could you please lift the Folk and hold them in a place in or near the shaft where you are certain you will not come to harm? Only place them at the bottom if you are sure you will not be harmed by doing so."

Between one blink and the next the bodies were moved and the imps were gone and Smythe and his mate were in their final resting place. Later she'd burn incense and pass his praise to the goddess; now she had to get the Wyrms to safety.

Mona turned to face Cart, who was divesting himself of his knapsack, coat, and utility belt.

"Next step?"

"You sure you want to watch?" He shrugged out of his sweater and shirt in one motion.

His shoulders were already widening, his body adding bulk as it prepared for the shift. He looked like a cartoon version of his usual heavily muscled self.

"I think I need to." Partly to convince herself it really was him, partly because she wasn't really sure what her reaction was going to be.

Unsnapping his pants, he leaned toward her. His scent and warmth made her want to wrap her arms and legs around him and…

Better not to go there.

Smiling, as if he knew her reaction, he kissed her nose. "Love you."

What?

He stepped back and green healthy magic swirled around and through him, spinning quickly and making a barrier she couldn't see through.

The barrier expanded and the edge reached her. The magic caressed her cheeks, leaving light prickles of magic in its wake, before brushing across her body intimately. Startlingly aroused from the contact, she blinked slowly in an attempt to regain her equilibrium.

A huge—huge! He had to be ten feet long—tiger stood on a pile of clothes. Black and orange with faint strips of white, he was both the most beautiful and scary thing she'd ever seen.

He stepped toward her, only to stop. Looking back over his shoulder, he lifted a hind leg and shook it free of the waistband of his pants.

"Oh!" Mona fought the need to back up, ignoring the part of her that was screaming, "tigers are carnivores" and the top of their food chain.

Another part was amazed at his closeness and beauty.

Good thing the latter part won the day.

Did he understand her when he was a beast? He had to, right?

"If you get off your clothes I'll pick them up so they won't get as cold and dirty."

He gave a solid shake of his fur, sending the stripes rippling, and moved over to a pile of rock in the corner. Setting his front paws on it, he quickly scaled to the top, his huge, padded feet not disturbing the pile. He stretched out over it, looking like a cat scratching a tree.

Mona picked up the clothes and absentmindedly folded them, trying to figure out how to scale his back. Not so easy, knowing that Cart was under there. Not under there, but in there.

No, that wasn't right either.

Unable to wrap her mind around the concept, she set the pants with the rest of his outfit before approaching him. His faintly musky odor was stronger, enticing. If this scent carried over when he changed back she'd have a hard time controlling the urges building up in her. Cart rumbled, and she knew he'd picked up on her body's reaction to his elemental scent. Damn the man.

She put one hand on his flank. The fur was thick like velvet but a little bit coarser. She burrowed her hand in, wondering if he had an undercoat. Cart shook his fur. Right, now was not the time to explore this.

Mona would work her way up along side Cart before clambering up him. Tigers weren't designed to be ladders and she had no idea how she'd scale him. Placing one hand on him to brace herself, she started climbing the pile.

The rubble shifted at her first step; a pebble skittered down, loosening several others in its path. The second step was worse.

Mona found herself sliding back to the floor. Cart's massive head was turned and his black eyes watched her every move.

Predator. Ignoring the thought, she examined his sleek back.

"I can't climb onto you when you're like that, Cart."

"Maybe climb on before, yes?" Rushka said.

If Mona didn't know better, she'd say amusement laced her voice.

Cart lifted his paws, turned, and with an audible oomph of fur, landed next to her. His head butted her hand and she caressed his ears, so soft, they reminded her of silk. With a rumble he lay down on the floor, his massive shoulders by her feet.

Mona look a deep breath, quelled her trembling limbs, and climbed on. His scent enveloped her, making her both relax and tense. She wrapped her hands around his neck, leaned forward, and whispered in his ear. "I will not forgive myself if I hurt you."

He shook his head, somehow making her think he was laughing at the thought that she could hurt him. He did have a point.

He reared up slowly, allowing her to adjust her weight and balance. Three carefully placed steps up the pile with his front paws and the rune was within reach. Mona grabbed it and he hopped down.

Sliding off Cart's back, she put the rune on the Wyrm's companion. Somehow she knew Rushka wanted him safe first. The Wyrm nodded in approval.

Mona glanced over at the beacon spell—still in stasis, good.

The other corner was past the pit and the ledge on either side was narrow. The good news was that the rough wall had plenty of handholds. Mona flattened herself against the wall and started to cautiously slide one foot out, figuring Cart would make it on his own the other side.

Her free wrist was gently engulfed in the tiger's mouth. Warm, not wet, with a faint rasp to his tongue, he gently pulled her away from the edge. Mona let him lead her away from the edge.

"I have to get to the other side, you know that."

He lay down, wrapping himself around her and again putting his shoulder by her knees.

"You're joking, right?"

His response was to curl himself more tightly, making it impossible for her to move.

"I am not going to sit on you while you jump over."

"Why not? You trust him." This from the Wyrm.

"Yes, but—"

"His way is safe, possibly safer than trying to cross yourself."

"Yes, but—"

"He is offering, you are not demanding. You are not demeaning him."

His head bumped against her hip, a bit hard, as if he was trying to knock some sense into her.

"Fine." Mona clearly was not going to win this argument. This time she settled herself just below his shoulder blades; she didn't want to impede his movement. Not worried about hurting him, she grabbed fistfuls of fur and leaned forward.

"Ready."

Under her legs she felt his muscles tense. A slight jerk and he launched himself at the other side.

Oh so briefly, Mona felt weightless.

With a thud they landed. She pitched forward, rattling her teeth as her chest hit his back.

"Ouch."

Before she recovered, he started to scale the pile on this side. Without thinking she grabbed the rune. He jumped down and was about to spring back across when she noticed something on the floor. The old book she'd noticed earlier next to one of the shrouds.

And set under it was what she knew to be Smythe's last log.

"Wait a sec. I need to get something else."

Mona slid off his back and reached down for the packet. The fizzle of magic worked close by hit her like a static shock. Quickly she tucked the two in the front of her jacket and then stood with her hand gripping Cart's ruff.

Across the pit, a woman appeared.

Mona blinked a couple of times to make sure she was seeing what she was seeing. The image didn't change.

The woman was older but still stunning, tight pants and cinched jacket with bosom spilling out aside. Something about her reminded Mona of an older starlet clinging desperately to the vestiges of her youth. The ski bunny attire only added to the impression.

This had to be Cart's mother.

Mona did her best to keep her face blank while the woman glared at her.

Cart shook her hand off and in an instant changed himself back, magic again swirling around both their bodies intimately. He stepped behind her, placing his hands on her shoulders. Whether it was out of modesty or not, she appreciated the gesture.

"Titania Margaret," Mona said as Cart drew his breath in to speak. "So pleased to meet you. Cart said to expect you."

Mona could see she debated whether to even answer. When she did she addressed her reply to Cart.

"Here I am." Her voice was rich with the resonance of southern gentility laced through it.

Cart took Mona's arm and they stepped across the hole to his mother, colors and stone blurring only slightly at the small jump.

"Mother, glad you could make it," he said as he slipped his pants on.

Mona wasn't sure how he maintained his dignity, but he managed to sound sincere and in charge. And not at all embarrassed by his nudity.

Leaving him to deal with the woman, she placed the rune on Rushka. The Wyrm was staring, eyes slit, at the Titania.

"Rushka, Titania Margaret is going to help you and your companion to get back home," Mona said as she stood and moved to Cart's side. "What information do you need from her, Titania?"

"She knows where it is," said Rushka.

"I know where it is," said Titania Margaret at the same time.

Cart paused for only a heartbeat. "Then this should be quick. Should we wait here for you, Mother, or have you set up residence yet?"

"With you owing me something, you can wait right here for me."

Somehow Mona got the impression she was using the singular you, and not "you both." Mona ignored her. They couldn't stay here, but now wasn't the time to push.

"Is there anything you need before you go?" Mona asked Rushka.

"No, thank you. May you and yours find comfort in safety."

Mona smiled at the colloquial Folk saying.

"And may you and yours prosper in peace," she replied.

As soon as she moved out of the way, Cart's mother stepped in and put her hand on Rushka's shoulder.

"Which will it be, the plateau or the cavern?" she asked.

"The cavern. I can ensure your safety."

"I was expecting you would."

They all disappeared in a shimmer of magic.

"I'd be interested to hear that story some day," Mona said.

Cart harrumphed.

"So, how long is she going to hold the 'you owe me' over your head?" Mona asked.

He threw his head back and laughed. "No beating around the bush with you, is there? I'd say she'll hold it over my head for less than a minute. This'll be fun. Watch."

I'm not sure how he knew his mother was on her way back, but as soon as he was done she felt the static charge of her magic again.

"There you are, dear, all done and settled. Now," she said, completely ignoring Mona's presence, "about that debt."

A feline smile stretched her mouth and she looked nothing so much like a cat about to get cream.

Mona saw the shudder Cart suppressed even if she didn't.

Shit, the spell. Mona looked over at the tracking spell. The runes were now solid enough that she could manipulate them. Given her previous history with these spells, she didn't want to do much.

"I assume you want to know if there is a male elf or elfling of sufficient blood to have rank that I could introduce you to?" Cart asked his mother.

Mona reached out and tweaked the location setting, just a touch. If she'd done it right, whatever was sent would now land in the middle of the ruined Warder's complex and not where they were.

Or, oh shit, they might go to Rushka. No, the spell was here, and hadn't disappeared when they had.

"As always, shugah."

Wait, Cart's mom wanted to meet an elfling—a not-as-yet-fully-come-into-his-powers male elf? Mona began to see where Cart was going to take this. She couldn't wait to see the fun.

"Before we take your mother to meet him, don't you think we ought to give her a chance to freshen up?" Mona smiled at her. "I'm sure you're going to want to put on an outfit more fitting for your introduction."

Titania Margaret's smile turned almost feral. "So right you are. I'll just pop over to the cozy shack Randall set up for me, and meet Cart, in say half an hour darling?"

Cart's mother narrowed her eyes and darted her gaze back and forth between the two of them. "And no contacting him before then, you hear?"

"No problem, see you then," Cart said.

She blinked out of existence.

"Well, I see where you get your firecracker determination from," Mona said. "Now let's get the fuck out of here. There's a spell about to go off and I want to change too."

"I'm going to focus on that last part." Cart cupped his hands around her face. "You don't take any shit from my mom, you hear? I love you and nothing will change that."

An uncomfortably hot sear of magic as the tracking working kicked in raced across her flesh and she gasped. He didn't give her a chance to respond, his lips devouring hers as the world slid by.

Chapter Seventeen

Thirty-five minutes later, after an all too brief stopover at her apartment, they were waiting by Cart's mother's front door. Cart had been initially disappointed that she'd nixed his plans, but understood why she wanted to light the funeral incense right away. He'd even added some of his own commendations of Smythe's character.

Mona looked around. Dried vines on wire trellises glowed blue from the setting winter sun. She knew this place—it was the abandoned stone house in the vineyard Nic's house backed onto. She'd spent many hours of her youth wondering who might have lived here and why.

A brownie peeked out from under the snow-laden bushes before popping back in. Vineyards were home to many non-human Folk creatures, grapes and wine being close to the goddess's heart.

Titania Margaret opened the door, the house lights spilling over and silhouetting her for a moment before she stepped out and glared at the pair. The look on her face could have peeled paint. Oh, this was going to be fun. Although Tania might not think it as fun as she and Cart did.

Mona tucked her hand into the crook of Cart's arm, watching the woman studiously ignore the action.

"I see you brought a sidekick. Trying to educate her on Folk customs and ranking?"

Titania Margaret wouldn't see any magic on Mona. Although why she thought Cart would be dragging a mortal around with him was beyond her.

"She has a right to be here," Cart said as he took hold of his mother's elbow. He looked at Mona.

She pictured the front steps of Nic's house. A brief sense of displacement and they were there.

Cart's mother stepped in front of them, placing herself squarely to be first through the door.

"Really, this is a private matter. We'll talk about it later." She pressed the doorbell.

"We'll talk about it now, Ms. Dupree," Mona said as she slipped in front of the woman and opened the door, intentionally not using the title Titania.

"She's part of his family, Mother."

"Yeppers, I am at that." Mona stepped in and shrugged out of her coat. "Hello!"

"In the sunroom," Nic responded.

"Sunroom? Why would you call it a sunroom?" Cart's mother's voice had lost a bit of its sultry edge. Hmm, perhaps she was annoyed. Well, so was Mona.

Ever polite, Mona took the coats and hung them up in the vestibule while Cart's mother's rant about sunrooms and solariums continued. Titania Margaret now wore black leggings, high heels, and a belted black tunic with a low keyhole neckline. With her styled blond hair, she looked like Ava Gabor getting ready for a pinup shot. Except she was older by a good century if Mona was any judge.

"What a useless phrase, since one clearly uses it when the sun is not around. Solarium means the same thing, doesn't it. Really, the proper name is a conservatory. Although, of course, they're not used as such anymore, are they? No need to be growing plants in the house for fresh fruit these days."

Mona was the only one who noticed Cart stumbled a bit on the step. Shit, with all the jumping and shifting he must have used a tremendous amount of energy. Food. She smelled something cooking. Good. They both needed it.

"Mother," Cart interrupted as she paused to take a breath, "Mona is staying. Not only is she with me, but this is her family's house. You are correct, she doesn't need to be here, but I want her here."

"I'm with Cart, so you might as well get used to it." At least for now, until they could talk over how Mona being a Warder affected their relationship and that "I love you" she'd still not responded to. Mona shut the closet and headed to the kitchen. "Hey, Nic, is there enough grub here for us to grab a bite? We haven't eaten yet."

Behind her, Cart stayed by the door, held fast by his mother. That conversation she ignored.

"Sure, there's enough for anyone who would like some." Nic rounded the corner from the sunroom and gave her a quick hug. He smelled like Tania and soap. You'd never guess from looking at him that less than two hours ago, he'd been completely paralyzed by poison.

"All right?" he whispered.

"I'm fine. You okay?" she whispered back.

He nodded.

"Get ready for fireworks," Mona replied, winking at him.

He stepped back and kept his face blank.

"Thanks," she said, louder. "You defrost some of my Salmon en Croute? Smells great!"

Taking two plates, she served generous helpings of the holiday sized puff pastry dish. Early in the fall, when she'd been worried about a test Smythe was getting her ready for, she'd come over and cooked up a storm. Nic had been left with a freezer full of food and no answers for why she was so anxious. Though that hadn't stopped him from complaining they'd never have enough people over to eat all of it—particularly this one, which normally might have fed ten people. Given how hungry she was, and she suspected Cart was as well, she'd bet between the five of them, they'd made a good showing. He'd also heated up the side she'd made, so she added equal sized portions of the root vegetables from the pan next to it.

She looked over the food. The meal needed something cool and crisp with it. She set them down on the counter and pulled out a cutting board from one of the lower cabinets as well as a metal bowl.

A quick fennel slaw with oranges did the trick. Making it relaxed her, even with the hissing argument ensuing in the hall. Mona stacked some on their plates, then gestured Tania, who'd come in from the sunroom, and put some on her plate well. Nic already had his out and hovering.

The whispered comments in the hall had gotten louder and harder to ignore.

"Really, Cart, I cannot see why she needs to be here. You know how…interested I am in meeting the male elf of rank in this backwater and her—"

Enough already.

"Yo, Cart, grub's ready," Mona called out, using her shout-over-the-crowd bartender's voice. She washed her hands and headed to the dining room. Out of the way, but with a decent view of the kitchen.

"Gotcha." Cart came through from the living room, walked over to where she stood by the sideboard getting out napkins, and kissed her.

Short, powerful, hard. He was clearly staking claim. She wished she could say she minded, but that was hard to do when her toes were curling.

"Now comes the fun," he said for her ears alone.

They grinned and sat down at the table. Tania stood in the doorway, blocking their view, but also out of sight from the front hall.

Titania Margaret's voice floated out from the kitchen.

"Well, hello." Honey had nothing on the sweetness embedded in that accent. "Aren't you the tall, dark, and handsome one? I'm Titania Margaret Dupree."

"Pleased to meet you, Titania Dupree." Nic's voice was entirely businesslike.

"Margaret, you may call me Titania Margaret. And you are?"

"Titania Margaret then. My friends, and I hope we will be friends, call me Nic." He'd picked up on the situation, all right. Nic wasn't slow. The way he said "friends" made it clear he was thinking platonic only. "Most Folk know me as Protector Niccolo Machiavelli Lombard."

There was a slight pause. He continued. "I would add at your service, however, I'm sure the elf I'm currently…attached to… might quibble with that."

"Oh, I doubt she'd give us much trouble, I'm after all a Titania."

And that, Mona realized, was Margaret in a nutshell. Beautiful, powerful, privileged, and not afraid to use any of it to get what she wanted. And right now she wanted Nic.

Nic chuckled. "Indeed you are, however she is all that and more. Besides, family squabbles can get very messy. Better to just let things stay the way they are, don't you think?"

"Tania!" Margaret's shriek of delight couldn't be faked.

He must have turned her to see Tania. Margaret came and embraced Tania, shooting the pair at the table a quick glare before stepping back.

"You wicked girl, you, taking this handsome gentleman before I got here." She put her arm though Tania's and turned back to the kitchen. "I don't suppose you'd be interested in sharing?"

Mona couldn't suppress her snort as she imagined the look on her straight-laced brother's face.

"Nope, sorry, can't do that to Nic," Tania said.

Cart's mother's back stiffened at her words.

"Is that a can't or a won't?" The sharpness of the words cut through her drawl like a knife.

"Oh-oh," Cart muttered and picked up his plate. She'd piled it high and every bite was gone. He rose and made his way around the table toward the kitchen.

"Nic is my protector. And yes, Randall already knows, and yes, I have pronounced him as such to the Folk here, including to our brethren the Weres."

"And is there a congress of the heart as well?" Cart's mother asked. Even Mona could hear the hope in the question.

"Mom," Cart said he entered the kitchen. "You don't need to put pressure on her or Nic."

"Of course I wouldn't do that Cart. Really. Hold that open, would you, sugah, while I get a plate for some of this 'grub.' Then I'll go meet this young lady you are so interested in. I can't leave either of you alone, can I?"

Oh my, Mona could tell she was in for a grilling by her tone.

"Mom, the 'young lady' is the Warder hereabouts, and one of my current interests is in training her since the old Warder died without finishing the job."

A dish shattered. Mona started up and out of her seat.

"Abner died?" Margaret said, her voice small and scared.

"Well, yes. I did tell you…"

A faint popping sound and a surge of magic hit Mona before she got to the doorway.

Margaret was gone.

"What was that all about?" she asked.

"Aw, hell, sorry about the mess. My mother has a flare for dramatics," Cart said. He looked at Mona then Tania.

"I'm sorry, Cart, I don't know where she went," Tania said. "And since it has to do with Abner, and possibly this whole mess with the renegades, I'm hesitant to ask an imp to follow."

Mona went over what had been said before she left.

"She knew Abner? She…wait…what is your mother's full name?" Mona demanded of Cart.

"Titania Margaret D'Anjou Dupree," Cart replied. "And no, despite what she might lead you to believe, she wasn't the wife of Henry the Sixth. That would be her great grandmother, whom she was named after."

"D'Anjou. Abner guarded Edward D'Anjou." As well as his mother. Mona had been shocked with the information earlier, when she'd read the last pages of Abner's missing journal. No name for his mother popped into her memory; the information Smythe passed along clearly very selective.

Tania and Cart started to say something but Nic held up his hands to stop them.

"Wait. Let's all get something to eat, then we can sit down and figure out who the ward might be and how you're connected," Nic said. "If we're heading out again soon, and it looks like we are, we'll need the energy."

Nic waved them back into the dining room. "You too," he said to Tania. "I know food isn't the best source of energy for you, but eating can't hurt. I'll clean up here and join you."

Mona blinked at this information. If Tania didn't need food for energy she was truly a Maven in her soul, and it was not merely an honorary title for the work she did. For her, only sunlight or the presence of naturally generated magic would replete her stores. Which explained why there was an elf of such power in their region—Niagara Falls generated more than enough energy to sustain her, provided she was close enough. The vineyard out Nic's backyard was probably a good, low-level source too.

Tania came in with a plate containing only salmon, and sat on the other side of Cart. Between bites they started going through the family tree to figure out who Smythe might have been Warding until Nic joined them.

"Fill me in." Nic pulled a chair to the corner of the table so it was right next to Tania's. "Is there a protocol for naming?"

Seeing Tania and Cart squirm was slightly amusing, although Mona understood their reactions. Nic watched them both with raised eyebrows.

"Any help here, sis?" Nic asked when it became clear neither was going to answer.

From what Mona had heard, if a full elf was fertile and conception was going to occur, the goddess's blessing raced through the pair during the climax of intercourse and the first name of their child was revealed. Elves, though, considered it bad luck, not to mention highly personal, to talk about the experience.

"Do you mean given names," Mona's voice squeaked slightly but she persevered, "or last names or earned names?"

"Wait!" Cart cut in, blushing. "I think you're mostly interested in the last name of this guy, right?"

"Right. Now, for Mona and myself, she has my mother's last name and I have my father's. Is that typical?"

"Yes and no. The mother has the entire decision on which last name the child will bear," Cart said.

Nic nodded. "Okay, but is there any protocol at all or is it merely a toss of the coin?"

"A lot of the mother's decision has to do with families and perceived social standing as well as the power of each elf in the relationship." Tania added. "Often, but not always, the mother will give the surname with a longer history. Which, most likely, explains why you are a Lombard and your sister is a Trubek. Both are old and honored families."

"So, anyway, D'Anjou's a family name. Tania and I might be able to figure out who it was,," Cart supplied. "Could Marty have had a kid before the girls? I mean, we all know Abner was old, could have been that, huh?"

Tania looked thoughtful. "You're right, I think we aren't going back far enough. As you said, Abner was old. Is there a sibling or cousin of Aunt Meg and Uncle Marty's it could be?"

Cart shrugged his shoulders and started listing people with Tania jumping in to fill names.

Mona didn't recognize any, not that she was sure she would.

"Is this something you could ask an imp?" Nic asked.

Startled into silence, Cart and Tania exchanged a look and then laughed.

"Thanks, Nic," Tania said. "An imp might be able to tell us— however, Randall *definitely* could. If he will, that's another matter. I need an imp, please."

Randall flashed into being in the middle of the dining room table, setting over the candlesticks and bowl of pinecones. He wore a twenties gangster outfit, pinstripes, spats, and hat complete with a dapper feather. Mona knew from experience that this meant he was out for vengeance.

"Where is she?" he said, stalking up to Tania. "I've trying to track Titania Margaret down and the imps won't go to her. She better have some answers."

Nic's voice overrode everyone else's. "Answers to what?"

They all quieted down and waited for Randall's answer.

"Why the hell she wasn't monitoring her uncle like she agreed to?"

"Edward?" Mona asked. Given how extensive elf families were, it was possible to have that large a generation gap.

"Edward? I'm talking about Abner. Weak link there, we all knew he was going to cave in, but we didn't think it'd be this catastrophic. Or, honestly, that he'd hold out this long. Wait, who the hell is Edward?"

"Edward D'Anjou, Abner's ward," Mona said, worry lacing through her at his description of things being catastrophic.

"No, Abner's ward was Elisabeth Dupree, Titania Margaret's mother's sister and Abner's wife. Edward D'Anjou? Aw, crap." He spun to face Tania, pointing his finger in her face. "You need to get going now! This is bad, bad, bad."

"Randall," Tania said, clearly trying to maintain her calm, "it would help me if I knew what ability Elisabeth manifested or if you know what ability Edward has."

"Is she serious?" He turned to fire the question at Mona. Not even waiting for a response, he leaned forward and placed his face where his finger had been, his voice dropping to become a hoarse, harsh whisper. "You can't figure out the ability he has? Does the fact that Weres are being forced into their animal forms tell you anything? And think about this, princess, there are more Weres who are now animals than there were half bloods."

Everyone at the table, except Nic, paled and gasped. Smythe's memory provided images for Mona. The darkest and bloodiest of Folk tales involved possession by the wicked and insane spirit of the first Were.

"We've got ourselves a Lycoan. And this one looks almost as strong as the first Were he's named after. You," Randall's gesture took in everyone in the room, "need to go after him and soon."

He straightened up and immediately disappeared.

They all sat blinking at the space he'd recently occupied.

Tania started to shake, and Nic scooted his chair over and wrapped his arm around her shoulders.

"What the hell is a Lycoan and how can it convert people into Weres who aren't?" he asked.

There was an awkward moment of silence before Cart cleared his throat. "You know anything about Weres?"

Nic shook his head.

"There are three types of shifters. The rarest is a first generation. They are the offspring of a full elf and a mortal. That's me. My bloodlines are exactly half of each, which, with the amount of crossbreeding in the past, is getting rare. Because I'm a first generation I carry my den's totem inside me. I can change into my beast, anytime, any place, although the moon call is still strong and the easiest time for me to change. I also have other abilities, but they're not relevant. Now a little more common, but still not so much, is a strong Were. That's someone who also has fifty-fifty blood lines but isn't first generation. They too can change out of cycle, but not so easily. The moon has a stronger influence on their ability because they don't carry their animals with them at all times, it's more of a displacement of their body with a magical beast from Elfhaven. Then there are what most Weres in the pack are—close to fifty percent elfblood and only able to change with the full moon. Of course, there are Weres who don't have enough magic in their bloodlines to call their beasts who are still part of the pack."

Mona hadn't heard that before. She must have jerked, because Cart glanced at her.

Tania continued. "What a Lycoan does is manipulate the body of a Were and supplement the magic in some way, making it so they can change into their totem even if they're not strong or first generation. Or a Lycoan attempts to supplement it, there's only so much he can add if the Were's innate magic is too low, the forced shift will kill the shifter. He also can hold anyone—strong, first, anyone he's successfully forced to change—in their beast shape until he chooses to release them. He can create an army that way if he so wishes."

They looked at each other. Was that what he was doing?

"This particular Lycoan has no discernment on who is close, and we've witnessed his attempts to force the change on Were who are too far away from the fifty-fifty split. As you can imagine, it's gruesome," Cart added. "Thank the fates the female version of the trait is far more benign given it's also far more common."

Nic sat for a moment looking back and forth between the three of them. Mona knew him well enough to guess his next question.

"How do you release the changed Weres?"

"The Weres? Short of killing them? Haven't heard of any way." Cart's voice softened. "You got any ideas, cuz?"

"Yes…no." Tania gestured vaguely. "I was planning to talk to Aunt Meg, but I'm not so sure how much of a help she is going to be. Sorry, Cart. I wonder though…do you think she knew this might happen? It would explain why she keeps trying to make more full elves."

"You mean…aw, heck, I don't know." Disbelief and shock laced Cart's voice. "I'd like to think that her screwing around and trying to elevate so many elves was noble. That'd be nice. But I'd never assume my mother does anything for a single reason."

"You do know I have no clue what you are saying, right?" Nic said.

"Cart's mom has the female version of the trait," Mona explained. "She can elevate male elves to full ranking, and somehow supplement their ability to work magic to make their workings closer to the level of a full elf. Unlike a Lycoan, this is considered a good thing, especially since full male elves are very rare."

"What ability do you think she was looking for?" Nic asked Tania.

"That's just it, I'm not sure," Tania said. "It's only a rumor, but she has gone to the effort of making many men close to full elves. However, if you take a Titania's power and apply it to a full or almost full blooded elf, the theory is you'll get something…more. I don't know what."

Somehow Mona thought Tania did have a good idea, but was hesitant to say anything. Like her reluctance over naming conventions, there were things Tania would not speak about in Nic's company.

"Yeah, maybe if Mom had been more discerning or had a better grasp of who was an elf and who wasn't—" Cart couldn't keep the derision out of his voice. "Plus the change never stuck. Every single one turned back."

"Enough, speculation isn't going to get us anywhere." Tania waved off any further talk. "Nic and I think that the numbers in Abner's message were routes, directions to where the Were pack is being held up in Canada. I think we should gear up and head out. Can everyone be ready in about an hour?"

"No." Nic's assertion forestalled anyone's answer. "We're heading into unmapped woods, something we want to do in daylight if possible. Unless someone thinks the need to act immediately outweighs the need for our being better prepared?"

Cart raised an eyebrow at Tania, but didn't naysay Nic. Nic seemed to take the silence as acceptance. "Everyone gather what information they can, anything you think might possibly be useful. And be sure to rest at least six hours. We'll meet here and head out an hour before dawn."

Mona contemplated how the change Tania implied, which was clearly already working on Nic, was going to affect her brother. Because, try as he might to deny it, and despite the fact that he had not had a talent evince itself, he was as close to a full blood elf as possible in this day and age.

"Good," Nic said. "It's eight p.m. Be back here at six a.m. Unless you're planning to stay here? You're welcome to stay."

"No, that's okay." Mona wanted to find out more about Lycoans and Titanias and their powers, which meant she'd have less than six hours of sleep, but for once she was feeling caught up.

"I'll go with you, there's some stuff I want to look up too." Cart stood and pulled out her chair.

"Tania." Cart's grip on Mona's arm tensed as he addressed his cousin. "If you hear anything from my mom, let me know. I suspect though, that we'll both hear from her soon enough."

"If not," Tania replied, "she's probably done the smart thing and headed to Elfhaven until all this blows over. Your mother never did like direct confrontation."

Mona didn't think Cart believed her, but he didn't say anything as they helped clean up.

Once in the car, they settled on going back to headquarters first, and Mona tried to sort through her racing thoughts. While she knew and had learned a lot of Folk mythology and history it was clear she didn't yet know enough. Although she had a strong guess. Who else came to mind when you thought of Titania?

"So, tell me about Oberon," she said to Cart.

He jerked the wheel slightly, but didn't leave the lane. "Crap. How did I miss that?"

"Too close to the situation? Plus, since my mother didn't have much to do with Folk, the first name I associate with Titania is Oberon."

"Drama club in high school, right?"

"English major in college before I dropped out to go to culinary school. So, what's the scoop?"

"Besides the fact that he's a powerful elf who's the enforcer of Folk justice—or his interpretation of it—on mortals and other Folk? Not sure."

Mona thought through what she knew about Titania and changes.

"I realize that this might be awkward, but how do most Folk react when they find out they've been changed by your mother?"

"Worried about Nic?"

"But unlike the others, this would be permanent, right?"

"If that's what's happening, yes." Cart was silent a moment, negotiating the darkened stretch of rural highway as he thought. "I can't say there was any 'one way' or that everyone reacted in the way you thought they would."

Who knew, if Nic would be in charge of meting out justice, he might actually take the change well. Plus, it was clear he was very attached to Tania, which would help. But that he'd been coerced into the position? That might outweigh both the others.

"Hmmm, what about the Lycoan? Any insight on him?"

"Beside what Randall said about changing Weres, no."

"Will he affect you?" she belated asked. She didn't think she could stand to see him forced into transforming.

"I don't think so, since I'm already a strong Were. Guess we'll find out tomorrow." He pulled into a parking spot behind the building. "Maybe there'll be something in the books you picked up at the compound too."

So much for thinking he hadn't noticed since he'd been in tiger form. "It's in code. I'm not sure we'll have a luxury of the time to decipher it.

After a good hour of reading, they hadn't come up with much.

"Do you think Nic is going to be Tania's first?" Mona asked as she flipped through Smythe's tome. They'd settled on the couch and had the large book on the coffee table in front of them. Cart was reading through the last couple of journal entries, making notes on a piece of paper on the miniscule space not occupied by the tome.

The other book Mona had found was still an indecipherable mystery.

"First what?"

"You know, first lover?" She couldn't help blushing. "Because if he is, and they're already bound, from this passage it seems more likely the change will occur and be permanent. Although, he's already pretty much a full elf."

Mona showed him the passage Abner had written that, after wading through archaic language, did seem to say Nic's change was likely to be permanent if they were bonded and Tania was a virgin.

"It's pretty likely he'll be her first. She's a bit scared of changing people. But as embarrassing as she'll find it, I can't imagine she won't say something if that's the case."

Yes, Mona could imagine Tania, no matter how uncomfortable the conversation might make her, standing her ground to make sure things were clear before anything happened. Mona read further down the page. "If that is the case, we may not get out tomorrow. According to Smythe, he'll have a 'sleep of a deep and restorative nature whist his body accepts the changes spectral to his magical essence.' I need to rewrite this into modern English."

"We should show up at the right time anyway, we can't be sure if and when it'll happen. Speaking of which…" He pushed the table aside, placing the book out of reach. "We have some unfinished business of our own. Now, where were we earlier? Right."

He wrapped his arms around her, bringing his hands up to cup the back of her head.

"Here," he gently kissed the corner of her mouth, the tip to his tongue darting out and teasing, "is where we were."

He traced the seam of her lips, while he leaned them both down onto the couch. The weight and heat of him felt incredible. Mona grabbed the front of his shirt, pulling him even closer, and chased his tongue back to his mouth. When they came up for air, Cart had nestled himself between her legs and was working his hands up the inside of her shirt.

There was a reason they shouldn't do this.

Mates. Warders.

Mona needed to talk to him before his wicked hands made thinking about anything but pleasure impossible.

"Cart, wait. Talk to me about wards and Warders."

"Not much to tell." He kissed his way down her neck. "If there's an elf who needs to be warded, a Warder will be around to ward him or her."

"Yes, but—" Mona bit her lip. How could she ask this without exposing her concern? "How do Warders' mates fit into all of this?"

Cart stopped kissing her and leaned away a bit. He looked her in the eye. "Typically, but not always, they're the mate of the Warder. Since that's not the case with us, I'm thinking your ward may need both of us to contain him or her. I'm hoping it's not this guy. Him, I just want to take down."

"Oh." She couldn't meet his gaze and glanced away.

"Wait." Cart extended his arms and pushed himself all the way off her. "Did you think I was going to be your ward?"

She looked back at his now blank face. Cautiously, she tried to explain her reasoning. "I know that wards are typically born with the imbalance of evil but nothing about my training has been typical."

Cart slid down to his elbows, his face now inches from hers. "You, know that's a very good point." He turned his head to the side and yelled, "Oh, Eternal Keeper of Folk memory, we needs ya!"

Randall flashed into being, sitting on the open pages of the tome. He tilted his head and wagged his grayed eyebrows at them. Gold chains glittered through his thatch of chest hair—other than that, his dark blue, mechanic's jumpsuit with a Puck patch on the chest was remarkably restrained.

"I don't do threesomes with elves anymore, although if you want to tempt me, by all means get undressed." He sat back, propping his arms behind him and swinging his legs as if he was going to sit and watch the show. "Oh, and thanks for the new imps. The way that Lycoan is burning them out, I'm running short."

His legs ticked faster.

"Oh!" Mona sat up, forcing Cart to turn and sit along side her. "That's how he does it, isn't it? He's found a way to siphon off the energy from imps for his spells. I'd wondered how he'd gotten so much. No wonder the imps won't go near him, he's killing them off."

"Like I didn't already tell you that when I put the geas on Tania," the Puck said.

"You said he was hurting them, this is a bit larger than that," Cart said. He looked over Randall speculatively. "We knew he somehow managed to put tracking on them when he shouldn't. I've never heard of anyone besides you being able to do anything that would affect imps in that way."

"Yeah, well anyone who figures out where imps come from can control them." Puck hopped down from the table. "Life was a lot easier when information was harder to come by and you could control who knew what."

Where imps came from. Mona thought the imps they'd created looked like the specters she saw when they did long jumps. Could it be that simple?

Mona stood up and grabbed their jackets. "Cart, we need to jump."

"Randall, what crazy—" The Puck was no longer in sight. "Shit."

Mona handed Cart his leather coat and shrugged into hers.

"I'd like you to jump us to the furthest place you can comfortably jump us to and back from tonight."

"Hold on." Cart slid his coat on, despite his words. "I'm sure there's a good reason you want me to use up energy we need to face the Lycoan. Mind telling me?"

"I want to see the beings in the time between the jumps."

"Beings? I've never seen beings." He paused, arm half in his sleeve, brows furrowed as he looked at Mona, confusion clear on his face.

"Well, maybe 'beings' is too strong a word. You know, those multicolored essences." Mona stomped on her boots. She was going to be prepared for the Buffalo weather no matter what this time.

"I've never seen anything while jumping, except the swirl of the locations coming and going. Nothing in between."

Mona blinked at him. "Nothing?"

"Nothing."

She thought this through. "And, I'm guessing, you've never heard of anyone seeing anything?"

"Nope."

She slumped against the side of the couch, perching on the arm. "The information I have from Abner is remarkable in its lack of information about imps. Any suggestions on who we could ask?"

"Yeah." Cart finished putting his jacket on, his face *grim[AA4]*. "Except you're not going with me to ask her."

"Oh joy, it's your mom, isn't it?"

Cart didn't bother answering, and instead rummaged in the desk. "Give me a list of questions and I'll do my best to get your answers."

Chapter Eighteen

On the way to her brother's, in the boxy, military-looking SUV which somehow they'd been assigned, Mona flipped through the papers Cart brought back. He'd been surly and cranky, and ferociously intent on sex when he'd returned and she'd not gotten a chance to read through until now. The first page had a dozen questions, only one of which Titania Dupree answered. Cart's mother agreed there was a strong chance Nic would be the Oberon but left every inquiry about his power and strength blank. The second page, covering other topics, had more information. According to Titania Dupree, the void they passed through when Cart jumped was a special space the goddess created which held shards of the life force of deceased Folk. And since imps were created from those shards, of course the two were connected. The last two pages about Smythe and his ward were entirely blank.

Mona now understood Cart's frustration the previous night.

"You believe what my Mom said?" Cart asked as he turned off the highway.

"Which part?" She knew full well he was having problems grasping the imps as partial embodiments of spirits.

"The part with the imps being dead elves."

"They're not dead elves, they're just linked to that spirit. Like a tendril of magic from them, not the whole self."

"But it's connected." Cart pulled on to Nic's driveway and turned off the engine.

"I think so, yes."

"I have a question then." He turned and looked at her, his finger tapping on the steering wheel in agitation. "If this Edward guy, and I have to think it's him, is killing off imps, how is that affecting the spirits? Are they gone then too?"

Mona stared at him. She'd been so caught up in discovering where imps came from, she hadn't thought about what the Lycoan was doing to them. If Cart was correct, and there was a tie-in with elf spirits, they had their explanation of why the Puck and goddess were involved. She didn't mention her suspicion that someone was augmenting the Lycaon's spells. When they tracked him down, she'd confront whomever helped him and deal with them there.

"I don't know. I guess the question going forward is, does the answer make a difference?"

"No, I guess not. We want him to stop, no matter what. Lets get these guys and get going." Cart opened his door, letting in a blast of ice cold air.

The lights were out and no on seemed to be up so Mona let them into Nic's house.

"Thinking he's got the sleep thing going on," Cart said.

Mona sure hoped so, because she didn't remember Nic oversleeping, ever. She headed up the stairs.

"You sure you want to do this?" Cart asked as he followed her up.

Her first chance ever to wake her brother up? Okay, she might be waking Tania up too, but she'd take the chance.

"Nic?" Mona called when they reached Nic's bedroom door.

"Just a minute!" Tania called. They heard a bit of scrambling then, "Come in."

In the middle of a bed draped with flowers and flitting with pixies, Tania sat, trying to shake Nic awake. He wasn't budging.

Mona and Cart's gasps echoed across the room. This scene, Mona knew it. The quote from Shakespeare sprang to mind.

I know a bank where the wild thyme blows,
Where oxlips and the nodding violet grows,
Quite over-canopied with luscious woodbine,

With sweet musk roses and with eglantine:
There sleeps Titania, sometime of the night.

The pixies danced as she recited the lines, then swooped up to blink out of sight.

"Holy moly, cuz, what'd you do?" Cart had stepped into the room and stood, arms akimbo, surveying the imps' decorations.

Tania copied his stance and raised her eyebrows at him. Really, they stood in the middle of Nic's bedroom, she was clearly only wearing a robe…what did Cart think his cousin and Nic had done?

He had the grace to blush. "Yeah, okay, about that, you all going to be ready in about half an hour? I'll rustle up something for us to eat on the way."

"Once I wake Nic up we shouldn't be long."

Mona came and stood by the bed, knowing full well nothing was likely to work, but unable to help herself. She leaned over his ear and yelled, "Yo! Bro! You kidding around here?"

He flinched some, and he turned away from her, mumbling something dark.

Mona kept her face impassive, although a little bit of worry did seep through. "He's never like this. I mean never. After drinking, after he got his tonsils out—which he did at twenty-five—he always just springs up wide awake. Usually it's rather annoying."

She started to bite on her fingernail and looked around the room, her other hand tracing lines in the air. Oh my, but was there a lot of magic in this room. She remembered what the tome had said. He might be out for hours and they didn't have hours.

"Um," Mona was sure she turned beet red as she asked the question, "if you don't mind my asking, was this your first time?"

Tania, she was sure, now matched her blush.

Cart muttered something about checking downstairs. He and Tania exchanged a look before he headed out. Mona didn't want to ask what that was all about.

Still not looking at Mona, Tania replied. "Yes."

Mona gritted her teeth and pursued the question. "I mean, not just with Nic, but your very first time?"

Tania nodded.

"Oh dear, he may be asleep for a while then."

The Maven looked over at Nic and back at Mona, curiosity clearly giving way to her discomfort.

"Okay, tell me why." Tania sat on the edge of the bed.

"Well, I was talking to Cart last night. You'd both said that perhaps his mother had been trying to accomplish…something during her trysts. So I thought 'There's Titania, Puck, where's the Oberon?' As you can guess, I'm a huge fan of Shakespeare."

"There hasn't been an Oberon in almost five hundred years," Tania replied. She blinked and looked back at Nic. "An Oberon is like a Maven and Titania and Puck all rolled into one, able to do all of their magic and more."

She managed to look both scared and thrilled at the thought. Mona wondered if she knew more. If so, she wasn't sharing.

"Yes, that's what Cart said too."

Tania gazed off into the distance for a minute before turning back to Mona, her face scrunched with perplexity.

"I'm not sure I agree with you, but I'm also not sure I disagree." Tania laughed uncomfortably. "I guess I'm just not sure about any of it. Wait," she added, jumping up and grabbing Mona's arm. "How long do you think he's going to be asleep? We need to get going."

Mona watched her steel herself, clearly coming to a decision before Mona could come up with an answer. Not that Mona had any clue how long the sleep would last.

"Never mind." Tania let go and straightened the collar of her robe, then retied the sash. "We're going to have to go on without him. He can catch up. He knows the coordinates and the Folk will help him. Even more so if what you think is true." She shooed Mona out. "Go, I'll join you as soon as I get ready."

Mona headed downstairs to find Cart pacing the hall.

"Your brother wake up?" Cart headed back to the kitchen. He'd already started a carafe of coffee..

"No and my guess is, due to the circumstances, it may be a bit."

"Shit. Do we wait? I have to tell you, I don't want to. I'm itching go, to even as tired as I am."

Mona agreed, she was fighting the compulsion already to jump in the monstrosity of a vehicle and head out.

"Tania's all for going now."

Cart merely grunted as she coffee into a thermos. Before she'd put the cap on, Tania's footsteps were on the stairs.

"Ready? Let's go."

Mona and Cart scrambled to follow her. She was already in the car before they made it out the door.

"This yours?" Tania held up a posy of flowers from where she sat in the middle of the back seat.

Mona glanced at them. They were not rudbeckia or daisies or any flower she knew, although they looked close.

"Nope. Maybe the imps left it?"

Tania took a tentative sniff at the small bouquet and wrinkled her nose. Mona watched in the rearview mirror. Over half looked like they'd died and dried already. The flaking leaves were crumbling all over the upholstery.

"A very odd gift, but welcome," Tania said as she carefully set it down. From one of her pockets she pulled out an empty sandwich bag. Placing the bag over the top, she shook the dried flowers and leaves causing them to fall off the stem and into the bag. She patted herself down before slipping the bag into the cargo pocket on her right thigh.

They drove north in the rosy tinted chill of the dawn. The first time Tania jumped them all in the car Mona bit back on her squeal. She had no idea you could move a whole car. Tania only did it twice more, both times, Mona realized as they arrived, to markers she'd placed along the road sometime in the past.

After they crossed the border—in record time, but then it was clear imps were rearranging things to their liking—they found themselves on a rural highway. Soon the signs on the roads made it clear that they were heading up to Algonquin.

The monstrous beast of a car needed gas so they stopped and stretched. Mona looked around. A bank of blue-gray clouds sedately moved toward them, coming from the direction they were heading. Snow, she was sure. No magic in sky that she could see, thankfully, but the heavy weight of the clouds seemed to indicate there'd be plenty of snow without any interference.

Mona headed over to Cart, to find him crouched down between two cars and talking to a Feeorin. Notoriously shy of women, the squirrel-sized human-like creatures loved the northern cold and the wooded areas around here. Mona hung back, not wanting to scare the blue-black being. The small man nodded at Cart, then bowed to her before scampering off under the chassis of the parked cars.

"Salamanders came through en masse about an hour ago."

"We missed that clue, didn't we? We could have just stayed and followed them."

Cart threw his arm over her shoulders as they headed back to the car and Tania, who was standing on the far side. "Only if we want to get there after them. I'm still hoping to get there before."

Twenty minutes later, the snow started. A light dusting of flurries that soon became dense white and shimmered in the headlights. The only good news was that nothing was accumulating. Yet.

"So," Tania asked, "what information did you all find out last night?"

"Well…" Mona stretched the word to see if Cart wanted to jump in and say he'd visited his mother. He didn't say a thing. "You mean aside from the Oberon thing? I tried to look up more information on Lycoan. That was a little difficult, given the title wasn't used last time."

"Last time they just used the name the non-Folk gave him. I'd only ever heard him called Jack the Ripper." Tania looked thoughtful.

"I think naming him is helpful," Cart added.

The big vehicle slowed down more and they kept their eyes on the road and woods. By the time Cart turned up the last route, everything had been recoated in new snow and anything loose was being kicked around by the wind.

"If nothing else, knowing his name helps us know his powers." Tania clearly had been thinking on the naming thing the whole while.

"Unfortunately, from what we could track down, his powers weren't really clear," Mona said. She mentally placed the people she knew with powers in a hierarchy, using her hands to help her go through the levels. Hopefully she was right in placing her brother at the top of the heap.

"Did you find out if Puck's using the name means there is truly a possession by the first's spirit or is it merely a title? I really, really hope it isn't possession," Tania continued before they could answer. "The stories warn of the spirit splitting every time it was cleaved and going forth to possess more Folk."

She visibly shook herself from the horror she'd just described. "I am the Maven for this area and I will protect and oversee justice for the Folk."

Cart and Mona exchanged looks. They hadn't known about the splitting thing. Shit, no wonder he wanted to make more Weres—more bodies for him to control if he wasn't truly killed.

They should have waited for Nic.

"We think this is just a title," Cart said. "Either way, there are very limited ways to kill him. He can't die by loss of blood or any death blow that would cause bleeding, because he'll heal too quickly. Drowning, suffocation, starvation…although drowning would be tough right now."

"Hypothermia might work, but it'd be harder if he's in his wolf form," Mona said. She was again biting her nails.

"Asphyxiation, poison, heart failure would do the trick too." Cart swore as they skidded.

Mona couldn't help but notice that all of the options, except possibly poison, were lingering ways to die. His demise wouldn't be swift or painless. She wasn't sure if she had the stomach for that. She looked over at Cart. He, too might not have to stomach for it, but she knew without a doubt that he'd see if through because letting the Lycoan live was a far worse option.

Mona looked in the rear view mirror. Tania was staring out the window and looked nothing so much as an angered Queen, maddened by events and ready to do justice.

Mona looked out window again and saw the sign for their turnoff briefly flitter before becoming obscured by snow again.

"TURN LEFT HERE!" Tania and Mona both shouted.

Cart jerked the wheel and they did a one hundred eighty degree spin, the slushing sounds of the tires punctuated only by Mona's slight squeal. Cart maintained control of the car and got them straightened out with only a little fishtailing.

"There'll be a split coming up. Stay to the right," Tania said. Mona didn't question how she knew.

Cart took the turn, slowing down further on the unpaved and unplowed road. Fir trees lined each side, helping to block the wind and making it clear that the snow wasn't falling as rapidly as it had been. The swirling white they'd been witnessing was from loose snow. Tania leaned forward over the console and peered at the white wall that was the world outside. She seemed to see some sign.

"We should stop the car here. The road doesn't go that much further and we'll be leaving it before then." Tania kept her voice quiet as if she could be heard outside the car.

Cart pulled up a bit, attempted a three point run that quickly became far more, and parked facing the way they'd come.

They looked at the snow-covered road, trees and hills. Mona had no clue what to do, although with the trace of spells she could see Tania had been right to make them stop. "Do we attempt to circle around? Which way? Damn, I wish Nic were here, he'd know how we should go."

"He's still asleep." Tania shrugged her shoulders at their stare.

Cart cleared his throat. "Nic strikes me as a 'meet your foes head on' kind of guy anyway, not a 'skulk around and sneak up on them.'"

Tania and Mona turned to look at him.

"Why not?" Tania asked what Mona had been thinking. "Why don't we just go up the drive and call him out? It is the quickest route. Mona can manipulate whatever spells are set to keep the Weres bound, wherever it is he has them."

"Aw, hell, if we were going to do that, I wouldn't have parked," Cart said.

"We couldn't drive it up anyway," Mona said. "There are spells here to block any vehicles. Let's just go."

Tania made to move but Cart locked the doors, forestalling her.

"I go first," Cart said.

"You can't see spells, I'll go first," Mona corrected. It did make a lot more sense.

"I can see spells and work magic, so I should go first," Tania said. They couldn't argue with that, much as Mona wanted to. "Plus, this is my fight."

They didn't contradict her, and she nodded. "Once we get out of the trees I'll take us to a clear spot and you can stand wherever you like."

"Gotcha. Bundle up."

Once out of the car Cart pulled a carbine out of the back along with some rope. He had them string themselves together for safety, the show was falling in blindingly heavy. The walk was a blur of simply pushing themselves forward through the cold wind and blinding snow. Mona felt the fission of a spell and suddenly the snow and wind ceased.

"Untie yourselves!" Cart frantic whisper had Mona scrambling to undo her knot.

"Why?" Tania was practically bouncing with the need get going.

"If we get attacked, being tied together will work to their benefit, not ours." Cart's rope came undone and he helped Mona with hers.

Tania didn't take the time to untie herself, and merely wrapped the extra rope around her waist. She crossed to the side of the lane opposite the drifts. Mona, expecting a trap any minute, kept stumbling into the snow as she tried to see through it to the ground beneath.

Tania led them to a large arborvitae hedge on the edge of the circular driveway, and screening it from the road. Glancing back at both of them, she stepped out from behind the bushes and onto the pavement.

There, standing in the center of the driveway circle in a ring of prowling Weres, was the Lycoan. Red streams of magic flowed from him in many directions, most vanishing down under the snow, making it difficult for Mona to trace. Behind him were two buildings, a large barn that glowed with spells and a house with a small, attached shed that shone less brightly. Beyond both, Mona could see the smooth, flat surface of a pond.

Excellent, there was a spell she could alter on the barn to keep those inside trapped for a bit. She reached out and moved it around as Cart cursed and scrambled through his clothes for something.

The Lycaon stood on a platform, giving him a clear view of the area. Hatless, despite the snow and cold, you could see the relationship between him and Cart. They had the same hair, although the Lycoan's was a bit longer and very, very straight, unlike Cart's. Some ancestor had graced them with the same high, slightly narrow forehead with thick brows beneath.

The Lycoan looked right at Tania, and Mona could see his spear of magic burrow into her, pulling out energy. Tania did something that aborted the flow. He jerked and took a half step back.

Oh! The red tint to his magic was because he consumed the energies of Folk and creatures, not just imps. Forget her squeamishness at a possible prolonged death, this man needed to be taken out.

Mona looked at Tania's strength and the Lycoan's. The Maven's was stronger, but only just, and he'd certainly proved himself wilier. She really, really, wished Nic was there.

Mona tweaked the last rune and every door and every window to the house and barn slammed shut. Tania took a step forward and pointed at the Lycoan. What was she doing?

"Lycoan Edward, release those Weres to me!" She pointed to the Weres then herself as she said the request. Mona could see the faint beginnings of a spell. Oh, this looked to be old magic.

The Lycoan just laughed. "A bold statement from someone who is clearly at a disadvantage here. Besides, I cannot release them to someone unnamed, can I?" A deep, seductive baritone carried the words across the snow.

Mona saw the sigils almost embedded in his voice. She was thankful, very thankful they would not affect her. She glanced at Cart. He was glaring at the man, the carbine rifle hidden out of sight behind Tania's back.

Mona looked at the lines emanating from the Lycoan. Concentrating on the larger lines, she worked on cleaning them. She saw a faint spark of an imp next to a deeply shadowed bole of a tree. Hoping she was right, she sent blood tinted portions straight into the blackness, turning lines from glowing red to a pumpkin orange. She stopped before she got too close to Edward, she didn't want him to become aware of what she'd done. On to the next line.

"I am Maven Greymantle. You, Lycoan Edward D'Anjou, shall release those Weres to me."

Again, Tania used gestures to emphasize what she said. The spell took a more solid shape. If it was like any traditional magic, the third recital would be the charm. Mona continued to clean the lines, hoping that whomever they led to would no longer be under the control of the Lycoan.

"Ah, Maven, I have heard of you and expected as much. Did you think I was so unschooled that I wouldn't know of you? My dear father, while he had many other faults, did at least teach me some of my own heritage."

They stood quietly and the silence grew. Tania was clearly waiting for something. The Lycoan just stared at them while the beasts below him paced back and forth, reflecting his anger, perhaps.

"What?" Incredulousness laced his voice. "You really expect me to release them to you?"

"Those Weres will be released to me, Maven Titania Isabella Meissen Greymantle, by you, Lycoan Edward Smythe D'Anjou." Tania paused, and smiled back at his smirk. "Now."

The spell took hold. The red lines of his magic holding the Weres vanished and were replaced by the golden glow of Tania's magic. Mona watched as a surge of energy rushed out of Tania to envelop the Weres close to him.

A slightly perplexed look crossed the Lycoan's face as the Weres' pacing lessened. Then another smirk and a slight bow toward us. "As you say. Now."

He waved his hand.

By the goddess, he was sending a death rune straight at Tania. Mona flipped it and sent it to the ground, severing several of his lines. She staggered a step back, heart racing like she'd run up a dozen flights of stairs, and just as tired. He cursed at her and Mona ignored him. There were three strands untouched and she didn't have the energy to do anything to them.

"Sorry," she gasped. "I couldn't sever all the connections."

She looked off to where the three strands led. Lumbering out of the woods came two grizzlies and a wolf. The wolf immediately slunk low to the ground, almost vanishing in the snow.

Cart shouldered his gun, taking a deep breath as he sighted. Two soft hisses and the two grizzlies batted at the darts that imbedded in their fur.

"I had to pick a middling dose, since I didn't want anything lethal. Hopefully it's strong enough to slow them down," he said as he placed the gun on the ground next to the bushes besides them. Mona only then realized that he'd stripped down to his thermals. With a stretch and a swirl of magic he shifted into to his Siberian tiger shape and leapt in a flurry of tan and white and shredded clothes toward the wolf.

Tania muttered something and sent a simple but effective protection charm after Cart. He met the wolf in a flurry of snarls and snaps. The bears turned toward the sounds. Mona looked at their spells. She reached out, and for the first time ever, her hands simply drifted through the runes and did not touch them.

There was a tingle of magic as Tania did something but Mona couldn't take her eyes off the fight.

Tania cursed. "Mona, move closer and put your hand on my shoulder. I'm bringing Cart back."

As soon as Mona touched her, Tania sent out a lasso of her power, wrapping it around Cart, and hauling him back. The strength of the magic changed him back. Tania screamed with the effort and Mona felt how low her reserves were getting. Mona looked to see if there was any clean magic she might give to the maven, but everything she saw still had tints of evil she no longer had the ability to clean.

Cart landed on the road fifteen feet away and they both scrambled toward him. As soon as his knee hit the ground, Mona grabbed his pack with his clothes and moved to his side. Around them she could see Tania putting up a buffer so the Weres couldn't get in. Why? She glanced over at the milling group as she pulled Cart's clothes out. The fight had made them too agitated. Tania must be spending too much energy trying to keep them contained. She needed to let the Weres go.

While the Maven was expending energy dealing with the agitated shifters, the Lycoan was drawing power from their anger. Shit, they'd played right into the Lycoan's hands.

Cart groaned and rubbed the side of his face where it had smacked the pavement. Mona set his things next to him and turned to watch Tania as she put a buffer around the Lycoan and set the Weres free.

In a flurry of nips and growls from wolves, badgers, and cougars, they turned to the Lycoan, only to stop short as they hit Tania's barrier. Several turned their way, baring teeth at the Maven before moving off toward the barn. A wolverine was particularly persistent and the last to go.

"What now?" Cart had slid on pants and his jacket and nothing else before standing and leaning on her.

They all looked over at the Lycoan. His face was contorted in rage and anger emanated off him. Even the Weres who wanted to watch were behind the barn with just their heads sticking out.

Mona wasn't sure how they were going to beat him. She was exhausted, Cart pretty beaten up, and Tania's power was dwindling away from keeping up the barriers. Mona looked over the Lycoan. His energy level was still high. She watched as he tested his buffer. Magic couldn't go out of it. He took a couple of paces and found he could move, slowly, in whatever direction he wanted; the buffer gradually changed to accommodate him. He looked at them assessingly, then started walking toward Tania.

Tania cursed and reached into her pockets, pulling out two bottles.

"Mona, use the lighter fluid to create a circle around us. Quickly!"

Mona took one while Tania took the rope from her waist and followed behind her, She placed the rope down on Mona's line and muttering a spell and dousing it again as she did so.

Their circle was barely ten feet round. Tania's plan was going to make them very toasty.

"Hey, cuz, remind me to never complain to you about being cold," Cart said.

Mona tucked her empty can in Cart's bag then stood next to him. The Lycoan was close enough they could see that his eyes were no longer human and had shifted to wolf.

Tania lit the rope, flicking her hand to activate the spell.

"Stay in contact." Her voice was low.

The Lycoan laughed, a deep cruel laugh that succeed in making Tania stumble. Cart and Mona grabbed her before she'd done more than slightly dip. Mona had a feeling Tania had no more back up plans.

"Do you think something so small and petty as a fire will keep me out? Even in wolf form, that excuse for a charm won't work on me."

They stood their ground, moving closer together as the flames lapped higher. The Lycoan grinned and stepped into the circle, merging the two.

Mona screamed as Tania shoved her and Cart ahead of her and out of the circle. They headed through the fire toward the snow-laden bushes at the same time Tania dropped the barrier and created a new one integrated with the flames. Mona turned as she fell, not wanting that beast to be behind her where she couldn't see it. Cart had done the same thing.

Tania hesitated before going over the circle as well. Her hesitation cost her, as the Lycoan leapt and grabbed her ankle. She fell with one foot still in the circle. Her shoulders were next to Mona and her shin still in the magical flames.

The snow pants over the flame burned off, sending a billow of black smoke to the sky along with the acrid scent of melted plastic. Tania's skin, though, didn't seem to be burning from the flames, just from the melted pants. Mona scooped up some of the snow they'd dislodged and packed it against Tania's knee so the flames wouldn't go higher while Cart grabbed her arm and pulled.

He and the Lycoan, whose insane cackle hovered over all they did, were practically playing tug of war with the Maven. Cart looked at the flames assessingly.

Tania wiggled her arm out of Cart's grasp and grabbed onto the base of a bush instead. "No, you can only go through once."

Cart looked at her then back at the Lycoan and nodded, as if something just clicked. "We'll get help, cuz."

Mona wasn't sure what he was up to but scrambled up to join him as he sprinted to house. At the last minute he swerved to the tool shed to the side.

Once inside she found herself slammed against the door and Cart kissing her, his hand grasping at her jacket and fumbling at the zipper. His scent was wrapped around her, fogging her senses. Until a whiff of burnt plastic crept in.

Tania.

She pushed at him. "What are you doing?"

He leaned in and kissed along her jaw. "Giving you enough energy so you can summon your brother."

Oh. Sex to reenergize her. She looked at him again. The scrape on his face was almost gone and he was practically burning up with energy. The adrenaline from his need to fight must have kicked everything into high gear. So full of energy, even his kiss helped bolster her. But no, she looked at the riding mower, the shovels, the cobweb covered watering can, she wasn't going to have sex here. Particularly with Tania alone with the Lycoan.

"Kiss me again and I'll think of Nic and you think Oberon. Between the two of us we should call him." His response to her suggestion was to pick her up and wrap her legs around his bare waist.

"But no sex," she said.

He nodded and leaned in. "I'll do my best."

Mona wasn't sure how he meant that, and didn't have time before he plundered her mouth. Nic, she needed to think of Nic, which just seemed so wrong right now. He was her big brother, always protective of her. If he found her like this, pressed up against a wall by Cart, he'd separate them. Then argue with her over all the reasons this was a bad idea. She'd argue back, and he'd pull that "I'm your big brother" line out…

A frisson of energy and he was there.

Cart stepped away, chest heaving, and, while clearly reluctant to do so, set her down.

Nic took a step toward them, eyes narrowed. He was filled with brilliant blue magic. Far stronger than even Tania's, it permeated his skin and gave him an eerie glow in the dark shed. Mona thought he could make magic work for him without even needing runes, the sheer strength of him would force the magic into submission.

"The Lycoan has Tania!" Mona yelled, pointing out the door. Nic turned and ran for the door, slowly opening it and slipping out once he'd taken a look.

Mona slumped against Cart even though she felt a whole lot better.

Huh.

She removed her hand from where it rested against Cart's bare back. She felt a lot worse. She slipped her hand back around his waist. "I think I have the energy I need to deal with the Weres."

Cart was already heading to the door. "We need to go help Nic and Tania."

"No, we don't," Mona said as she hurried to his side.

"Yes, we do." Cart put his hand on the door to open it but Mona put hers over his, stopping him.

"Nic has as much power as the all of the protectors you brought combined. He makes Tania's look like a lake to his ocean. If he can't beat the Lycoan, we're all screwed."

"If he fails…" Cart didn't say anything for a minute. "If he fails, he'll still have damaged the Lycoan. We need to be there to attack then, before he has a chance to recover."

"And if he's not beaten and he's able to call all those Were's back to him because they're still linked since he made them, we'll never win. I need to truly sever the bonds, so we have a chance. Plus I think he may have someone here he's coercing to help make his spells stronger. If we can find that person, we'll weaken his ability further."

The indecision was clear on his face. "Let's see how Nic is doing before we decide."

Mona took her hand off of his. They opened the door just enough to ease out, then ran, hunched over in the hopes of remaining out of sight, to the edge of the Lycoan's platform to get a better look. They needn't have worried, the beast had its back to them.

And beast it was. The Lycoan didn't change into a true animal like other Weres. Instead he'd become the tall, hairy, fang snapping half-human Werewolf figure that nightmares were made of. He leaned over, fangs bared. Tania must be on the ground.

They could see that Nic had the rifle with the darts aimed at the beast, even if he could not. He got off two shots. The beast rose and snarled in fury as Nic said something they couldn't hear. Nic set down the gun and walked into the ring of fire.

Nic's energy was spilling out and making the fire cackle around him. There was another short exchange then Nic's foot lashed out and slammed into the Lycoan's shoulder.

"We need to go," Mona said. "I need time to work on the Weres."

Cart watched as Nic did a couple more kicks and drove the Lycoan back. "It goes against my better judgment to leave, but you're right, you need to do your job."

Mona felt a glow of admiration for him. His understanding her need to do her duty was one of the things she loved about him.

Oh crap, she did not just have that thought.

"You just want to see him fight," she said, in a jocular attempt to ignore the revelation.

"No shit."

Neither voiced any worry over Nic's being defeated. As soon as they rounded the corner of the barn they were met with a phalanx of snarling animals.

Cart snarled back.

"Not helping," Mona muttered. She took a step forward. Creatures flitted around the edges of the group, unnoticed by the Weres, who were entirely focused on Cart.

Salamanders. Here. They were natural healers. Hopefully they'd help.

"I am Warder Kubrek," she said loudly over their growling reaction to Cart. "I'm here to break your links to the Lycoan."

She paused. The attention of most of the group was on her. "I do not know the long-term effect of doing this. It may mean you will never change back to human. But you will be free of him and not killed by his senseless actions."

There were a couple of whines quickly followed by more snapping and growls.

"If we can't change you back," Cart said, his voice low and calming despite his earlier reaction of snarling at the group, "the protectors will arrange for you to be moved to a safe territory near Elfhaven, and help you however they can. You will not be abandoned, you will always be pack."

It was as if a collective sigh went through the group. Cart's words brought them a reassurance Mona would not have thought to offer.

"We now have an Oberon," Mona informed them, trying to match Cart's tone, "which gives me hope that if I cannot change you back, he can. First, though, I must sever your bond. I need to touch you to do this."

No noticeable reaction.

"And I need the help of my partner. So you must let him near too." A few of the animals reared up, not liking her restriction. Once she did a couple, she hoped they'd get over it. "Who wants to go first?"

The huge wolverine who'd been the last to leave the Lycoan by the platform lumbered up. Mona looked at him.

"I think I've met you before. In the hospital, you were sent after us, and when the Lycoan called you back you turned and attacked him."

His black masked snout nodded while his brown eyes remained steady on her.

Mona looked over the spell on him. He was a strong Were, he'd needed no help to change. From what she could see, the affect the Lycoan had on him was to make him freakishly large in his animal size. And kept him there until the Lycoan changed the spell otherwise.

She reached out to touch him, but he took a step back. Like a grouchy aunt, the wolverine petulantly turned his side to her so she could reach him. Mona placed one hand on him, while keeping the other in contact with Cart's skin. A soft brush against her ankles let her know at least one salamander was there as well.

Running on instinct, Mona thought of the cleansing she'd done for the protectors. She ran her hand along his side and went over the spell on him as if it were the same thing as cleaning his inner essence, and stripped as much of the Lycoan's imprint on the sigils as she could all the while searching for one that might contain something like a signature.

She didn't see one.

Shit, all she saw was the angry red where someone had supplemented the spell. No one here had enough magic to have helped the Lycoan. His helper was somewhere else.

Maybe, she was going about helping the Weres the wrong way. Maybe, instead of concentrating on the actual pieces she saw, she should see if she could change the color of the working, get rid of the Lycoan and his helper's color. Could she do that? Would there be a way to disassociate the spell caster by changing the color, their personal mark?

At the end of the lines of rune, Mona concentrated on the color. Nic's hue came to mind and there was a jolt as she realized she'd somehow connected to him. It was the salamanders, she realized, they acted as a conduit for the energy, keeping it clear and steady. As she worked her way back, the angry red of the original spell's sigils and markings was now a blue. The red pooled in front, as if it was being scraped off, although she was certain it was being replaced.

Halfway through there was a tug and the rest of the runes rushed through. So focused on the work, she hadn't realized the wolverine had shifted until she reached the end and stepped back.

Cart was growling at the naked man.

"Cool it, dude," the tall, muscular man said to Cart, his voice low and gravelly. "I don't have designs on your lady."

He ducked his head at her. "Thank you." He turned his back to the pair and stepped into the crowd of animals.

"Do the pair of bears next, they're bothers and were caught together in the spell," he tossed over his shoulder, clearly looking around the group for someone. "You might even be able to do them at the same time."

Cart looked at the man, a grin splitting his face. "Any chance I could talk you into training to be a protector?"

"Rather not go through the training again, thanks all the same. Need to go find the rest of my group."

Cart snapped his fingers. "You're with the Reno group."

The man nodded still looking through the crowd. The bears had worked their way to the front and the man slid out of sight behind the large animals.

Mona set her hands on the bears. With Nic's added help she didn't need to touch Cart for energy. She did both, a little more quickly, since she knew what to expect and do this time. They too changed back to their shapes, ducking their blond heads and murmuring thanks as they stepped back.

"How many can you do at once?" Cart asked looking at the good two dozen left.

"I think if the spell is the same I could do several," Mona said after a moment's thought. With the salamanders' help and Nic's magic she should be good. "If they're not the same it could get slowed down quite a bit."

"Last five Weres who were changed up next, Reno," Cart called out.

"Okay, New York."

Reno pointed out the animals to the brothers who helped push them forward, including one extremely reluctant badger. They went quickly, too, although as the badger transformed, it became clear why she'd been reluctant. Mona handed over her jacket without a word.

Mona now had a pile of hostile magic residue at her feet, ribbons of anger and evil. The salamanders, she noted, were keeping the tendrils confined so nothing would leach out. She needed to get rid of it. She leaned over, and the ground spun and dove at her. Cart reached out for her but she shouted "NO!" and he stopped. A rush of energy was coming back along the line from Nic, and she worried what would happen if Cart touched her. The magic was all evil, as if Nic had stripped someone of the taint—but who? The Lycoan. She squatted down, setting her forearms on her knees and bowing her head against nausea.

"Don't touch me, just…give me a sec," she managed to get out when Cart knelt down beside her.

She watched as the color leached out of her fingertips and drifted to the ground, threads of magic making crazy looping patterns on the hard packed snow. By the time it was done she was taking shallow breaths through her nose and swallowing against the bile in her throat.

"We need to get rid of this," Mona said before she remembered Cart wouldn't be able to see the residue.

"It looks pretty nasty," Cart agreed.

She lifted her head and blinked at him. "You can see it?"

"Only when I'm around you."

Something else to figure out. Later. She gathered the red up, the strands feeling, and looking, like cold, slightly slimy noodles. The Weres, she noticed, had stepped back and were warily watching her.

"I think the Lycoan is gone." Her pronouncement set of a series of reactions, not all good. Reno and the group she'd cleaned moved to create a barrier. She couldn't help but notice that the bear brothers had hairy asses. Right at eye level.

Cart took her elbow and helped her stand. She swayed a bit before getting her balance.

"Can you jump us somewhere? Maybe the Maven's old place?"

"I don't know if I can, my energy is fluctuating a lot." Oops, Mona hadn't let him know she was drawing on him, she'd assumed he knew. "Let me try a short one, back to the shed."

"I—" She was cut off by Nic.

"Mona! Cart!" But his call was too late, the darkness surrounded them as Cart hauled her forward a step. Mona stumbled, her feet almost too tired to lift. Her elbow slipped out of Cart's grasp.

She let go of the red strands, reaching out to grab where Cart should be. His energy, the aquamarine she'd never consciously associated with him was right…there…

The strands she'd let go were squiggling like worms in the blackness. Distracted, she watched as one of the faint streaks of color creating specters of dark on dark wrapped itself around the thread and dimmed its light. She looked around. It was as if she'd acclimated herself to the dark and could now see so many colors where there'd be none before.

Go!

The idea pulsed in her brain, not her thought and clearly an order. Cart's color was there, right there! She flung herself at the glow, colliding with him and causing them both to tumble to the ground as he stepped out of the jump. The landing bruised them both.

Cart didn't seem to notice. He wrapped his scraped arms around Mona and held her close. His kiss was strong and domineering, and more than a bit frantic. When he broke off the kiss, Mona found their rapid breaths fogged the air between them.

"Don't ever let go of me during a jump again!" His voice shook. "I couldn't find you. I thought—"

His body shook, and he didn't continue.

"I don't plan to," she said.

He lifted off her. "I—" he started but was distracted by something. "Shit, the fire circle's still in place." He looked around. Mona, under him, couldn't see what had made him tense. "We need to get up."

He scrambled up and dragged Mona with him. Hand in hand they raced to the fire, cutting off the Weres so they were in front.

"Tania!" Cart's worried voice carried over the fire.

"She's safe," Nic called out.

Mona watched as the energy of the fire disappeared and the flames melted down to tiny flickers before fading away. Nic was standing over Tania, braced as if for another fight. There was no sign of the Lycoan.

Tania struggled to rise but fell back.

"Your ankle?" Nic leaned over, his hand outstretched. Mona could see his power gathering.

Tania, though, waved him off. "Save your energy for the Weres. I can heal myself once I have my power back."

He nodded and pulled his hand away. With a half smile, he tucked something into in an inner pocket in his vest then pulled out small plastic bag, which he offered to Tania.

"Salmon jerky? I'm told the vitamin D in it works wonders, but isn't as good as the real thing."

"Thank you, I think I will." Tania took several large pieces

As she ate, Nic picked Tania up. He strode past Cart and Mona to the platform the Lycoan had been standing upon when they'd first seen him. He carefully set her down. Mona looked around. The sun hung its golden disk just above the horizon—perhaps an hour had passed since they'd arrived.

Closer now, Mona realized there was another series of spells under the contraption. The lime-green color of the original casting was overlaid with the angry red with tints of deepening vermillion. Actually, there was a bit of the red spells on the top too, on what looked to be a rack or something the Lycoan may have used to… she wasn't going to go there. He had used death magic.

Chapter Nineteen

Nic frowned at the construction as he paced around the rectangle one way and then back the other. Looking up, he waved Mona over to him.

"What is that?" He pointed to a particularly large bump of orangey red.

Mona looked through the sigils to the runes. Both were linked through a containment rune. The top one also had the death rune, but it was on its side, which would mean a curse of some sort.

"A couple of things going on. The foremost is the top containment spell—it has a nasty counter curse imbedded in it. I can't be sure what the curse does; the symbols are all under the top portion.

Nic nodded and poked at the knot. Mona watched his finger slide through and tap just the green portion of the containment rune. Sparks shot out and Nic caught those and absorbed them. Mona watched as he converted the wild energy into something he could use. He shared some with Tania, given the thread between them, but that was probably not on purpose.

He poked again, this time tilting the death rune, flipping it over so it would be ineffectual. A loud keening occurred causing every Were in sight to drop and roll around in an attempt to cover their ears. Mona reached out, flipped the rune all the way over and the keening stopped.

Nic nodded at the work she'd done. "Can you tell now?" he asked her.

Mona peered at the spell again. Yes, just that little flip had exposed some major workings. The bit she could see under the containment looked similar to the memory spell on Smythe's journal. But also a bit like the spell Tania had used to show them where the 'traitor's gate' was back at the compound.

"Some ancient…half beast…is in place to keep you from opening the top holding spell. There's definitely a tie there and I can't do anything to change the second one, it's too ancient a spell."

Tania came over and peered around Nic's shoulder at the knot of magic. Mona glanced around—Cart was over with the Were he'd called Reno, talking quietly while they worked this out.

"That's what I see. There's a weak spot here," Tania said, pointing to a place where the sigils were slightly less vibrant. "If you trigger the spell there, it could be whatever is trapped below gets out that much faster."

"Okay." Nic yanked at the spell.

Mona scrambled back as the platform erupted, sending shards of wood everywhere and making everyone duck. Everyone except Nic and Tania, who stood side by side behind a vibrant blue energy shield. Mona blinked at the shield—the energy was from the spell. He'd taken the magic and forced it into another shape. Cracked acorns, he had crazy power.

A great bovine head, with bronze clad horns and a ringed nose, arose from the wreckage. Once on solid ground he stomped his unclad feet then shook his wrestler's arms and body like an animal shedding water. Snout high in the air, his massive shoulders under the pelt skin shifted and stretched, then some scent caught his attention. Still now, except for the twitching tail over his bare buttocks, he breathed in the smell deeply.

Slowly, his nose leading the way, he turned his bull's eyes toward Nic and Tania.

A growl was all the warning they had before he charged right at them.

Mona turned and ran toward the shed, Cart by her side, although she had no memory of when he got there. Behind her, she felt a surge of magic. A jump. She looked back over her shoulder. Tania and Nic were now behind the beast who again scented then turned around.

"We need to find some weapons," Cart said. "The only known method of killing them is to separate the head from the body."

Mona thought of that massively thick neck. Defeating it would be very difficult. Cart headed into the shed while she watched from behind the safety of the building. Tania jumped them again, this time closer down to the pond.

"We aren't here to hurt you," Nic's voice rang out.

Apparently the beast disagreed, because it lowered its head and ran at them again.

Nic sent out a lasso of magic and jerked its feet out from under it. Mud and slush and gravel spattered when it hit the ground.

"We did not trap you," Nic clarified.

The beast shook his head, snowy mush flying in a ten-foot arc around him, and roared. Mona watched as the half man rose, mud and magic sliding off him. She squinted. The minotaur had a natural resistance to magic, but there looked to be something else going on here. A spell on him that made only one person's magic stick to him. She'd remove it but there was no way to do so without touching him. If needed, she would, but she sincerely hoped it wouldn't be needed.

The minotaur swung its head from side to side and Mona realized there was a whole lot more than that spell on him. The earthy tones had blended into his skin, making it difficult to see. Except for the faint red pulses. Red pulses like the areas on the Lycoan's spells. Someone had manipulated this working too.

Tania and Nic turned from their whispered conversation.

"I can help you get revenge." Nic's voice was full of power and promise.

The great shaggy head stilled, although his shoulders twitched as if he fought against the urge to move.

"I can also send you back so no one would ever know you've been gone." Nic's voice was lower this time. "You tell me. One hand up for revenge and both hands up for return." Nic demonstrated what he wanted as he spoke.

A foot pawed at the ground, causing Nic to pull Tania tightly against his side. The beast stood, toes scuffing the ground.

"You want to do both, don't you?" Tania asked. "I'm not sure we can promise that."

"She's right, I can't promise you that we'll be able to do both," Nic said. "Not because I don't want to, but I don't know what and who you'll find when I send you to get your revenge. However, if I can, I'll help you get back. My word." He smacked his fist on his chest twice then did a half bow. A ritual Mona didn't get, but the minotaur seemed to be reassured; he knelt and raised one hand in the air.

"Okay, I'll take your word you won't harm us and you have our word we won't harm you. We need to get close enough to undo your bindings." Nic took a step and the half man jumped up, arms cocked to fight. Nic stopped. "I can't do this if you don't trust us."

Tania took a step forward and bowed. She flicked her fingers and Mona saw a set spell tornado around her, then her crown was plopped on her head. Mona thought this was supposed to change her into the finery she'd worn at the Puck's binding, but without imps around, this was what she got.

"I'm the ruler of the Folk in this area and this is my…consort," Tania said. "Our promise to help you binds us to do you no harm."

The fists lowered.

"I'll stand here, next to you, while my consort works, if that'll put you at ease." Tania slowly walked toward him then stood with her back half to him, trust implicit in the stance. Mona did notice she'd gone to the side where she'd be standing in the sun.

Nic waited half a heartbeat and joined them.

Tania was saying something to the beast that Mona couldn't hear.

"Must be an Asterion, they're smart. A regular minotaur acts on animal instinct alone." Cart gave a dry chuckle. "An Oberon who doesn't fight first and ask questions later, this'll be new."

"Stop doing that!" Mona hissed.

"What?"

"Showing up at my side with no warning!"

"You want me to warn you that I'm at your side? How?"

Mona just shook her head and looked back. The beast had his arms raised and Nic was examining the workings etched into the underside. Tania kept up her low-key banter. Cart might be able to hear it but she couldn't.

Whatever she was saying must have been funny because Cart started to snicker then almost doubled over with suppressed laughter. Tania shot them a glance, not breaking her banter with the beast.

Nic approached Tania, who turned and bowed her head regally at the beast before stepping away. Nic elegantly pulled at each strand using a small hook of magic and gathered together the lines that were binding the Asterion to this place. He then wrapped the hook of his magic around them and brought them to his fist.

Cart and Mona moved closer as Nic spoke to the being.

"I want to grant you some power to help you and so that whoever you face knows I sent you," Nic said. He flicked a bit of magic at it, marking its brow with a symbol Mona couldn't make out. "When you are ready to for me to get you, what movement do you want to make?"

The minotaur clapped his hands three times.

"No, something simpler that you can do even if disabled. Not that I think that'll happen, but I want to plan for any eventuality."

The shaggy head nodded then stilled. He touched his chest three times, going across, down, then up to make a triangle.

"Yes, I can use that. Touch any place on your body to make a triangle and I'll either come get you or pull you out. Good idea. Now let's see…"

Mona watched as her brother—her brother, the one who'd never used magic and who had suppressed his heritage until less than two weeks ago—created a spell of amazing simplicity and beauty. She remembered thinking that Tania's spell was like looking at copperplate after reading block letters. Nic's elegant sigils and three-dimensional runes, were like the most elegant of calligraphy, simple, clear but so well structured and shaped there was joy just in the formation of the pieces while the whole became a work of art.

"Either hand, Nic," Tania pointed out, her voice soft so as not to break his concentration. When he was done she added, "Nice job."

Mona thought this was a bit of an understatement.

"Thanks. You ready to send him?" Nic's voice sounded tired.

"Yep. Here," Tania wrapped a hand around his wrist and Mona saw the swell of energy she sent into him. "On the count of three. One, two, three!"

The spell literally pushed him away. The effect was odd to watch as he shrunk toward his middle from top to bottom. Then he was gone.

"That's different, I've never seen anything like that," Cart murmured.

It made Mona feel better that she wasn't the only one who thought the method odd. With the minotaur gone the hole under the platform drew her attention—there was one more containment spell. About to tell Nic and Tania, she found them heading over, Nic carrying Tania in his arms as he fed energy he'd cleaned into her. That's what it was, Mona realized, he cleaned energy like a Warder but could also make spells.

Oberon. King of the Elves and able to do all magic. Mona watched as he set Tania down, worried over his reaction when he found out exactly what these new powers meant.

"Shouldn't you wait?" Cart called to them, his disbelief that they were doing this now clear.

Mona agreed—they had low energy and who knew what else was in the pit? She stepped closer, until she could see below the edge of the ground. No more angry red, just the lime green of the ancient spell, the one that looked so much like a memory spell.

"Finishing the job while we're here," Nic called back. "Want to help?"

"This one is safe," Mona assured Cart, knowing it was true but unable to put her finger on why. The color? The intent of the sigils? Something.

"Nah, call me if you want backup."

Nic and Tania stepped right up to the edge of the hole. Mona watched as the edges of the spell swayed as if drawn by their presence. The one tendril curled up and unraveled, leaving a bright blue and a goldenrod yellow.

Tania and Nic's colors, but not put there by them. The pair looked at the strands and seemed to come to a decision.

"What is it?" Cart asked under his breath. He stood behind Mona, hands on her shoulders, a sense of excitement vibrating off him. Even the Weres who'd crept back out were standing still, as if aware that this might be a momentous occasion.

"It's a memory spell, similar to the one Smythe used on me."

"A memory—"

At that moment Nic and Tania counted to three and each grasped a strand, belatedly throwing a shield up.

Two figures formed in front, semi transparent but clearly there. The woman older and in the raiment that Tania had worn not so long ago when the Puck had bound her to find the Lycoan. The man in a brief kilt of leaves and bark vest that did nothing to cover his very hirsute body. Even the tops of his feet had a pad of brown, curly hair. They were life sized and frozen as if in mid-action.

The last full Titania and Oberon stood there, ready to impart something to Nic and Tania.

A loud crack and Randall, Cart's mother, and…by the goddess, that was Dad!

"Dad!" Mona couldn't help the exclamation from escaping her lips.

He turned just his head and winked at her before quickly looking back. Nic's expression at seeing him was less than pleased. Mona knew he had issues with their dad's seeming abandonment, but when the Queen of Elfhaven had called, he'd had to go.

"We're waiting here!" Randall said.

"That's your father?" Cart said, distracting Mona from watching Nic and Tania trying to figure out what they were supposed to do. The pair looked flummoxed, then took a pose mimicking the holograms.

"Yep."

Cart's reply was a soft chortle. Mona didn't have time for figure out what that meant as the pair dropped their shield and together proclaimed, "Welcome."

Mona watched as the colors surrounded the couple, entwining and meshing with their magic. Imps started blinking into existence. But something, something was still off. Like an off-tune instrument in a band, a faint buzz of evil played on her nerves.

Mona looked around. There, on the top edge of the askew lumber that had once been the Lycoan's torture rack. A last little bit of vermillion still hung despite the fact all of the ties for the Lycoan's workings should have been cleared from this area when Nic had freed the minotaur.

"Come on," she said to Cart. "There's some of the residue from the person who helped the Lycoan I want to look at."

A couple of the Weres looked over at them as they moved closer, before turning back to watch the light display of new imps being created.

"Here, give me a boost up. I want to touch it." Something about it made Mona think the spell had been placed by whoever was helping the Lycoan. Although, it wasn't really a spell, just a bit a magic residue with the marking of the person who'd worked it.

"You sure that's a good idea?"

"It should be okay." The only other magic in this area was the residue of Nic and Tania's spell to send the minotaur away. "Plus, spells shouldn't affect me."

Although, come to think of it, they had been affecting her some. But this probably wasn't the time to mention that.

Cart knelt his six foot plus frame down, wrapped his arms around her thighs, and picked her up. Mona grabbed onto his shoulders for balance.

"You could have warned me!"

Cart was nuzzling her stomach. "This going to take long?"

Mona ignored his question and stared at the splash of color. It wasn't a sigil or rune, more like it was a little bit of energy left from a working. The same deepening color appeared on many of the Lycoan's workings.

She reached out and touched the piece.

The remnants of the transfer spell Nic and Tania created for the Minotaur swirled in a blue and yellow cyclone around them. Cart's grip loosened and Mona slid a fraction before the familiar blackness of a jump swallowed then. There were, she noted, less of the faintly tinted black specters today. In fact, as she watched, one with a slight orange shade coalesced to a pin point then popped out of sight with a slight spark.

Imps, this was where imps came from. She looked around at the magical sparks created when elves' souls returned to the goddess.

The light returned like the flash of a light bulb. They were at the edge of a road curving down a hill in a lazy "s," barely visible through the trees. The air was slightly less chilly then it had been in Canada, but much, much windier.

"I know this place." Cart turned and looked around at the trees and the small lot behind them. He let go of her and jogged down to a sign facing away from them on the road, read it, and jogged back up. "We're in New Jersey."

Mona looked around at the forested hills. Cart didn't give her a chance to observe much before he hustled her away from the road and across the parking lot. The purr of a motor explained his actions.

"You sure?" She'd never been, but from what she'd heard this was not what she'd expected it to look like.

"Absolutely," Cart said as he continued down to the trailhead marked at the end of the parking lot. "This is the South Mountain reservation. The local townships have a deer problem and they contract us to cull the population. They think we use rifles, instead every year we have a tracking and training exercise for the New York City protectors. It's about three square miles, all of it hilly."

"And clearly you have an idea of where to go."

"There's an abandoned estate on the very northern edge. Huge place, looks like an English country estate—formal gardens, viewing ponds, the whole deal. Think the heirs are fighting over the land. Anyway, unless whoever placed that bit of magic is at the remnants of the mill, which I doubt, as it's pretty close to the road, I'm guessing that's where we should head."

"Can we jump closer?" They'd slowed down as the trail rose steeply. The path curved around the sprawling upturned roots of a giant felled tree. Holes and furrows marked the debarked wood.

"No, I—" Cart stopped as Mona grabbed his arm.

There was a shift in the wind. She felt the power rushing toward them as the wind began to shriek. The scent of wet leaves and snow raced in front of it. Cart turned around and ran back down the trail, pulling her down and behind the rotting tree. He tried to slide her in the small hollow below and cover her with his body. Mona stepped to the side.

"No, I need to protect you!" Mona said, whispering frantically. "There's magic in that spell, magic intended to harm. It won't affect me, but it could affect you. I need to be on the outside so I can shield you."

"But there'll be debris and branches, you need to be on the inside," he hissed back.

"The tree will protect me." The leading edge of the windborne spell hit them as a sapling tangled in the roots of their shelter then crashed down. Cart wedged himself as far back in the hollow as he could, then wrapped his arms around her waist and pulled her in front of him.

"No, I need to face out, I need to see the spell," Mona said, squirming and trying to move.

He snarled, and in the gloom of the now overcast sky she could see the magic he'd need to change building up. She put both hands on his face. "Josiah, stay with me. I need to do this, and you need to trust that I can."

A second passed, filled with the now howling wind and clatter as smaller bits of debris bounced and pinged against her back. Cart closed his eyes and loosened his hands. Mona brushed his lips with hers before she rolled over.

The sky swirled with sigils and runes, huge amber shapes tinged with vermillion. The distorted images were hard to read. Wind, speed, shield, all clearly moved from their original places in the working. Mona reached out and nudged the speed rune.

Abruptly all the twigs and papers and debris of a forest in winter plummeted. Mona squealed and attempted to shield her head with her arms.

"Dammit, Mona!" Cart pulled her closer.

The loud clattering as something very solid tumbled down on the log stopped Mona's reply.

Then silence.

No birds, no wind, no sounds even from the not so far off road.

"GO!" Cart shoved at her and she scrambled out, bumping on the half dozen bricks now littered over the path.

She watched back up the trail, in the direction the wind had come from. Something, some thing was coming down that path. A faint hissing built up and moved toward them, slowly stalking their way.

Cart slipped out of the hollow, his jacket ripped and streaked with blood.

"Help me get this off. I want to be ready to shift." He was carefully pulling his arms out of the jacket.

Mona reached over and realized splinters of wood were embedded through the fabric and into his back.

"Let me pull out the worst of these," Mona said softly. Knowing they didn't have much time as the hissing become more distinct, she grabbed a jagged edge of fabric and pulled out the ones with the most blood around them.

Cart leaned over to undo his boots, grunting in pain. Mona kept an ear out, listening again for the shushing sound she'd heard earlier, but except for their whispers nothing was moving. Whatever was coming had stopped. Was it close enough to see them? She looked around, she didn't see anything or the glow of any spells. A small window then, to help Cart heal before they faced whatever was coming after them.

"Ready?" Mona whispered. Without waiting for his response or for him to straighten, she grabbed opposing corners of the ruined coat and yanked it up, following the direction of the scrapes.

"Cracked—" Cart bit off the rest of his exclamation. The copper scent of his blood filled the air. Mona plucked out the larger bits she could see, tossing them under the tree.

"Shoot!" She shook her finger after a particularly barbed piece pierced her.

Cart started to stand up. "You okay?"

"Stay there. Two more and I'll be done." Mona braced her sore hand on his back and pulled with the other. Done.

Cart stood and grabbed her now bloody hand in his own scraped ones.

Energy, a bolt of pure, electrical, hair-raising energy went through her. Both she and Cart jerked from the shock, although he managed to retain hold of her hand.

Mona shook her head and looked around.

The Earth glowed, trees a slumberous emerald green, the ground with streaks of umber. And Cart, Cart was a blue so close to purple she wondered why she thought of it as blue.

"I've never seen magical essence this clearly, I can always see a little, but this…" Cart trailed off in wonder.

The understory saplings quivered. Mona turned toward them and a deer skittered out, veering off with a leap when it saw them. Mona could almost see the beat of its heart in the pumpkin colored life force.

"Let's go, I'd rather be uphill from whatever it is than downhill." Cart headed up the trail, keeping his hold of her hand.

Mona was glad for his help, the change in perception was making her a bit dizzy. She had no idea why her sight had shifted. Would she still be able to see spells?

"Are you going to shift?" she asked as they neared the crest of the hill.

"No, I'd lose the advantage of the sight. I need to stay in contact."

"The sight, don't you always see like this?"

"Not this strongly, and if I'm right, I'll be able to see a bit of what you see."

Pulling on their joined hands, she stopped them.

"Why is this happening?" she whispered. She didn't see the beast but somehow her brain was reading the shifting patterns of energy, she knew it sat, unmoving, just over the ridge.

"It's the blood." He held up their joined hands. "Somehow we've each absorbed a little of the other's, so we've gained a bit of each other's abilities."

"It wasn't that much!" Mona said. Well, at least on her side, just a bit more than a pin prick.

"Right, so I'm not sure how long it'll last. I want to wait until it's done before I shift."

They both tensed as the energies around them stirred. As one, they headed off the path and up toward higher ground, crashing through underbrush when it was in their way. There, at the top of the ridge they looked down on the lizard whose scaled snout was turning toward them. Not a Wyrm, but something similar. He stood a good twenty feet down, his head was almost parallel to their feet. Mona looked over the runes wrapped around his body, distracted by the additional lines of his life force—Cart jerked her down. They slipped a few feet back along the ridge. With a whistling sound, a blast of air and ice frosted the trees around them.

Only one side of the trees. Not the other. It was as if someone had painted frost across the bark and not completed the task.

"Okay, so is this a different kind of Wyrm?" Mona asked. Something seemed off about its movements and actions, its life force. Even with the little she'd seen there was a feeling a misplayed note in the middle of a song.

"Not a Wyrm, pretty sure it's not sentient, just an animal. The closest thing I can think of is a basilisk, but it's far too large and basilisks turn things into stone, not freeze them."

"The spell on it probably did that," Mona said. She was reasonably certain she'd seen the markings that would have changed the size of the creature.

There was a scraping sound on the other side of the hill.

Not looking to see what it was, Mona and Cart ran further into the woods.

"If I can get a good look at it, I could probably change the spell back," Mona managed to get out as they rounded a boulder and stopped.

She leaned her back against the cool stone and tried to catch her breath. Cart paced, arms crossed and hands tucked against his side, his muscular shoulders hunched against the cold. Mona unwrapped her scarf and took off her hat and handed them over. Somewhere, she wasn't sure when, they'd lost Cart's knapsack.

"I want to see the spell," Cart said. "If we got a good view, would you be able to explain it to me?"

Far behind them they heard a crash. Cart looked down the trail. "It moves very slowly," he said, frowning at the noises "I don't think it's meant to be out in this cold."

"But if it breathes freezing air, wouldn't it be used to it?" Mona asked.

"I'm guessing it's a cooling mechanism for the dessert. Something in the spell must be ramping up the chill factor and causing the ice laden breath. What we need is a diversion, something to distract it so we can get a look."

Another crash and they peered around the edge of the boulder. The half frozen trees they'd stood by earlier swayed as the reptile forced its way through.

"I think we need an imp," Cart said. "It can provide a distraction so we can get a look."

"No!" Mona was as surprised as Cart at her vehement reaction. "If this person's been working with the Lycoan they might also be striping imps of power. We can't risk it."

"We could outrun it," Cart said thoughtfully. "Ignore it and keep going."

Mona nodded, liking the idea. "Whoever sent it to delay us expects us won't expect that."

Without a word, Cart started off. Mona followed, hoping they'd get back to the trail soon. Although seeing the forest through the filter of Cart's view was informative—she could spot where small critters hid from them—blazing a new route across the frozen ground was taking valuable time. At least now the sounds of the forest had returned. The birds calling, the chittering of squirrels, and the intermittent hum of cars nearby all resumed, as if they'd been turned on with a switch.

After a half hour's walk they reached a road, on the other side of which was a large grassy hill. Mona looked at the open space with trepidation. After seeing the life force in the trees and bushes, the sloping field looked barren.

"There's a better place to cross a little further down."

Wait, were his teeth chattering?

"You should shift," Mona said. "You're using up too much energy just trying to stay warm."

"I'd planned to risk shifting once we crossed the road."

Risk? "Why risk?"

The purring of an oncoming car had them both moving off the berm and standing in the woods waiting for the vehicle to pass.

"Given how this person manipulates magic, I could see them doing something to lock me in my beast for a while." Cart shrugged as if it wasn't a big thing. Mona, though, heard the worry in his voice.

"Imp, if you can do so without exposing yourself to danger, please bring a winter coat for Josiah Cart Dupree," Mona said. "I apologize for not waiting for you to appear before stating the request, but you understand the necessity. Thank you."

"Are you crazy!" Cart whispered as the purr of the car's engine morphed into the rumbling of a truck's as it passed them.

There was a dull thud. They looked at each other before heading back to the road. A charity donation pickup truck disappeared around the bend, its back door flapping open. And on the salt dusted road a plastic bag lay, split open, with winter clothes spilling onto the black top.

Hauling the load to the side, they picked through, finding an enormous thermal shirt, which hung large on Cart, and a down vest with a tear along one seam. And a dark green rain poncho with a partial roll of duct tape in the kangaroo pouch. They tied the bag back up over the remaining items, and set it on the side of the road.

"You always this lucky?" Cart asked.

Fine for him to blame it on luck—Mona was more worried about how much of their circumstances seemed to be being manipulated. And, unless the goddess was using her hand directly, she had an idea who was dealing the card.

"It's either luck or something that rhymes with it," she said, reluctant to use his name, here.

Cart's step hitched, then he kept on, acknowledging her comment with only a grunt. She didn't blame him. If the Puck was as heavily involved as he seemed, then the goddess' hand may well be being played too.

Chapter Twenty

After they crossed the road it took another half hour to get to the edge of the property Cart had been aiming for. She knew they were getting near once they started skirting the path again. Finally they reached a basin. Here huge pines marched up both sides of the trail, uniform and evenly spaced; their age made her wonder just how old the property was. The deep presence of the life force from the collective group had her in awe. And a presence it was, a power almost as strong as an ancient sentient being.

Cart stood looking at the pines too. "Every time I come here, I am reminded of the goddess's power. This place has always seemed to be close to her heart."

Yes. That was it exactly, the feeling that a small part of her was here, in this place.

Cart took her hand and gave it a squeeze before detouring around the trees and heading up the hill. Even to the side their power almost pulsed at her. Only when they were past did Cart speak.

"There's a barn here, a tractor shed really. We might be able to use that to climb up and over the fence."

Now that she looked for it, Mona saw the thin metal wires of the fence running between the trees at the end of the pine lined promenade. A strand every foot and a half and the top one, in the lower branches, faintly outlined with a spell.

For once it was a spell that didn't bear the deep crimson markings of the person they sought.

"Oh, there's a spell on the top wire isn't there?" Cart squinted at the nearly invisible line. "I—" He stopped.

Silence again descended on them. Goose bumps raced up Mona's arm and she shivered at the eerie sensation. Yanking on her hand, Cart took off at a run. They raced along the fence, the noise of their struggling through the brush the only sound in the still air. Around a corner and then ahead, faded white washed wood perched on a stone foundation came into view. Cart didn't go to the door, instead he pulled Mona into the narrow space between the building and the fence.

They ran through and came out the other side and kept going, moving away from the wire fencing. Cart led them over cleared ground, making the hair on the back of Mona's neck rise as they left the concealment of the building. He held them to walking quickly and their passage was almost silent. She didn't like feeling so exposed but clearly the plan had changed.

Once again in the forest Cart stopped just inside the tree line behind another towering pine. He pulled a small army knife out of his pocket and opened it. He ran the edge over his palm, creating a thin line of blood. Mona, steeling herself against the pain, held her hand out so he could do the same. They each would need the boost to face this enemy. Plus, she sincerely hoped some of her immunity would rub off on Cart. The idea of his being badly hurt made her nauseous. Cart slid the blade across her palm and she bit down on her hiss of pain. Noise was the enemy here.

He clasped her hand in his. In the silence she could hear his heartbeat. His golden eyes looked down at her.

Hers. This man was hers. She could only hope and pray to the goddess that he was not going to embrace evil, because doing so would be an anathema to who he was. If he turned she would not be able to live with herself. No, she could not believe this man, whose soul was now part of hers, would ever turn.

Cart tensed and looked back down the path. Between the low branches Mona saw a woman—blond, beautiful. She stood in the path, her head cocked, looking at the building they'd slid by. Dressed eye-catchingly, if inappropriately, in low riding white cargo pants and a cropped fur trimmed jacket, she looked like she'd stepped off the pages of a fashion magazine. If one discounted the tension in her shoulders and the tattoo up the side of her face.

Radiating around her was a cone of silence. Mona looked the runes and sigils over—crimson markings modified the working, making it suppress all animal sounds. Oddly, the spell wasn't anchored on her, but was linked to something she wore, perhaps a necklace given where the power lines emanated from.

Mona didn't see any evil in the woman; instead it was as if it was painted on her, layer after layer, until some stuck and clung and embedded itself in her flesh. Strange because Mona didn't sense much ability to handle magic in her at all, but then with all the out layers distorting her view, she couldn't be sure.

"What am I seeing?" Cart whispered, his voice so soft she barely heard it.

Mona assumed he meant the silence spell. After reading through everything again she leaned over to him, keeping her eye on the woman. No way was she going to not keep an eye on her.

"The larger forms are runes," she whispered in his ear. "They are the what the spell is built on. This one has four—wall, sounds, silence, and one that can be manipulated to specify a distance. The squiggly links between the runes are sigils. They're what the caster uses to create an order and hierarchy that give the spell its shape and purpose. The intent of the actions and the way the sigils are written aren't something I can easily change. However, I can rotate the runes, modifying their strength or sometimes switch runes within the working to change the scope of the spell."

He looked back. Given how his head swiveled slightly, following the parameters of the spell, she guessed he was sorting through what he saw.

The woman pulled out a small spiral notebook from her hip pocket. Mona hissed as the cacophony of magic embedded on the book flared. Cart squeezed their joined hands, either in sympathy or warning, she wasn't sure. Snow bunny seemed unaffected and flipped through until she found what she was looking for. Tearing off the page, she closed the book and slid it back into her pocket.

Mona blinked, unable to process what she was seeing.

"She's got a spell on that page," Cart murmured. "How can she do that?"

However she did it didn't matter, as the woman pulled the paper through her fingers, removing the spell. As the working lost its inertia she tweaked the runes and flung her creation at the house. A fireball formed and exploded as it hit the building, projecting shards of white washed wood into the sky.

Cart used the noise to cover their moving to a better position to watch the woman's movements. Mona knew he was waiting for an opportunity to confront her. Hiding until she left was not going to be an option.

Watching the woman, they ignored the rain of splinters. Her mouth was open and there was a gleeful, anticipatory expression on her face. As the remainder of the building collapsed in on itself, the fingers of one hand stroked the inside wrist of the other. Magic pooled there, too. The woman seemed to have a number of magical pieces. They'd need to get close enough to disarm her.

A furious look crossed the woman's face.

"Where are you?" She looked around, then focused on the trees they stood in.

"Stay here," Mona whispered. "I can manipulate the spells while you work out how to take her down."

Without waiting for his response she walked out of the trees. Good thing Mona kept her eyes on the woman, because she'd whipped out a spell from somewhere and flung it right at Mona. While she knew the spell should slide over her, there was a chance with Cart's blood now mixing with hers she'd be vulnerable.

So she kept walking and flipped the speed rune over and the whole thing tumbled to the ground, now moving at a snail's pace.

Closer, she needed to get closer. She stepped around the working now sitting on the ground.

The woman laughed. "Oh, you're going to be fun to kill."

Another spell came at Mona, her opponent pulling this one off an index card she took out of her hip pocket. The working was not directly aimed at Mona. Instead, exactly like the spell she'd encountered at Smythe's complex that had almost killed her early that morning many days ago, it was pulling slabs of stones out of the ground, which were racing up to crush her between them. Mona turned the rune, giving the working direction and the rumbling under her feet subsided as the stones headed down.

Ten feet away now. Cart was circling around behind the woman. Huh, she didn't realize she'd feel him that well. Not only could she feel him, she knew anger and worry for her seethed under his calm calculations.

"We're close enough that anything you send might turn back on you," Mona said, moving closer.

"True." The woman pulled a gun out of her parka. "Stop right—"

Mona kicked out, knowing she couldn't let her bring the gun up and brace it for a shot. While she'd not gotten nearly as far as her brother, the couple of years of lessons weren't forgotten. Her foot connected with her adversary and she felt a backlash of energy as she came in contact with the spell on the woman's wrist.

The gun went off, startlingly loud this close. Shit, she hadn't kicked it free. Then Cart was there, pinning the woman's shoulders and arms to her side. Mona reached out and grabbed her wrist before she could react and raise the weapon.

Pain. The spell there sent shards of pain through Mona's hand and spearing up to her elbow.

"You okay?" Cart asked as her knees buckled and she yelped in response. Mona nodded, although, really, she wasn't. "Get rid of the gun if you can."

Mona held on, squeezing and twisting to get the woman to drop the firearm. The woman stood there laughing, not trying to fight. Finally the gun dropped to the ground. Mona kicked it away.

Mona slid her hand up and away from the wrist, confused because she didn't feel any jewelry under her now tingling palm. Cart's hiss echoed hers as the tattoo and its magic were exposed.

"Pretty, isn't it? Edward suggested I get it." The woman flexed her wrist, making the dark markings writhe.

No, it was revolting. Mona looked over the woman's shoulder at Cart, who looked as disgusted as she felt.

The tattoo was an ugly, nasty spell, one that pulled energy out of Folk and stored it for later use. Mona let go, repulsed by the images of people and creatures she was getting simply by looking at the design.

"I'd never consider killing others pretty," Mona said.

"And you have so much experience, do you?" the blond sneered. "No, you're too goody-goody, using your gift to Ward folk. They've got you brainwashed. 'Your powers mean you serve to protect us.'" Her voice deepened, mimicking someone. "They've got it wrong. Our powers mean we can't be touched. If you're invincible you're on top. And I intend to stay there. With or without Edward."

The woman was looking at the tattoo, grinning in pleasure.

By the goddess, she was a Warder. Edward's Warder, although not his Mate, or at least if she was they hadn't completed their mating or she'd be tied to his fate. More importantly, Smythe had not been responsible for his son, this woman was supposed to have been. Somehow, some why, Smythe had missed training this woman, and she'd gone rogue. His ego? His denial? Mona would never know.

The woman looked up at Mona again. Eyes now narrowed. "I know you, you're the bitch who tried to prevent me from ridding the world of that mother and her baby. The child destined to have all the powers. Too bad you didn't succeed. Now you'll have to wait years for another to be born. You were too late for that, Miss Goody Two-Shoes." She bared her teeth in a feral snarl. "You made me lose several good men, something I'll not forgive."

Mona didn't look at Cart. Didn't want to give away that they were sure they'd saved the child. Wasn't even certain it was true anymore. When was the last time she'd heard anything?

The woman was muttering under her breath. Mona saw a spell being built up. How many of these tattoos did the woman have? Remembering her brother's advice she stepped back and aimed her fist at the woman's jaw, easy to do as the woman was looking away, putting her weight behind the hit and following through. Cart loosened his hold and the woman's head snapped back before she was knocked out. He kept the woman upright, despite her lax body.

"Shit, that hurts!" Mona shook out her hand.

"Get the Swiss army knife out of my vest pocket."

Mona's eyes went wide.

"You can't mean..." She didn't know how to finish that sentence.

"I could kill her now."

Mona saw the truth in his eyes—he'd do it if she said he should. But Mona couldn't make the call. Wouldn't make the call. Part and parcel of her being Warder, perhaps, but she didn't think killing the woman, at this juncture at least, would solve anything.

He nodded, and she sensed his agreement. "You can use the knife to mar the tattoos and make them unusable and we'll bring her back for Nic and Tania to judge. And we should start with that one."

Dizzy with nausea at the idea of cutting the woman, Mona reached under the poncho and into his vest.

"Clean it first, I got most of our blood off, but there's no reason to take chance on there still being some."

Mona looked the compact knife over. The casing had a rough black texture and there were at least two blades. "Can't I just use the smaller blade?"

Cart had the woman down on the ground and was wrapping her forearms together behind her back, being sure to keep her wrist clear.

"Yeah, might take longer, but sure." He tore off a short piece of duct tape and placed it over their captive's mouth. There was barely enough to tape her ankles together before he ran out of tape. Still kneeling, he looked up at her.

"I can't do the work." His voice was soft, calming, and Mona knew he wished he could. "I can be here, help you, but you know what the runes mean, how to nullify the spell, I don't."

Mona looked down at the knife in her hand, unable to fathom that she might use it on a person. "Will it be permanent? I mean, are we just going to do this and have it all go back?"

"You tell me. *Can* you change the spell? Rework the runes in a way she won't easily be able to change it back?"

Kneeling next to him she looked over the tattoo, trying, trying not to think about cutting into this woman's flesh.

"Moving the runes wouldn't do anything. Flipping them, rearranging them, she'd just move them back. I could probably take a rune out." Would she have to slice it out? Better to not think of it. "Which might collapse the whole thing or not, I'm not sure with the more permanent elements of this spell."

Cart cupped her neck in one hand and brushed the tear she hadn't realized she'd shed with the thumb of his other. The blood link was still strong; she felt his love and worry, his fierce protectiveness and his angst-ridden acceptance that there were some things he had to let Mona do.

"Is there a way for me to do this?" he asked anyway. "No, never mind. Look, do you remember when your brother cut Tania, then had to suck out the poison? Think if it that way. Having a spell with that evil an intent on her, it's got to affect her in some way."

Mona knew that to be the case. With all the spells their captive had embedded on her skin—and there were definitely more than the one on her wrist and collarbone—layers of evil were sinking in and permeating through her being. Mona placed a finger on the woman's palm and tried to assess her magic beneath the layers of workings. Cart clasped her other hand, bringing their already healing scars into contact.

What she saw was very different than an elf's or a Were's abilities. Closer to what she'd seen on Kofi, the witch who had all her energies concentrated in her head. But unlike the witches, where magic only appeared that one place, and unlike those with elven blood, where the essence streamed like arteries throughout their body, her magic showed as if through a fine mesh, innumerable pinpricks at every single point on her body. Had Smythe looked like that? Mona didn't think she'd ever thought to see how Smythe looked to her inner eye.

And the thread of evil was scattered through the microscopic dots via the ink in the tattoos. There was no way she'd ever get them all clear. Perhaps Tania, or Tania and Nic together, but she couldn't do it.

"You don't look like that," Cart said. "You look like you have delicate swirls and curls of magic. When you look closely you realize each line is made up of many more, even finer lines, running next to each other to give the curves shape and depth. It's quite pretty. Sexy even."

Mona smiled at him, knowing she didn't have to express her gratitude for what he'd told her, he'd feel it like she was feeling his joy. He leaned over and kissed her salt-laden cheek, for again she found herself weeping.

The woman twitched. Mona couldn't delay any longer.

Folk.

Energy.

Death.

Mona wasn't sure which rune to remove. Any pairing she'd leave—death with folk, energy with death, energy with folk—was still a potentially dangerous spell given they could all be manipulated to harm others.

She closed the knife and handed it back to Cart. "I need to try to take the whole spell off. Once I remove it we'll need to jump away from here, immediately. Oh!" A stray thought popped into her head. She looked over the various spells and saw the thread she was looking for. Pulling on it, the spell that had changed the lizard came into view. Mona yanked, flipping the runes around until the creature was once again the right size. The ten inch reptile landed with plop by Cart.

Cart picked up the now comatose creature and put it inside his vest. "Any sign of the minotaur?"

She checked the lines that seemed most likely. "No. Hopefully Nic called him back."

Cart nodded. "Can you do this standing up? That way if we have to leave in a hurry, we can."

Mona shook her head. "I need to touch her. Unless you want to prop her up, I need to be down here."

"Is there any economy of scale? I mean, if you're taking off one spell is it just as easy to remove more at the same time?"

"No, I don't want them getting entangled. It's got to be one at a time. Ready?"

Cart reached down and grabbed her upper arm. Clearly he thought he might need to yank her along with him.

"Ready."

Mona placed her hand above the working, concentrating on pulling the markings away. The wrist reddened as the first rune came free then blistered with the second. The marks repeated themselves on Mona's palm, sending pain again shooting up her arm.

Cart's hand tightened on her arm. He had to know the agony she was in.

By the goddess I can't get sick!

"Breathe through your nose," he said quietly.

Mona followed his advice, thankful she was as the last sigils and rune came free. Now the skin was raw and openly wept with ooze and blood. She forced herself to look at the wrist and ignore her discomfort. Using her free hand she turned their captive's forearm to make sure all the sigils and markings were done, difficult with the bindings.

A jerk, then a muffled scream. Their captive awoke, rolling onto her side and clamping her bound hands around Mona's ankle. Mona fell back on her ass, breaking Cart's hold. Mona instinctively clasped the other hand over the spell, keeping it in place.

Pain!

He slid his hands under her arms and pulled her away from the thrashing woman.

"Jump!" Mona screamed. She needed to get rid of this spell *now.*

The dark with its faint shushing of colors surrounded them. Mona shook her hands, freeing them of the magical residue.

Freeing her ankle of its additional weight was going to be more difficult. She grabbed Cart's bicep before she slid out of his hands. Reaching down, she tried to pry off the fingers with no success.

Not much time. She didn't want to bring this woman to wherever Cart was taking them.

She slammed her booted foot on the bound wrists, using her grip on Cart's arm for balance. Then she kicked out, shoving the body away. Mona had to believe that the woman wouldn't be in this in-between place for eternity. That she'd come out somewhere, some short distance in the future if what Mona suspected about what lingering in the non-space would do was correct.

But for now she was gone.

They stepped out onto a dock that jutted out into ice-laden waters. The same place they'd jumped to once before. Cart stumbled a step.

"I thought she was still latched onto you." He looked around the dock as if she'd appear there.

"No, I got her off while we were jumping." Mona looked around. They were by the coal plant, so not too far from home, but plenty far from New Jersey.

"You left her in the void?" Cart frowned. "I'm not sure that'll hold her, eventually she'll come back out."

"When she does, we'll need to be ready."

"Good job, you two."

They turned around to see the Puck in a yellow rain slicker and rain hat and holding a pipe leaning against a pylon. He grinned at them, clearly pleased he'd startled them.

"Hi, Warder," he nodded at Mona. "And you too." His hand flicked in dismissal at Cart.

Mona felt Cart still beside her. If they weren't still linked together she might have missed it, but she knew his mind was racing even though she couldn't get a grasp on what his thoughts were.

"You keep doing that." His voice was flat, unemotional.

"Cart, he's just trying to yank your chain by not greeting you."

Cart shook his head. "No, that's not it. The Puck, he's said the truth the whole time and we've missed it."

"Knew you'd catch it." The Puck's small, pointed teeth glinted in the afternoon sun.

"What are you talking about?" Mona looked back and forth between the two of them, but they were too caught up in a staring contest to notice her. She clenched her fist in annoyance, only to hiss in pain as her fingers dug into her healing skin.

Cart immediately reached out for her.

"Never mind this." She waved her hands out of his range. "I want to know what all you are talking about!"

"I—" Cart hopped and jerked. "Cracked acorns, this is not a good time for you to wake up."

He pulled the lizard out of his vest. "Here, you take it."

The Puck was already holding out his hands. He inspected the creature's toes and tongue before flicking it into oblivion with a wave of his hand and a sparkling of imps.

Mona was not distracted. "Care to fill me in on the big secret?"

Cart walked over and stood behind her, placing his hands on her shoulders and leaning forward so his mouth was by her ear.

"Have you ever noticed how casually the Puck greets you?" He squeezed her shoulders gently when she would have said something. "It's never hello, or hey, it's always…"

He trailed off and let her fill in the gap.

"High Warder." Mona stared at the small man. He'd snuck it in so subtly she never thought anything of it.

Love, worry, menace all rolled off of Cart. "So, what does it mean?"

The Puck ignored his question and focused on Mona.

"You're going to be fine." He nodded as if reassuring her. "We just needed someone a little stronger. With less elves being born, and therefore less wards, more evil is leaking out and affecting Folk. And you," his gaze shifted to Cart, "you better be damned good at the protecting business, because she's going to need it once the people gathering evil figure out who she is."

He popped out.

"Wait!" Mona's yell echoed out over the harbor. "I hate when you do that!"

She turned in Cart's arms.

"I can't." The thought of him turning evil, that there was more evil leaking into people, and he might be one made her toughen her resolve. "I can't do this. I can't let you get hurt."

Cart just grinned. "Did I ever tell you about how I met Randall?"

"No. I assume this is relevant?" A cold wind came off the lake, making her shiver.

Cart wrapped his arm across her shoulders and started them walking to shore.

"When I was in training, the Warder in Tallahassee—Marina, you'll like her—nick-named me 'Teflon.' It seemed that even when my teammates came back with bits of evil residue I'd have none, and she'd started to notice. Then she happened to mention this to the Puck."

Oh, Mona could only imagine Randall's reaction. He'd want to test Cart, see if it was true. "That can't have been good."

"It wasn't. Most of the guys thought I just had shit luck for assignments. Some of the crap he threw at me…" He didn't finish the thought. "I don't know that I'll ever forgive him, even though knowing how much evil is out there helped me keep perspective when even my superiors were flipping out."

"And nothing ever stuck."

"Nope. It's not that spells don't work on me, I'm not a Warder. But when I got hit and then the spell was removed, you couldn't tell I'd been around evil."

They walked a few paces in silence, off the pier and onto the ground. If evil couldn't stick to him, and she was High Warder, what the hell was coming down the pike?

Cart pulled her in closer, his warmth spreading up her side. "I don't think we should dwell on the future. It's out there, waiting for us. I want to live in the now, and I want that to be with you."

There were no barriers now. Cart would not, could not succumb to whatever evil they would face.

Joy, the rapid, giddy beating of her heart and the lightening of a load off her shoulders. This was joy.

She could be with Cart and he'd be safe.

Only then did she realize they'd stopped and she was standing there grinning like a fool. He hadn't asked a question, but seemed to be awaiting an answer. No way was he going to get off that easily.

Although she could tell by his answering grin that he'd read her emotions already.

She raised an eyebrow at him.

Cart rolled his eyes then knelt down.

"I didn't—" She stopped, Cart's raised hand forestalling her saying anything else.

"If I'm going to do this, I'm going to do it right." He took her hand and held it against his heart. "Mona Lisa Kubrek—"

He stopped and Mona felt his desire, joy, welcome.

She put a finger from her free hand across his lips. "I know."

He turned his head and nudged her finger aside. "I'm still going to say it anyway."

Mona didn't realize how delighted she'd be that he persevered.

"And that's why," he continued, clearly picking up on her feelings. "There will be times when we don't agree, when things will be tough, and I want you to always have this moment to look back on, to remember, no matter what, I love you with all my heart. You are etched onto my soul, stronger than the even the moon is entwined in my spirit. You will always be the center of my universe. Even when I may not show it or have time to be with you, you will be in my thoughts and in my deeds. I will protect you and ours with every fiber of my being. And I hope I will always be worthy of your love."

Mona sniffed, tears of joy trailing down her face.

"I love you, Cart," she said. "For everything you are, and that you will be, that we will yet become. My future would end today if you were not with me."

Cart stood and wrapped his arms around her, holding her as tightly as she now held him. "I will always be with you, in spirit if not in body."

"I know, I know, but there will be times you need to leave and I'll worry. And there will be times I need to leave and you'll worry. And, oh my goodness, what if we have kids? Who'll stay around to protect them? There's no way I'd ever leave them with—"

Cart cut her off with a kiss, deepening it and pressing her close until she wasn't sure where she ended and he began. He broke it off, leaving them both breathless.

"Why are you nervous?" Cart asked, dipping in for a quick peck to show he wasn't expecting an answer. "Could it be you've heard rumors about mating sex?"

Best. Sex. Ever. Mona nodded, then gasped as the level of lust and need radiating off of him spiked to the point she thought she'd melt right there.

"Room, we need to get a room." He grabbed her hand and headed left this time, to the hotel.

Unlike that night not so long ago when they'd gone to the diner instead, Mona knew this was right. This was the time to start her life with Cart. Some bad shit was coming down the road, she had no doubt, but they'd face it together. Somehow she thought they'd have help, and not just from Tania and Nic—she had a feeling this was a time when many new skills would come to the fore to face new adversaries.

"I hope they have room service," Mona said.

"If not we'll ask some imps to bring us food. We can indulge this weekend, nothing is going to happen to them."

Cart was right, nothing was going to happen this weekend, they were more than due for some down time.

"Shit, I need to give a report. It's what, noon? Yo, imp. I know you're hanging around." Cart stopped them halfway across the deserted parking lot. A blue green spark appeared between them.

"Tell Tiffany we're okay and to contact the Maven for more details. I'll be in day after tomorrow with a full report. Got to do this mating thing first."

"Got to do this thing?" Mona, interrupted, laughing, because while it so wasn't romantic, it was so Cart.

"Got to, desperately want to, need to before I explode. And thanks for letting my whole crew know that. Cause you know Tiff will be opening that one in a crowd." The imp blinked out.

"Oh!" Mona hadn't meant to embarrass him in front of his group. He looked at her and they both laughed so hard they bent over, out of breath. "Shit, Cart, sorry."

"Not like they haven't figured it out." He straightened and took her hand. "So, now can we go?"

"Yes," Mona said. "Because, you know, Cart, I got to do this thing too."

Epilogue

Mona looked at the pink-wrapped bundle in her arms. Soft swirls of dark hair delightfully capped the newborn's head. She turned her head, futilely attempting to swipe her tears with her shoulder. Cart reached out and dried them with a tissue.

Raine's baby had still been premature, but the extra three weeks she'd managed to hold on had made a critical difference in the child's development. Raine had never told them, but Mona and Cart suspected the baby was Edward's. According to the woman they'd left in the void, the child was destined to have phenomenal powers. All the more reason to make sure she was raised by someone who would keep her grounded.

"Don't worry, Maya," she whispered to the sleeping baby. "We'll take care of you."

There was a soft knock on the door. She looked over at Cart. They'd discussed this and both agreed it was the right track, hard as it was for Mona to let the baby go. If—when—the renegade Warder came back, Mona was a target and a child would not be safe with them.

She nodded and Cart opened up the door.

Averill stepped in, confusion on her face at the request for the four a.m. meeting, but smiling in delight when she saw the infant. Dressed in a hospital gown over her clothes, the fabric shushed as she walked over to Mona.

"She's beautiful," Averill said. "What's her name?"

Mona cut her eyes to Cart, who nodded in reassurance. This was even harder to do than she'd thought it would be.

Mona cleared her throat. "Her first name is Maya."

Averill looked down and cooed at the baby, who, Mona realized, had awakened and was staring up at Averill.

"Hi, princess. You are one lucky lady, yes you are," Averill said, keeping her voice soft but didn't slide into to squeaky baby talk.

Mona couldn't go on. Cart came over and wrapped his arm around her shoulder.

"Averill," Cart said, and the pack leader's head shot up. "Maya's Folk, and we need someone to take care of her."

She frowned and looked off, clearly running through her head who in the pack might be able to take the babe. Her pack was much smaller now. Many of the shifters the Lycoan had changed had been too far gone for Nic to call them back. And several of the men who had been turned back left rather than have a woman as a pack leader. Mona estimated the pack was half the size it had been, and mostly women. Nurturing, caring, resilient women, the strongest of whom stood before her.

"We want you to take her," Mona said. "She's special. Very special."

Averill was weakly shaking her head.

"Her mother was the focus of much of the attacks, including the bridge collapse." Cart's baldly stating the fact didn't make it any easier to hear.

"The mother could—" Averill waved her hand at the pink bundle.

"She died right after giving birth." One month and the pain still sliced through Mona. By the time Raine had reached out to her, there was nothing Mona could have done to change the outcome, but it still hurt. Made her almost wish she'd let Cart kill the woman when they could have.

"What would I...How would I explain..." Averill's voice drifted off.

Mona knew then that Averill would take Maya, that she'd care for her with the determination and love she'd shown when taking over the pack.

How would they explain? She and Cart hadn't thought through more than convincing Averill she needed to do this.

"I can do this," Averill said, nodding and thinking. "My brother's pregnant wife moved back to her family in St. Paul. I can put out that the depression she was dealing with before her child was born has gotten to the point the family wants me to care for the child. Good thing I know that's not true because I'd hate to wish her ill, she's been through enough."

Averill looked down at Maya, who blew a bubble. "I need a couple of days, though. Do I have them?"

Cart nodded. "We can do that."

"Averill," Mona said, looking down at Maya's face and already seeing magic swirling through her even though she was far too young for any to be showing yet, then making sure she looked the other woman in the eye. "Protect her. There are people who, as her powers grow, will try to use her."

"You have some time, though, I think," Cart said, squeezing Mona's shoulder in reassurance, "before you need to worry. She's only a month old."

"Just remember, Cart and I will always be an imp away any time you might need us," Mona said. "Tania and Nic too."

"Me too."

Mona had known the Puck was there, hiding. The thought had niggled in the back of her head, waiting to be brought forth but had bloomed too late.

Cart must have too because he hadn't tensed up in anger like he usually did when Randall appeared.

"Thanks, all of you," Averill said. "I'm pretty sure once she starts showing some power I'm not going to forget who she's got looking out for her. May I?"

She held out her gloved hands and Mona placed Maya in her waiting arms. Averill held her like a pro.

"Hey, princess," Averill said. "You are going to come with me, okay? I have a big old bedroom I just painted yellow. I think you'll like it. And the old ladies of the pack are all going to coo. It's going to be a while before you have playmates though, not a lot of kids being born into the pack right now with there not being a lot of guys around."

Averill looked up and grinned at Cart and Mona. "Did Tiffany tell you of the latest contretemps? One of the few able bodied men suggested we allow polygamy for a period. The women almost hounded him out of the pack."

Cart frowned. "Did you send out a notice to the National Council? They'll help."

"It's on their agenda. Anything you can do to hasten it being announced would be good."

"If you open up the pack you'll have a three year period to bring the pack up to minimum. If you don't, you may have to agree to merge with another pack."

"I know, we'll have to cross that bridge when we get there. Right now, we just need able bodies. Perhaps not as small as this," Averill smiled down at Maya, "but we'll take anyone who passes the Maven's inspection."

With a sigh she handed the bundle back to Mona.

"Two days. I'll be back in two days. Will I see you at the falls?"

"We're heading there next."

"Good. Just don't mention anything yet, I need to lay the ground work." Without a look back she left the room.

"What are you two going to do?" Randall asked as he reached up and took Maya from Mona's arms. The baby's arms flailed in excitement.

"You've been visiting her, haven't you?" Mona asked. Of course he had. With things quieter and the imps no longer in danger he had more time.

Randall grimaced. "Been called back to Elfhaven a lot and she's my present to myself when I get back." He grinned down at the infant. "Yes, you are. And when you get older, I'll take you to

Elfhaven with me and they can see how strong we make them up there."

"I don't think I wanted to hear that."

"They're not happy that there is an Oberon here when there isn't one there. While we've lost many of our ties, we've always had a parallel ruler." Randall had found a bottle, or more likely conjured one, and was feeding Maya as he gently swayed.

"They'll get over it, or someone will step up. We'll see. You two should get going. I can handle Maya until Averill can take her." He did seem to have things under control.

"You'll not take her on any visits? You'll keep her here?" Cart asked.

"No, she's too young, needs another year at least, probably two."

Mona didn't know if he was teasing them or not but it didn't matter. She and Cart did need to go, the Maven had called a convocation of all Folk in the region up at the falls and they needed to be there.

"Thank you, Randall. And yes, I know that may mean an obligation on my part. I'll take the chance." She leaned down and kissed the baby's cheek. "We're off to get ready for the Maven's convocation. We'll see you there."

Whether he knew it or not, leaving Maya when she was in the Puck's arms was easier then when she was asleep in her crib. The child needed more human contact, which is why they'd picked Averill, who would wrap her arms and heart around Maya.

"You ready to see if your brother has come to his senses yet?" Cart asked as they headed down the nearly deserted hall.

Nic had not accepted his changed role very well.

"If you're ready to see if Tania will come down off her high horse."

He laughed. "They are eminently suited to one another."

Mona opened the door to the cold wet air of early spring "Funny how fate works."

About the Author

Ellie lives in SW Ohio with her three kids, two dogs (one of whom thinks he's a cat), and one cat (who thinks he's a dog). She's thankful her kids have no such issues. When she's not writing she's encouraging other writers to submit their stories and follow their dreams. Or cleaning dog hair off, well, everything.

You can find Ellie on the web at *www.EllieWrites2.com* and follow her on Twitter @EllieWrites2.

In the mood for more Crimson Romance?
Check out *By the Light of the Moon* by Laila Blake at
CrimsonRomance.com.